"You cannot take what the sea is not willing to give."

-Birde Isles proverb

TO KISS THE SEA

KINGSPORT CHRONICLES BOOK 1

C.H. CARTER

C.H. CARTER BOOKS

Paperback ISBN: 979-8-9888820-0-8

eBook ISBN: 979-8-9888820-1-5

Book Cover & Chapter Graphics by Maldo Designs – https://maldodesigns.com

Map Design by Cartographybird – https://www.cartographybird.com

Edited by Rowe Carenen – https://www.thebookconcierge.com/

First edition 2023

Take your time. Let the words flow.
Writing is whatever you want it to be.
And *you* are a real author.
Don't let anyone tell you any different.

Notes & Content Warnings

Notes:

The full cast of characters, including name and birthplace pronunciations, can be found in the Index at the back of the book. (Seriously though, I'm not a stickler for name pronunciation, this is just how they sound in my head!)

To Kiss the Sea is a high **romantic fantasy,** meaning it is a fantasy epic first and foremost with romantic subplots that develop over time for various characters. If you are looking for **fantasy romance**, or "romantasy", where the plot centers around the romance between characters set in a fantasy world, this may not be the book for you. Though I hope you will be able to enjoy TKTS either way, I understand if you need that bit of spice in your life! The next book I have planned after the Kingsport Chronicles (currently dubbed "Project Staircase") will be a historical fantasy romance with a lovely dash of spice, that might be more your cup of tea.

Content Warnings:

To Kiss the Sea contains themes that may be distressing to some readers including serious injury, physical violence and bloodshed, character death (on and off page), child abandonment, drowning or near-drowning, aquaphobia (fear of water), panic attacks (on page), parental manipulation, implied assault (off page), mention of coerced sex work (off page), consensual sex work (off page), and consensual sexual relationships (off page).

As much as I hope everyone who picks up this book will be able to read and enjoy the whole story, please be kind to yourselves.

CONTENTS

THE KNOWN WORLD

FRAOLLKIN FLEET
THE PASTURES
HORN
ZAVATLEO
FRAOLLISH TERRITORY
FRAOLLAND
LAIVASTHO
THE SPLIT SEA
LALESEIR
TJORDUN
MIDTHE
EHLAFI
BALAH
SAPREA
MEREDIA
PRAVIL
UEVAT
AGRIYA
MYRRE
SAN AVETH
EAST TO THE BIRDE ISLES
THE SOUTHERN STRAIT

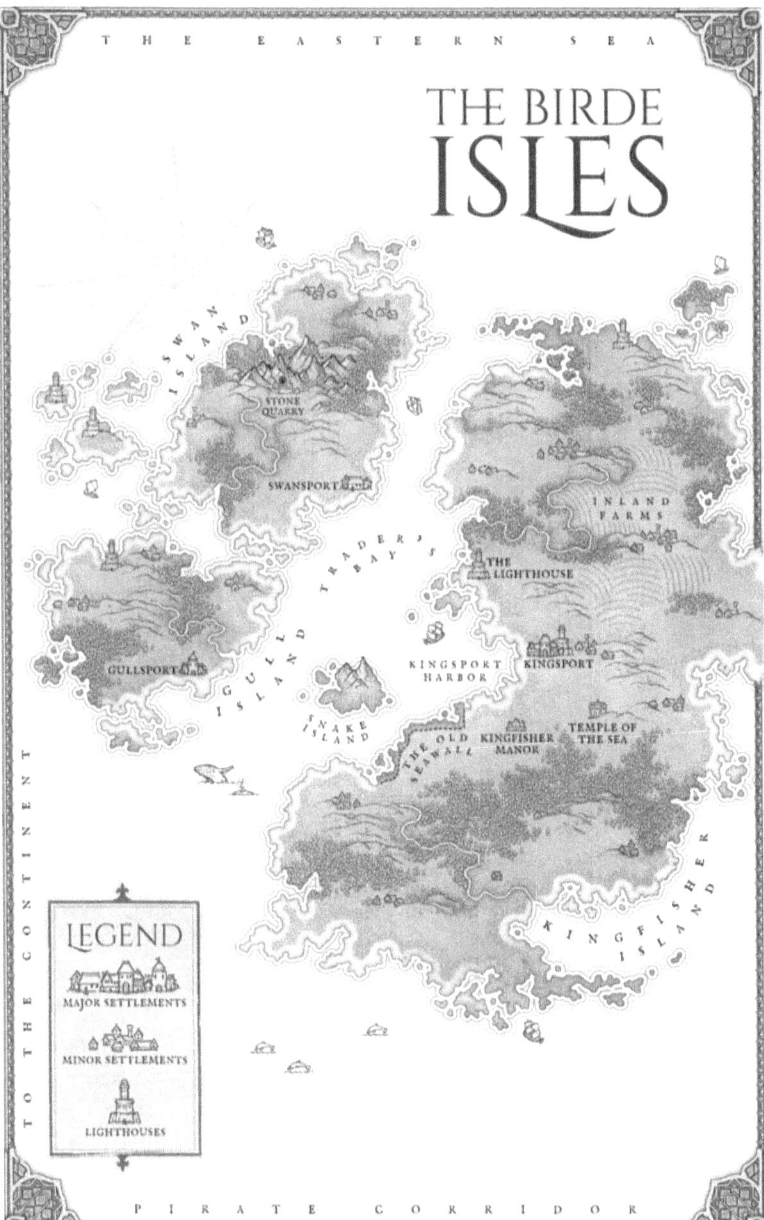

THE EASTERN SEA
THE BIRDE
ISLES
SWAN ISLAND
STONE QUARRY
SWANSPORT
INLAND FARMS
THE LIGHTHOUSE
GULLSPORT
ISLAND TRADER'S BAY
KINGSPORT HARBOR
KINGSPORT
SNAKE ISLAND
THE OLD SEAWALL
KINGFISHER MANOR
TEMPLE OF THE SEA
TO THE CONTINENT
KINGFISHER ISLAND
LEGEND
MAJOR SETTLEMENTS
MINOR SETTLEMENTS
LIGHTHOUSES
PIRATE CORRIDOR

PASHA

PROLOGUE

She was nearly gone, when the young priestess called her to the surface.

The pulse from above, as blood touched the water, was so far away she almost didn't hear it.

Drifting. She'd been drifting for so long, soon sleep felt like the only answer.

They weren't coming back. Pasha didn't want to admit it, but it had to be true. Too many years had passed. They'd left her, and they weren't coming back.

It took a long time to open her eyes. The blood was calling, they'd taught the priestesses how to do that, and she wanted to answer. Pasha's eyelids were so heavy. When had she last opened them? Salt and sand crumbled away, clinging to her lashes and stinging the corners of her eyes. The pain forced her to blink hard, more sand slid down her face.

The pulse called again. The faint smell of liquid copper broke through the film muffling her senses.

Raising an arm took a while, but by the time she'd lifted it her vision was less blurred. Pasha moved her fingers in front of her face. Salt coated every inch of her like a second skin. She stretched both arms over her head, white powder cracked off and flitted around her like chunks of ice.

The pulse called a third time. How long would they wait before giving up?

Sand had blown through with the tides, her lower half was buried. With all the strength she had left, Pasha twisted and pushed until she was free. Too much like hatching.

Floating for a moment, she took stock of herself. Everything was stiff, but it was all there. Her home had kept any curious, larger creatures away and she was lucky there were no mollusks or other hitchhikers to remove.

The call came again, softer this time. They were going to leave!

Fighting the ache that had settled into her bones, Pasha flexed her fins and propelled herself through the water. The last of the salt and sand broke away as she swam. The water rushing over her face was glorious. It made her feel almost alive.

When Pasha's head broke through the surface, the blast of air into her nose sent her reeling. Her vision sharpened as she adjusted to the difference between seeing underwater and seeing above it. Scanning the shore, Pasha found the one calling her. The girl was young, pale from the loss of blood, but she wore the blue robes of their priestesses. Slumped forward, the girl's hand was still in the water, but she was barely awake.

It had been more than a century since they wanted their goddess to appear. The pain of going onto land, after so long in the sea, would be excruciating. But, if they were desperate enough to call for a goddess after all this time, then Pasha would give them a goddess.

ESA

CHAPTER ONE

A shout echoed down the hallway as Priestess Esa rushed to Lady Rochelle Kingfisher's private birthing room, a stack of fresh linens clutched against her chest. Her new robes, which were slightly too big, trailed the floor behind her.

The head priestess had personally asked Esa to assist her when it was time for her ladyship to give birth. At twenty years old, the youngest priestess at the temple of the sea, Esa questioned if one of the more experienced priestesses might be a better choice. But Aithne had assured Esa she needed her youth and speed to fetch anything that might be needed. She was getting older, and this would likely be the last birth she attended as head priestess. The manor physician and a midwife would also be stationed nearby, in the event of an emergency, but it was always a priestess of the sea temple who delivered the Kingfisher children.

Esa pushed the double doors open and nearly ran into Lord Gaius Kingfisher III. He hardly noticed her as he paced through the antechamber to Lady Kingfisher's room, hands locked behind his back. She knew how concerned his lordship must be. His first wife had died not long after giving birth to little Calder.

"My lord," Esa paused long enough to bob a curtsy, then continued on through the next set of doors. The head priestess was helping Lady Kingfisher into the large copper tub that was moved into the room in preparation for the baby's arrival.

Their new lady of the manor had balked at the idea of giving birth this way. She was from Balah, a large country on the southern end of the continent across the sea, and hadn't been aware of this particular Birde Isles practice. Finally, they'd convinced her this was their safest method for bringing her child into the world. The baby would arrive in a soft, warm environment much like her own womb.

Lady Kingfisher cried out again, gripping the rim of the tub.

"Pray to the goddess of the sea, my lady." Head Priestess Aithne urged. She sat on a low stool beside the tub, using a sponge to gently trickle the heated water over her ladyship's shoulders.

"I do not follow the goddess of the sea." Lady Kingfisher ground out through her teeth. "If I pray at all, it will be to the Moon."

Esa glanced at the small altar her ladyship had placed in the corner of the room. She knew little of the Balahn trio of deities, they had no exact shape or appearance like the goddess of the sea. They were important to Lady Kingfisher, though, and his lordship was so in love with his wife that he now worshiped both the goddess of the sea and the Balahn gods.

"Esa, bring the linens over here," Aithne said without taking her eyes off the woman in the tub, a lock of her graying hair fell across her forehead and she swept it back. "Then, I want you to draw back the curtains so her ladyship can see the moon."

"Yes, Aithne." Esa quickly deposited the linens where the head priestess sat and hurried to the large bay window that offered a view of the cliffs and the sea beyond. Moonlight flooded the room when she pulled the curtains aside, mixing with the light from the candles and the fire blazing in the hearth. The room was almost stiflingly warm.

"There, my lady," Aithne said gently. "Now the moon can see you."

Some of the tension left Lady Kingfisher's body as she murmured a Balahn prayer under her breath. Aithne's gnarled hands lifted the brunette curls, heavy with water, from her ladyship's neck and draped them over the edge of the tub. Rivulets ran through them and soaked into one of the cloths Aithne had laid out on the floor.

"It's nearly time, Esa." Aithne beckoned her over. "Stay by her ladyship and pray to the sea."

When the baby was safely delivered and the cord tying mother and child together severed, Aithne took the child to a table by the hearth to clean and wrap it in a fresh blanket. All Esa could see was a crop of dark, loosely curled hair, just like her ladyship's, plastered against the baby's tiny skull.

Aithne stood unmoving at the table for a long time. Esa shifted uneasily in her spot by the tub. Was something wrong with the baby?

"Is something wrong?" Lady Kingfisher voiced Esa's own question, her head lifted from the rim. She reached a hand towards them. "What's happening?"

Priestess Aithne looked up, eyes shining with both hope and uncertainty. Her voice filled with an emotion that Esa couldn't place. "Congratulations, my lady. You have a daughter."

AITHNE

CHAPTER TWO

"I will *not* send my child away!"

"Rochelle, darling..."

"No, Gaius. I would rather leave and take her back to my country, than to lose her because of some mad decree by your grandfather!"

Aithne stood with her ear pressed to the doors of Lady Kingfisher's birthing chamber. They'd just gotten her and the baby into bed to rest, when Lord Kingfisher couldn't wait any longer to see them. Her ladyship had kept the baby close and ordered the priestesses out. Aithne sent Esa away with the soiled linens so she could try to hear what was being said in the next room.

Lady Kingfisher's strong voice carried through the door, her words made sharper by her Balahn accent. "I can't believe you kept this from me, Gaius. Who in their right mind would believe such a thing?"

Aithne glanced back to make sure Esa hadn't returned yet. She was the last priestess at the temple of the sea who knew the real reason why there seemed to have been no Kingfisher daughters in generations. Deliberately keeping the truth from the new priestesses who came after her.

Everyone at the temple who'd lived during Aithne's youth knew the story, how the honored Head Priestess Eschina had used the old ways to call upon the goddess so that Gaius Kingfisher I could garner her favor. Many had seen the faded scar on Eschina's hand, and they'd all witnessed the prosperity that steadily built on the islands after that night. But when the elderly Eschina chose her to take on this burden, Aithne thought surely Gaius I must have gone mad. Sending away his own daughters and granddaughters to unknown futures? What exactly happened that night, what drove him to make that choice? At the very least could they not have been given to childless families on Swan or Gull Island instead? But the head priestess had been adamant they follow his lordship's orders exactly.

It never sat right with Aithne. And the old man only sent away the children who were born daughters. What if any of the others had come to know themselves and became daughters later in life, like young Esa? What would Gaius and Eschina have done then? Ripped a child or adult away from the only home they'd known? Was that better or worse than sending the infants away to live as fosterlings on distant shores?

Gaius I was off his head, there was no other explanation. She wasn't sure how many children had been taken from this family, but she vowed when Eschina and the old lord were both gone from this world the practice would die with them.

Perhaps she'd exaggerated a touch when she revealed Gaius I's practice of sending daughters away. This was what was needed, though. Lady Rochelle was an outsider, the perfect person to bring the family out of this archaic mess.

"Please," Lord Kingfisher begged his wife. "Let me see her?"

"No! I will not let you–"

"By the goddess, Rochelle! Will you please listen?"

The following silence lasted for several minutes. Aithne tucked her hands into the pockets of her robe to stop herself from grabbing the door handles. The baby fussed for a moment, then quieted down when her mother soothed her.

Aithne held her breath. She'd wanted to speak to the current Lord Kingfisher about this before. But the other three children born to his first wife, before her untimely death, were all sons. There never seemed to be a right time to approach him.

Lord Kingfisher spoke gently, "I have no intention of sending *our* daughter anywhere."

"Gaius... You really mean that?"

The bedframe creaked; he must have sat next to her.

"I know, I should have told you about this before we were married. If I'm being honest, I forgot about it. I wasn't sure if I would love again after losing Glenna, and then I met you, Rochelle. I was so besotted nothing else entered my mind."

Lady Kingfisher laughed softly. Aithne smiled, hope fluttering in her chest.

"When you told me you were pregnant, this ridiculous superstition crossed my mind, but I didn't want to worry you or cause you anxiety. I thought to never bring it up at all and let it die." His tone sharpened, "I never expected the priestesses would still believe it. I should–"

"Gaius don't blame them. I believe Priestess Aithne told me so that I could be prepared to protect our child. They are smart, your sea priestesses."

"If you're sure... Please, may I see her now?"

"Of course, Gaius." The blankets rustled. "And I'm sorry for assuming you would... the thought of losing her..."

"I understand, I do. I've had a long time to think about my grand-father's actions. He must have been more disturbed than anyone realized. After barely recovering the Birde Isles from ruin, it must have taken a toll on his mind. At least we can take comfort that there weren't many daughters born after Grandfather took leave of his senses. There were a few, my own father said, and none from the time I was born until now. If I knew how to find them, I would. I can only hope they lived good lives, wherever they ended up."

"Here," Lady Kingfisher shifted. "Meet your own daughter."

"She's beautiful. She looks just like you, darling."

"Almost. I think she'll have those green eyes you're all so proud of."

Lord Kingfisher chuckled. "What shall we name her? Something special, for the first Kingfisher daughter in two generations."

"I was thinking, Alphonsine. After my father's mother."

"Lady Alphonsine Kingfisher. That sounds perfect."

Aithne rested her forehead on the door as relief washed over her. The strange hold over the Kingfishers was broken.

"What's going on, Aithne?"

Spinning around, Aithne collided with Esa.

"Esa!" She hissed, pulling the girl into the hall. "How long were you standing there?"

"Only a moment. Is everything alright?"

"Everything is wonderful." Aithne hugged the young priestess. "Everything is wonderful, and the child has a name. Lady Alphonsine Kingfisher."

News of the birth of Lord and Lady Kingfisher's daughter spread quickly through the Birde Isles and beyond, carried out on the trade and fishing vessels. Kingsport was alive with excitement. Offerings of fruit and fish were brought to the temple to wish the child well. Aithne saw to it the food was given to those in need. Though the three Kingfisher boys hadn't warmed much to their new sister, Aithne was sure they would grow to love her, especially once Alphonsine was old enough to talk and play with them.

It felt good to be sitting on the sand again, though Aithne was also starting to feel her age. It took longer than it used to for her to lower herself onto the beach and find a comfortable position. Finally, she relaxed and closed her eyes. Her hands rested in her lap as a cool, salty breeze brushed over her face. Colder weather would be upon them soon. Aithne let her chin drop and opened herself up to listen to the sea. One of the responsibilities of the head priestess was regular time spent communing with the sea. Listening to the sound of the waves, the calls of the sea birds, and the trickle of sand as it ebbed and flowed from the shore. Taking that sense of peace back to share with those who came to the temple seeking comfort. Since Lady Kingfisher entered the last cycle of her pregnancy, Aithne had been lax in performing this task. Now that things had settled down after Lady Alphonsine's birth, she was taking a long overdue afternoon alone on the shore.

A chill ran through Aithne as she opened her eyes. The sun was nearly set. Had she become so relaxed that she'd fallen asleep?

Trying to uncross her legs proved difficult and she wondered if she'd be able to stand on her own. Esa wouldn't come looking for her until night had truly set in. Aithne rubbed her palms over her thighs, urging the blood to flow.

"Do you need help standing, priestess?"

Startled, Aithne looked up. She hadn't heard the woman walking on the sand. The setting sun was to the woman's back, leaving her face in shadow.

"Yes, it appears I do. My legs aren't quite as good as they used to be."

The woman took both of Aithne's hands and helped her stand, keeping hold of her arm until the priestess found her balance.

"Thank you, very much my dear." Aithne shook the sand from her robes. "I might have been stuck if..." Looking down at the hand steadying her, Aithne saw a flash of multicolored scales against the sleeve of her robe. Dragging her gaze up, daring to hope she was wrong, Aithne met a pair of pitch-black eyes shining at her in the twilight. "You... you are... It can't be."

"I am the sea."

Aithne's knees buckled, and the goddess kept her from falling.

"Careful, priestess. Can you stand on your own?"

Aithne took a bracing gulp of air and nodded. When the goddess was satisfied Aithne wouldn't fall, she let go and backed away.

Aithne's heart raced. Was this truly happening? There were some written details about the goddess of the sea that didn't match the creature standing in front of her, but those accounts were hundreds of years old. Aithne was a priestess, a woman of faith, but her imagining of the goddess had always been more of the natural spirit and power of the sea itself. The resources it provided. Not an actual physical presence that could walk on land when it chose, no matter what story Eschina chose to tell. It was how Aithne trained all the young priestesses to think of the goddess.

"W-why are you here?"

"I've heard that Lord and Lady Kingfisher have welcomed a daughter into their family. I wanted to send my congratulations to them, and a gift."

Aithne stiffened. "Why bring a gift now and not for the other children?"

"I wasn't waiting for the others. The first Gaius Kingfisher and I made a bargain. He promised me the next daughter born to his family."

The priestess pressed her hands to her chest. "That's why... It can't be true. Gaius I was mad, but he couldn't have really promised a daughter to the sea."

"But he did." An oddly shaped object lay in her palm, but it was already too dark for Aithne to see what it was. "Will you not deliver my gift?"

"No! I will not. Take my life instead if you want, I will not allow that child to be taken away from her home." Her voice caught. "Not again."

"Again?" The goddess closed her fist. Her eyes shuttered, blending her face back in with the shadows. "I always wondered, but I never actually thought... How many?"

Aithne swallowed against the fear constricting her throat. She knew what the goddess meant. "I'm not sure. Maybe three."

"*Three*?" She growled low, eyes snapping open. "That *idiot*."

"Please. Please, let this child go. I don't know or care why Gaius I did this, but please spare her."

"Spare her?" The goddess' harsh laugh made Aithne cringe.

"She's only a child! A baby!"

"I didn't ask for a child!" She hissed. "Gaius was supposed to send a daughter to me when she came of age, not before."

"Why wait until she came of age?" Aithne's mind was swimming. She'd pored over the records transcribed by the priestesses when Gaius I was lord of the Birde Isles, looking for a way to convince the Kingfishers to stop sending their daughters away. She'd read how the early islanders sacrificed young people to the sea, but had always questioned that. Why wait until a person was old enough to know they were going to be a sacrifice? The act itself was bad enough, why put an innocent through the fear of knowing what was going to happen to them?

"Aithne?" A faint shout reached them.

Esa. Aithne couldn't let her see this.

"My aide has come for me, please, let me go to her."

The goddess had turned towards the direction of Esa's call. Now, she stepped close, speaking low so only Aithne could hear.

"I'll make you this promise. If the Kingfisher daughter comes to me of her own free will, *after* she's grown, the bargain will be complete. If she's forced to come, or rejects the bargain on her own, it will be broken. I will release my claim on her, but my protection of the Isles will be forfeit."

"Protection?"

"And, *you* have to tell her the truth, so she can decide for herself."

"The truth? How could I possibly tell that child her own great-grandfather was willing to sacrifice her to the sea?"

"Priestess Aithne!" Esa was getting closer.

The goddess whispered into Aithne's ear, "It's your choice, priestess, but don't think you can drag her down here without explanation, just to break the bargain."

Aithne shuddered. "I understand."

"One last thing. Even if we were to meet before she comes of age, I swear I won't tell her who I am until the day she comes freely to settle the agreement."

"Aithne! There you are!"

Aithne turned and shielded her eyes from the glow of Esa's lantern.

"We got worried when you weren't back by sundown." Esa stumbled over the sand. "Are you alright?"

"I'm fine, Esa." Aithne peered over her shoulder, but the goddess was gone. "Help me up to the path. I communed with the sea for so long, my legs became stiff."

"Oh! I wish I'd thought to come sooner." Esa linked arms with her, and they made their way back to the path that led to the temple.

"Thank you, dear Esa." Aithne kept their arms together even after they were far from the shore. Esa's warmth helped chase away the chill left by the encounter with the sea goddess.

"You must have had an exceptional experience, to stay so long."

"I did." Aithne gripped Esa tighter. They were nearly back to the temple, could the goddess hear them there? Or was she bound to the shore? This couldn't happen again. Not another child lost because of one man's rash actions. Perhaps there was a way to keep the girl from encountering the goddess until she was grown? Then Aithne would have more time to prepare her for the truth of what her great-grandfather had done.

She stopped in the middle of the path and held Esa's shoulders. "I communed at great length with the sea and received an important vision."

"A vision?" Esa's brown eyes widened. "What kind of vision?"

"One I will need your help with, Esa, when we deliver it to the King-fishers. Swear you will help me."

She nodded quickly. "Of course. I swear, Aithne."

"Good. Now listen carefully, Lady Alphonsine will always be happy and safe on land, but she must *never* go into the sea. If that child sets even one foot onto the shore before she comes of age, she will know only suffering."

ALLY

CHAPTER THREE

"But I want to go too!" Ally chased after her older brothers, all headed for an afternoon of sailing around the harbor and to Snake Island just beyond. Three sets of matching moss green eyes, and varying degrees of frowns, turned on her at once.

"You know you aren't allowed on the water." Gai, actually Gaius IV, said for the tenth time that day. At eighteen he was the oldest of her siblings and, as such, had declared himself in charge when Lord and Lady Kingfisher weren't around.

"You're still too little, anyway." Thirteen-year-old Calder, the youngest brother, said gently. "It's not safe for a seven-year-old on the open water. We'll take you sailing when you're older. Maybe in a few more years, for your tenth birthday or something."

"You're lying," Ally sulked.

"Of course he is," Luthais said. The middle Kingfisher brother hardly spoke to anyone, unless he felt it was worth the effort. The surly expression that seemed permanently fixed to his face had earned him the nickname 'the Pike' among the servants. Not that Ally would ever mention it. "Father is never going to let you past the seawall, you might as well accept it." Luthais walked away, grumbling about annoying little sisters.

Ally sucked on her bottom lip. She wanted to stomp and yell after him that grouchy brothers weren't so great either. Instead, she took a deep breath and reined in the urge to throw a fit. She already stood out next to her brothers, the last thing she wanted was for them to think she was a brat as well. They were the spitting images of their father, all dark sandy hair and green eyes. Freckles that multiplied with each summer spent in the sun stood out on their skin, more so on Cal than the others. The bridge of his nose and tops of his cheeks looked like they'd been dusted with cinnamon.

"It's not fair," she tried again, appealing to the two kinder brothers. "Everyone else gets to learn to swim and sail. Why can't I?"

Gai cleared his throat, "Not everyone learns those things, Ally. There are plenty of people here who don't swim or sail at all."

"That's not true! *Everyone* learns to swim. We live right next to the sea!"

"Ally," Cal started.

"What about the selkie women who dive for oysters?"

The selkies, named after legendary seal creatures who could shed their seal skins and walk on land as humans, were famous in Kingsport for how deep they could dive and how long they could hold their breaths. Visitors to the islands would take time just to watch them work.

Ally caught a glimpse of a group of them once from a high terrace that faced the harbor, when she'd gone into town with her mother for tea at an ambassador's house. They'd stripped down to nothing but loin cloths and breast bands, nets and knives in hand, and disappeared beneath the waves that crashed against the docks. Some of them even kept their hair shorn off, so they'd be faster underwater. The days spent in the sun and sea had deepened their complexions into varying shades of reddish tan, rich ochre, and golden brown. Even from so far away, Ally could see the many scars they'd picked up over the years of harvesting oysters bare-skinned and barehanded.

They were beautiful.

She'd begged Priestess Esa for stories about them, often while they were supposed to be focused on Ally's lessons. They weren't all Birde Islanders, Esa said, some of the selkies were from the continent across the Eastern Sea, like her mother. Or the lands far beyond the Split Sea that carved its way through the continent, places that took three months to reach by land and even longer by ship. A few even came from the isolated group of islands everyone called The Riddles, where the sands were pink as the peonies in her mother's garden, and the water was always warm and said to be clear as glass. Not anything like the gray sand and cold, murky depths that surrounded Ally's home.

"Not the selkies again." Gai passed a hand over his face. He was growing a blond mustache beneath his upturned nose, like their father. Ally thought it looked like a pale sea urchin was sitting on his upper lip.

"We have to go." Gai gave her shoulder an awkward pat and headed the same way Luthais had gone. "We'll bring you back a pretty shell from Snake Island."

Ally snorted. There were no shells on Snake Island. Only rocks. Snake Island got its name because the stone that made up its base had formed into curving, scale-shaped slats over the years. Nothing grew there and nothing lived there.

Cal shook his head. Kneeling down to Ally's eye level, he ruffled her hair. "Give it a little more time, squirt. I'm sure when you're a bit older Father will let you come with us."

Ally watched her last brother walk away. She was done begging them for permission.

If they weren't going to take Ally with them to the sea, then she'd go by herself.

CHAPTER FOUR

"May I say again, how terribly sorry we are for your loss, Mrs. Dare."

Foraoise gazed at the Meredian lawyer across the desk, fiddling with his papers and seals. Her late husband was sewn into his hammock over a month ago. She'd put the final stitch through his nose herself, to make sure he stayed dead. The process of transferring everything to her name had taken entirely too long, and now this idiot was wasting more of her time with condolences. She longed to free the knife hidden in her bodice and hold it to the man's throat, but that might not hurry him up so much as make him faint. Then she'd have to find another lawyer to finish the paperwork.

"Thank you, it was indeed a shock to lose him so suddenly." Foraoise's gravelly voice belonged to a much older woman. Years of salt air and shouting orders at her late husband's crew had taken their toll. She took a deep breath and locked her hands together to stop them from unbuttoning the lace around her wrists. This frippery would be coming off the moment she returned to the ship, it was hot as blazes and the brown wig she'd forced over her own hair smelled like wet horse. The crew had barely recognized her when she'd left that morning to handle the last of Jon's effects. This was the image the lawyer expected, though, the grieving widow in her black skirts and veil.

The lawyer finally placed the documents in front of her and pushed his pen stand to her end of the desk. "If you'll sign each of these, Mrs. Dare, then our business will be concluded. You will have Captain Dare's certificate of death and all relevant business contracts with the Meredian government."

"And the ship?" Foraoise dipped the nib in the ink pot and scrawled her name across the bottom of each page.

"Yes, of course. The deed to the *Tide's Last Revenge* is on the bottom, along with the form that was requested to change the name."

"Good." She reached the last page, the one that would finally give her ownership of her own story. Crossing out the ship's original name, Foraoise wrote in the new one and signed beneath it.

"It's probably best that you're renaming the ship." He arranged the papers she'd already handed back. "Especially since…" The lawyer cleared his throat, running a finger through the top of his puffy cravat. "You've signed your name as Captain For…" He stumbled over her first name.

"Fora-shuh." She rasped.

"Yes, thank you, as *Captain* Foraoise Dare?"

"That's right." Foraoise handed him the deed and tapped a finger next to the ship's new name: *Maiden's Revenge*. "It's what Jon would have wanted."

ALLY

CHAPTER FIVE

Ally crept through the dark manor grounds, pausing each time she heard boots on the gravel paths. There wouldn't be any guards close to the seawall. Not when the stretch of beach below belonged to the Kingfishers and there was no safe way to sail around to that point without first crossing through Trader's Bay. And no one made it into Trader's Bay without being seen by a hundred other ships and their crews.

Pebbles and bits of shell pinched Ally's bare feet as she climbed down the stone steps. Cal told her they were left over from when a castle once stood where the manor was now. The wind plastered her nightgown against her back. It would have been smart to bring a cloak, and shoes, but she promised herself she wouldn't stay long.

Ally wanted to touch the sea, just one time. Father had never explained why she couldn't go down to the shore. Neither had Mama, or Esa, or anyone else she'd asked. All they ever said was that she wasn't allowed, or it wasn't safe.

Why? Was she deathly allergic to jellyfish? Dolphins? Sand?

Ally stopped playing with the children who sometimes accompanied their parents on visits to the manor. They only teased her. Lately she'd been learning to sew from Mama's seamstress. It was fun, watching something beautiful emerge from bits of fabric and thread. The seamstress said Ally was doing very well for a beginner.

When she reached the dry sand at the base of the steps, Ally's eyes widened. She wiggled her toes and wished she'd thought to bring a light so she could see the rough grains sliding over her feet.

Looking out at the sea, Ally heard the gentle shushing as the waves broke against the shore. The closer she got to the water's edge, the coarser and colder the sand became. She shivered and jumped when the first wave nipped at her toes. The dark waters stretched out forever until they blended in with the starry sky above.

Walking in a bit further, Ally gasped as the wavelets wrapped around her ankles, urging her farther into the sea. It was wonderful, better than she'd imagined. It was everything that made her pause at every high window for a glimpse of the rolling water. With each step her nightgown billowed more around her. Water splashed up and soaked her sleeves, the fabric clinging to her skin. Gooseflesh raced up her arms and legs, but she didn't care. The chill was nothing compared to the rhythm of the waves.

Ally trailed her fingertips over the surface, the sea foam tickled her palms and a giggle bubbled up in her throat. She wanted to stay all night until the sun rose, so she could look into the water and truly see it up close.

Whether it was the tide hugging her waist, the numbness that had settled into her legs, or the joy of finally, *finally*, touching the sea... Ally didn't know how far she'd gone until the first wave broke hard against her chest. She teetered; the wind nearly knocked out of her. Turning in place, Ally couldn't see the shoreline clearly in the dark.

Where was the seawall? Where was the manor? Another high wave slapped against her back, seawater gushed up her nose and she coughed against the sting. How was she going to find the shore... There! She locked onto a dot of light in the distance. A lantern that had been left farther down the beach. She dug her heels into the sand and pushed towards land.

Ally felt a harsh tug as the water pulled back around her middle. She heard the rushing growl of another wave cresting. The wave broke over her head and pulled her under.

Turning end-over-end beneath the water, salt burned in her eyes and scorched down her throat when she opened her mouth to scream for help. Ally dug her fingers into soft, squishy sand as the tide tried to pull her out to sea. Every time she thought she'd stopped herself, the sand broke away and another wave tossed her back. Darkness crept around the edges of her mind, she didn't know if her eyes were opened or shut. Her fingers relaxed and her body went limp as she rolled back and forth with the tide.

She hoped Mama wouldn't be too upset when they realized she was gone.

Ally felt the arms wrap around her and the water rush over her skin as she was pulled towards the surface. The slap of fresh air hit her face and she passed out.

When Ally woke, she was laying on the dry sand farther upshore. Dark, glassy eyes shined above her as a cool hand swept the tangled hair from her forehead.

"You gave me quite a scare. You must be careful if you come to the sea at night." A voice whispered. Something warm and smooth was pressed into Ally's hands. "I want you to hold onto this, take very good care of it for me." The voice laughed softly. "It's the oldest treasure I have."

Ally couldn't speak, she couldn't even blink. Everything else had faded away. Her hands closed reflexively, and she felt a sharp point dig into her palm.

"When you're ready to meet again, I'll be here." The shadowed face disappeared, leaving her to stare up at the fading night sky.

Ally lay there for a long time, filling her lungs with air and waiting for her heartbeat to slow down. Her mouth tasted sour, and she somehow knew she'd already coughed up a lot of seawater. As the brine on her skin and clothing dried, both felt itchy and tight. She felt as if she were coated in sand.

The sky was shifting to the hazy, purple light that came just before dawn when Ally found the strength to sit up. She'd made it all the way back to the seawall steps?

Something sharp pricked her palm again and Ally looked down at the thing clutched in her hand. It was the biggest shark tooth she'd ever seen. Taking up her entire palm, the tooth was polished black like the onyx stone in one of her father's rings. A steady trickle of warmth seeped into her skin, and she hugged the tooth to her chest. On shaky legs she climbed back up the stone steps, hoping she could make it back to her room before anyone saw her.

Ally only looked back at the sea once she reached the safety of the top of the wall. Tears slipped down her cheeks. Everyone was right, as much as she wished it wasn't true, the sea wasn't a safe place for her to be.

PASHA

CHAPTER SIX

The sea must have called to her.

They wouldn't have let the girl come down to the shore alone, at night.

Had they told the child about the bargain already? It was impossible to know, but at least now Pasha could keep a better eye out. If she hadn't been close by when the waves pulled the girl under... Shaking her head, Pasha watched the girl climb the stone steps and pause at the top. The shark tooth pulsed in her hands, growing fainter as it moved farther away, but it would still reach back to the sea. Pasha wouldn't have let the girl drown regardless, but the moment she grabbed her Pasha knew who she was. The scent might have been dulled by the sea, but she was Gaius Kingfisher's descendant rightly enough.

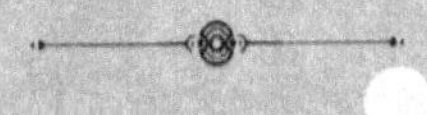

A hundred years had passed since the young human priestess woke Pasha from the sleep that had nearly been her death. She'd used the old way after all, slicing a blade across her palm and sacrificing her blood to the sting of the sea. When Pasha made it to land at last, the girl truly believed

Pasha was the sea goddess. It had been so, so long since Pasha had spoken to anyone. Tears welled up in her eyes for the first time in centuries and she'd gladly given one to heal the priestess' hand. If only it had been the priestess who wanted to speak to the goddess.

Gaius Kingfisher I, the arrogance of him, standing on her shore as if he owned it. Even in the dark of the night, she could see the frayed edges on his once fine clothes. How the supple leather of his boots had dried and cracked from neglect. Demanding, then begging for, her help to save the humans that remained on the islands from a famine of their own creation. Pasha nearly refused, she wasn't even supposed to be on land. The elders had been so severe in their instructions, *stay put and stay out of sight*. But how long had it been since they left? Too long. What would they care if Pasha left the sea when they'd forgotten about her so easily?

When Gaius hit his knees and pleaded again for the *goddess* to aid them, something cold settled into Pasha's heart. If they were determined to abandon her, then she'd find a companion of her own.

"There's only one thing I want." Pasha said to the human groveling in the sand.

"Name it."

"Your daughter."

Gaius lurched to his feet and stumbled back. "I... I have no children."

"But you will, I'm sure, and when you do, you'll bring me your first daughter the very day she comes of age."

"What if I never have a daughter? I am newly married, but..."

"Then you will give me the next daughter born in your family." Pasha tapped a pointed nail against the crest embroidered on his tunic. A kingfisher bird, his family's namesake, frozen mid-dive with two twisting fish in its long beak. "Is it really such a large price to pay for mastery over the tides? For knowing that more of your ships will return safely, laden with as many fish as they can catch? To secure your family's place?" She offered a hand to him. "Do we have a bargain?"

Gaius stared at her as the wind shifted and the light from the moon was blotted out. The man's haggard face hid nothing as he wrestled with the prospect of promising his own blood to save his skin. An idea, a desperate idea, came to him and Pasha saw it in his eyes when Gaius latched onto it.

Triumph surged through Pasha's veins, she had him.

Breathing in sharply, he clasped his hand with hers and sealed the agreement.

"We have a bargain."

"Good."

Lightning flashed around them. For a split-second, in the dark, she let Gaius feel a slick, bone crushing pressure wrap around his wrist. He jerked back, but Pasha's hold kept him anchored to the sand.

When the sky cleared and the moon shined down again, all that was left was her small hand eclipsed by his.

Her grip tightened again when he tried to pull away. "Don't think to deceive me, Gaius Kingfisher. I'll know if you bring me a daughter that is not your own."

When the deal was struck, Pasha'd been grateful it happened, at first. But over time, when she'd fulfilled her own promise and no companion appeared...

Even before she encountered that priestess on the beach, Pasha'd begun to question if the bargain had been a good idea. It seemed like the perfect answer at the time, but to learn that fool had sent his own flesh and blood away? When she'd kept to her end of the deal from the start? Her teeth ground together; threads of white light danced down her arms. Clenching her fists to snuff them out, she told herself this would work. It had to work. The girl was already called to the sea, Pasha was sure, and she wouldn't make the same mistakes as... But there was no point thinking about that. Not anymore.

It could work.

When she felt sure the girl had made it safely home, Pasha dove beneath the surf. Swimming down, down, down farther than the humans could reach, she slipped into her home and waited.

CHAPTER SEVEN

Maher Villaon hustled down a side hall in the Kingfisher manor. He would not be dragged out on another boat with Lord Kingfisher's sons.

Three months had passed since his father accepted this post on the Birde Isles, they'd arrived just shy of his thirteenth birthday, and all Maher had heard about was fishing, boats, trade, and more boats.

The only remotely interesting member of the Kingfisher family was Lady Alphonsine, and she spent most of her time cooped up with her sewing instructor. At least she was interested in an activity besides sailing, but there was something uneasy in her. Maher never saw her go beyond the base of the sea cliff slope that rose behind the manor. Any mention of the beach or the ocean and Lady Alphonsine's hazel eyes would glaze over. Something must have happened to her, Maher tried asking her brother Luthais about it. That hadn't gone well. He quickly figured out why people called the middle Kingfisher brother the Pike when he wasn't around.

Maher was almost to the front end of the manor. Despite the simple outward appearance of the house – a massive, red brick rectangle with dozens of glass-paned windows and a sloping gray roof – it still took him weeks to memorize the inner layout of this place. If he could make it out the garden doors in Lady Kingfisher's front parlor without being seen, he could hide in the hedges or the tall grass on the cliff slope until the brothers were gone.

Reaching the double doors of the parlor, Maher slid one open a few inches to check if Lady Kingfisher was inside.

"Let's see what you're doing, then." A shrill, unfamiliar voice floated out of the room.

"It's not finished…"

That was Alphonsine.

Maher slowly pushed the door open. Three girls around his age had ten-year-old Alphonsine cornered. One look at their expensive clothes and the satin ribbons woven into their hair, and Maher knew they must be the daughters of the trade guild members who were meeting in his father's study at that very moment. That private meeting was why Maher was told to go sailing again with Lord Kingfisher's sons.

"I said, give it here!" The tallest girl, the ringleader if Maher were to guess, snatched the embroidery hoop and fabric out of Alphonsine's hands. Her fiery hair was woven through with a complicated web of white ribbons.

"Give that back!" She reached for her sewing as the tall girl held it over her head. "You'll ruin it!"

"It already looks ruined to me." Another girl in a long goldenrod dress laughed, high and nasal. Maher knew her, Safiye, her family was from Saprea too. Which meant the third girl, with the same jet-black hair and a matching dress in a shade of burnt orange, was Safiye's twin sister, Latife.

"You're right." Latife took the hoop and squinted at it. "Looks like one big, ugly knot."

Alphonsine's small hands curled into fists. "That's the *back*. Just because you're too stupid to know the difference..."

"Shut your mouth!" Latife threw the hoop across the room.

"It's not nice to call people names." The tall one loomed over her. "I think you should apologize."

"I think you should leave me alone, Beitris." Alphonsine snapped.

Maher grinned. Alphonsine had more spirit than he thought. He wasn't going to leave her outnumbered, though.

Beitris lifted her nose and gave an exaggerated sniff. "Do you smell something Safiye? Latife?"

"Sure do." Safiye propped her hands on her hips. "I heard a rumor that little Lady Kingfisher doesn't take baths anymore. Turns out it's true."

Maher slipped into the room and shut the door without making a sound.

"Maybe getting clean would improve her attitude." Latife giggled.

Alphonsine pressed back against the wall. Her face went gray, and her eyes took on the glaze which Maher understood now was complete terror at what they were saying.

"I suppose she can't smell herself anymore with that nose." Safiye added.

"Why don't we take her down to the ocean for a swim?" Beitris reached for the smaller girl.

Marching up behind them, Maher summoned the voice he'd acquired after years of following his father through the Saprean trade floors.

"*What do you think you're doing?*"

They all spun around. Latife shrieked when she saw Maher.

"Maher!" Safiye plastered a fake smile on her face. "What are you doing in here? This is the ladies' parlor."

Maher's upper lip curled back. "I couldn't help but notice the three of you picking on a child not half your size."

"W-we were only playing around." Latife said, twisting the front of her skirt in her hands.

"I doubt that." He put himself between them and Alphonsine, who still didn't seem to be aware of what was going on around her.

"Maher, was it?" The ringleader flipped her long red hair off her shoulder. "I'm Beitris Tapper. I'm sure –"

"I don't care. Now I suggest *you* apologize to Lady Alphonsine and leave, before I go interrupt your parents' meeting to show them what you've done."

"No!" Latife gasped. "Please don't!"

Beitris' pretty face crumpled into a scowl. "Do you even know who my father is?"

"Do you know who *my* father is?" Maher arched a brow. He'd never had to throw that line out before, but Beitris sounded like she used it often.

"Please, Beitris, let's go." Safiya tugged on her sleeve. "Maher's father is the Saprean ambassador!"

"Fine." Beitris turned to leave.

"And the apology?"

"I'm sorry," Beitris tossed over her shoulder. "That we were interrupted." She flung the doors open and flounced out of the room.

The sisters backed out after her, apologizing over each other.

"We're very sorry…"

"Lady Alphonsine, really…"

"It won't happen…"

"Again. We swear it."

They hit the threshold and stumbled out.

Sighing, Maher turned and knelt in front of Alphonsine. Some color had returned to her face, but her pupils were still unfocused.

"Lady Alphonsine?" Maher said softly. "Can you hear me?"

Her lips parted, but no sound came out. Slowly, Maher placed a hand on her shoulder. "Alpohns..."

"NO!" She snapped back into the world. Her arms flailed and Maher narrowly avoided taking an elbow to the face.

"It's alright!" He backed up, hands held out by his sides. "They're gone. No one is going to hurt you."

"Gone?" The moment she realized he was right, Alphonsine slid to the floor and sobbed into her hands.

"Ah! Don't worry, please." Maher pulled a handkerchief from his vest pocket and offered it to her. "Those girls don't deserve your tears."

The cloth trembled in her hands as she took it from him and covered her face. Maher scanned the room and found where Alphonsine's hoop had landed. He picked it up and trotted back over to her.

"Here, I don't think it's damaged." Maher smoothed the free edges of the fabric aside. His fingers traced the delicate floral embroidery pattern, the stitches were impeccable. "You have a real talent." He looked up to find her staring at his handkerchief.

She turned the dark green square at several angles, studying the white tulips sewn around the edges. "I've never seen a pattern like this."

"My aunt made that for me." Maher smiled. "I have others with that pattern if you'd like to have one?"

"Really?" Her face lit up. "That would be wonderful! I can make you a foxglove one to replace it, if you like."

"It's a good trade." Maher helped her stand up. "Do you feel better now?"

"Yes, I... thank you, for helping me."

"Those sisters won't bother you anymore. Though I can't say the same for that Beitris."

She made a face. "Beitris is always nasty when we're alone. She's nice when my family is around because she wants to marry my brother Calder."

"Poor Calder." Maher laughed.

"But that's the first time she's…" Alphonsine trailed off and she rubbed a hand against her chest, as if her heart hurt.

"Lady Alphonsine?" Maher tensed, ready to catch her if she left him again.

"Call me Ally, please." She shook her head. "I'm fine, I just didn't think many people outside the manor knew I was afraid of water."

"Some people are prone to gossip. The trick is not to let anyone think you care if they talk." Maher led the way to one of the parlor couches and they sat down. "Can I ask, why are you afraid? I thought most Birde Islanders loved the water. And sailing." He rolled his eyes. "So much sailing."

Ally smiled. "I had a feeling you weren't enjoying yourself with my brothers. A few years ago," she looked down at the hoop in her lap, "I almost drowned. I went down to the beach alone, it was dark, and I went too far out. Since then, the thought of being under water…"

"I'm sorry, Ally. Making light of someone else's fear is a coward's way of feeling important." When she reached up and touched the lump on the bridge of her nose, he asked, "Did that happen that night?"

"Huh?" Ally let her hand fall. "No, it didn't, but not long after. A maid tried to put me in a tub. I didn't handle it well." She pursed her lips. "I still take baths, they're just small ones."

"You look perfectly clean to me." Maher grinned. "In fact, I think you might be too clean. The glow of your skin hurts my eyes." A small throw pillow hit his shoulder and he stroked his chin. "You also smell quite lovely. Like fresh, red roses, and sunshine, and–"

The next pillow hit his face.

CHAPTER EIGHT

Ally stared at the ceiling above her bed, awakened yet again by the same dream she'd had every month, without fail, for nearly a year.

The dream first came to her on the night of her sixteenth birthday and it always began the same way. She was sitting on top of a steep hill, watching the wind blow through the tall grass in the valley below. Then, the wind would shift, and the green grass blended together until it became a sea. A sea in a brilliant shade of blue that she'd never found in the real world.

The water scared her; it always did. Her heart would beat faster, and she'd dig her fingers into the soil on either side of her legs. But then something would happen that never did when Ally was awake. The longer she looked at the gently rolling surface, the calmer she felt. The thing that frightened her most would soothe and murmur until her body relaxed and her fear was reduced to a small, insecure thing in the back of her mind. In the next blink she'd find the hill had shrunk into a soft dune just above the water.

What came next varied. Sometimes, she'd hear the splash of an unseen creature swimming towards her. Other times, there would be a dark shape gliding smoothly beneath the surface. Or she'd hear a soft voice whispering on the edges of the waves, but couldn't make out what was being said.

Ally would stand, brush the sand from her clothes, and walk closer. Just as she reached the water's edge, every single time, she would wake up.

When Ally mentioned the recurring dream to her mother, Lady King-fisher had assured her there was nothing to worry about. Mama even offered it could be a symptom of her monthly cycle. Ally didn't think that was it, though. The dream was too real, too powerful to just be a trick played by her body. Besides, she was starting to suspect, and dread, what dream Ally wanted.

It was happening more often, something compelled Ally to seek out the highest manor windows for glimpses of the sea. Her steps would slow whenever she and Maher passed the trading port in town, though she didn't dare set foot on the docks. Last summer, she tried to attend a ship dedication with her parents. Ally's tutor, Priestess Esa, was to lead the ceremony, where she would dip her hand in red paint and leave a print on the bow of the ship. The symbolic gesture represented the goddess of the sea's blessing for the crew's protection. Arriving in the wharf district for the ceremony set Ally's heart racing. One step onto the dock where the new ship waited, and her vision went gray. Had Gai not caught her, Ally would have landed face down and likely busted her nose. Again.

Still, glancing out of windows wasn't working anymore.

Sitting up, Ally made sure her shark tooth was still securely around her neck. Often the dream made her pull on it so hard she untied the cord. The fire in her room had died down to glowing embers. Shivering, Ally wrapped a shawl over her nightgown and stepped into a pair of slippers. She still had a few hours before anyone else would be awake.

Tall, dry grass brushed against her legs as she climbed the slope that rose up behind the manor. Tiny pebbles and bits of twig dug into the thin soles of her slippers. A chilly breeze tugged at her shawl, but her necklace kept her comfortable enough. The one thing she'd never told anyone about her good luck charm, and thankfully no one else had noticed, was that it was always *warm*. Ally couldn't explain it, but the low, steady stream of heat soaking into her skin only made her more certain the fossil was something special.

Ally's heart sped up with each step, but she didn't stop walking. When she reached the top of the slope, Ally inched closer to the edge, mindful of the cliff that dropped off into the sea on the other side. There was enough pre-dawn light to know when she'd gone far enough. Ally sat down in the thick grass, heart pounding now as she wrapped her arms around her knees and waited.

The sound reached her first, distant waves breaking against stone. She was already used to the salty air and smell of the water, living so close, but up here the air felt cleaner, crisp. Her lungs filled as much as they could with each breath. The sky grew brighter and finally Ally could see the water rolling away into the horizon.

Like in the dream, Ally grabbed handfuls of dirt and hoped her pulse would slow down. It wouldn't do if she'd made it this far, only for her heart to give out. She didn't feel as calm as she'd have liked, but this was far enough from the sea that she didn't feel in danger of being pulled in. There were no shapes swimming towards her or whispers trickling out of the foam, but Ally hadn't really expected that part to come true.

This was good. This was close enough.

The dreams didn't stop after that, but they became less intense. They didn't startle her awake in the middle of the night, tugging at her until she got out of bed. As long as Ally didn't go too long without visiting her perch over the sea, the dreams would play out and then float away.

FORAOISE

CHAPTER NINE

Foraoise waited alone in the captain's cabin, a letter in her hand.

Light from the candlesticks bolted to the map table illuminated the half of her hair that was shaved down. A jagged scar wrapped around the exposed side of her skull.

A leaving present from dear Jon.

The letter had arrived by way of a Meredian pigeon several days before. Foraoise read the handful of lines again, absorbing each word and storing them away for later use. The paper itself would have to be burned, there was too much risk in keeping it.

"Captain?" The quartermaster, Swain, knocked on the cabin door before sticking his head inside. "We're coming up on the trade ship. We should be upon her in less than an hour."

"Good. Even if they spot us, they'll be too weighed down to make full sail." She held the paper over one of the candles, catching the corner on fire. Watching the words from her mysterious new friend burn away, she dropped the remnants onto an empty plate.

"It's right where you said it would be and no mistake. The Fraollish don't usually sail this far south," He tugged at one end of the gray-streaked mustache that hung down to his chin. "How'd you come to know that, Captain?"

"That's not important right now, Swain." Foraoise turned, catching his eye. "What's important is that we take the ship with as little damage as possible."

A slow grin spread across his face. "Why'd that be, Captain?"

"I'm going to keep this one." Foraoise jerked her head towards the door. "Go tell the crew, I want that ship in one piece."

After the quartermaster left, Foraoise bolted the door and strode back across the cabin. Against the wall, beneath the table, sat an old wine crate. Crouching down, she lifted the lid and pulled out one of the corked clay jars that sat in the bottle slots.

Standing in the middle of her cabin, Foraoise uncorked the jar and tipped it over her head. Thick, red liquid poured onto her hair, running over the grooves of her scar and dripping down the sides of her face.

It wasn't blood. Blood spoiled, no matter how well she tried to preserve it. This mixture was her own creation, adjusted over the years until she had something that would keep for months at a time. She went through several failed versions, until the day they took a prize carrying a large shipment of carmine powder exported from Agriya. Made from thousands of crushed red insects, the powder held the color of real blood and wouldn't slowly poison her like some of the other pigments she'd researched.

Jon gave her the idea. The day he tried to kill her, the day he gave her the scar that made her famous. When she'd stood over him with her own blood coursing down her face, soaking into her hair and clothes... The fear she'd seen in his eyes lit a fire in her soul she'd never felt before. If she could frighten the great Captain Jon Dare, imagine what she could do as captain of her own life.

When a prize was in sight, Captain Foraoise Dare would douse herself before they caught up to the other ship. Years of using the liquid had stained her hair and scalp until it really appeared that she bathed in blood before each attack. Some of her more seasoned crew liked to tell new recruits it was the blood of sailors who disobeyed orders. They tended to believe it, once they saw the red stained floorboards of the captain's quarters.

Foraoise used the empty jar to grind down the charred remains of the letter. The anonymous writer had given her the ship's exact route without asking for anything in return, a play to gain her trust. If the cargo on this ship was everything the letter implied it to be, she would write back.

The barrelman's whistle blew, high and sharp. They were closing in on the other ship. Captain Dare secured her weapons and pulled open the cabin door. This might prove to be the most fruitful friendship she'd ever had.

CHAPTER TEN

"There you are." Maher wandered into the parlor, hands tucked into his trouser pockets.

Ally barely looked up from the embroidery hoop balanced on her knee. "Don't shut the door."

"I wouldn't dream of it." Maher stopped in front of her. "Come on, we're going to the market."

"I'm busy."

"What are you going to do, sit in here and sew for the rest of your life?"

Now she glanced up at him mid-stitch. "So what if I do? Who else will keep you in fancy waistcoats and handkerchiefs? Before I met you, Maher, I never knew one person could own so many clothes."

"Are you saying *I'm* the one keeping you in here?" He snorted. "And my wardrobe is not that large."

"You had the room next to yours converted into a closet."

"The rooms on that hall only come with one small cupboard!"

"You could go a month without wearing the same outfit twice."

"Then stop making things for me, if it's so much trouble."

Ally scowled at him. "Face it, darling, you're becoming quite the popinjay."

Maher's mouth dropped open. "You…That…"

Ally's shoulders trembled. She buried her face in her lap but couldn't stop the snort of laughter that escaped.

"You little imp!" Maher laughed, his head tipping back. "You nearly kept a straight face. I'm impressed."

"I learned from this Saprean boy who keeps hanging around." She set her hoop aside and stretched her fingers. "Why do you want to go to the market?"

Maher sat next to her. "For one thing, you need to get out for some fresh air."

"Didn't we just spend an entire day out in the woods east of Kingsport?"

"Not everyone is blessed with this beautiful complexion." He swept a hand across his brow. "You need all the time outside you can get."

Ally's head tilted. "Aren't you taking credit for something that happened purely by chance?"

"Will you please just come to the market with me?" He sighed. "Your birthday is almost here and I want an idea of what gift to buy for you."

"You always pick out nice gifts on your own." She kept glancing past him.

Maher turned, but there was no one there. "Yes, my taste is legendary, but this is your coming-of-age birthday! The entire house is bustling to get everything ready for the celebration. I want to be sure you'll love what I give you." He paused. "Is there some reason you don't want to go? We can avoid the streets that run next to the wharf."

"It's not that." Ally pulled her curls back and tied them in place with a bit of ribbon from her pocket. "I can go anywhere in the market, as long as I don't have to actually set foot on the docks." She lowered her voice, "I overheard Gai and Luthais talking…"

"About what?"

"Another of our trade ships is late returning from the southern end of the continent. What if it was attacked like the one from last summer?"

"Have they any proof it was attacked?"

"I don't know. They went into the sitting room where the representatives from the trade guild were waiting."

"The sitting room?" Maher glanced through the open parlor doorway to the closed double doors just across the front hall. "You're waiting for them to come back out."

"Now you're catching on." She held up the embroidery hoop and only then did Maher notice she wasn't even following a pattern. It was a random assortment of shapes. She just wanted to look busy.

"Clever, aren't you?" Maher grinned. "Hold on."

He nipped across the front hall, checked that no servants were nearby, and pressed an ear to a seam in the door frame. The voices were too muffled to hear well, but there had to be at least half of the trade guild leaders in there. All talking over each other. When he heard a brusque call for order that had to be from Luthais, Maher rejoined Ally in the parlor.

"I couldn't make anything out, but they are most definitely upset about something."

Ally frowned, picking at loose threads on her fake project. "Even if I asked them, they probably wouldn't tell me anything. Gai acts like I wouldn't understand just because I never learned to sail. Or have ever even been on a ship."

Maher thought for a moment. He grabbed Ally's hand and pulled her to her feet. "Let's go to the market."

"What? Still? I don't think my seventeenth birthday present is as important as what's going on in that sitting room."

Maher took the hoop and dropped it into her sewing basket. "There's more than one way to gather information."

When they reached the Kingsport market, Maher took them down to the row of shops lining the docks. Starting at one end, they entered each shop under the guise of Ally deciding on a birthday present. Ally would browse through the wares being offered while Maher chatted with the clerks and shopkeepers.

As they worked their way down the street, Ally began to give him curious looks.

"How often do you come here?" she asked, after the fifth stop.

"What do you mean?"

"How do you know all of these people so well?"

"You know I sometimes run errands for my father to the guild headquarters. It makes sense that I'd become acquainted with a few people along the way."

"This is more than a few," she pointed out. "Every shopkeeper has called you by name the moment we walked in, as if you're down here all the time. Is this what you do while I'm in my lessons with Esa?"

Maher sniffed. "It would also make sense, given how well I've grown up, that I've picked up a few admirers. Word travels fast when you turn out this handsome."

"Old Mrs. Ekmekci at the bakery is sweet on you, is she? It all makes sense now. When should I send a gift to congratulate the happy couple?"

"I'll not have you mocking my relationship with Mrs. Ekmekci, her walnut pastries are incredible. Keep it up and I won't invite you to the wedding." He opened the door to the next shop. "After you. We're losing daylight."

There were only a handful of businesses left on the row. Ally was suggesting they switch up their story, - who would believe she wanted a shaving kit for any birthday, let alone her seventeenth? - when the bell above the barbershop door dinged.

Out of the barber's walked a tall girl with dark red hair. When she turned to face them, they saw she'd just had one entire side of her head shaved down from her temple to the back of her skull.

"Beitris?" Ally blurted out. "What in the goddess' name have you done?"

Beitris Tapper looked down her nose at them. "Don't you presume to judge me *Lady* Alphonsine. There's nothing wrong with a woman changing her hair. Half the selkies shave all theirs off!"

"You're really comparing yourself to the selkies?"

Maher smirked, proud of his friend. When they first met, Ally only spoke her mind to someone like Beitris when forced.

The trader's daughter sneered. "Don't you know? This is the style worn by the great pirate maidens of the Eastern Sea. It's a symbol of their independence. They do what they want, go where they want –"

"Steal what they want," Maher muttered.

Ally crossed her arms. "You're copying the supposed hairstyle of the women who just last year, along with other pirates, attacked one of our ships? Stole our supplies? Killed our sailors?"

Beitris faltered, red splotches appeared on her cheeks. "They're... they're free! They govern themselves."

"They murder people," said Maher.

"They're unafraid to make their own way!"

"Make their own way?" Ally scoffed. "You've never worked a day in your life! You probably can't even make yourself a cup of tea and you think you can be a pirate maiden?"

"The docks are right there you know." Beitris stalked closer. "Keep insulting me, *my lady*, and you just might fall in."

Maher felt Ally stiffen next to him. Beitris Tapper might have been the tallest among them when they were children, but Maher had that advantage now. He stepped in front of Ally, but not so much that she couldn't see what was happening.

"Do you know where your father is right now, Beitris? I'd wager he's at the Kingfisher manor with the other guild members, trying to figure out if one of our largest trade ships has been captured by one of your precious pirate maidens." Maher let his eyes roam over the section of hair missing from her head. "What do you think he'll say about your new hairstyle?"

The color drained from her face. Without another word, Beitris turned on her heel and headed straight for the milliner's shop at the end of the street.

As soon as she was out of sight, Maher turned back to Ally. Her shoulders were hunched, and she was breathing a little fast, but her eyes were clear.

"Let's handle the rest of the shops tomorrow." Maher looped his arm through Ally's and turned them down a side street, away from the docks. "I'd love to be a cat on the windowsill when Mister Tapper sees his daughter's daring new aesthetic."

The farther they walked, the more Ally relaxed. As they crossed through the main square with its brightly colored tile mosaics, she looked up at him and smiled.

"Forget the cat. I wonder if she'll find a hat big enough to cover that side of her head?"

CHAPTER ELEVEN

Ally sat nearly hidden in the grass that grew above the sea cliff, watching the sunrise crest over the unending stretch of water. Waves rolled and broke against the rocks down below.

This was still as close as Ally dared to get and, if she was being honest, the sea was the last place she wanted to be. But she was pulled to this spot each morning. As if something were calling to her from beneath the waves, and it only grew louder as time passed. She'd been coming for six years now and had hardly missed a day. She *had* to lay her eyes on the sea, even if from a distance. From her little nest of grass, she could see beyond the cliffs and the old seawall to the stretch of beach that belonged to the manor grounds, and even beyond that to the edge of Kingsport harbor. The anchored and moored ships floated quietly next to each other; their furled sails left the masts standing like a forest of bare trees. The people who made their living along the harbor were starting their day, already she could see movement on the docks.

The large, black shark tooth dangled from her hand by a leather cord. Ally didn't remember much about that night, when she nearly drowned, but when the waves had spit her back on land the tooth was clutched in her hands. It became her good luck charm, a talisman she wore every day around her neck, the necklace tucked safely beneath her clothes.

Only those who were closest to Ally knew about it. When she first started wearing the tooth as a necklace, Luthais had plucked the cord out of her hands to examine it. Ally became so hysterical she nearly passed out. The tongue lashing Luthais received from their father was heard by most of the manor. Possibly throughout Kingsport.

Ally hadn't planned on telling *anyone* about that night, about how foolish she'd been to go down to the sea alone. She thought she'd be able to keep that secret too. Until a few days later, when one of the maids tried to give her a bath.

Panic, instant and all-consuming, had washed over her. Instead of a cozy tub of scented water, Ally saw black waves trying to pull her under. Her vision blurred and she couldn't breathe. She struggled so hard the maid dropped her, and Ally's face bounced off the edge of the copper tub. Blood was everywhere. Her nose was broken, and twin bruises soon blossomed under each eye. Ally had to tell her mother what happened that night on the beach, to save the already guilt-stricken maid from losing her position.

Since then, Ally only used a kettle and basin to wash herself. It took twice as long, but she could handle small amounts of water. The thought of submerging herself in anything larger than a bucket-full still set her head spinning.

Ally caught herself running a fingertip over the long, crooked knot that ran down the bridge of her nose. A reminder to the world of her fear. She'd tried to break the habit early on, thinking it would only draw more attention. Then, one day she overheard a visiting dignitary say to their attendant, "Lord Kingfisher's daughter is pretty enough, I suppose, but she's ruined the Balahn nose her mother gave to her."

After that, Ally didn't give a barnacle's backside if anyone saw her touching her nose. They were going to think what they wanted either way.

The sun was over the water now. Sliding the shark tooth back around her neck, Ally pressed it against her skin a moment before standing and brushing the dirt from the loose trousers she'd thrown on to come outside.

The wing of the manor that held the living quarters was still quiet, but the lower levels would be bustling by now. Ally slipped inside through her mother's parlor. Cutting down a hall that was near the front gallery, she spied a familiar figure peeking around the corner ahead. Even with his back to her, she'd know Maher anywhere.

When Maher and his father first arrived in Kingsport, she'd assumed the gangly boy with wide, chestnut-brown eyes would spend most of his time with her brothers. To her surprise, and occasional consternation over the years, Ally and Maher found they had far more in common. He was an exceptional artist, mostly uninterested in the more athletic activities her brothers favored. Ally helped bring many of his drawings and paintings to life with needle and thread. Their shared love of art and creative pursuits soon had them spending hours together each day. They became fast friends, so much so that Lady Kingfisher suggested the Villaons stay at the manor rather than find their own house in town. There was only Maher and his father, after all, and so they stayed.

What Ally wanted to know that particular morning, was Maher sneaking out of the house or sneaking back in?

PASHA

CHAPTER TWELVE

Pasha braced herself against a low rock that jutted out from the sea. The hunk of stone shielded her from the waves that were drawn towards the cliff and from any humans that might be on the hill above. The beacon cast by the shark tooth drifted farther away, the girl was leaving.

The Kingfisher daughter came to this spot often, it was the closest she'd gotten to the sea since the night Pasha dragged her out.

Her coming-of-age birthday had passed some years ago. Was it four? Or five? Pasha was starting to lose track. Either the priestess hadn't kept her word, or worse, the girl knew about the bargain but had no intention of coming.

White hot threads wrapped around Pasha's fingers and bounced from knuckle to knuckle. She swam beneath the cliffs and ducked through one of the many tunnels that led into her home, ending up on the side of the island where most of the humans' ships were docked. Floating farther out from the big island, *Kingfisher* Island they called it, Pasha eyed the banded current she'd put in place the very day the bargain was made. It took all the strength Pasha had back then to create, after laying still for so long. The current hovered around the bay, a halo of energy drawing enough fish to feed all three islands and more.

For a century that current had slowly leeched energy away from her, never allowing her to fully heal or recharge. No more.

Pasha dipped her hands into the current. It shifted and clung to her like ribbons of seaweed. She grabbed the middle strands and *pulled*. Electricity arced through Pasha's bones, the water around her crackled. Every creature within range of the shock darted away.

When she ripped through the last of the threads holding the band together, a pulse shot through the water. High waves crashed against the edges of the big island and battered the sides of ships that got in the way. No doubt, even the smaller islands would feel the ripple of what Pasha had just done.

They weren't coming back, and the girl wasn't coming either. Not even to see what the bargain was about.

Pasha was alone and she was going to stay alone.

Fine. If she was going to be alone, she'd take back all that was hers since the beginning.

Chapter Thirteen

Ally moved quietly, glad that she'd chosen a soft, worn-in pair of boots that morning. Leaning over Maher's shoulder, she whispered, "Where do you think you're going?"

"By the gods, Ally!" Maher's back hit the wall. He slapped a hand against his chest and scowled down at her. "My hair is going to gray before my time and it's going to be your fault. Why are you up so early?"

"Why are *you*?" She glanced at his simple black trousers and waistcoat, white shirtsleeves rolled up over lean, dark brown forearms. No rings on his fingers or in his ears. It was a far cry from the bright colors and intricate embroideries he usually wore, often stitched by Ally. "You went down to the Lantern last night, didn't you?"

"So what if I did?" Maher straightened his waistcoat and ran a hand over the side of his head. The careful waves he'd styled and pomaded into his thick, coal black hair were mussed. The close-cropped beard that hugged his jawline was freshly trimmed. Everything about him at that moment announced he'd gone down to the Lantern for a tumble, or two.

The Lantern wasn't just one place, but a section of streets close to the trading wharf that slanted into a shape not unlike an oil lamp. The close-set buildings were nondescript brown brick, nearly identical, but in Kingsport they weren't allowed to openly advertise certain after-dark entertainments. To get around the law, each building hung a lantern with glass panes tinted a specific color to indicate what was being offered inside. Red for gambling halls and games of chance. Green if you were seeking women, orange if you preferred men, there were as many options as there were colors of glass. There were even blue lanterns for those who wanted a place to relax and have someone talk to them, brush back their hair, express concern. Maher said there were times the blue lanterns did more business than all the rest.

Maher was becoming a known patron at several of the establishments, but Ally knew which ones he frequented the most. He'd shown her in case something ever happened to him, and he didn't make it home. They went during a safer time of day, before the sun set and the flames were lit.

"You see that one? Never go in there." He'd pointed out a building tucked back in a dead-end street. The frame of the lantern out front had been painted gold and black soot was smudged all over the panes. It couldn't have been real gold; someone would have stolen it already.

"Why?" Ally asked as he led the way back out. "What's that one for?"

Maher cleared his throat and kept his eyes ahead. "You don't want to know."

They never spoke of the black lantern establishment again. Since it wasn't one Maher visited, Ally didn't worry that he'd get into anything he couldn't handle. Not much, anyway.

"Come on. I'll walk with you." Ally made sure the next corridor was still empty and waved him out. "Your father will keel over if he ever catches you."

He fell in step beside her. "We can only hope."

"Maher Villaon! You don't mean that." Ally swatted his arm.

"I suppose not." He gave her a cheeky grin. "You can always come with me next time. You know I'll keep an eye on you if you run into trouble."

Ally's face grew hot, and she seriously considered pushing him into one of the statuary alcoves. See if the sound of cracking marble would rouse his father.

"I have no interest in going to the Lantern district with you." She raised her chin. "If I were to go, I'd much rather be by myself. I don't want an audience, as I suspect you do."

Maher stumbled, but quickly righted himself. His long legs caught back up to her in a few strides.

"Very good." Maher had been her teacher in, as he called it, the art of verbal sparring. "Let me know which night you'd like me to cover for you, my princess."

"I'm *not* a princess. How many years have I been telling you that?"

"Let's see… that would be nearly twelve glorious years I've been blessed with your company."

"So you should have remembered it by now. Do I need to stitch it onto your underwear?"

"You might as well be a princess," Maher pointed out. "The Birde Isles have been independent practically since your ancestors landed here."

Ally sighed. "Father believes that staying a lord will…"

"Keep him closer to the people…"

"…than crowning himself a king or an emperor."

They stopped outside Maher's room. He felt along the edge of the door, below the lock, and withdrew a tiny scrap of silk. "Good, no one's been here."

"Politics and art are not your calling." Ally shook her head, "You should train as a spymaster instead."

"Spymaster of the Birde Isles. I like the sound of that." Maher winked and slipped into his room.

Ally stuck her tongue out at the closed door and turned back the way they'd come. This hall was mostly for visitors, foreign dignitaries and the like. Maher liked the privacy of not having any permanent neighbors and had persuaded his father to let him move from the Saprean ambassador's quarters when he came of age.

"Ally!"

"What?" she turned; Maher's head was sticking out into the hall.

"Are we still going to the market today?"

"Of course," she smiled sweetly. "As long as you bathe first."

The door slammed shut and Ally resumed the walk back to her own chambers. It was good they had time to visit the market, she wanted to buy a few things for her mother. The Lady Kingfisher's birthday was coming soon.

FORAOISE

CHAPTER FOURTEEN

Captain Dare stood at the quarterdeck railing of the *Maiden's Revenge*, watching as the sailors under her command swarmed the captured trade ship, the *Gull's Flight*, rounding up what was left of her crew.

"We've taken the ship, Captain." Swain appeared at her side and confirmed what she already knew. His face was streaked with soot and blood that was not his own. When they realized they were outgunned by the two ships Foraoise sent to flank the prize, the traders tried to set their cargo on fire.

This vessel was smaller than the others she'd taken, lighter on the water. It would make a useful addition to her budding fleet. She scanned the rigging until she spotted the sailor taking down the ship's flag with its diving bird and replacing it with her own. The banner snapped in the wind, a cracked black heart with a dagger pierced through, on a field of red. Foraoise smiled.

Another crew member approached and got Swain's attention. She was a signaler, trained to use different colored flags to relay orders to the other ships. "Quartermaster, we've got about a dozen of the trader's crew who want to jump ship."

Foraoise glanced at the sailor, who quickly avoided the captain's eye. She swept off her cap and mopped her brow before shoving it back over her head. A fresh tattoo of Dare's heart and dagger emblem stood out on her forearm.

"Captain?" Swain asked.

"Aye, they can join up. Since they volunteered, they can be tasked with gathering any goods to be auctioned off at the mast." She pushed her long braid back over her shoulder, it was heavy with the latest coat of fake blood. "Let one longboat go. We'll need someone to take the news back home."

"And the rest?"

"We have plenty of sailors from the last prize to crew this one." Foraoise turned back to watch the activity below. "Feed the sharks."

"Aye Captain!" The signaler grinned, showing the number of teeth she'd lost to scurvy, and took off for the flag post at the bow of the ship.

"You're sure, Captain?" Swain asked carefully.

"Questioning my decision, Swain?" She shot back. "Care to put it to the crew?"

"Course not," he shrugged. "I only ask 'cause you left those that wouldn't join up from the last prize to fend for themselves."

"That was a Meredian ship. This one isn't." Foraoise thought of the newest letter that had arrived the week before, waiting for her in her cabin. She owed her friend a reply. "Kill the rest."

CHAPTER FIFTEEN

Ally threw on a cream-colored shirt that had once belonged to Maher, until he outgrew it. Tiny blue flowers embroidered across the neckline and around each cuff were the reason she hadn't wanted to part with it. A skirt in the same periwinkle shade was next, hemmed above the ankle for easier walking. Her usual daytime belt with its attached pouch, a gift from Cal, and the same boots from that morning went on last.

Maher was waiting for Ally in the front hall of the manor.

Now he looked more like himself, in a cobalt blue waistcoat and trousers with a daffodil yellow shirt. Small gold hoops glinted from his earlobes and a wide gold band wrapped around each thumb. It was warm enough that he'd left off the jacket for that suit. Ally was glad, it showed off the gold tulips she'd embroidered on the front of his waistcoat. The pattern drew the eye away from Maher's waist, making him appear slightly broader than he was. He'd always been on the thinner side of slender and very aware of it. After each growth spurt, Ally would tailor Maher's clothes to fit in a way that made him feel more confident. It was the least she could do, after he'd seen her through countless bouts of panic brought on by her fear of water.

"Don't you look nice? I must know who your tailor is."

"So sorry, dear. Can't give away all my secrets." Maher handed Ally a market satchel he'd grabbed from the kitchen, and they left the house.

The walk from the manor to Kingsport market wasn't very long. Open fields and the neatly kept gravel paths that lead to Ally's home soon gave way to farms and wide cart roads. These were smaller farms that mostly fed the manor and the city workers, the large farms were all inland. There were some who might spend extra money on inland beef or pork, but most Birde Islanders lived on the bounty of the sea.

Soon the water on their left narrowed into a thin strip of blue, before disappearing altogether behind the steadily rising buildings of the Birde Isles capital. The ground beneath their feet shifted again from cart road to cobblestone, dotted every block or so with bright mosaic tiles. As they entered the outskirts of the marketplace, the smells of seafood being salted, roasted, and fried wafted from the stalls already open for the day.

They stopped by one stall where a man and his son were shucking oysters with practiced speed. A small tub of ice sat between them, keeping the shellfish cool while they filled their orders.

"First oysters of the season, brought up fresh by the selkies this morning," said the man, pausing to wipe his short knife on a rag.

"We'll take four half-shells." Maher placed two coins on the counter.

"Coming up, if you'll step to the end there."

They moved to a small wooden table at the side of the stall. Bowls of seasoning, sliced lemon, and grated horseradish sat under the awning. Within minutes, a tray appeared in front of them with four newly shucked oysters. Maher squeezed lemon juice over them before handing one to Ally. The rough, oblong shell took up her entire palm. Ally sprinkled a pinch of horseradish onto hers and tipped the oyster into her mouth.

A wave of pure flavor hit her tongue, briny and sharp, and Ally immediately reached for her second one. Maher was right behind her. He'd been wary of the idea of eating raw oysters when they were children, only trying his first one on a dare from Ally. The mollusks were now one of the first treats they sought out on a market day.

"Ready to go?" asked Maher as the oyster man's son took back the tray with their empty shells.

Ally licked a drop of lemon juice from her thumb and nodded. "We'd better, or I could stand here all day."

They thanked the stall owner and moved on. More people drifted into the market as the morning passed. Ally loved seeing the old, familiar wares next to the new and exciting clothes, food, inventions, and people that arrived each year. Whether they were from their closer neighbors on the continent like Saprea, Fraolland, and Meredia, or as far away as Nuvwaan, Char-range and Utollmir. Even the smaller, lighter ships from The Riddles were making the trip across the Unending Sea more often than ever before. Or that's what she'd overheard from Gai as he showed their brothers a model, the odd design looked like a ship's hull balancing with stilts on top of two longboats.

Despite the fact she'd never been off of Kingfisher Island, and likely never would, Ally felt like a citizen of the world each time something new came into port. And it was enough, most days.

They left the food sellers' end of the marketplace and Maher asked, "What are we looking for again?"

"I want to visit the soap carver and the perfumery."

"I wonder what I should get for your mother this year?" He scanned the stalls ahead. "Some Balahn wine, perhaps?"

Ally grinned. "Mama would love that. It's nice when she can get things from her homeland."

"How long has it been since she last visited?"

"Not since she and father were married. They stopped there on their wedding tour." Ally was sure her mother would have gone back to Balah before now, if she hadn't been so worried about leaving Ally. There was no way Ally would have been able to go with her, she couldn't even set foot on a ship...

"Hey," Maher looped his arm through hers. "None of that. I'm missing out on some much-needed sleep to help you choose a gift for Lady Kingfisher's birthday. It's your job to keep me entertained."

"Is it?" Ally squeezed his arm. "That's funny, considering you were the one who chose to stay out all night."

"A minor detail."

Their stop at the soap carver didn't take long. Ally selected a rose oil soap carved into the shape of its namesake flower for her mother, and a bar of lavender soap for herself. Su's Perfumery, with their vast selection of oils and mixed scents, was only a few stalls down. Ally greeted the owner, a Char-range woman named Su-Yonn, then picked three oils: rosemary, bergamot, and clary sage, for her mother's altar. The perfumer turned to measure them out.

"I thought you didn't follow the Balahn gods?" Maher picked up a vial, sniffed the contents, and quickly put it back down.

"Too strong? They're important to Mama, and she was just saying the other day that her offering oils were running low."

"Then I'm sure she'll appreciate them." Maher chose another vial, smelling it more cautiously than the last one. "How about this?" He held the vial under Ally's nose.

She breathed in the crisp, clean scent of pine laced with something else she couldn't readily identify. Like a spice she'd only had once before and could remember the taste but not the name.

"I like that one, it reminds me of something satisfying. Is it for you?"

"I thought so. I'm tired of the scent I've been wearing."

"You should get it then."

The perfumer's daughter came out of their shop in the row of buildings behind the market stalls, arms full of fresh supplies. It had been a while since they'd seen her, but Ally recognized the high cheekbones and button nose that matched Su-Yonn's. Her silky black hair was pulled into a single braid, as she wasn't yet old enough to wear the upswept style of grown Char-range women.

When the girl saw Maher and Ally, her steps faltered and her cheeks pinked.

"Su-Minn? Su-Minn, bring that here." Su-Yonn didn't look up from the clary sage oil she was carefully dripping into a slender bottle. "Say good morning to Mister Maher and Lady Alphonsine."

"G-good morning." Su-Minn put the supplies down on her mother's workbench and gave them something between a bow and a curtsy.

"Good morning, I hope you're having a nice summer?" Ally asked, bringing her into the conversation. As she'd grown into her adolescence, Su-Minn had become increasingly flustered whenever Ally or Maher patronized her mother's shop. Ally felt for her, remembering those days when a kind word from the right person could send her own heart soaring.

"I am, thank you, Lady Alphonsine." She loitered by her mother, any other chores she might have had at the moment forgotten.

"I hope you're having some fun as well. Making friends? Maybe getting into a bit of old fashioned, yet harmless, trouble?" Maher grinned and her blush shifted from pink to red.

Ally stepped on Maher's foot and he glowered at the dusty print left on the black leather of his boot. "Pay no attention to him, Maher never learned when to stay out of trouble."

"Su-Minn has plenty of time for fun, when our work is done for the day." Su-Yonn smiled fondly at her daughter before turning back to them.

Next to Ally, Maher shrugged and winked at Su-Minn, who let out a squeak and busied herself collecting empty oil containers and used utensils.

Ally thanked Su-Yonn as she brought over the oils, wrapped in a cloth to protect the glass bottles. She slipped them into her bag. One for the sun, one for the moon, and one for the in-between. "We'll take the scent Maher has as well, please add it to my bill."

"Thanks, Al." Maher tugged on a lock of her hair before tucking it behind her ear. "Would you mind carrying it for me, since you're the one with the satchel?"

"If it's too much for you, darling." Ally pushed his hand away and tucked the scent bottle into an outer pocket of her bag. Looking up, Ally caught the forlorn cast of Su-Minn's face before she retreated into the shop.

Maher chuckled as they walked away. "Poor girl. I wonder which one of us she fancies now?"

"I don't know, but you mustn't tease her. Being that age is tough as it is and I'm sure her feelings are confusing enough without your meddling."

"Do I hear a bit of personal experience creeping in there?"

She sniffed indignantly, "Yes, and Su-Minn can benefit from it."

Ally's first infatuation, for she didn't quite think of it as love, had hit her hard. Like she'd been run over by a carriage. One moment everything in her life was as it always had been, and in the next she was done for.

Neylan Savva was Maher's cousin, on his mother's side. The summer Ally turned fifteen, she came to the Birde Isles to visit Maher and his father for the season.

She was the most beautiful creature Ally'd ever seen. With dark, hooded eyes set beneath strong brows that had been groomed into a fashionable, fanned shape. Every time they landed on her, Ally forgot how words worked. When Neylan's full lips tipped up into a smile or her bronze skin shone in the lamplight, an unfamiliar heat coiled deep in Ally's stomach. And her hair? Hair that hung in an unbroken, obsidian sheet down her back. How Ally longed to run her fingers through the strands every time Neylan's head turned and the resulting ripple ran through to the ends.

Neylan was also six years older than her, and only put up with Ally's company because she was the daughter of Lord and Lady Kingfisher. And she was Maher's cousin. A fact he'd never let Ally forget.

Still, Ally begged him to teach her more complex Saprean phrases than the few she'd gleaned from him over the years. Neylan only spoke a little Trader's Tongue and Maher had to translate for her most of the time. Ally wanted any excuse to get closer to her, learning Saprean seemed like an easy price to pay. But by the end of the summer, Ally'd learned enough to realize she had absolutely nothing in common with the older girl. Maher had probably tried to tell her, but it would have been in the early days when Ally was still mesmerized each time Neylan walked into the room.

These new, often disorienting, longings for Neylan never made Ally feel good about herself. That's why she didn't think of herself as being *in love* at the time. She was charmed by Miss Savva, would have fainted clean away if she'd returned even a fraction of Ally's interest, but not in love. Loving someone else was supposed to make you glad to be in each other's company, even on an average day. Or so she was taught. Her own parents were still as smitten as the day they'd married, and that's what Ally wanted.

When Neylan returned home, with little more than a wave in her direction, Ally decided to embrace the loss of the feelings that went along with her. The pain eventually eased and soon she'd been able to laugh at Maher's jokes that they could have been related, had Ally been a little older. And if Neylan had actually noticed her.

Circling around the other side of the market, they passed as close to the docks as Ally would get. There was still a whole street and a smaller row of buildings between them and the wharf, but they had a view of the ships docked into port.

Maher's steps slowed. A frown creased his brow. "Why are the docks so empty?"

"Are they?" Ally glanced in that direction. There were a few gaps between the ships unloading their cargo, true enough, but it didn't seem like much. Not that she'd been to the wharf often enough to know what a normal number of ships at any given time of year was, like Maher could. That was his territory.

"They are," he craned his neck, trying to see farther down the street. "Usually there's barely enough room to fit a dingy between the rows."

"Do you want to walk down there? I can wait here for you if you'd like to take a look. Is your father at the trade guild today? Maybe he knows what's going on."

"No, don't worry about it." Maher led them away from the docks. "Come on, let's cut through a side street. We'll reach the square faster."

CHAPTER SIXTEEN

There were fewer stalls in the narrow streets that shot off from the market proper and the wares were, at times, questionable. The sellers also managed to be twice as loud as the rest of the marketplace.

They were near the end of their chosen street when a middle-aged man in a worn apothecary apron popped out from behind a makeshift table. "You don't want to pass by just yet."

Maher eyed the hawker. "Yes, we do. Good day."

"But wait! I have the finest, the rarest, the *only* mermaid scales for sale on Kingfisher Island." The man shook a wooden mortar bowl in their faces. Bits of pink and silver and light blue rattled around the edges. "Shall I grind some into a powder for the lady? Mix it with your face cream and watch your skin become luminous like sunlight shining off the sea."

Ally's nose wrinkled. "They look like mother of pearl shavings."

"Smell like them too," said Maher.

"How dare you suggest such a thing! These are genuine mermaid scales."

"They look like you scraped the inside of an oyster shell into your bowl." Maher snorted. The woman at the next table laughed.

"Nonsense!" The man glanced around, as if to check no one else had heard.

"If those are mermaid scales, where is your mermaid?" Ally asked.

"Don't you know? She left them on his doorstep." Maher rolled his eyes. "Come on Al, he's lucky we don't report him for selling fake goods. I would, except I doubt he'll find anyone gullible enough to believe him."

Maher moved on to the next table, feigning interest in the mismatched dishes the woman had assembled into sets and repainted, and kept an eye out for Ally. She started to follow, but the hawker blocked her path.

"They have other uses." He leaned closer and leered in Maher's direction. "Add a little to your young man's wine and he'll–"

"What? Spend the next three days in the toilet?"

Maher's hand came down on the man's shoulder. "Watch what you say next. That's Lady Alphonsine Kingfisher you're speaking to."

"Lady Alphon..." His eyes bulged and he ducked back behind his table. "My sincerest apologies, milady, I meant no rudeness."

Ally and Maher exchanged a look. "Stop trying to cheat people, or possibly harm them with fake powders, and we'll forget this happened."

"Thank you, milady. Thank you." The man grabbed the bowl of pretend mermaid scales and dumped them onto the ground behind him.

They left the side street, but not before Maher made sure the whole thing hadn't been a distraction so someone else could pick their pockets. Satisfied they had everything, they walked out into the market proper.

"You didn't have to do that," Ally sighed.

"He was being disrespectful!"

"But I was handling it!" They sidestepped a fabric cart rumbling down the street. "And the point was that he was disrespectful to me as another person, not to me as a Kingfisher."

Maher shook his head but didn't argue the point any further.

As they crossed up onto the next street, Ally stifled a laugh.

"What's funny?"

"Imagine him trying to pass off crushed oyster scraps as mermaid scales."

"I know," Maher grinned. "When no one's seen a mermaid for centuries, I doubt one would choose to suddenly bless *him* with a visit."

"Do you think there really were mermaids?" Ally glanced up as they happened to pass one of the many stone mermaids carved into the portico of a nearby building. There were countless images of sea creatures, both real and out of their priestess' stories, all over the city. Carved into stone like the one they'd just passed, laid out in the street mosaics, printed on dishes and pottery. They were everywhere, and yet nowhere. Many of the carvings were quite old, but the mosaics were all redone after the rebuilding of the fishing and trading fleets in her great-grandfather's day. A mark of renewed prosperity.

"You don't?" Maher's brow rose.

"There's a reason no one has claimed to witness real magic of any kind in over a hundred years. We're becoming a world of science, we don't need magic, or gods, or mermaids to explain the things around us anymore. Just look at all the new innovations that have arrived on this island in the last five years alone."

Maher made the Saprean symbol against ill fortune over his heart. "Just because we haven't heard from them in a while, doesn't mean the gods might not still be listening. Take no chances, that's my philosophy."

They passed a clockworks shop where a small crowd had gathered to watch the owner demonstrate a new version of a lighting jar, a device that had arrived some years ago from Botsa University in Kharabo. The glass jar was wrapped in metal foil and sealed with a wooden lid punctured by a thin brass rod sticking through the center. The shopkeeper asked everyone to stay back, as the jar was already filled with an electric current, or a "captured bit of lightning" as he put it. With a gloved hand, he held a wand with a wooden handle that split into two metal prongs. When the prongs were touched to the brass rod and the jar, a bright flash arced between them and then disappeared. The people clapped, some commented on how this new jar was much brighter than the first one.

It was certainly a novelty, though Maher doubted it was good for much beyond allowing wealthy people to show off the flashy reaction to guests.

But Ally waved a hand at the shop, as if it proved her point. "Maher, you make blue paint by mixing the right minerals and pigments together. The Kharaboans have captured lightning in a jar. Soon, we'll harness even more elements to make our lives easier. It's science, not some mysterious wizardry. The planets and winds control the tides and create waves at random, not a so-called goddess who happens to be in a good or bad mood."

"Says the girl who wears a fossil around her neck to ward off evil."

Ally frowned, her hand sliding up to touch the necklace beneath her shirt. "That's different."

"Of course, it is. It's tied to a traumatic moment in your life. You know that, yet you feel it's good luck anyway." He shrugged. "Your priestesses all say the first Birde Islanders came from the sea."

"You know what else that could mean?" Ally nudged him with her elbow. "That we came to the islands on boats."

Maher brought them up short to let a large cart and four horses go by. Strapped in the back were massive barrels filled with rainwater collected during the last storms. Ally didn't like being caught in the rain but, as long as she wasn't expected to wade through standing water, she could tolerate it long enough to get to shelter. The wagon hit an uneven patch of stone in the road and water sloshed over the sides. Ally watched the small stream as it flowed between the cobblestones and disappeared into a drain.

"What happened to your sense of wonder, Ally? Your belief in the amazing?"

"It washed away."

CHAPTER SEVENTEEN

Pasha lay on the floor of the largest cavern in her home. Her fingers dipped into the sand as a fresh stream of electricity surged from the water through her body, mixing with her own energy before rising to the surface again to dance across her skin in white-hot arcs. Taking back the current all at once had flooded her with more power than she'd held in a century. It would take some time to readjust, to rein in the spikes of energy trying to break free. The corals scattered over the cave walls lit up in response, soaking up the arcs and storing them away for their own use. Everything in the cavern felt brighter.

Above Pasha's head, a sculpture of bones twirled, shifting into different patterns and shapes. Tiny, fresh white bones from the fish she caught for her meals. Older, larger skeletons from creatures who'd sought the safety of the caves while Pasha slept, dolphin and ray and serpent and eel. Ancient jaws that had blackened with age, settling in until they became part of the cavern. All dancing together along the ceiling. The bones had been quiet while the current took from her, now she twitched her fingers and a dozen rose out of the sand or broke free from the rock of the cave itself. They'd always listened to her, as far back as Pasha could remember. It never seemed odd until the first elder noticed a fish skeleton circling

Pasha's head while she giggled and gave chase. One horrified gasp from the elder and the fish broke apart. After that none of the others looked at her the same, even Pallagia seemed unsure how to react... The bones wobbled, a few rained down on Pasha as her concentration stuttered. She hadn't thought of Pallagia in... it had been so long Pasha couldn't remember. Before she'd gone to sleep, at least.

Stretching a hand up, she watched as a small collection of teeth broke away from the rest and cascaded down to her. Shark teeth ranging in color from light gray to mottled black, but none were as old or large as the one Pasha'd given to the Kingfisher daughter the night she'd pulled her from the sea. That one was special. Another flick of her wrist and the teeth flipped points-up before circling around the top of her head like a crown.

Queen of the Boneyard. Pasha chuckled to herself, remembering the name one of Pallagia's friends had thrown at her.

That same night, Pasha'd sent a pair of sea snake skeletons into the chamber where the older mermaid slept. Pallagia made her promise never to do that again, after she'd stopped laughing.

The wave of energy she'd been riding finally crested. Pasha swept her arms out, sending all the bones back to their resting places. Except for the teeth, those she left in a little pile on one of the stone ledges lining the walls. Carved into the rock above the teeth was the fading visage of a warrior holding a spear nearly as long as her tail. Her unseeing eyes gazed out from somewhere in the past, there were none of the old warriors left by the time Pasha was born. Only the stories. Still it was one of the few etchings that made Pasha feel safe when the others left, she slept beneath it for years before moving back into her own chamber deeper beneath the island.

Pasha left the teeth as a small offering for the warrior. It was the best thing she could give for now, but who knew what treasures were tucked away in this place? The charge still humming beneath her skin, Pasha set out to explore one of the long unused tunnels of her home, before the next wave came to claim her.

CHAPTER EIGHTEEN

When Maher walked into the Kingfisher family dining room, a more intimate version of the manor's formal dining room, something was missing.

He couldn't say exactly what, but there was definitely something off. The oval table was laid out with shining cutlery and fine plates edged with delicate painted seahorses. A low centerpiece of driftwood and bluebells sat in the middle.

Maher counted the chairs, but they had the right number. Enough for the family, the Villaons, and the head of the trade guild and his husband. After Ally and Maher became friends, he and his father were invited to all of the family gatherings. A favor Ambassador Villaon was quick to claim.

Several covered dishes were already on the table, with more to come no doubt. They'd be eating the Balahn way in honor of Lady Kingfisher, sharing each large dish together. Maher preferred this himself; it reminded him of how they ate in Saprea. The Birde Isles custom of serving each food on its own small plate, up to five plates per person, took some time to get used to.

"What's missing?" Ally came into the room behind him, her gift for Lady Kingfisher tucked beneath her arm.

"I'm not sure. You noticed it too?" Maher set the bottle of red Balahn wine by his place at the table. It had taken them all afternoon at the market to find a seller who had any in stock.

"It does seem that way, doesn't it?" Ally put her gift down in front of her chair, between her mother and Maher. Lord Kingfisher would be at the other end of the table, with everyone else spread out in between. "Maybe one of the others will know."

"Will everyone make it? When is Cal due back from Meredia?"

"I'm not sure, I haven't seen him today but he promised to do his best to be here."

Cal had been standing in as a trade delegate to some of their allies and Meredia did a great deal of business by ship. With their southern coast taking up a large swath of the strait and their entire western border spanning the mouth of the Split Sea.

Maher turned and admired the gown Ally had chosen for the party. It too was in the Balahn style, a nod to her mother. Pale blue with billowing sleeves that cinched at the wrist and layer upon layer of soft, paper-thin material to make up the skirt. She'd embroidered leaping Balahn deer in gray thread over the cuffs and down either side of the bodice. Maher smiled; Ally rarely made things for herself.

"You look lovely, Princess."

"That was almost a compliment." Ally reached up and straightened the neckline of his dark green waistcoat. Her fingers lingered over the delicate gold vines she'd only just finished the day before. Maher had suggested silver, but Ally'd insisted gold would offset the green better and bring out the warmer tones of his skin. She was right, of course.

"No more princess jokes after everyone arrives." She gave his shirt collar a sharp tug. "Understood?"

"Of course," he gently swatted her hands away. "I'm sorry Al, you really do look lovely." Maher pulled one of the curls that framed her face.

"First to arrive, I see?" Cal strolled into the room, an easy smile on his face.

Ally rushed to give her brother a hug. "Cal! You're back!"

"Did you think I would miss Rochelle's birthday?"

"That was a quick trip, even for you." Maher shook Cal's hand; he towered over all three Kingfisher brothers now. "Do you know where you're traveling next?"

"Not yet, but I hope to add Utollmir to my rounds. The ambassador is due to go back soon; she could give me some introductions."

"Where's your gift?" Ally teased.

"Not to worry, dear sister. Gai, Luthais, and I have gone in on a gift together." He sat in one of the chairs across the table.

"Bragging about your idea?" Gai asked as he and Luthais arrived. An oddly shaped, paper-wrapped bundle was hanging from one of Gai's hands by a loop of twine. "We know you only suggested it to save money." He looked more like their father every day, especially with his hair combed back and the blonde mustache that had finally filled in.

"Sounds about right." Luthais claimed one of the chairs next to their father's. His long, sun-bleached hair was pulled back into a tight braid. It did little to soften his features.

Ally shared a look with Maher, they took their seats as they waited for the remaining guests.

Soon Ambassador Khafra Villaon swept into the room, greeted all of the present Kingfishers and took the empty place next to Maher. His father always smelled of mint and the oils he used on his silvering hair and carefully trimmed beard. While he didn't share his son's love of bright colors and patterns, Khafra appreciated fine materials and quality craftsmanship. Tonight he wore a suit of apricot damask, high-necked with a series of silk thread knot and loop closures that went straight down the front. A style popular on the continent for quite some time, before it arrived on the Isles.

Mr. Pavan Dayal, the head of the trade guild, and his husband Edgar were the last to arrive. The Dayals were a middle-aged couple with a penchant for dressing in matching outfits. For today's celebration they were both clad in shades of violet and lilac, also popular in Balah. Mr. Edgar Dayal sported a mauve hat precariously perched on top of his dark blonde head and Pavan had wrapped a ribbon in the same shade around his walking stick.

The guild leader made a point of greeting Luthais separately. "My Lord of Trade, good evening."

Maher wasn't sure, but it sounded like Luthais grunted out something that might have been "Good Evening, Dayal".

When Lord and Lady Kingfisher entered the room together, everyone rose and clapped for Ally's mother.

"Happy birthday, Mama!" Ally hugged her before she sat down.

"Thank you, darling. Thank you everyone for coming to celebrate with me." Lady Kingfisher nodded to Ambassador Villaon, then to the trade guild head and his husband. "Ambassador, Pavan and Edgar, it's good of you to join us."

"It's our pleasure, Your Ladyship." Pavan bowed, showing off the beginnings of a bald spot in the middle of his black hair. "Isn't it, my dear?"

"Yes, we're so honored to be included in a family gathering." Edgar smiled warmly. His hat wobbled a bit but stayed put.

"You're very welcome here," said Lord Kingfisher as everyone found their seats. "Shall we follow tradition and start with the presents? Ally can begin."

"Here, Mama." Ally handed the small parcel over.

Lady Kingfisher held the delicate glass bottles up to the light, reading the neatly written Su's Perfumery labels. "Thank you, Alphonsine, this is just what I needed!"

Maher hid a grin behind his hand. Lady Kingfisher was the only member of the family allowed to call Ally by her full name, outside of official events. It was his turn, Maher passed down the bottle.

"Balahn wine!" Lady Kingfisher's dark, finely arched brows rose. "The kitchen staff weren't able to buy any. How did you find it?"

"Ally and I spent an afternoon scouring the marketplace. It was the last bottle the seller had." And Maher had to pay an extra coin to get them to part with it.

"What a delightful surprise. We must have it with our dinner tonight." She handed the wine to one of the servants attending them.

"Are you sure, Lady Kingfisher?" Edgar asked. "You wouldn't rather save it?"

"Of course not, it is my birthday after all."

Maher's brow knit together as his father's gift was sent down to the end of the table. *That's* what was missing. Or at least one thing that was missing. Lady Kingfisher's birthday celebrations were always filled with imported reminders of her homeland. Balahn wine, purple orchids from her hometown when possible, sweets wrapped in delicate layers of pastry and preserved in syrup. Maher didn't see any of those things this year. Even the dishes on the table, while mouthwatering, were less than the family would usually have for a celebration like this.

Lady Kingfisher graciously accepted Khafra's gift, a book on the history of Saprean fashion that Maher had tried, and failed, to talk him out of buying for her. The Dayals presented a set of lace trimmed handkerchiefs and also a bouquet of flowers on behalf of the guild. Lord Kingfisher passed his turn to his sons, wanting instead to go last.

Gai carried the bundle to Rochelle's end of the table and kissed her cheek. "This is from all three of us. We wish you the happiest of birthdays, Rochelle."

Maher caught the look of confusion that passed between the Dayals. They'd only been residents of Kingsport for a handful of years. It was common knowledge that Lady Rochelle Kingfisher was the boys' stepmother, but that she allowed them to call her by name was still a novelty to some. Maher thought it showed an understanding of how the brothers must have felt about calling a new woman 'mother'.

Holding the bundle in her lap, Lady Kingfisher untied the twine and pulled the brown paper apart. "Oh! How lovely." She held up a woolen cloak in traditional Balahn colors, sky blue trimmed with silver.

"That's beautiful," Ally looked to her mother for permission, then ran her hands along the hem of the cloak. "It's been rainproofed?"

"Good eye, Ally," said Cal. "You know how quickly storms can crop up here. This was made using a new water-resisting technique from Meredia, they've improved on the old linseed oil method."

Lady Kingfisher folded the cloak and put it to the side. "Thank you, very much boys. I'm touched."

Gai and Cal smiled at their stepmother. Luthais nodded stiffly.

Lord Kingfisher stood, "If I may, I'd like to give my gift now. Then we can begin the dinner you've all been waiting for."

Maher allowed himself a slight smile. Lord Gaius Kingfisher III was someone who truly loved to show his family how he cared for them. In public or in private, Gaius was very much the same man. Something that couldn't be said about his own father. Maher wasn't sure Khafra had ever hugged him in public, and the few hugs he did receive were stopped altogether after his mother died.

Reaching his wife's side, Lord Kingfisher withdrew a rolled piece of paper tied with a gold ribbon from inside his jacket. Ally's fingers twitched; Maher knew she'd reach for the ribbon the moment it hit the table.

"For you, my darling wife." Gaius bent to kiss her cheek. "You have made me happier these twenty-four years together than I thought possible. You love my sons as your own and our daughter causes my joy to overflow."

Next to him, Ally blushed. Maher glanced across the table at her brothers but was unable to read any of their faces clearly.

Gaius continued, "With all that in mind, I wanted to do something to hopefully show even a fraction of the love and respect I have for you."

Lady Kingfisher blinked back tears as she untied the ribbon. Without looking up, she passed it to Ally. "My dear, I don't know what to say, I really don't," she unrolled the paper. "What's this?"

"What is it?" Ally helped her mother spread the long paper out on the table. "A ship? You gave her a drawing of a ship?"

Maher studied, what appeared to be, a detailed diagram of a ship unlike any of the others belonging to the Birde Isles. It was modern, elegant, and more suited as a pleasure vessel than anything else. His eye caught on the name printed on the bow. The *Rochelle*.

"It's a building plan. He's going to commission a ship just for Lady Kingfisher."

"Oh my!" Edgar pressed his hands to his plump cheeks. "What a wonderful tribute, Lord Kingfisher."

Pavan Dayal stayed silent and Maher thought he saw the older man's eye twitch.

Ambassador Villaon came around the table to examine the drawing. "Having a ship named after you will be quite an honor indeed, Your Ladyship."

"Father," Gai shook his head, clearly working to keep his tone light. "I thought we discussed the cost of something like this."

"We did, son, but we have funds set aside to build new ships as needed. If there isn't enough allotted to cover this one, I'll pay the difference myself."

Luthais' jaw worked back and forth. Maher could guess what was coming next.

Cal tried to step in. "Let's all calm down and discuss it after dinner. This is Rochelle's birthday party, after all."

"Very well," said Lord Kingfisher. "Though, I don't see there is much else to discuss if the funds allow –"

Luthais leapt up. "Damn it Father, the fund does *not* allow for it! Refusing to acknowledge it doesn't change the fact –"

"Luthais!" Lady Kingfisher stood next to her husband. "You are a grown man and, I'm well aware, able to make your own decisions. But there is no need to speak so disrespectfully to your father. And in front of our guests, no less."

The middle Kingfisher brother braced his hands on the table and took a deep breath. "I apologize, I do, but there's missing information here. I don't want everyone to go on thinking we can spend funds we don't have."

"What do you mean?" Ally asked.

Lord Kingfisher answered, "Most of us are aware the fishing catches have greatly declined this year, but it hasn't been enough to keep us from feeding our own people."

"That's not all though, is it?" Gai brushed a hand roughly over his mustache. "We've lost more than that, much more. We can feed ourselves, but we're behind on our trade promises. How much is missing from the table tonight? How much has *been* missing that's usually brought into port from our trading partners?"

Ambassador Villaon moved behind his son. Maher felt his father's hand on his shoulder. "Some of the Birde Isles allies have withheld their goods as a result, it is true, but surely this can be made good by diverting more of the catch to our trade agreements?"

"You can say that?" Luthais spat. "You can say that without admitting withheld goods aren't the only problem? When pirates have been ravaging our ships more in the last ten years than we've ever seen before?"

"Pirates!" Ally gasped. "The same ones who attacked our ships a few years ago?"

"How did you know about that?" asked Cal.

"Enough," Gai sighed heavily. "Tell them, Mr. Dayal."

"We were going to wait until later to tell you, my lord, so as not to cast a damper on Lady Kingfisher's celebration." Pavan licked his lips nervously. "We learned just this morning, the *Gull's Flight* was taken... three days ago."

"Taken?" Maher winced as his father's nails bit through his jacket. "Not burned or sunk, but taken?"

Luthais nodded. "They took the whole thing, added it to their number."

"But pirates don't build fleets... do they?" asked Edgar.

Lord Kingfisher paced around the table. "How many made it off the ship?"

"One longboat," said Luthais.

"Only one?" Rochelle sank back onto her chair and took Ally's hand. "That can't be more than twenty sailors at the most."

"We're still trying to get more information out of the sailors who escaped." The trade guild leader tried to give what, Maher guessed, was meant to be a reassuring smile, but it came out as a grimace. "They're not quite lucid yet, after three days at sea with no food or water. They're saying strange things."

Ally asked, "What strange things?"

"Nothing to trouble you with, my lady…"

"Tell us, Dayal," said Lord Kingfisher.

Pavan shifted uneasily in his seat. "It's all hallucinations, I'm sure, but they keep talking about lightning shooting up out of the sea, and fires that wouldn't burn anything, and how the sea goddess had abandoned them, and…"

"And?" Cal prompted.

"And a pirate ghost rising out of the water, with a face covered in blood."

The candles had burned low, and the food was cold by the time they began to eat. Though it didn't appear anyone had much of an appetite.

Ally's father was casting strange, apprehensive glances her way. Maher wasn't sure if Ally noticed, but when Lady Kingfisher caught him looking she cleared her throat.

"*Gaius*," Rochelle hissed. "Leave it alone."

Everything ended on a somber note. Maher walked Ally back to her room, both too drained to talk about it anymore that night. They agreed to meet in the parlor the next afternoon.

He still had questions but knew he wouldn't be allowed in Lord Kingfisher's study where Gaius, Pavan Dayal, and the three brothers would likely lock themselves in for the next few days.

He'd have to find answers his own way.

CHAPTER NINETEEN

Nearly a week had gone by, and still no news of what really happened to the sailors from the *Gull's Flight*. Ally paced through the manor, unable to sit still or think of anything but what the delirious sailors had described upon their rescue.

Of course, they were dehydrated and scared, their story had to be a hallucination like Mr. Dayal said. There were no ghosts, or monsters, or lightning that came *out* of anything except the sky. The pirates who attacked them must have been so fierce, so brutal, that the experience became twisted in their minds. There was no other explanation.

After her third trip through the great hall, Ally veered towards the front of the house. She needed a task to distract her, and her new embroidery project could use some work. She would have asked Maher to bring his paints and join her, the light in the parlor was lovely this time of day. But he'd been scarce since the night of her mother's birthday. If he wasn't running errands for his father and the trade guild, he was taking off into the city at all hours of the day and night. When was the last time Ally actually saw him painting? Not since last winter, at least.

Ally reached the double doors to the parlor and met Luthais walking out of the room.

"Luthais?" Ally's head tilted. He never went in there. "What were you doing in the parlor?"

"I was…" He cleared his throat. "I'm looking for Maher. We need him to run a note to the guild headquarters."

"Ah, your guess of where he is would be as good as mine. He might already be in the city."

"Thank you." Luthais moved past her.

Ally watched him for a moment before turning into the parlor.

"I hope…"

Ally looked back. Her brother had stopped in the middle of the front hall.

"I hope," he said again over his shoulder. "You weren't upset about how your mother's birthday ended. We didn't want to bring it up until afterwards."

He meant the *Gull's Flight*. Ally took a step towards him, but Luthais didn't seem inclined to do the same.

"It's alright. Mama understood, the safety of our sailors is more important than a party."

Some of the tension in his wide shoulders eased. "That's right," he said more to himself. "I appreciate you saying that."

Luthais was gone before Ally could reply. She finally entered the room, puzzling over the interaction with her taciturn brother. It wasn't as though she thought he disliked her, not like when they were children. But Luthais wasn't someone she'd thought would ever warm to her. He only really seemed happy, expressive even, when he was working to make the sailors' lives better. Or so Cal had said. Ally'd never witnessed the transformation herself.

A large wicker basket held her embroidery supplies. Ally lifted the lid and found a new bundle of thread and linen sitting on top. The household staff regularly restocked her materials, she really only had to make a trip to the shop when there was something special she needed. The housekeeper, Mrs. Thorley, turned down her offer to reimburse them for the cost, insisting the embroidery supplies came out of the household fund.

Ally found the hoop she wanted and settled onto one of the sofas. This was a new pattern, seagrass and sand dunes. She'd been fixated on them lately. The frequency of her strange dream had gone down considerably the last few years, but she'd had some version of it every night since they learned the fate of the *Gull's Flight*. Not even her pre-dawn walks to the cliff seemed to help. And the shark tooth... the gentle stream of heat that always trickled out had spiked dramatically. Ally refused to think too much about what that meant.

She'd been mindlessly sewing, lost in thought, and in no way as distracted as she'd hoped. Ally looked down at the hoop in her hands, her needle had veered off from the tall grass pattern. And in the middle of the fabric, she'd stitched the outline of a shark tooth.

"Ally? Are you in here?" Cal's head popped into the room.

"Yes?" Ally looked up from the third new pattern she'd started that afternoon. With each one she'd begun with the seagrass, only to lose focus and stitch something else altogether. If it happened again, she was ready to chuck the hoop across the room.

"Looks like you've been busy." Cal eyed the growing pile of linen scraps at her feet.

"Don't ask." Ally sighed. "Did you need me for something?"

Cal sat next to her. "I thought you'd like to know your mother just received a special delivery from Balah. They sent a messenger and everything."

"Really?" Her mother often wrote to friends and family back home, but a personal messenger had never come before. "What about? Did she say?"

"Rochelle's been invited as a special guest for the Balahn Festival of the Moon being arranged next month."

Ally's stomach fluttered. "The one that's held every five years, for the eclipse?"

"The very same. They want her to preside over the opening ceremony. It's a great honor, apparently."

"Is she going to accept?"

"She didn't say, I expect she'll bring it up this evening." He grinned. "You should go with her!"

"Me?" The butterflies in her stomach turned to stone.

Quickly, Cal put a hand on her shoulder. "I know how you feel about the sea, Ally, but surely this would be the perfect opportunity to meet your fear." He peered into her face, freckled nose scrunched in thought. "Don't you want to see your mother's home country? It's part of your heritage too, squirt, just as much as the Birde Isles."

"I don't know," Ally gripped the hoop in her lap, the wooden edges bit into her palms.

"At least talk to your mother about it. I'm sure she'd love to show you around, introduce you to family you've never met."

"Why are you so sure I should go?"

"Ally, you've never been off this island." Cal squeezed her shoulder. "Not across the inlets to Swan or Gull Island, or even to Snake Island, come to that."

"I tried to get you to take me there." She laughed, even if it was a bit wobbly.

"I know, and I still feel awful about that. You deserve to see more of the world. I know living in such a busy city makes it easier to experience new things while staying put, but I don't want you to miss out on a chance like this."

"Thank you, Cal." Ally patted the hand still on her shoulder. "I'll talk to Mama about it, and I will seriously think about going. I promise."

"That's all I wanted."

Ally found Rochelle at her dressing table, preparing for a dinner in the city.

"Hello, Mama," she kissed her mother's cheek and sat on a nearby ottoman. As a child, Ally loved to watch her mother dress for an event or even for an ordinary day. Rochelle was the portrait of classic Balahn beauty, all long lines and defined features. Ally took after her in some ways, they had the same hair, the same squared jawline. They'd have looked more alike if Ally hadn't broken her nose, but she'd finally moved beyond that. She didn't have the pinkish complexion of her father and brothers, the summer sun was a little kinder to her. And Ally was softer, the curves of her figure only growing more rounded as she got older. She would never have her mother's height, but her legs were strong from the regular walks into town with Maher.

"Cal said you received a special invitation today."

"I thought he might have already told you." She used a pearl studded comb to secure the top half of her curls away from her face. "I wish Cal would have waited. I wouldn't have even told him yet, but he was there when the messenger arrived."

"It's alright, he was very excited about it."

Rochelle finished her hair and turned to her daughter. "He didn't worry you, then?"

"Not really," Ally's fingers twisted together. "He suggested I accompany you."

"Would you *like* to go with me, darling?" She paused. "Of course, I would love to show you Balah. Where I grew up and where our family lives. But I wasn't sure I should ask. I'd never want to put you into a difficult situation."

"So, you are going?" Ally asked.

"I want to, yes, but I'd stay if you needed me."

"It's such an important festival..."

Rochelle leaned forward and took her hands. "Not as important as you, my darling. And there's no need to rush into a decision. I have some time before they need a reply. First, decide if you're comfortable with me leaving, for two months at least. Then, decide if you'd like to join me, and we'll do whatever is needed to make you feel safe on the journey."

Ally stood and wrapped her arms around her mother's neck. Trust Mama to always know the best way to lay out her options. Some of the weight in her stomach eased, and maybe Cal was right. Maybe preparing for this trip would help Ally take that first step to overcome her fear.

PASHA

CHAPTER TWENTY

Pasha swam close to the shallows, a small net of fish dragging behind her. It'd been too long since she'd eaten anything. Taking back the current spiked her energy so high, she forgot all about food until her muscles and joints began to ache. It was a childish mistake; she knew better than to rely on a charge to sustain her for long.

The humans would be feeling the bite of the current's loss by now. Half the summer gone and only a third of the catch they were used to was brought in. A small consolation, but it was what she had. All that mattered now was keeping herself alive. Maybe the others weren't coming back, but Pasha wouldn't likely survive another long sleep. She'd barely woken from the last one.

Shaking off the memories before they could take shape, she counted the fish in her net again. A few more and she'd be set for several days. The oyster divers wouldn't be out until the next morning, maybe she'd go and claim some of the shelled creatures for herself.

With a flip of her tail, Pasha headed for the nearest dock, a small one set outside the bay. Might have better luck than under the bigger docks near the humans' port. She was nearly there when something plucked at the edge of her mind. The shark tooth. That had to be it, but the Kingfisher daughter never came this close to the sea. Surfacing just enough to focus on the shore, Pasha blinked the water out of her eyes and scanned the beach.

There she was at the edge of the road, just before the grass sloped down to meet the sand. Why was she here?

Pasha couldn't make out much from this distance, only the soft blue of her skirt and the long, dark brown hair being lifted by the breeze. But it was her and she had the shark tooth. Her hands were fisted into her skirt, she leaned forward as if she meant to walk down to the beach but was tied to that spot.

The shark tooth spiked again, hard, and Pasha winced.

Pasha let the current lift her until her head was above the water. She wanted to move closer, pulled by the tooth and a gnawing need to see the girl up close. In her mind all Pasha could see was the face of the child she'd pulled from the sea.

Was she finally here to meet Pasha? Had she learned the truth? The net slipped from Pasha's hand, the fish forgotten. Her entire body tensed, she wanted to swim to shore as fast as she could. Pasha doubted the girl could see her from there, she blended in well with the sea. Jumping out of the waves would only startle her. Pasha needed to think.

A scream hit Pasha's sensitive ears and a wave of bitter frustration flowed out of the shark tooth to strike her in the face. Ducking under, Pasha's jaw clenched as she rode the wave out. The tooth was picking up on her emotions? That shouldn't have been possible.

When Pasha surfaced again, the girl had turned her back to the sea. The tooth pulsed, but she couldn't feel any particular emotion anymore. As she wrestled with what to do next, there was a shout from up the road.

A tall, slender young man in bright clothing ran straight for the girl and pulled her into an embrace. Pasha watched as he said something she couldn't hear and led the girl away from the shore.

Short bursts of electricity arced from Pasha's hands and the emptiness of her stomach doubled. She dove underwater to find her net; it couldn't have gone far with the fish pulling in different directions.

Pasha was a fool to think the girl was there to see her. There *was* something else going on though, the reaction from the shark tooth was too glaring to ignore.

ALLY

CHAPTER TWENTY-ONE

She couldn't do it.

Ally stood there for over an hour, closer to the sea than she'd been in years, so paralyzed with fright and nausea that she couldn't bring herself to touch the sand.

There was no way she could go with her mother to Balah. Her heart would give out the moment she stepped onto the ship.

When Ally screamed, it wasn't out of fear. It was anger. Anger at herself for sneaking out to the sea alone. Anger at how she'd let that one night change her forever. And she'd admit to no one but herself, anger at her family for not encouraging her to conquer this obstacle before now.

She didn't blame them, not really, but why had no one talked to her about it? Or asked how they could help? They'd protected and consoled her, but not one of them asked her to try to face her fear or help her work through it until Cal brought the news of the invitation. No one but Maher, anyway, and Ally wasn't sure if he even knew how deep this problem ran. It was a part of her, flowing through her veins right along with her blood.

By pure chance, Maher was walking back from the city at that moment and witnessed her breakdown. Without hesitation, he'd wrapped his arms around her and let her cry it all out. His shirt front was soaked with tears, and sadly she'd wiped her nose on it, and stuck to his reedy chest by the time Ally collected herself.

"Are you ready to walk back?"

"I think so," she sniffled. "I'm sorry about your shirt."

"It's not a problem, I have so many of them." Maher took her hand and they walked towards the house. "We'll both change into something cozy, then we'll commandeer your mother's sitting room and light the fire. And when you're ready, if you want, you can tell me all about it."

The messenger was sent back to Balah with Lady Kingfisher's answer. Then it seemed like Ally blinked and it was time for Mama to leave.

Maher and Ally sat together in the grass at the top of the sea cliff. She'd said her own goodbyes to her mother that morning, in private, but couldn't bring herself to join the rest of her family at the wharf to see the ship off.

Even from their spot high up above the sea, they could make out the crowd that had come to watch Lady Kingfisher board the ship that would take her to Balah. The crew of the *Swan Song* raised a smaller version of the Balahn leaping deer pennant beneath the standard Kingfisher bird on its field of hunter green.

Ally hugged one knee to her chest, she ached to go with them. Maher, darling that he was, had offered to come too for support, once she'd explained her struggle. It was no good. She was a coward and gossip about her (unwanted) refusal to visit her mother's homeland was no doubt spreading throughout Kingsport.

A sharp breeze whipped through the grass, sending the last of the summer seed pods into the air. Maher sneezed.

"I never had this trouble before we moved here." He pulled out a handkerchief to dab at his watering eyes.

"Hmm..." Ally nodded, watching the schooner preparing to make way.

"They're going to be fine." He said, not for the first time that morning. "It takes only a week to reach Balah, sometimes less with a good tail-wind."

"I'm sure you're right," she sighed. Mama had promised to write as soon as they arrived. Assuming the ship carrying the post left on time, it would still be two weeks before they had word. Two weeks where Ally wouldn't be able to sleep until she knew the *Swan Song* had docked safely in Balah. It wasn't Mama's leaving that took up residence in the back of Ally's mind, it was being in that space of not knowing.

There was movement on the docks. The crowd split, like water flowing around a stone, to let the Kingfishers through. Ally couldn't tell exactly when her mother boarded the ship, but she saw the gangplank lift away. Her knuckles turned white as she gripped her leg tighter. A ripple went through the people gathered there, a silent cheer from this far away. The first sails of the *Swan Song* unfurled, filling with the same breeze that blew over their spot on the hill. Soon, they were sailing out of Kingsport Harbor and into Trader's Bay.

Ally watched the crowd slowly disperse and the carriage that had brought her mother depart for the manor. And she watched the ship until it shrank into a tiny dot on the horizon before disappearing altogether.

Maher tugged on Ally's elbow until they were lying side-by-side, looking up at the sky instead of at the sea.

"Thank you for staying up here with me." Ally leaned her head against his shoulder. Maher produced a second handkerchief and offered it to her, but Ally's eyes were dry. She'd cried out all the tears she had in the days since her failure to set foot on the beach.

"You're the only one I'd sit in this bed of sneeze-inducing weeds for." His voice already sounded thicker. "As thanks, I expect you to bring me a pot of hot tea later to open my nose back up."

"Gladly," she smiled, just a little. Having Maher around would help her through the next fourteen days, and she was grateful.

Ally listened while he mused on which paints he'd use to capture the sky currently above them. Maher rarely painted landscapes and nature, but when he did, Ally would try to copy them onto a runner or table-cloth.

It had been a while since Maher practiced his art, let alone talked about it. Ambassador Villaon never seemed too keen on his son's hobby, yet Maher always received paint supplies from him on his birthday. Maher's specialty was scenes of life. The fishers bringing in a catch, a sailor resting on a coil of rope, countless sights from the markets and shops around the city. Hanging in Ally's room was a small portrait of the selkies preparing to dive into the bay.

She'd also seen a few pieces inspired by his nighttime trips into Kingsport, but those were kept where his father wouldn't notice them.

"Say," Maher tapped her foot with his and Ally snapped back into the present. "Why don't we take a new tack? Go somewhere different this week?"

The sun was high above them now, Ally felt a bead of sweat slide down her temple. "Such as?"

"What about seeing a play or dining out? When's the last time we had a drink together away from the house?"

"Your birthday last year." She snorted. "The barkeep assumed we were a couple and made it clear he wished I wasn't there."

"Oh, right," Maher chuckled. "I forgot about that. So, we won't go to that pub again." He stretched his arms above his head, the joints of his long fingers cracking when he laced them together. "I'm going to the Lantern tomorrow night to see a friend, want to come with me?"

"A *friend*?" Ally poked his ribs and Maher's arms dropped to protect his sides. "I appreciate the invite, but I think I'll pass."

"If you're sure," he scooted away to avoid another poke. "I do know some lovely ladies... *Ack!*"

Ally managed to get a hand under his arm and dug all of her fingers in. "I can meet my own lovely ladies, thank you."

"I give! Stop, I give!" He curled inward and Ally immediately took her hand away.

She laughed properly for the first time in weeks. "You go to the Lantern tomorrow, and then let's see what plays are showing in town." Ally stood and offered him a hand. "We can find somewhere nice to eat afterwards."

Maher accepted the help up and wrapped one arm around her shoulders. "Sounds perfect. We'll have so much fun the days will fly by."

Ally glanced back at the empty horizon. "I hope so."

Chapter Twenty-Two

Maher strolled down the high street that led into the Lantern. Horses, carriages and carts gradually filtered down to foot traffic. The entry points into the district were too narrow to fit anything larger than a hand cart. A precaution from the early days to keep patrons from running out on a tab and making a quick escape. Now, there were more modern measures in place.

He passed a few of the smaller establishments crowding for room around the edges of the Lantern. The bigger, comparatively nicer, buildings took up the space around the border of a square that sat in the middle of the district. A handful of barkers milled around with the actual patrons coming and going through the square to their destinations. Some were trying to lure patrons into certain establishments, the rest acted as eyes and ears for their employers. Musicians staked out a spot by a fountain, fiddling, piping and strumming a lively tune to keep the crowd in motion. The petty thieves and pickpockets knew better than to linger very long around the square. The owners of the surrounding establishments had come together some time ago to form an unofficial guild. They kept prices regulated, somewhat, and ensured their patrons would make it in and out unmolested, as it were.

Maher headed straight for a large brownstone with a short iron gate wrapped around the front. He waited for a group of people to walk out, then slipped through the little door as it swung shut. The lantern hanging by the door was more ornate than most of the others. Silver filigree trees wrapped over the corners of the green tinted panes. A brass knocker shaped like a bear's head was at Maher's eye level, the thick ring hanging from its jaws. He ignored it. Twisting the oversized knob set into the middle of the door, Maher stepped inside.

The noise of the street instantly faded as the door shut behind him. The inner walls of this place had been stuffed with wool to give the impression of being far away from the city. Eyes adjusting to the dim lighting, Maher glanced at the figure reclined on a tall stool to his left. They appeared to be asleep, a flat cap tugged down over their face and arms loosely folded, but Maher knew better.

"Pimm." Maher leaned against the same wall.

"Maher." One slate gray eye peered up at him from beneath the brim of the cap. "Back so soon?"

"I had some free time." He watched Pimm pull out a tobacco pouch and roll a cigarette. The glow from the match lit up a sharp chin and wide mouth. Declining the smoke when it was offered to him, Maher let his attention wander around the ground floor.

The Bear's Den was done up like a rich person's idea of a mountain cottage. Gray stone from the mountains of Swan Island encased a massive fireplace on the back wall. A roaring fire, burning even in the summer, cast dancing shadows around the room. Heavy, dark wood furniture and cushions covered in wine red velvet were scattered around. Patrons sprawled about on the cushions and at the few small tables set up near a bar made of the same stone as the hearth. Maher caught the eye of the barkeep and nodded. The big man was one of the few residents of Kingsport who was actually from that region, Swan Islanders who didn't sail tended to stay where they were, he'd been consulted on every detail in the establishment. Maher's gaze swept twice around the room but couldn't find the one person he was looking for.

"Mama Bear's with a guest," Pimm said, guessing Maher's purpose for being there. "You'll have to wait."

"Fair enough," he shrugged. There was time to wait, this was his only stop that night.

Pimm stubbed out the cigarette in a standing brass tray shaped like a bear's paw, fingers dipping close but never touching the ashes. Maher smirked. So meticulous, even when not paying attention. Pimm was one of Maher's best contacts in the district. He'd even secured their job as door guard to the Bear's Den. In return, Pimm kept an eye and an ear out for things that might interest Maher. And did very well at it. Pimm was more observant than half the buskers out in the square put together. Slender and slight, they were often overlooked, and it worked out in Mama Bear's favor. Door guards tended to be brawlers, big enough to throw someone out or break up a fight if needed, but didn't blend in well. Pimm could slip in, pull a knife or a pistol from somewhere unexpected, and stop a fight before it really got started.

The knocker on the other side of the door clacked twice. Pimm slid off the stool and opened it just enough to look out.

"Tokens please," said Pimm. The Bear's Den was one of the few private establishments on the row. Tokens weren't cheap. A member could lend their token to someone, but they still would need one themselves to get in.

"Tokens?" A gruff voice slurred from the doorstep. "Ain't got no fucking tokens."

"No tokens, no entry." Pimm started to shut the door. A meaty hand belonging to the voice pushed it back open.

"Who says? This is Kingsport, innit? This is the Lantern, innit?"

Maher glimpsed three men dressed in rough blue-gray fabric and matching knit caps. Sailors. Obviously not from Kingsport, or they'd have known better.

"It is. And this is also the Bear's Den, which means, no one comes in without a token."

"Says you!" The door was wrenched out of Pimm's hand and banged back against the wall. "What's a mite like you gonna do about it?"

The conversations in the room halted. Maher shook his head at the barkeep, who'd already reached for the club he kept beneath the bar. Sliding a hand behind his back, Maher gripped the handle of the small pistol tucked into his trousers.

Pimm's calm voice floated through the room. "I suggest you try an establishment farther down the way. I doubt you could afford to buy a drink here, let alone anything else."

"I'd take that advice if I were you." Maher stepped behind Pimm.

The front sailor looked Maher up and down, then laughed. "They got nothin but a runt and a Saprean scarecrow at the door. Get outta my way!"

The sailor barely stepped across the threshold before a knife slid out of Pimm's sleeve and pressed against the artery in his groin. Less of a reach than going for the one in his neck.

"One wrong move," Pimm said softly, "and you won't live to make it back onto your ship."

Maher leveled his pistol at the other two sailors. "No token, no entry. You'd better leave now, before my friend carves the words into his flesh as a reminder."

They nodded quickly and grabbed their frozen shipmate by the arms. Only when they were outside the gate and stumbling down the street did Pimm put the knife away. Maher put his pistol back where it belonged, his heartbeat drumming in his ears.

"Don't mind the disturbance, folks." The barkeep pulled an expensive bottle of amber liquor from behind the bar. "Let's all have a drink, on the house, to toast our fearless door guard."

The patrons applauded, more for the free drink than for Pimm, and converged on the bar.

"Thanks, Maher," Pimm sighed. "I had a feeling something like that might happen, sooner or later."

"Why is that?" Maher shut the door while Pimm hopped back onto the stool by the wall.

"You haven't been to the wharf lately? The ships have been few and far between, both traders and fishers. Many of the captains docked here are refusing to sail until something's done about the rogue ships prowling the Eastern Sea. No sailing means no work, means idle sailors looking for trouble in town."

Maher rubbed his jaw in thought. "I noticed the docks looked emptier a few weeks ago. The captains are really refusing to sail?"

Pimm rolled a new cigarette. "Yep. Not even the trade guild has been able to make them weigh anchor." Another match was lit, soon blue smoke curled out of Pimm's nose. "A lot of the Birde Isles sailors think we've angered the sea goddess somehow and that's why the fishing catch has been shit. Divine retribution."

"Divine retribution." Maher echoed, thinking of his conversation in the market with Ally and the news broken at Lady Kingfisher's birthday dinner. He snagged the cigarette out of Pimm's hand and breathed in a slow drag. His eyes watered and his throat burned, he didn't do this often, but that's what Maher wanted. Something sharp to focus on. Clarity. Ally was already so worried about her mother's voyage, her own fears of the sea notwithstanding. If she got wind of the situation on the wharf? No, he'd wait until they heard from her mother to mention it.

Maher coughed as he exhaled the smoke from his lungs. Passing the cigarette back, Maher caught Pimm's mouth twisting up into as much of a smile as he'd get from them.

"It burns if you're not used to it."

"Thank you, Pimm. I'll remember that." Maher gave a small bow. A corner table had opened up since the scuffle at the door and Maher decided to claim it. "I'll be waiting over there. Tell your Mama Bear for me, won't you?"

Pimm chuckled behind Maher's back as he wove through the crowd. Sitting with his back against the wall, Maher observed the activity on the ground floor. Patrons in the Bear's Den were only allowed upstairs if they were escorted by an employee. Every so often, a woman would descend to the ground level to greet her guest and bring them up the stairs on the left side of the building. The second and third floors were all bedrooms. Maher wasn't sure what was on the fourth floor, but he'd made it a point to find out one day. A woman whose only job was to act as a guide would bring departing guests down a separate set of stairs on the other side. Every patron was made to feel like they were the most important, one of Mama Bear's talents. The rules were strict in this place for a reason, it was how Mama Bear kept all of her employees safe. It was also one of the reasons Maher trusted her judgement.

A full, throaty laugh drifted down the left set of stairs and the Mama Bear herself made her entrance. All wide hips, wide eyes, and wide smiles, she stopped to speak with the barkeep, then crossed right to where Maher sat. He hadn't seen Pimm move from the door but had no doubt they'd let her know she knew he was there. Swinging her hips and fluffing her fawn brown hair as she walked, she easily avoided the patrons who tried to pull her into conversation or to join them for a drink. They all knew to let her go by if she wasn't available. As amiable as she appeared, none of them wanted to be in range when the Mama Bear loosed her claws.

"Maher, so good to see you again." She bypassed the other two chairs at the table and squeezed herself into the corner with him. Looping one arm around Maher's neck, she settled onto his lap. Her crimson skirts and round bottom both spilled over the sides of Maher's legs as she leaned in and planted a kiss on his cheek. Looking around her shoulder, Maher saw several patrons shooting jealous glances their way. He wrapped both arms around the generous dip in her waist. Let them all think he was a favorite patron of hers.

"You look lovely, as always." It was true. She was nearly twenty years older than Maher, but he'd have had no idea if Pimm hadn't told him.

"Such a charmer you are." Mama Bear hooked a finger into the collar of his shirt. "Shall we have a drink? I have a new bottle of brandy from Meredia that you simply have to try."

Maher put his lips against her ear. "Sadly, I can't stay long and must hang on to my faculties. Tonight is for business, darling, not pleasure."

"Pleasure is business for me, silly boy." She sighed. "But if you insist." Shifting on his lap, she took his hand and slipped it up her skirts. There was a thick ribbon tied around one of her ample thighs. Maher ran his thumb beneath it and caught a folded square of paper no bigger than a copper coin. She rested her chin on top of his head. "For your collection, my little magpie."

Maher snorted. Magpie. She'd started calling him that last year and it was spreading throughout the Lantern. Though, he supposed it wasn't as ridiculous as the Pike he shared a home with.

"Thank you, darling." He slowly pulled his hand out, keeping the paper pinched against his palm with his thumb. When his hand was free, she turned to block him from the room so he could slip it into his inner vest pocket. "Can I trouble you with one more favor?"

"What's that?" She tilted her head closer; her perfumed hair fell around his face. Someone at a nearby table grumbled about Maher getting special treatment. Another patron told them to quit griping and enjoy the view while it lasted.

"Let me leave through your room?" Maher grinned. "How would it look if I walked out the front door after all of this?"

Standing up, Mama Bear took Maher's hand and pulled him to his feet. She purred, "Come on, then."

He let her lead him upstairs to the third floor, sending Pimm a wink as they went, and down to the end of the hall. Her room was the largest, by far, boasting a balcony with a vine-covered trellis that dipped down into the backstreet running behind the row of brownstones.

"Here we are." She closed the door with her hip. "Now, how long should I stay up here to preserve your reputation?"

"That's entirely up to you." Maher made sure there was no one in the street below. "Take a little time for yourself. Read a book. Have a nap. Whatever your heart desires."

"That's not a bad idea." She laughed. Catching the front of Maher's vest, she pulled him close and pressed a quick kiss to his lips. "Just smudging my lip color, we have to keep things believable."

Maher kissed her back, then pulled away before she could give him any other ideas. "Enjoy your rest, I'll be back soon."

"Looking forward to it, my little magpie."

Maher shot her a look, then disappeared over the balcony railing.

CHAPTER TWENTY-THREE

A roughly drawn map, notes scrawled around the edges, was spread out on Foraoise's desk.

The big prize was coming and now was the time to strike. There would be a few unavoidable complications, but there could very well not be another chance like this one again.

The capture of the *Gull's Flight* had been a rehearsal for this moment. Her crew, those loyal on each ship and the conscripted sailors alike, knew what to expect now. They'd learned to navigate a coordinated attack using multiple vessels. And the advantages provided by her letter-writing friend would ensure their success.

This last letter had been written in haste. Adjustments needed to be made before the prize crossed their path, but the *Maiden's Revenge* was holding steady. They had two days to prepare.

Crouching next to her bunk, Foraoise felt along the underside until she found the latch that opened one of the boards supporting the frame. Not even Swain knew about this compartment, only herself and Jon. And Jon wouldn't be telling anyone. She moved aside a small leather-bound book and a packet of letters, yellowed with age, until her hand closed around a velvet covered box. Inside was a small collection of rings. A jeweled ring taken off the captain of the first prize she'd ever claimed, one with the Meredian seal that came with their privateering contracts, the thin, battered wedding band Jon had given her, and a heavy ring of yellow gold. This last one she took out, trying it on different fingers until she found one large enough to fit. She'd waited a long time to wear this ring and wouldn't be taking it off again.

Foraoise found Swain at the helm, charting the coordinates she'd given him that morning.

"Swain." She joined him at his makeshift table. "Where's the helmsman?"

"Sent him down to do a cargo check." His mustache twitched as he examined a list of numbers scratched onto a scrap of paper. "If the back hold is full, it'll slow us down more than I like."

"You think we'll have to jettison the load?"

"Hope not, Captain, we might could make lagan of the lot and float it instead. But we'd have to call a vote either way."

"I'll leave you to it then." She hooked her thumbs into her belt, turned to leave. Swain knew what he was doing, he'd been the one sailor from Jon's old crew she was desperate to keep aboard. "Let me know what the helmsman finds."

"Aye Captain. Wouldn't be as much of a worry without that great bleedin' spinner taking up so much space in the bow hold."

Foraoise stopped. "And?"

"The crew haven't been thrilled having it below the forecastle. They don't trust it yet, s'all I'm saying."

"The great bleedin' spinner is going to make us the most dreaded fleet in the Eastern Sea. If any sailor isn't comfortable sleeping above it, tell them they can sleep in the rigging."

CHAPTER TWENTY-FOUR

Ally was in the middle of her dream. Only this time, she was running for her life through the tall grass.

Sharp edges nicked her legs as she passed, but she couldn't stop. Behind her, the field had melted into a storm-ridden, violent sea. The tide nipped at her heels. The roar of the water grew louder with each wave that crested and broke, eating up the ground between them. Ally reached the edge of the cliff. Below was a bare seafloor, jagged rocks rising out of the sand like teeth. A monster ready to swallow her up. The sea was closing in from behind. Ally turned, wild eyed with terror, as a great wave rose up over her head. Lightning flashed and she saw the shapes of giant creatures, whales and sharks and serpents, suspended in the water. The ground beneath her feet buckled, Ally lurched forward and grabbed onto the patch of grass left around her. White foam broke at the top of the wave, the wall of water came crashing down –

Ally bolted upright in bed; the blanket clutched in her fists like a lifeline. The room was pitch black. Her throat was raw, as if she'd been screaming; her pulse pounded against her skull.

The dream had never been like that before. Ally pressed the heels of her hands against her eyes, trying to blot out the image of the wave with the creatures trapped inside. The pounding in her head started again, she could actually hear it...

"Ally!" Someone really was making that sound, knocking rapidly at her door. "Ally! Are you in there? I'm coming inside."

The door swung open and Gai stepped into the room, only his face illuminated by a single candle. It looked like a floating head had come through the door.

"Gai?" Ally rubbed her eyes. When she opened them again, her eldest brother came into focus. "What time is it?"

His expression was grim. "You need to come downstairs."

Ally slid to the edge of her bed, still not quite understanding him. "Why? What's wrong?"

"Please," Gai used his candle to light the one on Ally's bedside table. "Just come downstairs. Father is waiting for us in the drawing room."

Pulling on her robe and slippers, Ally grabbed the candle and followed Gai through the darkened manor. Ally glanced at the tall clock at the top of the second-floor landing, it was just after one o'clock in the morning. They reached the bottom of the stairs, passing one of the servants who was lighting the lamps on the ground floor. Gai didn't stop, heading straight for the drawing room.

When Ally crossed the threshold, all eyes turned on her. Luthais and Cal were seated near the cold fireplace. Their father was standing in the middle of the room, talking to a woman Ally didn't recognize. Even Ambassador Villaon, in his elaborate silk dressing gown, was pacing by one of the windows. She didn't see Maher anywhere.

"Father?" Ally swallowed past the growing lump in her throat. "What's going on?"

"Ally, why don't you sit down?" Gai tried to steer her to an open seat next to Cal, but she refused to move.

"What's going on?" she asked again. The way they were all looking at her sent gooseflesh racing up her arms.

Luthais ran a hand through his hair and Cal shifted in his seat, but they both looked to Lord Kingfisher to answer.

Her father whispered something to the stranger, who bowed and quickly left the room. Crossing to where Ally stood, he gently took her candle and set it aside. His green eyes were red-rimmed, his face haggard. Ally sucked in a deep breath.

"A messenger came from the harbormaster's office, not half an hour ago." Lord Kingfisher took her hand, his touch was gentle but the fingers that wrapped around hers trembled. "The *Swan Song* was halfway to Balah when... they were set upon."

"Set upon," Ally whispered. The words lost all meaning.

"We don't know the whole story yet, but," Her father choked up. "They may have been attacked by the same pirates who took the *Gull's Flight*."

"They were..." her breath caught. "And Mama? What's happened to Mama?"

Lord Kingfisher brushed Ally's hair back from her face. "We don't know, Ally. Not yet."

Ally's vision blurred and her father's face swam before her. The drawing room tilted.

Luthais stood. "She's going to faint."

"Ally, you mustn't give up hope," Cal said. "We're going to find her."

"My dearest girl," Ally's father wrapped his arms around her.

"No!" Ally pushed him away, shaking her head back and forth. "No, no, no."

"Ally, please," Gai tried to step in.

"NO!" she shouted. "I knew something was going to happen, I knew it."

"This doesn't mean Rochelle is lost." Cal stood, too. They were all watching her as if she were a skittish horse. "We will –"

Unable to listen anymore, Ally fled from the room.

"Ally!" her father called. "Ally, come back!"

She bolted up the stairs, her thin shoes sliding on the polished wood. Ally ripped them off and ran, one slipper in each hand, the rest of the way to Maher's room.

"Maher!" Ally pounded her fist on his closed door. Why didn't anyone wake him when they came for her? There was no answer. Ally tried again, "Maher! Wake up!"

Done waiting, Ally tried the knob. It was unlocked. She pushed her way in. "Maher? Answer me, please." It was too dark to see. Ally dropped her slippers and ran to grab the nearest lamp she could find. When she came back moments later, the light confirmed what she already feared. Maher was gone. His bed was made, folded pajamas and robe waiting for him on his pillow. In the fireplace sat a stack of new wood, ready to be lit. He'd been gone all night.

Ally set the lamp on Maher's dressing table. The very blood in her veins had turned to ice, her fingers gone too numb to hold it any longer. The shark tooth was in her hands before she thought to reach for it. Steady, unnatural warmth pulled the feeling back into her fingers. Ally held the tooth out as far as the necklace would go. It glistened in the lamplight; a greenish blue sheen danced across the polished surface.

If only Ally had gone with her mother, she could have protected her. Or, at least, Mama wouldn't be alone now. Frightened and alone.

If she'd even survived.

Leaving the lamp and her slippers behind, Ally walked out of Maher's room and found the hall that led to the back stairs. She barely looked up, her feet carried her through the twists and turns until she exited the manor through the parlor garden. When she was past the view of the front windows, Ally broke into a run.

CHAPTER TWENTY-FIVE

"It's getting worse." Pimm took a sip from the glass of cider Maher brought over from the bar. It was the strongest thing Pimm would touch, even when not on duty at the Bear's Den.

"You're going to have to narrow that down."

"The rumors. There's been more talk of pirates taking ships and only sparing the crew if they agree to switch sides. Ships that can't leave port here or on the continent because there aren't enough sailors to make way. Logbooks pinched from the fishing trade clerk's desk, I won't say by who, proved the catches have plummeted. We're talking big numbers, not a few fish here and there. If it doesn't change, they'll have to choose between honoring our trade agreements with other countries and feeding our own people."

That matched what Dayal said on Lady Kingfisher's birthday. Maher scratched the long whiskers that tickled the underside of his jaw. He'd been running back and forth so much for the last week he'd barely had time to change clothes, let alone trim his beard. This was the first time he'd made it back to the Den since the day after Rochelle left for Balah. "Has there been any more trouble from the sailors staying on shore?"

The door knocker clacked three times. Pimm held up a hand - wait - and went to check the patrons' tokens. When they were seated at a table and out of earshot, Pimm rejoined Maher by the wall.

"Some. We don't have as much trouble here; they've learned they won't get in without a token anyway. But some of the other establishments have had huge fights break out, dishes or windows broken, people thrown into the street. And that's only if the owners are protecting those that work for them. The guild's going to call a meeting."

"I'm not surprised."

"I hope they discuss the street crews that take up the neighborhoods around the wharf while they're at it."

"Why? The crews have a decent arrangement with the Lantern establishments, don't they?"

Pimm snorted, "They did, but a large portion of their income came from providing safety detail for the night ships. Now there's no night ships loading or unloading cargo, they're testing other parts of the city."

Maher tucked that bit of information away but didn't offer any thoughts. He tapped their vest pocket. "What's the time?"

Pimm pulled out the silver pocket watch Mama Bear had gifted to mark their first year working together. "Quarter 'til three."

"Right, I'm going to head out. I have one more stop to make. Anything else I need to know right now?"

"Just one thing." They started to roll a cigarette. "We've been seeing uniforms walking the district. There were only a few the last time you stopped by, so I didn't think much of it. Now I see at least one or two a night."

"Kingsport guards?"

"No, that's the strange part." Pimm struck a match. "They're manor guards."

Maher walked out of his last stop of the evening, an orange lantern club one block down from the Bear's Den. While Maher wasn't on quite as friendly terms with this owner as he was with Mama Bear, the other man had been hinting for Maher to stay the night. It was tempting. Soon, Maher had promised, when he was no longer expected to be in his father's office at the crack of dawn each day.

Pimm was right, though, the establishments Maher frequented that didn't require membership were much rowdier than usual. Not that Kingsport was known for being a particularly quiet city, but the feeling in the air was different. Everyone was on edge, waiting for something to happen, whether good or ill.

Up ahead, at the edge of the square, Maher spotted the dark green uniform with a diving bird emblazoned on each shoulder. Just like Pimm said. What was a member of the manor guard doing in the Lantern, in *uniform*? What they did on their own time was their business. But in uniform, they represented the Kingfishers.

The guard's head kept swiveling, which would have given away that he didn't belong here even without the uniform. After another quick glance behind him, he turned down a narrow street that ran between two of the brownstones. Maher flipped up the collar of his jacket to shield the lower half of his face and followed. The sounds and lights of the square faded as Maher kept a slower pace behind him. There was a sharp turn ahead, highlighted by a faint glow at the end of the street. The guard practically hugged the wall as he went around it. Maher waited a moment before slowly peering around the corner.

Standing before a closed door, the guard fidgeted as he knocked and waited for an answer. While the door itself was nothing special, it was the lamp hanging beside it that caught Maher's attention. The glass panes were tinted purple, a color he had no knowledge of in the Lantern.

When the door finally opened, the guard snapped to attention.

A voice that struck Maher as instantly familiar said from inside, "You're late."

"I thought I was being followed." The guard's head bobbed in a short bow. "I took another lap around the square to be sure."

The voice growled, "If no one noticed you the first time you walked through, they most certainly would have caught you a second time."

Maher would know that tone anywhere.

"Begging your pardon, milord." He looked over his shoulder and Maher ducked out of sight. "But better for them to think a guard left his post to gamble than for anyone to follow me here."

Maher edged one eye back around the corner in time to see Luthais Kingfisher step into the open doorway. Holding his breath, Maher pressed close to the wall and hoped the Pike couldn't hear his heart pounding from the other side of the street.

"Did you bring what I asked for?" Luthais asked.

"Aye, milord." The guard patted his breast pocket. "It took some convincing that I wasn't already on the take, but I got it."

"Good. Come inside." Luthais clapped the man on the shoulder and the door shut behind them.

Maher peeled himself off the wall and retreated several steps before stopping to think. This was infinitely more complicated than a few rogue manor guards shirking their posts. What in all the gods' names was Luthais Kingfisher doing down there? The middle Kingfisher brother might have the personality of a ship's anchor, but he was also as straight-laced as Maher had ever seen. There'd be nothing, that Maher knew of, to interest him in the Lantern.

It was far past time for him to be back at the house and he didn't want Luthais or any manor guards to find him standing outside their door. Maher straightened his clothes and started back down the street. His mind turned over what he'd seen and what reasons Luthais might have for being there. He'd made it halfway back, when the light at the end was blocked by a large shadow.

"It's not safe to leave the square alone, lad," said the shadow.

Maher stopped, eyes adjusting. The shadow split into several smaller shapes and one struck a match against the nearest building. A child-size lantern lit up, and Maher counted five bodies blocking the exit.

"This whole district is protected by the establishment owners' guild." Maher slipped one hand behind his back. "You should know that. They don't take kindly to their customers being accosted."

The man who'd spoken first, his outline larger than the rest, spat on the ground. "The *owners* can't do a fucking thing."

"There's more of us than them." A wisp of a girl who looked to be about fifteen stepped closer, a rusted knife in one hand and a burlap sack in the other. "Hand over whatever you got, and we'll let you back into the square in one piece."

"I like that green jacket," another said. "I think I'll have it."

"I think not." Maher drew his pistol. He aimed for the biggest man in the middle and the light went out, plunging them back into darkness. Maher fired, heard the shot ricochet off a building. Someone tackled his waist and his back hit the brick wall behind him. The pistol was knocked out of his hand and something very solid struck him square in the face. He tasted blood.

Maher kicked as hard as he could, and his heel connected with something soft. Whoever he'd kicked grunted and tried to hit him again. This time the very solid thing hit the wall by his head. Maher pushed away as another pair of hands grabbed the collar of his jacket. Slipping his arms out of the sleeves, Maher ran for the square. A bullet shot past his ear and Maher hit the ground.

The big one closed in. "Wait 'til I fucking catch you, you little – ugh!"

Maher rolled out of the way as a heavy body landed next to him. There was another scuffle and the sound of glass and bone breaking before the rest of the thieves took off down the street. Spitting out a mouthful of blood, Maher pushed back against the nearest wall and waited to see who else was in the dark with him.

Something rattled to his left and another match was struck.

"Pimm," Maher sighed heavily. "I don't think I've ever been so glad to see you."

"I suppose that's a compliment." They tipped the broken glass out of the lantern and lit the candle still inside.

Maher accepted Pimm's help and examined the man lying in the street. There was nothing distinguishing about him, no sailor's tattoos or street crew patches sewn into his clothes. He couldn't see where Pimm had stabbed the man, but the spreading pool of blood beneath the body was clue enough to how he died.

Pimm searched the ground and found Maher's pistol. "I think they took your coat."

"You'll be able to recognize them then." Maher pulled out his handkerchief, miraculously still clean, and pressed it against the throbbing cut in his bottom lip. "I suppose that's what I get for wearing a new suit tonight."

"Come one, let's get inside before anyone else sees this."

"What about him? There are... other people in an establishment at the end of the street."

Pimm shrugged. "I'll tell Mama Bear. She'll send someone to take care of it."

PASHA

CHAPTER TWENTY-SIX

The days and nights were blending together. Pasha spent hours at a time exploring the depths of her home. Swimming through passages that had been empty for years, inspecting the things left behind, pitted with age and covered in grit. They reminded her too much of the state she'd been in not so long ago. So she'd scrubbed and polished and arranged until everything was neat again. Some items were beyond repair, but Pasha found herself reluctant to remove them. A mirror that was shattered when part of a tunnel crumbled away. Treasures that had lost their luster. One of the glass tapestry frames had cracked under pressure, the colors inside faded to shades of brown. Trinkets gathered from sunken ships that were rusted and bent over time. They were all broken bits of the past she wasn't ready to give up yet.

Underneath it all, like a tiny crab scuttling around inside her head, was the steady pulse and sudden spikes from the shark tooth. No matter how deep Pasha went beneath the island, she felt it. No matter how far out to sea to hunt or meet with the creatures who'd learned she was awake again, it was still there. The incessant hum wasn't so bad, she'd always been able to hear it to some degree. It was the sharp, out of context emotions that startled her each time they broke through. One morning, not long after

Pasha saw the girl on the edge of the shore, a feeling of such deep sorrow hit her that Pasha nearly went looking for her. It soon passed though, like they all did.

Pasha couldn't be sure how much of that was really coming from the girl and what was being twisted as it was amplified by the shark tooth. The more she thought about it, the less sense it made. That tooth wasn't a conduit, or it wasn't supposed to be. When Pasha gave the tooth to the Kingfisher daughter, she never imagined the energy infused into it would change on its own like that. It was purely to help Pasha know when the girl came to meet her. And if the priestess had taken the message to her grave, then the girl was always wearing it because... why?

Pasha wished she could squeeze the questions out of her mind. She could *feel* the emptiness of her home. The cavernous chambers and echoing passages taunted her as she swam through them.

Alone. You're still alone. You will always be alone.

Darting through each room, Pasha searched for something else to keep her occupied. If she had some task to focus on, the thoughts would stop for a while.

You brought this on yourself. You didn't stop Pallagia and so they left you. It's your fault, you knew she was going to do it. Why didn't you stop her?

"Quiet!" Pasha swam faster.

Queen of the Boneyard, indeed. What made you think the humans would actually give you one of their own? You could have demanded anything, and you asked that *of him?*

Pasha careened around a corner and screamed. She'd come face-to-face with an ancient suit of armor. Pallagia had dragged it up from a ship that sank near the islands when the humans first arrived. A growl started deep in her chest and rolled up into her throat. This wasn't her fault. It was Pallagia. She'd done this. And Pasha was the one paying for it.

Flipping around, Pasha slammed her tail into the human-shaped hunk of metal. It broke apart, clouds of red rust exploded from the joints. Pasha grabbed the head before it rolled away and smashed it against the wall. She hammered it over and over, until her arms were shaking, and the once-round head was a shapeless lump.

Letting it go, Pasha sank down until she was lying on the floor of the chamber. There was a sharp pressure behind her eyes, and she squeezed them shut. She didn't want to cry; it would only make things worse. The last time Pasha cried was the day she made the bargain. It had been so long since she'd spoken to anyone, it wasn't hard to produce a tear for the young priestess.

Something nudged her tail fluke and Pasha glanced down. A bone that had still been inside one of the leg pieces rolled away a bit with the current, then back to bump her tail again.

"Not now." Pasha focused instead on the glow of the luminescent creatures that lived on the cavern walls. It shifted and flowed through them. Perhaps they were telling their neighbors what they'd just witnessed. It must still be night; they didn't give off this much light during the day.

At least the thoughts had stopped. The voice. Her voice.

Better Pasha's voice than anyone else's.

That was the loudest it had been in a long time. Not since she'd gone into her long sleep.

Something hard was digging into Pasha's back. Rolling over, she found one of the metal hands from the suit. This she would get rid of; it made her think too much of Pallagia.

And Pallagia wasn't coming back either.

Pasha stuffed some of the smaller pieces into the torso and dragged it to the nearest tunnel leading out of her home. When she reached the mouth of the passage, where the drop off gave way to the open sea, Pasha shoved the armor out. It rolled away down the sand, startling a few creatures on the way. Time and the current would take it farther.

A spark flashed out of the corner of her eye. A pop of warmth that was there and yet not there. Slowly, she swam out from the tunnel. The water stretched out around her, dark and quiet.

Maybe she'd imagined it.

The light that pierced through the sea was like a ray escaped from the sun. Bright and hot, it struck Pasha with enough force to send her reeling through the water. Digging her nails into whatever she could, a rock, a hunk of coral, Pasha held on until the first burst of light faded. When she could open her eyes, Pasha saw a beacon of gold holding steady in the water. One end tied around her wrist and the other, she knew already, connected all the way back to the shark tooth.

This meant only one thing. The shark tooth had touched the sea.

She'd come at last.

CHAPTER TWENTY-SEVEN

"What do you know about a door with a purple lamp?" Maher winced as Mama Bear dabbed a pungent salve onto the cut in his lip.

"Is that where you were when Pimm found you?"

"I was nearby."

They were sitting on the sofa in Mama Bear's room. Pimm secreted Maher in through a back entrance and then upstairs without anyone else the wiser. As soon as Mama Bear arrived with medical supplies, Pimm disappeared.

"I heard a new lantern color had appeared recently, but I couldn't tell you what their specialty might be. No notice was given to the guild, and they seem to move around every few nights."

"Their specialty, right." Maher didn't say just who he saw at the purple lantern door. He wasn't sure he should tell anyone, maybe not even Ally, until he learned why Luthais was meeting Kingfisher guards in secret.

Mama Bear finished checking Maher for injuries and put a glass of brandy in his hand. Pimm slipped back into the room.

"Is everything taken care of?"

"Yes ma'am." They nodded and pulled something from an inside coat pocket. "He had these on him, sewn into the hem of his trousers."

"Again?" She held out her hand and Pimm dropped four heavy silver coins into her palm.

"What is it?" Maher asked. Mama Bear passed him one of the coins. "Saprean silver?" He held the thick silver disc up to the light. It looked brand new, freshly minted from the Saprean capital with a double-flower tulip stamped on one side and their queen's face on the other.

"Each time we've caught a member of one of these new crews, they've had these in their pockets," said Pimm. "I told you, Maher, they're going beyond the wharfs. I think someone must be paying them to organize and divide up territory in the city."

"But why would anyone do that?" Mama Bear sat next to Maher. "We've had a balanced system between us and the established crews for years."

"And who could have gotten their hands on this much silver?" Maher passed the coin from one hand to the other, testing the weight. "It looks real, feels real... Do you mind if I take this with me?"

"Of course, darling, go ahead." She gingerly touched the corner of his mouth. "This has stopped bleeding, thankfully. Why don't you stay here and rest a while?"

Maher squinted at the ornate little clock on the mantle. It was nearly five o'clock in the morning. The sun would be rising soon.

"I appreciate the offer, my dear, but I need to get back." Maher downed the rest of his brandy. "I might ask my father to take a look at this coin. He'll know for sure if it's real." Mindful of his cut, he kissed her cheek and stood. "Thank you for everything. I think I'll go out the back way, I'm not quite up to the balcony."

"I'll take you down." Pimm opened the door. "Shall I go back to the front after, ma'am?"

"Yes, that will do for now." Mama Bear brushed off her skirts and gathered the brandy glasses. "And, my little magpie?"

Maher sighed, turned back. "Yes, dear?"

"Do send me a note tomorrow, to let me know how you're doing."

Maher winked at her and followed Pimm down the hall. When they reached the bolted door that led to the back alley, Maher held out a hand.

"Thank you for your help tonight, Pimm, truly. I let my guard down and I don't know if I would have made it out of there alive without you. I'm in your debt."

"There's no need, you've helped me more times than you probably realize." They clasped his hand.

Maher nodded and stepped out into the quiet alley. The breeze plucking at his shirtsleeves reminded him that he'd have to replace that jacket.

"Wait a damn minute," Maher turned on his heel. "How did you know I was down that street?"

The sound of the bolt locking into place was the only reply he received.

CHAPTER TWENTY-EIGHT

Ally slid to a stop at the water's edge, chest heaving and tears streaming down her face.

She'd come to the quiet stretch of beach beyond the seawall, the place where all of her fears were born. On a night like this one, with the moon bright enough to light up the edge of the waves, Ally's life changed forever. The coarse sand beneath her feet was foreign and yet familiar.

A chilly breeze ruffled through her hair and Ally shivered. She really was reliving that night, standing in her nightgown at the threshold of the thing that both terrified and transfixed her. Even now, with the world crumbling around her, Ally felt an insistent and alarming urge to walk into the water. The wind changed directions and blew against her back, as if it were inviting her to take that first step.

Ally looked down at the dark water line mere inches from her toes. When her stomach rolled she was prepared for it, taking deep breaths in through her nose, out through her mouth. Legs tensing, Ally bent one knee and lifted up onto the ball of that foot. It was almost a step, almost...

She *still* couldn't do it. Even now. Even when her body had done what she couldn't make herself do a matter of days ago. Even when Mama was surely dead, or would be very soon, and Ally hadn't been there for her.

The soft whispering of the waves mocked her. *Coward. Coward. Coward.*

Ally tripped back up the beach. When she reached the top of the nearest dune, she closed her eyes and charged towards the sea. Sand kicked up beneath her heels, the sound of the lapping waves grew louder with each step. Ally felt the moment the sand changed from dry to damp and her eyes flew open.

Her traitorous body wrenched to the side, even as her legs kept going. Ally's feet sailed out from under her and she hit the dry sand hard enough to clack her teeth together. Pain shot through her head and the hip she'd landed on. With a groan, Ally forced herself to stand. The right side of her body was on fire, but she could still walk.

During the fall, her necklace had swung and wrapped around her neck. Struggling to untangle the cord in the waning moonlight, Ally stabbed her thumb on the point of the shark tooth.

"Damnit!" She yanked on the cord until it snapped. Blood smeared onto the tooth as she finally pulled it free. Why had she held onto this thing for so long? It was just another reminder of how weak she was.

"Why don't you take it, then! You took everything else!" Ally hurled the necklace into the sea, and it disappeared beneath the black water.

The moment the shark tooth was gone, a cold unlike anything Ally had ever felt sank down into her bones. Vicious and sharp. Like the strange warmth from the tooth was what kept her blood running. And she'd thrown it away.

Sinking onto her knees, Ally wrapped her arms around her middle. Every breath was an icy stab into her chest. She squeezed her eyes shut and ordered herself to wake up. This had to be a nightmare, another distortion of her dream. It had to be.

"Wake up!" Ally hissed. "Please wake up."

Waves rolled and sharp bits of shell dug into her shins and, deep down, Ally knew she wasn't dreaming. Her teeth chattered, *everything* hurt. What was happening?

"I thought I asked you to take care of this for me?"

Ally's head snapped up and the joints in her neck crunched, as if they'd been coated in a layer of frost. Her necklace was dangling in front of her. Ally focused on the shark tooth, neither knowing nor caring who was offering it to her.

"Would you like to have it back?" The stranger's tongue rolled over the words in an odd way.

When Ally nodded stiffly, the necklace was gently dropped in front of her. Hands trembling, Ally snatched the tooth up and precious warmth flooded through her arms.

"Are you alright?"

"Y-yes," She could feel her fingers again, at any rate. It was like someone had mistaken her hands for pincushions, but she could feel them.

After a while she said, "I was wondering when you were going to come to see me."

Legs aching from the cold, Ally slowly stood up. The world was still hazy. "You were... Who are you?"

"I am the sea." The last of the moonlight reflected off a pair of black eyes. "I've been waiting for you."

"Waiting?" Ally shook her head, sure mind was playing tricks. The moon was nearly gone, and she couldn't see clearly. A small, anxious voice in the back of her mind was telling her to *run*, but her body was stiff and sluggish.

"I'd like to ask, how old are you?"

"I, what?" What did that matter? "I'm twenty-two years old."

She snorted. "You're a few years late."

"What?" Ally's heart thudded harder against her chest. The pink light of dawn hit the sky and Ally blinked hard as her senses sharpened. "I don't understand. I don't know who you are."

"I told you, I'm the sea."

Ally's vision finally cleared, and she saw who, or what, was standing with her on the shore.

A scrap of fabric that might have once been part of a sail was wrapped around her torso, just enough to cover her body from collar bones to thighs. Her skin was the sleek, silvery gray of a shark's. Swaths of scales ranging from deepest green to brightest blue spread over her body like splashes of paint. A row of sharp, bone white teeth appeared when her upper lip curled into a smile that made the hair on the back of Ally's neck stand up.

"I'm glad to meet you at last."

Ally backed away. "What are you talking about?"

Her expression shifted. "You don't know? I thought they'd finally told you and that's why you were here."

"Told me *what*?"

"In short? Gaius Kingfisher I, your great-grandfather, made a bargain to save these islands from ruin. In exchange for my help, he was to bring me the next daughter born in his family. Clearly, it took a long time."

Ally's throat constricted, ice creeping back into her marrow.

The sea goddess was real, standing in front of her, claiming her great-grandfather had traded a member of his own family? And what did she mean that Ally was late? Her family was supposed to just... turn her over before now?

The goddess watched as Ally absorbed her words, her face serene in a way that set Ally's teeth on edge.

"I don't... this is..." Had everyone else known? Her father and brothers? Did Mama know? Did Mama... Ally gasped. "But, if you're the sea goddess... Did you help them? Did you help those pirates attack my mother's ship? Because of this mad bargain?"

"Pirates?" The goddess shook her head. "I don't know anything about any pirates."

"How could you not?" Ally shouted, not caring if the goddess decided to strike her dead then and there. "How could the goddess of the sea not be aware of everything that *happens on the sea*?"

She shrank back, appearing unsure for the first time. "It's not so simple."

"Please, I have to know."

"I'm sorry, I don't know anything about what happened to your mother." Her voice fell flat. "I'm not a goddess."

Ally's stomach dropped. "Wh-what do you mean?"

"I'm not the sea goddess."

"Then... how?"

"I promise I can explain everything to you." She reached towards Ally. "If you'll let me..."

"Explain?" Ally stumbled back, slipping on loose sand. "What is there to explain? That you tricked my family into believing you were a goddess? Do you know what you've done? Because of *you* I've spent my whole life terrified of..." Ally made a break for the stairs.

"Wait!"

"No!" Ally turned back at the base of the seawall. "You have no power to stop me. You're not a goddess, or a spirit, or even a damned selkie. You're..." She searched her memory for what this fake goddess could possibly be, reaching for the buried stories Esa had told. "You're nothing but a sea witch!"

Scrambling up the stone steps as fast as she could, Ally didn't look back again until she reached the top of the wall. The sea witch followed to the bottom of the stairs, but no further. Ally bolted for the house, feeling those black eyes watching her the whole way.

MAHER

CHAPTER TWENTY-NINE

It wasn't quite dawn when Maher slipped back into the manor. The rooms on the ground floor were fully lit, strange for the hour, but he didn't encounter another soul on his way to his wing of the house.

Maher stopped just outside his room. His door was ajar, the scrap of fabric he'd left beneath the lock lay on the floor. An oil lamp from the hall was sitting on his dressing table, nearly burnt out. As Maher entered the room, something soft squished under his foot. Picking up the embroidered slipper, he stared at it for a second before spotting its partner by the dressing table. They were Ally's slippers. But what would Ally have been doing in his room in the middle of the night? Setting the slippers aside, Maher lit his own lamp and snuffed out the other one. The room brightened.

"I see all that time spent with those degenerates in the Lantern district has finally caught up with you." Khafra Villaon was sitting in a corner chair, half-hidden in the shadow cast by the door.

"Father?" Maher backed up a step before catching himself. He unbuttoned his waistcoat. "What are you doing up here at this hour?"

"There's been an emergency, which you clearly are unaware of. The entire manor has been awake for several hours."

"What happened?" Maher's hands stilled.

His father stood, "Lady Kingfisher's ship was set upon by pirates."

Maher shook his head, certain he hadn't heard that right. "Pirates? But they obviously wouldn't have been carrying anything of value, not like a trading ship. That's why they chose to send her on a schooner like the *Swan Song*."

"The wife of the lord of the largest trade hub in the Eastern Sea sounds pretty valuable to me."

That's why Ally was here. She'd needed Maher and came in to find him gone. Forgetting about his clothes, Maher strode past Khafra. "I have to see Ally. She was worried something was going to happen…"

"She's left the manor."

He turned back. "Where did she go?"

"I don't know. I gather Lady Alphonsine came here looking for you and, when you were nowhere to be found, she ran outside."

"Does *anyone* know where she went?"

"I'm afraid not." His cool, ever-poised expression grated on Maher's nerves.

"How can you be so calm? And how is it no one has bothered to find Ally?"

"We're on an island, she can't have gone far." He brushed an imaginary speck of lint from his sleeve. "Before you go tearing off to search for her, there's something we need to discuss."

"Right now?" Maher shoved his hands into his trouser pockets and found the silver coin. "Actually, there was something I wanted to ask you –"

"Whatever it is can wait and so can searching for that girl. This is far more important, I assure you."

The coin slipped from Maher's fingers, landing at the bottom of his pocket. "What could possibly be more important than finding Ally, when you've just told me her mother's ship was taken by pirates?"

"We have an opportunity here, Maher." Khafra smirked, a cold sweat broke out on the back of Maher's neck. "Nothing throws a nation into chaos quite like the loss, or anticipated loss, of a ruler. We can use your close friendship with Lady Alphonsine to ensure there are seats at the table for *both* of us when decisions are being made. It's an entry into the type of position only this nation's most trusted advisors hold and more."

Ignoring his instinct for self-preservation, Maher made himself ask, "Did you have anything to do with the attack on the *Swan Song*? Father, did you plan this?"

"Even I couldn't have designed a situation that aligned so perfectly." He scoffed.

"And what position could you possibly hold that would help the Kingfishers at a time like this?"

Khafra folded his arms over his chest. "Lord of Trade."

"Lord of Trade?" Maher blinked at him. "You want to be Lord of Trade?"

"I don't believe I misspoke."

"*Lord of Trade*. The position currently held by Luthais Kingfisher, second son of Lord Gaius Kingfisher III. That's the position you're talking about."

"You're testing my patience, Maher."

"But one of Gaius' sons already has it! Has had it for several years now, in fact."

"Luthais is not a politician. I don't have to explain to you, there's a certain level of skill and finesse involved with any appointed title, which he does not possess."

"The captains and sailors all respect him." Maher bristled, compelled to defend Ally's family even when he now suspected the very same brother of plotting *something* in secret. In a place no one would think to look for him. In the middle of the night. Maher's building arguments were losing credibility before he even spoke them, though his father would have no idea why.

"He spends too much time with the ruffians sailing those ships and not enough time entertaining the officials representing our allies," Khafra sneered. "He's more likely to punch one of them for using a word he doesn't understand, rather than broker a trade agreement."

Maher frowned. He may have only gotten a handful of words out of the middle Kingfisher brother in the twelve years they'd lived under the same roof, but Luthais wasn't stupid. He was quiet. And that worried Maher more than a lack of small talk.

"You will do this for us, Maher. This affects your future as much as mine."

"This is madness." Maher stepped toe-to-toe with his father. "This is the most underhanded scheme I've ever heard from you, and believe me, there have been some contenders."

"How else do you expect me to rise out of this servile ambassadorship? With the Queen a thousand miles away and the Minister taking credit for every scrap of progress I've made? This is how legacies are built, how prominence is achieved when you must fight against the flood of incompetence and status given to others by pure chance of birth." His breath smelled of the mint leaves he was always chewing between meetings. Maher's stomach churned.

"What you're saying then, is you don't give a damn about Ally or her family. You only care about yourself and what they can do for you?"

"This is where you lack vision, Maher. Why else would you have spent years cultivating this single friendship, if not to use it when the time was right? When there have been dozens of children from far better circumstances coming and going from the Birde Isles since we arrived. Those were relationships we could have used as well. Instead you chose to devote every spare minute to the one Kingfisher who sits at the bottom of the inheritance ladder, with nothing to her credit but a damaged mind and misshapen nose –"

"Don't you dare say that about her!" Maher shoved both palms against his father's chest. Ambassador Villaon staggered, eyes wide, and caught himself on the dressing table.

Father and son stared, unmoving, as if they were strangers who'd collided on the street. Maher had never done anything like that in his life, always tolerating or finding loopholes in his father's demands instead, avoiding confrontation. Compromising. Giving in a little at a time until he finally realized, the only way to get out of the cycle was to make the path for himself. A secret weapon that would free him of a life of trade, or politics, or whatever else the honorable Ambassador Khafra Villaon of Saprea wanted his son to do. It was pure luck his father hadn't taken another post, especially before Maher came of age. Saved him the added burden of devising a plan to stay in the Birde Isles. He was so close to freedom, and with one momentary lapse of control, he might have just lost it.

Maher took an unsteady breath, "Father, I –"

Khafra grabbed the front of his shirt and shoved Maher backwards. The bruise that had been steadily spreading across his back hit the wall and Maher saw stars.

Ambassador Villaon's voice was a hot knife against his ear. "Listen to me, Maher. I have allowed you free rein until now. I let you have your painting, indulged your ridiculous and expensive clothing habits. I looked the other way while you shirked your responsibilities to run off with Lady Alphonsine when she called. And, most ludicrous of all, I've allowed you to cavort around the Lantern with thieves and whores, putting your reputation in untold peril, and for what? So you can disobey me when the time has finally come to put your friendship with that girl to use?" His grip tightened on his son's collar, and Maher struggled to breathe. "You will convince Lady Alphonsine I should assume the title of Lord of Trade. That I will use that power in a way her brother can't, to bring every ally of the Birde Isles to aid in reclaiming Rochelle Kingfisher. You will make yourself useful and you will make *me* indispensable."

Khafra released him. Maher dragged air into his lungs, eyeing his father as he checked his appearance in the mirror.

Straightening the front of his jacket, Khafra smiled coldly. "I'll wager it will take at least ten days to receive any further news of Lady Kingfisher's ship. That should be plenty of time for you to lay the groundwork."

Maher's voice cracked and he hated himself for it. "And if Ally refuses? What then?"

"It would be in your best interest to ensure that doesn't happen." His father left the room, closing the door with a snap.

Maher slid down the wall until he was seated on the floor and leaned forward over his knees. The pain in his back was enough to make him retch. Pressing his palms over his eyes until the feeling passed, Maher crawled to his bed and used it to pull himself upright. He had to stay in control. More than anything else, he needed to find Ally and remind his friend she wasn't in this alone.

He'd deal with Khafra later.

ALLY

CHAPTER THIRTY

Ally trailed sand through the manor, searching every room for her father.

When she reached Lord Kingfisher's second-floor study, she heard his voice and several others inside.

"Messengers have been dispatched my lord, to the governors of Swan and Gull Island, and to our allies on the continent."

"And the ships to retrace the *Swan Song's* route?" Lord Kingfisher asked.

"Preparing to make way as we speak," said Gai. "The wharf must be cleared to get the provisions through,"

"I don't care if they have to fire a cannon across the docks to make room, I want those ships ready to set sail by noon!"

Ally felt a pang of sorrow, her father sounded scared, angry, desperate. That melted away when she remembered why she'd come to see him. Pushing the door open, Ally knew how wild she must look – barefoot in her night clothes, covered in sand. She'd tucked the shark tooth away, but blood from the wound on her thumb had dripped down the front of her gown.

"Ally?" Lord Kingfisher stared at his daughter. Her brother and the advisors gathered followed suit. "What happened to you? Where have you been?"

"I need to speak with you. Alone." Ally surprised herself with how composed she sounded.

"Of course, dearest, let me finish here while you clean yourself up, and–"

"No, Father, we need to talk now." Ally stood at the other end of the table and eyed the people seated there. "If you will excuse us."

Unsure of who to listen to, some of the advisors stood while the rest looked to Lord Kingfisher.

"Give us a moment," he said, standing himself. "If you will all wait in the sitting room down the hall. Gai, please show them the way."

When Ally was alone with her father, she braced her shaking hands on the table.

"I have to ask you something, and I want you to tell me the truth."

"Of course, I will."

Ally took a deep breath. "Did Gaius I, your grandfather, make a promise to the sea goddess?"

Her father ran an unsteady hand over his face. "Where did you hear that?"

"Did he?"

"That's just a story, Ally, an outdated superstition,"

"That's the thing," she cut him off. "It's *not* just a story, is it?"

"I think your great-grandfather must have been very disturbed later in his life, he truly believed he'd met the goddess."

"So have I."

"What do you mean?" A deep furrow creased his brow.

Her head throbbed as she recalled the encounter. "I was on the beach,"

"On the beach!"

Ally talked faster, the words running together, "I was on the beach, and I met the same goddess as Gaius I, well, she's not actually a goddess – that was a lie – she's some kind of creature or sea witch, most likely a sea witch, but she's real and she's here and she said Gaius I promised her –"

Her father's large hands firmly held the sides of her face. "Breathe, Ally. Take your time."

"She," Ally hiccupped, "she said, in exchange for her help, Gaius I promised her the next daughter born in our family. That's *me*."

He waited until she was breathing normally before letting go.

"Was she right? Were you supposed to give me to her?"

"I never believed it was real," he said softly. "I swore this strange family superstition would end with me. There was no way it could be true, and we took such care with you. I couldn't have imagined sending you away like the others."

"Others? What others?"

The realization of what her father had said hit him and he looked away. "I'd hoped to never burden you or your brothers with this. Especially when there is nothing we can do about it now."

"With what? Father, what did Gaius I do?"

"After this so-called encounter with the goddess, he started sending any children who were born daughters away from the Isles."

"How... how many were sent away?"

"I'm not sure, Ally. It was all before my time, I didn't learn of it until after I was grown myself. By the time I married Glenna, both my father and grandfather were gone, and not once did I think that ridiculous arrangement was real."

"But *she's* real. I know what I saw. I *spoke* to her."

"I won't let this happen." Lord Kingfisher paced back to the head of the table. "Real or not, sea witch or not, I won't lose you too. We'll capture her or drive her away."

Ally was only half-listening. An unnerving thought had leapt to the front of her mind. "But, if you didn't believe Gaius I had truly met the goddess, then why did you keep me away from the sea?"

"What?" He froze.

"This bargain that you say you don't believe in, is that why you never let me near the sea?"

"Of course not. Our head priestess said it would be best for you. That the story my grandfather told wasn't a concern, but your health and happiness depended on your staying on land. At least until you were older."

"And you couldn't tell me any of this? If it was for my so-called health and happiness, I didn't have a right to know?"

Gaius held out his hands, but she didn't move. "After your... accident, you wanted nothing to do with the water anyway. We didn't want to upset you anymore than you already were."

Ally's fingers curled into her palms. "I have been petrified for years. I thought it was all my fault. Knowing all of this might have hurt, but it also might have shown me I wasn't entirely to blame. Don't you see that?"

"I'm sorry, Ally, we did what we thought was best."

"No one asked me what I thought was best," she snapped. "And if this bargain with the not-goddess turned out to be true? Would you have still only considered what *you* thought was best? Would you have still hidden it from me?"

"Darling, I never dreamed –"

"Would you?"

Her father was on the verge of tears, but Ally didn't care. "I'd never have agreed to it, Ally."

"I suppose we'll never know for sure, will we?" Ally's throat burned. "We'll never know if we could have faced it together because you let me be afraid."

"Ally…"

"You let me be afraid. Because it was easier than telling me the truth."

Ally changed into the first clothes she could lay her hands on, an old pair of tan trousers and a blue shirt, then threw her tangled hair into a loose braid. The knot she'd tied in the cord of her necklace would hold for now, but she wanted something more secure when she returned.

Any servants Ally passed avoided eye contact and hurried past her. What they were seeing was not their sweet, considerate young lady of the manor. Only Mrs. Thorley stopped and spoke when they met on the main staircase.

"My lady, are you going out again?" The older woman spoke gently, yet firmly. "We are all worried for Lady Kingfisher and pray for her safety. But perhaps you should rest now. Have you eaten anything today?"

Ally bit back the first reply that came to mind, that she could rest once her mother was found. Mrs. Thorley didn't deserve that, she was showing her concern the best way she knew how.

"I must go out, Mrs. Thorley, but I won't be long. I'm going to the temple, I want to… pray for Mama. I'll have a tray in my room when I return."

"Would you like someone to accompany you? I'm sure I saw Mr. Villaon not long ago."

"No, I'd rather be alone." Ally hesitated, then quickly kissed Mrs. Thorley's cheek. "Thank you, Mrs. Thorley. I appreciate everything you're doing to help us."

Ally left before anyone else could approach and found the lane that led from the manor to the temple of the sea.

Esa was seated on a bench in the temple garden. A pair of stone whales arched up behind her, providing shade from the mid-morning sun. Her tightly coiled hair was pulled back into a simple knot at the base of her neck. In her lap was a porcelain bowl of pearls in different sizes and colors. She was stringing them onto strands of wire. The finished garland would be draped above the temple doorway, a blessing on the heads of all who entered.

The lighter shades of blue trim on her robes and the silver medallion around her neck signified Ally's former tutor as Head Priestess now, but they rarely bothered with titles.

Though some of Ally's anger had burned off by the time she reached the temple, it was still there, simmering in her chest.

"It's been a while since I've seen you, child," Esa said without looking up. The laugh lines around her tawny brown eyes deepened. Ally tried to smile, but couldn't.

"I'm sorry, Esa."

"There's no need to apologize." Esa patted the empty space next to her. "Come and sit with me."

She sat, draping the growing lines of pearls across her lap so they wouldn't tangle.

"I've heard what happened to Lady Kingfisher. I'm sure many people have said this, but I'm truly sorry." Esa took her hand.

"You've heard already?" Ally's shoulders tensed.

"There are some who have already come to pray to the goddess for your mother's protection, yes. She is much loved by the people of Kingsport."

"As if the *goddess* would really help," she muttered.

"What do you mean, Ally?"

"Nothing."

Esa cupped her chin. "I know how upset you must be, but please don't give up hope. I'm not."

"It's not that." Ally gently extracted herself and paced in front of the bench. Esa gave her space and silence until she was ready to speak.

"I have to ask you something," Ally stopped and faced her. "Do you know why I wasn't allowed near the sea as a child?"

"It's been a long time since you've raised that question, but I suppose you are grown and there's nothing preventing me from telling you now." She resumed threading the pearls. "It was Aithne who urged your parents to keep you on land until you came of age."

"Aithne?"

"The head priestess who delivered you." Another pearl slipped down the wire. "She died quite suddenly, when you were still very small."

"But why would she do that? And why would my parents have listened to her?"

"Aithne never would explain exactly why you were to be kept from the sea as a child. She only said she'd communed with the sea and knew it was best."

There they were again, those words, *what was best*.

No one had told Ally it was only supposed to be until she was grown. None of them.

Part of her wanted to be angry with Esa as well, for going along with all of Aithne's assertions, but even now she couldn't muster those feelings towards the priestess. "She must have been very convincing, for my parents take her word even after she was dead."

Esa's expression turned thoughtful. "I never brought it up to Aithne, but I always wondered if you were Sea Kissed. If that was what she'd seen in her vision."

"Sea Kissed?"

"There have always been people who were called to the sea. Some of us became priestesses," she waved a hand at her robes. "Others became sailors. Some even joined the selkies, living most of their lives in the water. But, very rarely, there would be someone who couldn't seem to get close enough. It would become an obsession. A need they couldn't fulfill. We said they were kissed by the sea."

"What happened to them?" Ally thought of the sea witch waiting for her on the shore. Is that what had happened to her? Was she a Sea Kissed woman who'd become so obsessed that it somehow changed her into what she was now?

"In the old days, it was difficult to predict. Of the people called to the sea, it was those with more feminine energy who tended to be Sea Kissed. The unfortunate truth was some would become so despondent they would throw themselves into the waves and perish. We simply didn't know how to console them. Of course, it's been many years since we've had a true Sea Kissed person, none in my lifetime. I've heard it happened more often when the islands were still isolated."

"You mean, once they were able to leave the islands, they were cured?"

"Cured? I don't know if that's the word. I'd hope they found ways to stay connected to the sea that calmed the overwhelming feelings pulling them to it."

"So, you aren't Sea Kissed."

"I'm very drawn to the sea, it's true, but I'm not one of them." Esa sighed, "The goddess only knows why those few were chosen."

Ally was about to tell Esa exactly what the so-called goddess really was, but she couldn't bring herself to say the words. She couldn't take that away from Esa. Not today.

MAHER

CHAPTER THIRTY-ONE

Maher searched the entire house and the surrounding grounds, with no sign of Ally. He thought of going into the city, but couldn't guess where she might be, and it was impossible to search every street in one afternoon.

As he circled back around through the kitchen vegetable garden, Maher saw Mrs. Thorley speaking to the cook. He waited until they were finished, then caught up with the housekeeper.

"Mrs. Thorley! Do you have a moment?"

"Of course, Mr. Villaon. How can I help?" She paused at the kitchen door, her kind blue eyes settled on him.

"I'm looking for Ally and she's nowhere on the grounds. Do you happen to know where she's gone?"

"She's at the temple of the sea."

"Really?" He'd never thought to check the temple. Ally only went there on feast days with her family, or to pay the occasional visit to the head priestess.

"Yes, she wanted to pray for Lady Kingfisher's safe return," Mrs. Thorley nodded solemnly.

Ally? Praying? She must have been truly desperate to pray to a goddess she didn't believe in.

"I suggested she invite you to join her, but she wanted to be alone. Mr. Villaon?"

"What? Yes!" Maher snapped to attention. "Thank you, Mrs. Thorley. Did she say when she'd return?"

"She wanted a tray sent to her room for lunch, so she should be back soon."

Maher thanked her again and backtracked to the front of the house. If Ally took the private path connecting the manor to the temple, she'd have to come back by the base of the cliff slope. He settled down there against the abandoned remnants of a stone wall, another relic from the island's past.

His father's demands from that morning echoed through his head, as if Khafra was there whispering them into his ear. It wasn't hard for Maher to understand why this was the position Khafra'd set his sights on. As an ambassador he was there to look after Saprea's interests. But as Lord of Trade? The holder of that title had full control over every facet of the Birde Isles trade from policy to negotiation, holding the power to make decisions without consulting Lord Kingfisher. Placed above everyone from the lowest ranked sailor to the ambassadors sent by other nations. That had to be part of it, Khafra Villaon must detest the idea of someone as young as Luthais holding a position over him. There was nothing to be done if it were an inherited title, but this was one of the few appointed titles within his father's reach. They'd known the previous Lord of Trade, of course, but Maher hadn't understood the true stature of that position until Luthais took over.

How, in all the gods' names, could he possibly talk Khafra out of this mad plan?

Mrs. Thorley was right; he didn't have to wait long. Ally spotted Maher from down the lane and veered off to meet him. Her face was pinched and there were dark circles under her eyes.

"Al..." Maher wanted to hug her, but was she angry with him for not being there last night?

Ally saved him from wondering when she wrapped her arms around his waist. He hugged her close, not caring that one of her hands was pressed against the bruise on his back. Her face nestled against the hollow between his collar bones. When she let out a heavy sigh, Maher felt her frame shake with the effort.

"I'm so, so sorry, Al." He tucked his chin into her hair. "I'm sorry I wasn't there for you."

"There's nothing you could have done," she said, her voice muffled.

"Still, you needed me, and I wasn't here."

"You can't always be exactly where everyone needs you." Ally slipped out of his arms and looked at him properly. "Maher! What happened to you?"

"Oh, huh, you noticed." Maher tried to grin and winced when the cut on his lip pulled. "I had a slight disagreement in the city last night."

"Slight disagreement? It looks like someone disagreed with your face."

"They might have." He coughed. "Listen, I'm fine. What I want to talk about is your mother. Can we do that?"

Ally chewed on her bottom lip, a habit from childhood that usually meant she wanted to say something she wasn't supposed to.

"We can wait, if you want to eat something and rest for a while."

She glanced towards the house. "Let's stay out here." They climbed the slope. Everything was beginning to dry up in preparation for autumn, Maher's nose twitched.

He ought to tell her what he saw in the Lantern, Maher had at least decided on that while he was waiting. Ally deserved to know if one of her brothers was up to something. If the news really came in at the time Gai told him, then Luthais went into the city *after* they learned about the attack on Rochelle's ship.

Yes, he'd tell Ally about Luthais, he might even tell her about the street crew that jumped him, but he would most definitely not tell her about the conversation with his father. Not yet. Not ever, hopefully, if his plans all came through.

They sat together in the usual spot. Maher made himself as comfortable as he could and waited for Ally to begin. She pulled her shark tooth necklace out of her shirt and rubbed it between her palms. The cord was damaged, he couldn't help but notice, and had been tied back together in a ragged knot.

Finally, Ally put the necklace back and looked at Maher.

"She's real."

"Who's real?"

"The sea goddess."

When Ally finished her story, Maher sat there in silence. Holding out hope that she'd say it was all a joke. Or a dream. She didn't.

Instead, she looked out at the waves and waited for him to speak.

"This is impossible."

"I know," she said, wearier than he'd ever seen her.

"Where has this... sea witch been all this time?"

"Out in the water, I suppose. I didn't stay to ask."

"This is –" Maher scrubbed his hands over his face and hissed in pain. "What are you going to do?"

"I don't know."

"What do you mean, you don't know?" He touched her shoulder, "Ally, now is not the time for you to leave the world. Stay with me!"

"I am with you. I just don't know what to do. All I can think about is Mama and whether she's alive or," Ally choked up, "or dead. Compared to that, deciding what to do about the sea witch my great-grandfather sold me to is lower on the list."

"Al, we won't let anything happen to you."

"We?"

"Me, your friends, your family."

Ally's laugh was bitter. "My family are the ones who've gotten me into this mess."

"Then they should also be the ones to help you get out of it."

"I don't see how."

"We'll figure it out. If I were you, I'd bring the rest of them into it, so there are no more secrets and everyone is aware of what you're up against."

"And what about Mama?"

"Your father will stop at nothing to find her, you know that. We'll save her and we'll get you out of whatever deal that sea witch made. To be safe," he added, "you'd better stay well away from the shore until we know more what she's capable of."

"No problem there, trust me." Ally's stomach rumbled and they started back down the hill. "Do you really think we'll find her?"

"Yes, I do. In the meantime, we'll keep an eye on…" Maher stopped before saying her brother's name. This didn't feel like the right time to add to Ally's worries, not after everything she'd just told him.

"Keep an eye on what?"

"We'll, uh, keep an eye on the horizon. One of our allies might find Lady Kingfisher before the missives even reach the continent."

The look on Ally's face was skeptical at best, but she didn't say anything else as they entered the house.

Ally looked ready to collapse by the time they reached her room. He pulled the cord to ring for Mrs. Thorley and helped Ally get comfortable. The housekeeper arrived with food, a pot of tea, and a wash basin of heated water. Maher silently blessed her for knowing exactly what to do and left Ally with the hope they both could get some much-needed sleep.

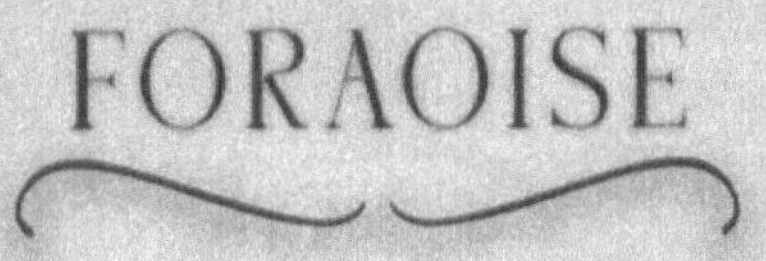

Chapter Thirty-Two

Foraoise paused outside the locked door to the captain's quarters. Tugging on the wide brim of her hat until it blocked the top half of her face, she pulled an iron ring of keys from her belt and let herself in.

Rochelle Kingfisher was sitting on the floor in the far corner of the cabin, head bowed with her bound hands resting in her lap. They'd left her free at first, but she tried to knock Swain's skull in with a mounted compass and the ropes became necessary.

"Good evening, Lady Kingfisher." Foraoise stopped a few feet away, just outside the light cast by the lamp hanging on the wall. "I'm so glad you could accept my invitation to join me aboard the *Maiden's Revenge*."

When the woman's head lifted, she was glaring daggers. Foraoise was impressed with how tough this great lady turned out to be. She'd been prepared for more wailing and crying, or fainting. That bottle of smelling salts was going to go to waste.

"I don't know what you're talking about. I never agreed to come on board this ship and I'm not Lady Kingfisher."

Ignoring the lie, Foraoise drew a narrow dagger from her boot and used the point to clean her nails. "I hope you're finding your accommodations comfortable. We aren't accustomed to hosting nobility, but we try our best, Lady Kingfisher."

"I'm *not* Lady Kingfisher," she snapped. "Whoever you're looking for, you took the wrong ship. I'm not her."

Foraoise took in her disheveled, yet costly, travel clothing. Reaching down, she took the hem of the blue and silver cloak and rubbed the fine material. "Yes, you are."

She spat at the captain's feet and Foraoise chuckled. Far more resilient than she'd expected.

"If I am Lady Kingfisher, then you must know every ship in the Eastern Sea will be looking for me."

"I should hope so." She enjoyed the confusion that crossed the other woman's face. "I want as many ships as they can send."

"You also want the Birde Isles and their allies as enemies? They're expecting me in Balah, what do you think they'll do when I don't arrive as planned?"

"Why should they expect you? It's not as if they knew you were coming."

There was a knock at the door, just as she'd planned. A sailor came in, carrying a pitcher of water and a hunk of hardtack bread.

"Is now a good time, Captain?"

"Yes, come in Frossard." Foraoise grinned. "Lady Kingfisher, I'm sure you recognize the *special* messenger you received at Kingsport? I admit, I never expected it would be so convenient having a Balahn sailor in my own crew. There were other options, but Frossard cleaned up better than the rest."

Rochelle gasped when he deposited the bread and water in front of her. "What... you sent the letter?"

"As I said, I'm glad you could accept my invitation."

"And you, you traitor!" She swung her tied hands at him, but the heavy ropes tipped her off balance.

"Can't be loyal to a place that threw you out," he sneered.

"Enough, Frossard. You can go."

"Aye, Captain."

When they were alone again, Foraoise knelt down to Rochelle's eye level. "This journey we're on together can go one of two ways, my lady. You can behave and stop trying to bash my crew's brains out, and you'll be made comfortable. Or, I can have you bound to the figurehead for the rest of the voyage and maybe you'll survive long enough to make it home." She pointed the dagger at her. "Which will it be? Will you behave?"

The muscles in Rochelle Kingfisher's jaw twitched. Eyes locked on the dagger, she slowly nodded.

"Good girl." Foraoise took hold of her wrists and sawed through the rope holding them together.

As she rubbed the blood back into her fingers, Lady Kingfisher's gaze landed on the heavy gold ring sitting on Foraoise's hand. "Which of our ships did you steal that from?"

"I didn't steal it." Foraoise grabbed a bottom corner of her cloak and sliced it off.

"Ah! How else would you have gotten it?" She spat.

Tucking the dagger away, Foraoise pulled off her hat. "It was a gift. Left to me by a kind soul who ensured I wouldn't forget where I came from."

Lady Kingfisher recoiled; her dark eyes went wide. "You... you're..."

"Captain Foraoise Dare, at your service." She stood and pushed the jug of water closer with the toe of her boot. "Fret not, I'm sure you won't be with us too long. Your husband will receive our demands soon. And I have special plans for the delivery."

CHAPTER THIRTY-THREE

The days that followed were agony, as each hour passed with no news of her mother or the crew of the *Swan Song*. Ally bounced between utter exhaustion, barely able to drag herself out of bed, and sudden bursts of energy that sent her prowling through the manor at all hours, hunting for something to tame her racing thoughts.

There was only so much she could do, following Maher on errands to the trade guild or listening in on the meetings in her father's study. All of the Birde Isles had heard by now of Lady Kingfisher's capture. Letters of condolence and offers of aid flowed in, but Ally couldn't bring herself to answer the notes addressed to her. In the end, she authorized her father's steward to draft replies of thanks. She read and signed each one, and immediately forgot about them.

Ally did take Maher's advice, telling her brothers about her encounter with the sea witch. Their reactions were mixed, to say the least. Gai didn't believe her at first, the set of his face showing he clearly thought she'd cracked under the pressure of Lady Kingfisher's capture. In a rare display of emotion, Luthais had openly gaped at his sister before moving to look out the nearest sea-facing window, as if he'd be able to spot the sea witch on the shore. Cal, to his credit, had been the only one to take Ally at her word and immediately began to pepper her with questions. Once they all settled down, and their father confirmed the story, the gravity of the situation sank in. Even with the initial excitement, it wasn't really mentioned after that first conversation. Ally suspected they didn't know what else to say to her until more was learned about the sea witch. Or perhaps they were having doubts on whether their prosperity was by their own hands or because of the creature lurking in the water around the isles.

Ally stopped her morning walks to the cliffs, she had no idea how far inland the sea witch could travel. Now that she'd made herself known, Maher had pointed out, what could stop her from simply grabbing Ally the next time she got close? Though not entirely sure such a thing would happen – she'd kept her distance during that first encounter – Ally stayed away from the cliffs to ease Maher's mind.

An ache settled deep into her chest, one not even the shark tooth could soothe. She wanted her mother and, Ally soon realized, she missed seeing the sea. The glimpses from high manor windows or the streets by the wharf weren't enough. Her dreams evolved into jarring nightmares of her mother being pulled underwater by a dozen scaled hands.

On the morning of the seventh day of waiting, Ally accompanied Maher to deliver a packet of letters to the trade guild. It was faster and more secure than handing them over to the post. The streets of Kingsport had grown quiet and subdued. Ally avoided the pitying looks of those who recognized her and instead focused on how long it took them to reach the guild. She added that time to how long it might take an offshore message to make its way into the right hands, and then to the manor. Even if word of Mama arrived at that very moment, it would take at least two or three hours to reach her family. Assuming the courier knew what they had and how urgent its contents were.

They crossed through the market district on their way home. It was nearly empty, with very few stalls set up. None of the sellers were calling out their wares or waving to customers. It was as if the entire city were holding its breath, waiting to find out if they would be celebrating or mourning.

Maher and Ally made the walk there and back with little said between them. Ally was grateful, it was a comforting silence. When the house came into view, there were several horses and carriages waiting out front. That wasn't unusual, given the daily meetings Lord King fisher was holding, but there was someone pacing impatiently by the nearest carriage.

Ally could just make out a flushed, freckled face.

"Is that Cal?" Maher asked.

"I think so, what's he doing?"

Cal spotted them and came running down the road. "Ally! Ally, where have you been?"

"What is it?" Ally's pace quickened. "Is it Mama? Have you heard something?"

Cal reached them. "We heard about an hour ago, a longboat from the *Swan Song* was found just outside Trader's Bay. A sailor on board was chained to a small chest. Before he lost consciousness, he said it was for Kingfisher eyes only."

"Where is it now?" Maher asked, squeezing Ally's hand as they went inside.

"The harbormaster sent for a blacksmith to detach the poor sailor. Gai went with the captain of the manor guard to meet them and bring the chest back."

"We were just down by the guild," Ally panted, trying to keep up with them on the stairs. "No one there said anything about a longboat."

"They brought them in on the northern end of the bay, to avoid a panic or someone trying to steal whatever is in that chest."

They made it to the study and Ally went to her father. She let him hug her for the first time in days.

Luthais and her father's five key advisors were already present. Mr. Pavan Dayal and Ambassador Villaon, indeed all of the available ambassadors residing in Kingsport, arrived soon after.

"Is there any word on when this message will arrive?" Ambassador Villaon stood next to his son. Ally noticed the clench in Maher's jaw.

"As soon as they can extract the sailor from it, Gai will bring the chest here." Gaius kept one arm around Ally's shoulders. "I want it understood, no word of what we find in that chest is to leave this room. Lady Kingfisher's safety may depend on it."

"Of course, my lord," said Mr. Dayal, and the rest agreed.

Ally wished they would leave her family, and Maher, to see the contents first. That was unlikely to happen, now that they were already discussing possible actions to take.

Another hour crawled by. Mrs. Thorley arrived with a line of servants bearing water, tea, wine, whatever the occupants of the room might like to drink. Ally accepted a cup of tea from Mrs. Thorley and thanked her. The cup and saucer clinked together as she tried to hold them steady.

When Gai finally burst through the door, Ally nearly threw her empty cup across the room. Maher deftly took it from her and stepped aside to let the captain of the guard through with the chest. The Kingfishers all gathered at the head of the table, and Ally was suddenly afraid. What if they opened that lid and found nothing, or worse, some piece of her mother the pirates had hacked off? She swayed on her feet and Maher put a steadying hand on her back.

"The lock has been broken, but not removed," said Gai. "I watched the entire time the blacksmith was at work."

"We owe those sailors from the longboat a commendation for their bravery." Luthais said, more to Gai than anyone else. The eldest Kingfisher brother nodded, not looking away from the chest as their father removed the lock.

The lid lifted, and relief washed over Ally. No severed hand or head in sight, only a stack of papers beneath a scrap of cloth.

Lord Kingfisher lifted the ragged-edged piece of fabric out. A stripe of silver caught the light.

"That's from the cloak we gave Rochelle for her birthday." said Cal.

"Proof they have her," Lord Kingfisher ran a hand over it.

"What do the papers say?" Gai asked.

Opening the folded letter on top, he read aloud. "Intended for Lord Gaius Kingfisher III, the safe return of Lady Rochelle Kingfisher depends on the meeting of the enclosed demands. You will find evidence that we have taken the ship known as the *Swan Song*, and Lady Kingfisher along with it."

Gai pulled out a sealed roll of thick parchment. "It's one of the *Swan Song's* trade permits. Seal unbroken."

"Enclosed is a list of ransom goods and coin to be traded for the return of Lady Kingfisher, unharmed and whole. Failure to acquire each item listed may cause her to be returned in a lesser condition than she was found."

"This reads like a parliamentary agenda," Maher whispered. "Not a ransom note."

Luthais took out a stack of pages, listing everything the pirates were demanding. "This will take some time to go through. Some of these lines make no sense. Thirty barrels of lamp oil?"

Lord Kingfisher's grip threatened to tear the letter apart. "Finally, you have been given a set of coordinates and a specific route that must be followed. Straying from this course will be considered an act of defiance and will be treated as such... *godsbedamned pirates*!" He slammed the letter down. The silence that had settled over the room broke, and everyone began talking at once.

"This list must be some sort of callous joke." The polished wooden bracelets stacked on the Kharaboan ambassador's wrists clacked together as she took a closer look at one of the pages. "Forty bolts of brocade? I ask you!"

"If I were you, my lord, I wouldn't even entertain these demands," the Fraollish ambassador said. "One letter from me, and Fraolland warships would be ready to hunt these criminals down."

"And then what, madam? Kill her ladyship in the process?" Khafra scoffed.

Her icy blue eyes narrowed. "What are you implying, Villaon?"

"This is not the time..." said Mr. Dayal.

Ally gripped the edge of the table. The arguing voices around her all jumbled together. Her father looked ready to murder whoever had done this... Wait.

"Father? Father!" Ally gripped his arm. "Who sent the letter? When do they want the ransom?"

He looked at the paper crumpled under his hand. "Silence! My daughter has asked an important question that doesn't seem to have occurred to anyone else." He scanned the rest of the letter. "If the date written here is correct, taking into account how long it took the longboat to reach us... We have fifteen days to secure the ransom and sail to the meeting point."

"Only fifteen days?" Gai asked as he and Luthais both reached for the coordinates.

"And, who's done this to us?" asked Ally.

"There's no signature, only a sketch of a flag. I don't recognize it."

Her brothers moved closer. Luthais stabbed a finger at the paper. "I know that flag, the broken heart and dagger. It belongs to Foraoise Dare."

"Foraoise Dare?" Gai took the letter and examined it. "Why do I know that name?"

"Her ships have been attacking the Eastern Sea trade routes for over a decade, at least, and she's likely been the one targeting Birde Isles vessels. She was the wife of Captain Jon Dare."

Khafra Villaon showed a hint of surprise. "Jon Dare, the privateer? How did you hear of him?"

"Even though he kept to the southern end of the continent, and never attacked our trading ships, we'd still hear tales," said Luthais. "Jon Dare was ruthless. The Meredians kept him on payroll to defend their interests from other pirates."

"You said she was his widow," Maher added. "What happened to him?"

"Dare was killed on his own ship, in broad daylight, in full view of his own crew. Yet they all claimed they never saw a thing."

"How is that possible?"

"There was a rumor floating around that a handful of sailors who'd been loyal to Dare were planning to tell the Meredian government the truth about their captain's death."

"Did they?" asked Ally.

"They never made it back onto land. His widow inherited his ship, his contracts, what was left of his crew –"

"And apparently his penchant for violence," Cal muttered.

Luthais ignored him. "She was able to bring several smaller pirate crews under her flag. They've been growing bolder, not even bothering to hide their colors when they target a prize."

"And she has Rochelle," Lord Kingfisher's fists clenched.

Cal frowned. "Does that mean Meredia is behind this?"

Everyone looked at the Meredian ambassador, who'd been steadily turning a dark shade of purple as Luthais spoke.

"Absolutely not!" He sputtered. "Meredia would never condone such a thing. I've warned our provost not to trust these so-called privateers, but would they listen to me? No! Not if it meant protecting their own interests."

The Fraollish and Utollmir ambassadors shuffled farther away from him. Ally's father and brothers were stone faced.

"You must believe me! I would never... Meredia would never... those pirates have doubtless gone off on their own!"

"I believe you had no knowledge of this, Ambassador," Gaius said at length. "However, until the truth is uncovered, I think it best that a guard be stationed outside your home. For your safety and that of your family."

"Um... that is, of course, my lord."

"Back to this list," Gai gathered the pages. "Is it possible to collect even a fraction of its value in fifteen days? Less than that, if we factor in the time it will take to sail to these coordinates. Will it all fit on one ship?"

"I'll take it," said Cal. "It will fit on my ship and my crew can be ready to sail at a moment's notice."

"You're certain, son?" their father asked. "We don't know what you'll be sailing into, you could very well lose the *Wave Skipper* in the bargain. We can send a ship with equal speed, but less personal value."

"I want to do this. Rochelle has been more of a mother to me than anyone."

Lord Kingfisher hugged his youngest son. Gai and Luthais shared a long look, but Ally couldn't guess what it meant. Cal was very young when Mama came to the Birde Isles. Perhaps he thought of her as more of a mother than Ally realized.

Tears gathered at the corners of her eyes, and she blinked them away. Searching her trouser pockets for a handkerchief, Ally spotted a tiny, folded piece of paper at the bottom of the chest. It was small enough to fit in the palm of her hand. While her father, brothers, and everyone else discussed the pirate's demands, she unfolded the note.

Ten words were written across the page. The paper trembled in her hands and Maher appeared at her shoulder.

"Are you alright, Al?" He read the words for himself. "Great gods!"

"What is it?" Gaius turned around.

Ally handed him the final note. She didn't need to read it again. The words were burned into her memory.

Lady Alphonsine must deliver the ransom. Or her mother dies.

CHAPTER THIRTY-FOUR

This wasn't what she'd wanted at all.

Young Lady Kingfisher was smarter than her great-grandfather ever was. One meeting and she saw right through Pasha.

Pasha stayed in the shallows by the seawall, waiting to see if she'd come back. By the time the sun was at its highest point, she slipped beneath the waves.

When the beacon first led her to the shark tooth, floating by itself in the water, Pasha feared the girl had lost it or had been swept out to sea again. Then she saw her, hunched down on the sand. There was something very wrong, her entire body was trembling, her face contorted with pain. Pasha's worries about how much the tooth had changed were confirmed, it was connected to the girl somehow. The loss, whether intentional or not, had hit her harder than Pasha could have predicted. Was it so tied to the girl's own energy now that she couldn't do without it? A sick feeling settled into Pasha's stomach; she hadn't meant for that to happen. Her education on individual energies and how they reacted together had barely started when... when the others left. The little understanding she did have must not have been enough.

Everything had gone wrong. The bargain with Gaius I went belly-up the day she'd made it. And her chance to *finally* meet the girl, whose name she still didn't know, was doomed from the start.

Pasha shouldn't have lied to her. Maybe if she'd been honest about who she was from the beginning, the girl would have stayed to hear her out. Maybe not. But at least she wouldn't think Pasha was a liar or, what had she called her, a sea witch? Pasha had never met a sea witch, wasn't sure what one looked like, but she'd met the girl on land. It must have been easier for her to grasp than to think of what Pasha really was. To her, a mermaid was probably a story told by the priestesses, not something real.

Swimming into her home beneath the island, Pasha went straight to the room that housed all of the history and knowledge that had been left behind. Most of it was carved into the rock walls of the chamber itself. A few of the tapestries still held out, created when her ancestors were freer to move on land and retrieve materials to make such things. These weren't made there; they were brought from other places far away. Pasha scoured each one, though she already knew many of them by heart. There was nothing written about an energy-infused object taking on a mind of its own. Nothing about one creature's energy tying itself to another, except for a few rare cases that had nothing to do with this one. An injured member of her family saved by another, sharing their energy store and giving too much. A young one got stuck during hatching and required a jolt from an adult to get them out.

Would the girl tell her family what happened? Pasha didn't feel herself to be in any danger. Not yet. The girl seemed more shocked than afraid, and angry. Then to hear her mother had been attacked? No wonder she was already upset, then Pasha appeared out of nowhere with the news of the bargain... The least Pasha could do was find a way to detach that tooth from her.

A few days after their meeting, after Pasha had read every text many times over, she was no closer to an answer. Only the girl could say how long the shark tooth had been affecting her or offer some clue of how it started.

Pasha went back to the same place on the shore, but there was no sign of her and the rough location of the shark tooth stayed well away from the sea. There was no sign of an angry mob or line of soldiers guarding the beach either. Pasha took that as good news. Maybe she hadn't told anyone about Pasha or, more likely, they were all focused on the fate of Lady Kingfisher.

Resolved, Pasha returned to the shore each afternoon and stayed well into the evening, in case the girl should appear. She'd only gotten a brief glimpse of her face in the dark but was sure she'd recognize her now even without the shark tooth's help.

No matter how long it took, Pasha would find a way to speak to her again, as herself. Not pretending to be some goddess. Pasha could be patient; she'd had plenty of practice.

CHAPTER THIRTY-FIVE

Everything Ally had come to rely on had been turned on its head.

After discovering the final instruction for her mother's release, that Ally must be the one to make the exchange, the meeting dissolved into chaos. Advisors and ambassadors argued their own opinions on the ransom, none of them in agreement with any of the others. Behind her, Maher let out a string of such colorful language, some of which she was sure he'd just made up on the spot, even the captain of the guard turned a vibrant shade of red. Only Ambassador Villaon appeared calm, looking from Ally to the note in her father's hand and back again with a peculiar expression on his face.

For her part, Ally felt a strange sense of relief. They had an exact plan of what was needed to save Mama, and the one person on the Birde Isles who'd never set foot on a ship was expected to carry it out. It had to be a cruel jab at their family. The pirates must have heard of Ally's fear and were using it to show how powerless the Kingfishers were to argue with their demands.

With no hope of resolution in sight that day, Lord Kingfisher asked everyone to leave and await further instruction. Maher tried to stay with Ally, but his father hooked him just outside the room and demanded his assistance. Assuring him, and her family, that she was alright, Ally walked alone to her room. She stared out her window until the silence began to close in, then grabbed a cloak and left the manor.

Not entirely sure where she meant to go, Ally soon found herself on the path leading to the temple of the sea. When she arrived, a younger priestess escorted her to Esa's private rooms to wait, as the head priestess was currently in a meeting with representatives from the Kingsport citizen's council.

Sitting on a cushioned chair by the small hearth, Ally thought over what she wanted to ask Esa. The more she analyzed what happened when she'd thrown her necklace away, the more the story of the Sea Kissed had been on her mind. And she couldn't help but think about the bargain Gaius I made. What exactly could the sea witch have given him in return that was worth giving away a member of his own family? Just how powerful was she? Powerful enough to save the Birde Isles from near ruin, but not enough to simply come and take Ally when she wished.

When Esa came into the room, Ally stood and hugged her. "Thank you for seeing me."

"You know you're always welcome here, Ally." She brushed an errant lock of hair out of Ally's face. "What can I do for you?"

"Could you tell me more about the Sea Kissed?"

Esa waved a hand to a table across the room, piled high with books, loose papers, and scrolls. "I thought you might want to know more, once you had time for everything to sink in."

Ally gingerly picked up the nearest scroll. It was delicate, the edges browned with age. "All of these documents are about the people kissed by the sea?"

"Not directly, some of these volumes reference accounts related to those who were merely called to the sea. There were more, I found a great many records as I advanced in my own studies here at the temple. But they must have become too old to be legible."

"What's done with them then?"

"We try to copy what we can, but the records that can't be saved are eventually burned."

"That's a shame," Ally put the scroll down and picked up a volume with a priestess' name stamped on the front. "Is this a diary?"

"Yes, many of our past priestesses kept journals detailing their days here. They can prove to be as valuable as any historical record. Take your time, Ally, these will stay here until you've finished with them."

"Thank you, Esa, very much."

Esa smiled. "I'll leave you to it."

"Wait," Ally put the diary back. "There's something else I need to ask you and... something I need to tell you."

"What is it?" She took a seat at the table and gestured for Ally to do the same.

"How much do you know about sea witches?"

15 Days

Ally stayed at the temple well into the night, poring over the documents and asking questions. It grew so late that Esa insisted she spend the night, and a priestess was sent to the manor to inform the Kingfishers.

The revelation of Gaius I's bargain with the sea witch wasn't a complete surprise to Esa. If anything, it answered the doubts she'd harbored about Aithne's supposed vision and Esa admitted her regret for keeping

Aithne's orders from Ally for so long. They traded theories on what the sea witch might have done for her end of the bargain. Without knowing exactly what her powers entailed, they couldn't be totally sure, but Ally was certain the sudden drop in their fishing catches was connected. There was very little in the temple library on sea witches, far less than the references they had on the Sea Kissed. Mostly stories or reports made by fishers and sailors over the years.

By the next morning, Ally had made a decision.

She bid Esa goodbye after breakfast. Walking straight back to the house, Ally washed and changed, then went in search of her father. The sooner she disclosed her plan, the less time she'd have to change her mind.

In the hallway outside Lord Kingfisher's study, she ran into Maher.

"I feel this strange sense of role reversal. Where have you been all night?"

"Not to the Lantern, if that's what you were thinking." She gave as much of a smile as she could.

"I love you for that," he gave her a quick hug. "Seriously, how are you? I looked for you yesterday after Khafra released me and you were already gone."

"I think I'm alright, or I will be. I was at the temple with Esa. We talked everything over, and I've come up with a plan."

"What plan?" His apprehensive brown eyes searched hers. "You're not going to do anything dangerous, are you?"

"I have to talk to my family, then I promise I'll tell you." She nodded at the study door. "Is he in there?"

"He is. Your brothers are with him."

"Good. I can tell all of them at once."

"They said they didn't want to be disturbed."

"Well, they're about to be anyway." Before Maher could stop her, Ally went into the study and shut the door behind her.

Gaius looked up; his face careworn. "Ally, you're back."

A map of the Eastern Sea corridor was spread out on the table. Model ships and other markers were placed at various points. Gai was adding up a list of figures on a sheet of paper.

"Yes, I am, and I need to talk to all of you."

"Can it wait?" Cal asked gently. "We're plotting the coordinates sent for Lady Kingfisher's rescue, to see if we can extend our allotted time for gathering the ransom."

"No, it can't wait. That's what I want to talk about." She looked at each of them in turn. "I have a plan."

Gai said, "Ally, I'm sure you want to help, but it's best if you leave this to us."

The pity in her eldest brother's eyes made Ally feel sick.

Their father nodded. "Don't worry, dearest. You won't have to go on the ship with the ransom, no matter what those pirates think they can demand."

"Let's hear her out," said Luthais.

"What?" Gai's pen skipped, leaving a splotch of ink across the numbers.

"If she didn't have something important to say, she wouldn't be here."

The others still looked doubtful.

Ally couldn't believe *Luthais* was the one who wanted to listen to what she had to say. "You all know about the encounter I had the night we learned of the attack on the *Swan Song*."

"With the sea witch, yes," said Gai. "We haven't forgotten."

"How could we?" Luthais grunted. Cal kicked him under the table.

"I've done some research with Head Priestess Esa, that's why I stayed at the temple last night. We tried to figure out how the sea witch could have convinced anyone to enter into a bargain like that, what could she have offered. I think she's behind the drop in our fishing catches, that she was the one who increased the number of fish around the islands in the first place."

"Of course this has been on your mind," said Cal. "You have enough to worry about already. We won't let her anywhere near you."

Their father said, "You must know we won't let that mad arrangement stand. Let us focus on getting your mother home safely, and then we'll deal with the sea witch."

"That's the point," Ally cut in before her nerve totally deserted her. "I'm going to accept the bargain."

CHAPTER THIRTY-SIX

Her father sliced a hand through the air. "No, I will not allow you to put yourself in danger or sacrifice yourself to that witch."

Ally stood her ground. "I haven't made this decision on a whim! She can be made to help us save Mama and restore our fishing trade. Everything I've read suggests she'd have at least some power over the sea, not as much as an actual goddess would, but still –"

"I said no! May I remind you, Ally, that barely a week ago you stood in this room in a state of terror at the very thought of being promised to a sea witch. Now you're volunteering to hand yourself over? Your grief for your mother has clouded your judgement. I don't blame you for that, but this is out of the question!"

The anger and resentment toward her father that had finally begun to simmer down roared back to life, licking up Ally's spine like a flame to a fuse. Would he ever take her seriously?

"Why not let her go?"

All eyes turned to where Luthais sat at the other end of the table.

"*What* did you say?" Lord Kingfisher braced himself on the arms of his chair.

"Why not let her go? If it will solve some of the problems that have been plaguing the islands, because this deal was never upheld, and Ally is going of her own free will, why not let her?" Luthais nodded at Ally. "It would allow us to help our people and devote our resources to rescuing Rochelle."

No one dared to speak for several breaths. The tension in the study hung over them like a heavy mist.

Ally found her voice first, "I think that –"

Her father pushed out of his chair so hard it tipped and hit the floor, breaking one of the legs. Gai paced away, raking both hands through his hair. Cal started shouting.

"Have you lost your mind? She's our sister! I know you've never cared for her company, Luthais, but even you should want to protect her from whatever that creature has in mind!"

"I think…" Ally tried again.

"Luthais!" Gai broke in. "That was a heartless thing to say. We have to think of the greater good, it's true, but not at the expense of our own family."

"*I think –*"

Lord Kingfisher loomed over all of them. "Leave us, Luthais. Clearly this is not a discussion you should be a part of."

Ally grabbed the nearest model ship and pounded it on the table. "I THINK LUTHAIS IS RIGHT!"

Lord Kingfisher, Gai, and Cal were looking anywhere except at Ally. Luthais was the only one giving her his full attention. He gazed up at her, face as unreadable as always. While the other men all appeared to have forgotten how chairs worked.

Ally put the ship down. One side was dented and the mizzen mast bent at a sad angle.

Sitting down in an empty seat next to Luthais, she folded her hands on the table. "Saving Mama and helping our people are what matter most right now. By honoring the bargain, we can demand the sea witch to help us. If she has the power to make the islands prosper, then she can help Mama as well." Ally stopped herself from touching the shark tooth for comfort.

Gai and Cal eased back into their seats. Lord Kingfisher looked back at his ruined chair and moved to the one across from his daughter.

"Think about the fishing catches, the way they just dropped off at the start of the summer. The sea witch said I was *late* in meeting her. What if she's been the source of our good luck in trade all these years and when I never showed up to satisfy the deal Gaius I made, she took it all away? I'll go down to the shore tonight and tell her our terms."

Gai spoke up, "I hate to admit it, but this makes sense. No other nation has been able to account for our success, not when the near ruin of the Isles wasn't so very long ago. Three generations were all it took to rebuild us to where we are. Whether we believed ourselves to be blessed by the goddess or not, from every angle it defies logic."

"And instead of a goddess, we were blessed by a witch and a dirty deal," Cal turned his head, as if he were unable to look at his sister.

Gaius took Ally's hands in his. "Ally, I appreciate you want to help, I do, but you don't have to do this. We'll find another way."

"There's not enough time." Ally shook her head. "I still don't agree with what Gaius I did, but now we're in this mess and the sea witch might be our best hope for Mama and our home."

CHAPTER THIRTY-SEVEN

When the voices inside the study became too quiet to hear, Maher retreated farther down the hall. Waiting, partially hidden behind a large vase, he thought over the parts of the conversation he'd caught through the door.

Ally couldn't really be serious about this, could she?

The minutes ticked by; Maher made a mental note to start carrying a pocket watch. It was careless of him, really, not to have one before now. Especially with all the hooks he currently had in the water.

Luthais and Cal exited the study first, walking in the opposite direction from where Maher crouched. His calves started to cramp just as Ally stepped into the hall. He stood too quickly and one of his knees locked up.

"Ally!" Maher hobbled out from behind the vase.

"Have you been waiting here this whole time?" She let him brace a hand on her shoulder and stretch his legs.

"Of course I have! You tell me you've come up with a plan with an unspecified level of danger and then leave me stranded outside." The burning in his muscles subsided and they left that wing of the house together.

"I know, I'm sorry, but I needed to tell them before I had any more time to doubt myself." Ally glanced up at him. "How much did you hear?"

"Enough to understand why your father was upset. And that you may have broken something in there."

"I knew you weren't going to like it," she bit her lip. "Just promise that you'll hear me out."

"That's not at all reassuring. Can you tell me what exactly this plan entails, Al? What good could possibly come from accepting?"

"She may not be a goddess, far from it, but if the sea witch was powerful enough to pull the Birde Isles out of ruin, then she can damn well help us get Mama home safely. I'm going to give her my terms and we'll see if she agrees."

"In exchange for what?" Maher didn't like how calm Ally was about this.

"I don't know yet." Ally took them around the corner that led to the family's quarters.

"Surely you're going to ask before agreeing to anything?"

"To be honest, I'm not sure I want to know right now."

"Ally, that's ridiculous. And reckless. You can't –"

"I don't want anything to distract me from what I have to do to save Mama!" Her pace picked up.

He easily kept up with her. "I think you've made this decision too quickly. There's time to find other options."

"We need her."

"No, we don't!" Maher grabbed her hand. They stopped outside Ally's door. "Ally, what else could she want except to harm you?"

"I'll deal with that after Mama is safe."

Maher was floundering. "But... you... you're afraid of water!"

"Do you think I don't know that?" She snatched her hand back. "Out of everyone in this house, I expected you would understand how hard this was to decide and could believe I know my own mind."

"I do believe you; I believe you are strong enough to face anything. I just... I don't want to lose you. I couldn't bear it if you sacrificed yourself when there might have been another way out of this."

They stood in silence for a while. Maher couldn't remember them ever being at odds like this before.

Ally opened her door. "If we had time to find another way, I'd agree with you. But we don't. She might not even accept a new arrangement, so it wouldn't matter anyway."

"When are you going to speak with her?"

"I'll go this evening. I think it'll be easier to find her close to dark."

He didn't know what she meant by that. "I'm going with you."

"No, Maher, you're not."

"You shouldn't go down there alone! What if she hurts you?"

"I think if she wanted to hurt me, she'd have done it already." Ally gave him a hug but pulled away when he would have held her longer. "This was my choice and I need to handle it myself."

She slipped into her room and shut the door.

Maher wrestled with his desire to talk Ally out of this and the knowledge that it would only distance her from him. What more could he do? If Ally really wished to remain ignorant of what her half of the bargain would be, how could he help her avoid it? Confronting the sea witch himself didn't feel like a smart idea. There had to be something else.

Perhaps it was time to call in a few favors.

CHAPTER THIRTY-EIGHT

Ally dozed restlessly for the rest of the afternoon. Rolling out of bed just before sundown, she rang the bell for tea and something to eat, then changed out of her sleep-rumpled clothes. What was one expected to wear to bargain with a sea witch?

After settling on her favorite blue skirt and a gray shirt, Ally hunted through her closet for her short wool jacket. She left her hair down, rather doubting the sea witch would care either way. Going through the steps of getting ready distracted her enough until a maid arrived with a tray.

Forcing herself to eat slowly, Ally finished every scrap of food and the whole pot of tea.

"If I die tonight, at least I die full." Ally couldn't remember where the saying was from, but hearing it come out of her own mouth made her pause. A near hysterical giggle followed, and Ally shook herself to clear her head. Now was not the time to snap her mainsail.

Grabbing a lantern with plenty of oil and wick, she wouldn't be caught out without a light again, Ally went down the back stairs. The grounds were strangely quiet. She didn't meet a single servant or guard on the walk between the house and the seawall. Ally lit the lantern before descending the steps to the beach.

How was she going to get the sea witch's attention? It was unlikely she lived on land, someone would have seen her long ago. Until a better plan made itself known, Ally was resigned to walking the beach until she found her. Or until the sea witch found Ally.

Ally stayed close to the seawall as she moved down the beach. When the stairs were barely visible behind her, she turned back. She didn't want to go too far from the house. If only Esa had found a way to signal the sea witch, but the temple records were limited. Switching the lantern to her other hand, Ally stopped a fair distance from the stairs and watched the sun slide down into the sea. So much depended on this plan working, assuming the sea witch even agreed to a new arrangement. Ally didn't know what to do next if she said no.

There was one detail of her plan Ally'd kept from both her family and Maher. The real reason she didn't care to know what the sea witch wanted from her.

After reading every note and story and diary entry Esa provided, Ally was almost certain she was one of the Sea Kissed. It explained why she felt pulled there even though the thought of getting too close could send her into a panic. Nearly drowning as a child likely kept her from feeling the effects too deeply. Her fear always matched, or exceeded, the call.

Her necklace was another piece of this puzzle of unknown size and shape. Whatever properties the shark tooth possessed, it also kept the call to the sea at bay. If the pain she felt after throwing it away was what the other Sea Kissed experienced... no wonder they tried whatever they could to ease it. No matter what the sea witch wanted, it couldn't be worse than that.

"You came back."

Ally jumped, nearly dropping the lamp. The sea witch stood in the shallows. Ally's free hand wrapped around the tooth. The warmth calmed her, and she set the light down. "Yes, I wanted to speak with you."

"About?" She stepped out of the water. A line of tiny, gray crabs making their way down the beach stopped and circled her feet. Ally might have found it funny if she weren't trying to remember everything she had to say.

"I want to talk about this deal you made with my great-grandfather."

"Did they finally tell you?"

"Not exactly," Ally worked to keep her tone neutral. "The only person who knew everything was a former head priestess, and she's been gone a long time."

The sea witch sighed, "Aithne."

"That's right, Aithne. She never told anyone."

"I should have guessed. I can tell you..."

"No, I don't care about the old terms, whatever they were. I want to make a new bargain."

Her head tilted. "You want to strike a new bargain when the first one was never fulfilled?"

"You've stopped your end of it, haven't you? I don't know how you cut off our fishing catches, but you're taking food out of people's mouths."

"Why should I continue to hold up my part when the payment was intentionally held back?" she hissed.

"*Payment*? I'm not a sack of coins or a barrel of oil. I'm a person!"

"And you were promised to me!" The water ebbing along the shore trembled and the crabs scuttled away as fast as their tiny legs would take them.

"*I* promised you nothing! He had no right to make that decision for me."

The flame in the lamp flickered, sending shadows across the sand. It occurred to Ally she'd brought nothing to defend herself with, but what good would a weapon have been when she'd never picked one up in her life?

Rather than attack her, the sea witch looked Ally over and smirked. "You kept my gift."

"I don't have anything of yours!" Ally spat. Her body tensed, unsure if she should stay or give up and flee.

Slowly, the sea witch walked closer. The scales on the side of her face lit up like stars in the lamplight.

"What is it that you want?"

"There are three things that I want." Refusing to be cowed, Ally looked her in the eye. "I want my mother rescued from those pirates and returned home safely. The ransom letter demands I make the trade myself. You're not a goddess, but you could still help get her back. Second, I want you to do whatever magic you did before to bring the fish back to the Birde Isles. So we can feed our people and honor our trade agreements."

"And the third thing?"

"I want to stay in my home, with my family, until everything is done. We have fifteen days to gather the ransom and sail to meet the pirates. When my mother is home and our people are secure, I give you my word I'll keep my end of the agreement." She held up a hand. "Before you ask, I don't want to know what my end will be yet. Nothing else matters to me right now. Those are my terms."

"And, if I refuse?"

Ally shrugged. "Then we'll be back to where we were. You've already broken your half of the old deal, and I wasn't aware of it. I don't think that binds me to anything."

The sea witch was so still Ally could have mistaken her for a statue, except for the dark eyes that searched her face like a captain studying a map.

"What's your name?"

"Alphonsine... Ally."

She waited a moment, as if Ally were meant to say something else. Then she held out a hand. "Alright then, Ally. We have a bargain."

With only a slight tremor, Ally clasped hands with the sea witch. The skin against her palm and beneath her fingertips was unnaturally smooth, the sharp edges of her nails grazed the back of Ally's hand. A slight tingle traveled up Ally's arm and she tasted metal. "We have a bargain."

PASHA

CHAPTER THIRTY-NINE

A new bargain.

Pasha stood on the beach long after Ally had gone.

Ally. She had a name for her now. Alphonsine was becoming, but Ally suited her.

The request for a new agreement wasn't what Pasha had expected when she saw the girl waiting on the shore. After their first encounter she thought Ally would only come to break the bargain, if she ever came back at all. Listening to the proposal, she'd quite forgotten to ask about the shark tooth.

And Ally didn't care to know what Pasha wanted of her. Would rather give an open promise if it meant saving her mother.

Try as she might to ignore it, the spark of hope was back. No more loneliness, no more isolation. No more...

"She probably thinks I'm going to eat her," Pasha sighed. That's why Ally didn't want to know what Pasha desired, she expected only the worst.

Even with that renewed hope, Pasha felt unsettled. What if the girl's mother was killed before they reached her? Or died on the journey back?

What she'd agreed to was far more involved than before. It was too precarious and could easily go wrong.

Maybe that was why, when she'd gotten close enough to see Ally properly, Pasha tried to commit her to memory. Dark brown curls framed her face and she'd held her strong chin high as she gave her own terms. Sharp eyes in a shade Pasha didn't have a word for – not quite green and yet not quite brown – had met hers without flinching. If Ally was afraid, she hardly showed it.

Pasha was curious about how she'd injured her nose, it hadn't been like that when she was a child. Clearly the bone had been broken and not healed right. It bulged out at the bridge and twisted to the left at the end. Not that it made her any less intriguing, not to Pasha.

What did Ally see when she looked at her? Pasha glanced down at the scales wrapped around her forearms, the black claws at the end of each finger. Every childhood nightmare and bedtime tale meant to warn her away from the sea. Ally hadn't even asked for Pasha's name, and Pasha couldn't give it until she did. What if she never asked? That in itself should have been enough to convince Pasha to drop this whole thing. But the new bargain had only just been struck. Pasha caught herself rubbing the jagged scar running nearly from her left wrist to the crook of her elbow. A long-forgotten burn started deep in Pasha's chest and traveled up behind her eyes; she pushed it down. It didn't matter what she saw, Ally needed her and... it was nice to be needed.

CHAPTER FORTY

14 Days

The next morning, Ally found Cal walking to town on the seawall road.

"Teach me how to sail."

"Good morning to you too, Ally."

"Good morning. Teach me how to sail."

Cal ran a hand over his short, sun-bleached hair. "I know why you're asking, demanding really, but you can't possibly master sailing in less than a month. It took Gai, Luthais, and I years to learn."

"Then teach me as much as you can," she gripped his arm. "I don't want to just sit on the ship like a barnacle and watch the crew do all the work to get us to Mama."

He sighed, extracting himself. "Your commitment to your mother is admirable, but you haven't even been near the sea in years. I'm more worried about actually getting you on the ship without you losing consciousness, let alone teaching you how to unfurl a sail."

Ally chose a section of freckles on his face to stare at and took a deep breath. "Please, Cal. You're the only one I can ask. Father is too distracted. Gai won't take me seriously. Maher is barely able to sail. And Luthais..."

"I know." Cal's nose wrinkled in thought. His eye snagged on the small, private dock below them that belonged to the manor. "Alright, if you can walk out onto that dock without fainting or becoming sick, I'll teach you how to sail."

"Fine." She turned on her heel and marched down the seawall.

Standing at the edge of the dock, Cal waiting a few paces behind her, Ally willed her feet to step onto the weathered planks. It wasn't even a large dock. There were a couple row boats tied to one side, and Cal's personal sloop anchored at the end. That would probably be what he'd use to teach her. If she could get her damn feet to move.

All she had to do was take one step to satisfy Cal and get what she wanted. She'd stood on the beach with the sea witch twice now, she could do this.

One step. One step onto the dock. One step off the edge and she'd be in the water...

When Cal touched her shoulder, Ally's body curled inward. Her hands instinctively caught his sleeve in an iron hold.

"It's alright, you don't have to do this." Cal wrapped his other arm around her shoulders and backed them up until they were on the path again. "This is what I was worried about. Let's just concentrate on keeping you calm and safe during the voyage."

Ally focused on his face, those concerned green eyes filled with pity.

Pulling out of his arms, Ally turned back towards the house. She didn't trust her voice to stay steady long enough to tell Cal what she was thinking, but this wasn't over. Ally was going to prove to everyone that her fear wouldn't make her useless.

CHAPTER FORTY-ONE

After dropping off yet another pack of letters to the trade guild and picking up a logbook of sums for his father, Maher detoured into the Lantern.

The Lantern at midday was a more composed place than the Lantern after sundown. Some of the establishments kept daytime hours, but most were sleeping or handling other business. There was a lone musician in the square, strumming lazily on a guitar. They didn't even look up as Maher passed, though the tune sped up when a coin landed in the upturned cap sitting on the edge of the fountain.

Maher went down the side street where he'd caught Luthais at the purple lantern. They'd moved a couple of days after, but he still looked to see if they were using the same place again. No such luck.

Doubling back, he went to the Bear's Den and knocked on the door. The heavy bolt inside slid back and the barkeep fixed a bleary blue eye on him.

"Not open righ' now," he mumbled.

"I know, sorry to disturb. Is Pimm here or at home?"

Barkeep grumbled at him to wait and shut the door.

Maher rocked back on his heels, occasionally glancing up and down the street until the man came back.

"S' here." The door opened enough for Maher to come inside. "Top floor. First door on the left."

"Many thanks," Maher clapped him on one burly shoulder.

"You can thank me by not waking me up again when you leave." Tugging roughly on his red beard, he shuffled back to his small room behind the bar. "Man's gotta get enough sleep to deal with them..." grumble, grumble, "'valued patrons' my ass..." The door slammed shut.

"Oh dear," Maher climbed the stairs. "The old boy sounds like he's having a tough time." He'd find the kitchen maid and ask her to lock the door behind him when he left. She should be awake.

So, Pimm was on the top floor? Maher couldn't remember Mama Bear allowing anyone up there, he'd certainly never seen it. Hopefully Pimm wouldn't be as grouchy as the barkeep. Maher was just glad he didn't have to journey all the way to Pimm's rented rooms across town.

The fourth floor looked no different than the others. Not that he'd expected anything spectacular, but Mama Bear had made it clear those rooms were off-limits. Maher knocked on the first door on the left, as instructed. There was some shuffling and a soft curse from the other side. Then the lock turned and Pimm's surprised face was looking up at him.

"Maher? What are you doing here this time of day?"

"Good day, Pimm. I hate to bother you when you're resting, but I was already in the neighborhood."

Pimm glanced down the hall. "Does Mama Bear know you're up here?"

"Our cheerful barkeep told me where to find you. I assume that means he asked her first."

"Come in, then. What's brought you out so early?"

"A long list, my friend." Maher found the room similar to the others he'd seen there, except for a large table that took up one wall. It was covered with maps dotted with pins and scattered notes. There was a small wood stove in the corner opposite the bed, where Pimm had clearly been sleeping before Maher arrived. Pimm threw on a loose jacket and slicked their sandy hair back before sliding on the usual flat cap.

Seeming more comfortable now, they offered Maher a seat. "Would you like some tea? I can warm the kettle back up."

"Only if you'll be joining me."

Pimm moved the kettle sitting at the back of the stove to the front burner. Two cups and a tea tin were produced and Pimm sat next to him while the water boiled.

"Let's start at the beginning."

"Right." Maher straightened his waistcoat. "You know, of course, about Lady Kingfisher's capture."

"All of the Birde Isles know by now, I'm sure."

"Yes, but they don't know what I'm about to tell you and it can't leave this room."

"To the grave," Pimm slid a finger over their lower lip.

"To the grave," Maher did the same. "Thank you. The ransom demands arrived, which you probably already know as well. My concern is this, they've ordered that Ally, Lady Alphonsine, must be the one to deliver it."

Their eyes widened a fraction. "The Lady Alphonsine who can't be near large quantities of water?"

"The very same."

"Well, sure as shit they knew what they were asking."

Maher rubbed his temples. "I've been trying to figure out a way to get her out of this, but they'll expect to see her on board the ship."

"A decoy wouldn't work?" The kettle whistled and Pimm went to get it.

"If they know as much as I suspect, I'm sure they have a good idea what Ally looks like."

"And she is distinctive." Pimm poured the water into their cups through a silver strainer. "Don't look at me like that. You know she is, and I mean no insult by it."

"I know you don't," Maher sighed. His father's recent comments ran through his mind, and he shook them out. "It was a reflex, I'm used to calling out those who do. That's beside the point, Ally's determined to go, fear of the sea or not."

"Of course, she is. She wants to protect her mother and who can blame her?"

"You're too astute for your own good." Maher took a sip of tea. "So, if I can't keep her from going, and let's assume this is the one circumstance that will actually get her on a ship, what can I do to make sure she gets through safely?"

"Besides going with her?"

It wasn't only that. Of course Maher wanted to go with her. What worried him more than the voyage was the creature lurking beneath the waves. Ally had sealed her new bargain with the sea witch. Maher knew because he'd waited until she made it safely back home that night. He didn't need to ask how it went, the resolute set of her face was enough confirmation.

Telling Pimm about the sea witch was out of the question, at least for the time being. Ally hadn't said either way if she wanted anyone else to know, and would Pimm even believe him? Maher wasn't sure *he* wanted word to get out. They lived in modern times, but Birde Islanders were a superstitious lot. More than he'd realized when the Villaons first moved to Kingsport. The night they'd celebrated Maher's coming-of-age birthday, after several drinks, Cal told him the early islanders sacrificed people to the sea goddess. Just tossed them into the deep, screaming all the way down. Whether that story was true, or the product of too much whiskey, Maher didn't care. It had been said. In Saprea, they believed telling a story instantly gave it more power.

"Maher?" Pimm nudged his knee. "Where'd you go?"

"I was organizing my thoughts. What was I saying?"

"Will you join Ally on the ship?"

"I want to, but I also want to give us an advantage."

"How so?" They rolled and lit a cigarette.

"Think about it. Those pirates – or privateers, or whatever they call themselves – knew which ship Lady Kingfisher was on and likely knew of Ally's fear of water when they demanded she deliver the ransom. How did they know?"

Smoke trickled out of the corner of Pimm's mouth. "They had someone feeding them information."

"Exactly! Kingsport is the biggest trade hub in the Eastern Sea, possibly the world, it could have come from anywhere. Even by accident. Sailors are some of the worst gossips I've ever met."

"Scuttlebutt. I assume you're building up to a theory?"

Maher tapped one of the maps that detailed the streets making up the Lantern. "The purple lamp. No one knows what they do or why they're always moving around. No other establishment does that."

"And that's where you followed that manor guard, the night you got knocked for six."

"Right. I also saw someone else there."

Pimm tapped ashes into an extra tea saucer. "The Pike."

Maher almost tipped his cup over. "How did you –?"

"There isn't much that happens in this district that stays a secret for long. Not many know the Pike's been around, but Mama Bear asked me to find out who was running the new place."

"I should have just told you that night."

"You think he's the leak in the boat? A Kingfisher?"

"I'm not sure, but it's obvious he never warmed to his stepmother, or to Ally for that matter. Even if he's not the leak, he could still be involved. What else could he be doing down here?" Maher downed the rest of his tea. "I want to know everything we can find out about the purple lantern. I doubt there's a way to get one of our people inside, and I don't trust any of the guards not to double cross us."

"Hmm... Anything else?"

"Yes, the Saprean coins. Are you still finding them?"

They nodded. "We are. It's getting harder to catch any of these new street crewmembers alone, but when we do they usually have those coins on them."

"Are they spending them anywhere?"

"Of course, but you won't find a business willing to just hand them over. Saprea has good money, it spends well no matter where you are. What did your father make of them?"

"I decided against asking him." Maher still cringed when he thought about Khafra's demands. His only bit of luck was the news of the ransom kept his father too busy to corner him again. For now. "As far as I can tell, they're genuine. I did show one to a friend at one of the Kingsport banks. The silver is real, if nothing else, it's the newness of them that still bothers me."

"Agreed. Everywhere you see a silver pin, we've found the coins," Pimm waved a hand over the map.

"What do the others mean?"

"Green and black for the two original crews that have worked the wharfs for years. The others are all new since the spring."

"Five new street crews in two seasons? Where are they all coming from?"

"I told you, sailors and other workers whose income suddenly dropped off. Between the ships refusing to sail and the low catches, I'd bet it's close to a thousand in Kingsport out of work alone. Never mind the smaller ports and towns."

"I had no idea," Maher counted the silver pins. "Most of the coins have been found in the sections of the city controlled by the crews?"

"I'd say someone's funding them. They've started harassing patrons, even once they get inside the Lantern. The owners have called the meeting for next week. Mama Bear wants the maps ready by then."

"No wonder you're sleeping here. I think that's enough for now, I'll let you get some rest."

"Bring food next time," Pimm yawned. "Barkeep won't be half so cross if you give him something to eat."

"I'll remember that." Maher shook their hand. "I appreciate your help and I'll keep you informed when I know more."

"I hope everything goes well for Lady Kingfisher and Lady Alphonsine, truly." They followed him to the door.

"Thank you, Pimm." Maher checked that he had everything he came in with and headed for the stairs.

"Maher?" Pimm's soft voice made him stop on the landing. "I don't know if I should tell you this, but there might be someone to help us get inside the purple lantern door when it opens again."

"Who?"

"The owner of the black lantern."

ALLY

CHAPTER FORTY-TWO

Waiting until after dinner, when her father and brothers retreated once again to the study, Ally changed into a loose shirt and breeches and slipped outside.

Part of her thought, belatedly, she should have told Maher where she was going. Or asked him to come with her. But he'd been coming and going more than ever since confronting Ally about her decision to propose a new version of Gaius I's bargain. She wasn't even sure where he was, he'd missed dinner at the house. Maybe it was better to do this alone, having Cal watch her during the last attempt had made it even harder to walk onto the dock.

The sun was just starting to set, a brisk wind whipped Ally's hair around her head. Summer would be over soon, would they have Mama back by then?

Before she knew it, Ally was stepping onto the coarse sand of the beach. She'd bypassed the manor dock. If she was going to make the journey to free Mama, then she needed to be able to touch the water at the very least.

Shuffling closer, Ally left her lamp on a dry dune and eyed the waves as they broke gently on the shore.

Just touch the water, she coaxed herself. *Just reach out and put one hand in. You don't have anything to worry about.*

Ally's fingers flexed at her sides. *It's only water! You drink it. You clean your body with it. It's only water...*

A tightness started in her chest and spiraled outwards. What if Cal was right? Would they have to nail her into a crate just to get her onto the ship?

"Are you alright?"

Ally yelped, stumbled backwards, and landed on her ass in the sand. When she looked up, the sea witch was standing calf-deep in the shallows, still wearing the same makeshift dress as before. Ally's heart raced as she walked closer, the water barely moving in her wake.

"I didn't mean to startle you." She offered a hand up.

Ally shook her head and pushed herself to her feet. "Must you always sneak up on me?"

"I thought you might have heard me coming this time." She watched as Ally dusted herself off. "What were you doing?"

Ally backed farther away from the sea and the sea witch. "I was trying to touch the water."

"Trying?"

Ally cleared her throat. She was used to everyone already knowing about her problem. When was the last time she had to explain it? "I never learned how to swim. I'm... afraid of the water." She forced the words out. "I want to help save my mother. I thought, if I could at least touch the water, it would help me be less afraid."

"They kept you from the sea, didn't they?" the sea witch asked softly.

Ally glared at her. "Yes, they did."

If she noticed Ally's clipped reply, she didn't show it. Looking out at the waves, she ran the tip of her tongue across the points of her upper teeth.

Ally shifted her feet, unable to stay still. Her fingers itched to wrap around her necklace.

The sea witch looked at her again. "I can help you."

When Ally only stared at her, one corner of her mouth turned up. "I may not be a goddess, as you say, but I can help you with this."

Ally's mouth went dry. "How?"

"I'll teach you how to swim."

"*Swim*? Right now?"

"Now is as good a time to start as any." She tugged at the knot holding the scrap of sail around her body.

"Whoa! What are you doing?"

"This will only get in the way. You should remove your boots and whatever clothes you feel comfortable leaving on land. Too much fabric will become cumbersome and weigh you down.

"Weigh me down?" Ally squeaked.

Weigh me down. Down. Down. Down under the water...

"Ally." The sea witch snapped her fingers in front of Ally's face. "If you're not ready to try this, we can start another day."

"No, I need to know if I can do this. It's only a matter of days before the ransom is due and I need my brother to teach me how to sail. How can I do that if I can't even step into the water?"

"Alright." She pointed to a small grouping of rocks above the tideline. "Leave your things there."

Ally walked numbly back up the beach. Sitting on the lowest rock, she pulled her boots off and stuffed her stockings inside of them. The dry sand felt strange and unsteady against the soles of her feet. Like standing on a pile of sugar.

There was a heavy slap as the sea witch's clothes landed in a heap somewhere. Ally kept her eyes averted as she took off her jacket and tucked it between the rocks with her boots. She was wearing a short shift and bloomers beneath her shirt and breeches but couldn't decide whether to take anything else off. She didn't want to be heavy in the water, but something about having no barrier between herself and the sea was too much to think about.

"Are you planning to look down the entire time?"

Ally could hear the amusement in the sea witch's voice and her cheeks grew hot. She was making a fool of herself. For the goddess's sake, Birde Islanders were more comfortable with nudity than most. Something Maher found delightful after the stuffy Meredian court where his father was previously stationed. With a huff, she faced the sea witch with her head held high.

At the sight of her, waiting there in the warm glow cast by the setting sun, Ally's mouth fell open. What she'd taken for random patches of blue and green scales on the sea witch's skin were actually wrapped in a distinct, swirled pattern that started around her waist and spiraled out from there. They spiked up between her small breasts like a waterspout and down over slender hips, spreading until they glittered like stars across her shoulders and down her legs. Ally thought of tiny jewels sewn onto a gown or a suit.

"Are you doing an impression of a fish on land?"

Ally's jaw snapped shut so fast her teeth clacked together.

"Ready to try again?" The sea witch turned and walked to the water's edge. The swirled pattern continued up her back and disappeared into the dark blue hair at the nape of her neck.

Ally pulled herself away from the imaginary garments she was already building in her head. Could anyone have the skill to truly recreate those scales?

"I think so," Ally followed, stopping just beyond the tide's reach. The colder, packed down sand stuck to the soles of her feet and the gentle lap of the water did nothing to calm Ally's nerves.

"Take one step in. Your feet won't be any wetter than when you wash them."

Something pulled at the edge of her mind, the same feeling that called her to look at the sea every day. Only now it was stronger, more insistent, and she found herself moving closer. Ally clenched her fists and stepped into the path of the next wavelet.

I can do this, Ally thought the words over and over.

The water running over the tops of her feet was cool, but not icy like she'd imagined.

I can do this. I can do this. I can –

Then the wavelet pulled back, circling around her ankles, and the world tilted.

"Ally." Someone was talking to her. "Ally! Look at me."

Ally opened her eyes. She was still standing in the water, but her hands had seized the sea witch's arms. Ally didn't remember her being close enough to grab.

"This was a bad idea," Ally gasped, unable to think of anything except the water trying to yank her in. Another wave tugged at her ankles, and her heart stuttered.

The sea witch's forearms turned so she could wrap her hands around Ally's wrists. Ally focused on the sharp black nails making small indentations in her skin.

"Look at me, Ally," she said again.

Ally dragged her eyes up. "I can't do this."

"What are you afraid of?" The sea witch kept her at arm's length, their feet still in the water.

"I..." A bigger wave than the last rushed around them and Ally realized the sea witch's hold was the only thing keeping her standing.

Her voice lowered, matching the sounds of the surf. "What are you afraid of?"

Ally pried her tongue from the roof of her mouth. "Dying."

"Just dying?"

Just dying? Was there something worse?

"Drowning."

"What is it about drowning that frightens you?"

Ally started to ask if the sea witch knew what a ludicrous question that was. Then she thought, sea witches probably couldn't drown.

"Drowning is... being pulled under. Not having any control. Being crushed, no matter how hard you try to get out." The tears she'd held back until then rolled down her face.

"How do you know?"

"How do I know?" Ally blinked at her. "Because it happened to me."

"It almost happened to you."

"Almost?"

"You were pulled under, you were close to drowning, but you didn't drown."

"I know, I made it out, but what if I hadn't? If the sea didn't spit me back out I *would* have drowned. I would have died! Are you really telling me to not be afraid of the thing that, by some turn of fate, happened to not kill me?"

Ally was shouting. She was ankle deep in the ocean and shouting in a sea witch's face.

"It wasn't fate. I pulled you out, Ally."

"You?" Ally took one hand back and pressed it against the necklace beneath her shirt. The sea witch's words, that hadn't made sense to her at the time, came back.

I thought I asked you to hold onto this for me?

You still have my gift.

"That's what you meant."

"Yes. When it was clear you didn't remember, I decided telling you could wait." She glanced away. "You already had enough on your mind."

"Right." The edges of Ally's vision sharpened back up. She was standing in the ocean and nothing bad was happening. "I did. I still do."

"That's why I think this is a good place to stop for tonight."

"But, I made it in."

The sea witch's lips twitched. "You did indeed, but that doesn't mean you're ready to go any further. We've been standing in this spot for a long time. You should get some rest."

Ally looked down, she could just make out the sunken pool that had formed around them. A layer of sand covered the tops of her feet, the grains shifting around the whole time, and she hadn't noticed.

There was a gentle tug on Ally's wrist. Her other hand was still locked around the sea witch's arm, where impossibly smooth skin was interrupted only by a ribbon of scales here and there. Then her fingers brushed against something just below the inside of the sea witch's wrist. It felt like a scar, wide and jagged, the uneven tissue so different from the rest of her skin.

Ally stopped herself from running her hand any farther down the scar. "I didn't hurt your arms, did I?"

"I'm fine." She kept her hold on Ally's wrist until they reached the rocks.

"We'll try again tomorrow." The sea witch backed away, giving Ally space to pull her jacket back on. Her boots were tucked beneath her arm, she didn't want to fill them with the sand that coated her feet.

"Do you think I can learn to swim in time?" Ally asked, her mind racing at the very idea.

"I believe so, and I have something that will help."

"What is it?"

"Let's get you past your ankles. Then we'll see."

CHAPTER FORTY-THREE

"Ally?" Maher stuck his head into the parlor. It wasn't likely she'd be there this time of night, but it was his first stop on the way back into the house. The fire lit by the servants earlier in the evening was nearly burnt out and the air felt stale. No one had really used this room in a fortnight, not even Ally.

Maher did a quick circle around the parlor anyway. There was a fine layer of dust on the lid of Ally's sewing basket. She hadn't touched any of her projects since Rochelle was taken.

By the time Maher reached Ally's room, he wondered if he should leave her be. She wasn't sleeping much, none of them were. There was no light coming through the bottom of her door, if she'd managed to go to bed early he wanted to let her rest. Perhaps they'd all retired after dinner.

Resolved to speak to her in the morning instead, Maher turned around and promptly choked on his own tongue. Luthais was standing in his own doorway a few rooms down, wearing nothing but a pair of breeches, the candle in his hand casting warped shadows across his face.

"Luthais," he whispered, keeping to the safety of the other side of the hall. "You could scare a man out of his boots, lurking around like that."

"I didn't expect to find you out here either." He rested one brawny shoulder against the doorframe, loose hair falling around either side of his neck.

"Right, of course not." Maher cleared his throat. "I came to talk to Ally, but it seems she went to bed early. I decided not to disturb her."

"She's not in there."

"What? Where is she?"

"She left after dinner, saw her through the study window."

It wasn't like Ally to take off so much on her own, she'd teased Maher often for doing the same thing.

"I see, and no one was concerned about where she was going?"

"Ally's an adult, she's free to come and go as she pleases."

Maher felt as if he was trapped in some strange dream. He kept seeing Luthais standing in the open purple lantern door, instead of a manor hallway. This might have been the longest private conversation they'd ever had. It wasn't surprising that Luthais was unconcerned about his sister's whereabouts, but something still felt off.

"What do you make of this bargain she's made?" Luthais asked. "I'm sure she's told you everything."

Maher chose his words carefully. "She has. I'd hoped Ally would reconsider, but since she hasn't, I'm going to find a way to get her out of it."

"You think it's possible, now that she's agreed?"

Maher bristled at Luthais' ambivalence. "I don't think it, I know it. And I know I'm not going to let anyone hurt her. Anyone."

"You hope so, but we aren't in control of everything, are we?"

"No, we're not."

Silence stretched out between them until Luthais shifted off the doorframe. "Well, I won't keep you any longer. Goodnight, Maher."

The candle went out and Maher's eyes readjusted to the dark. "Goodnight."

As soon as Luthais' door closed behind him, Maher quickly made his exit from the family wing. The encounter left Maher feeling strange, like Luthais had been trying to get something from him. He'd given nothing away that he could think of and was convinced more than ever there was something else hidden behind the middle Kingfisher brother's stony expression.

Maher hoped he'd meet Ally coming in on his way back through the house, but when he crossed the landing of the main staircase he met another Kingfisher instead.

Cal paused on the stairs. Maher couldn't decide if he was coming or going.

"Maher, you're up rather late."

He doesn't know my habits very well. Maher thought.

"I could say the same to you. If I manage to run into Gai between here and my room, my night will be complete."

Cal frowned slightly. "What does that mean?"

"It's nothing." Maher noticed the bag slung over his shoulder, the same kind he used to run messages for the trade guild. "You're an unlikely messenger. Is there anything I can help with?"

"No. That is, I'm already finished. Father sent me with some papers to the wharf."

"Oh? I could have taken them on my first run in the morning."

"I know, but father wanted them put into Mr. Dayal's hands tonight. You were already out, Gai and Luthais had their own tasks, so I went."

"I see, well, I'm glad someone was able to receive them this late?"

"Absolutely. We must do what we can to get Rochelle home." Cal passed by him. "Goodnight, Maher. If there's anything else that needs to go out in the morning I'll find you."

"Goodnight, Cal." He waited until Cal was gone to make his way to his own room. Whatever documents Lord Kingfisher sent to the guild that late must have been important. Hopefully Cal hadn't passed the papers off to the wrong person. Evidently, he wasn't aware Mr. Dayal received night messages directly to his home.

ALLY

Chapter Forty-four

Sleep wouldn't come easily that night. Ally's entire body buzzed every time she thought about what happened down on the beach. She'd stood in the ocean for the first time in fifteen years. It was only up to her ankles, but she'd done it. With the sea witch's very unexpected help, she was facing her deepest fear.

Ally rolled onto her back, sliding the shark tooth between her palms. If her revelation was to be believed, the *sea witch* was the one who had saved Ally from the waves. Hearing it had been such a shock, Ally hadn't even thought to ask her why. Had she known who Ally was? She must have, why else would she have given Ally the shark tooth?

Briefly Ally thought about giving it back, but didn't want to risk that unbearable, soul freezing cold again. Besides, the fossil was still such a comfort to her, did it really matter where it came from? The steady, never-ending warmth soaked into her hands. It was securely wrapped in silver wire now and attached to a metal chain instead of a leather cord. Cupping the tooth against her chest, Ally shut her eyes and thought again of how the water felt rushing over her feet. She could handle that, at least.

Maybe it would be enough to convince Cal to help her.

Their father had already decided to send Cal's ship and crew to deliver the ransom. The *Wave Skipper* was one of the fastest ships in Kingsport and Ally was going to be on it.

13 Days

It was almost noon by the time Ally crawled out of bed. She'd finally gone to sleep shortly before dawn, lulled by the heat of the shark tooth and exhaustion from the last few days.

Dressing quickly in a pair of comfortable breeches and a loose-sleeved shirt, Ally pulled on a pair of high boots that tied at the knee. Knotting a handkerchief around her neck, like she'd seen her brothers do before a day of sailing, Ally assessed herself in the mirror. There were dark circles beneath her eyes and her curls were already escaping the knot she'd crammed them into at the nape of her neck. She didn't particularly look like a sailor, but it would have to do.

Ally's stomach growled as she walked through the house, and she detoured towards the kitchen. As if she'd known Ally was coming, the cook had set aside a plate filled with freshly baked buns stuffed with ham and potatoes. After wolfing down two, Ally wrapped up a third in a spare cloth and thanked the cook again on her way out the kitchen door. Cutting through the vegetable garden, she soon rounded the front corner of the manor. Her steps slowed when she realized she had no clue where Cal would be today. She'd already looked in her father's study on her way downstairs, it was empty for the first time since the *Swan Song* was taken. She was debating who to ask about Cal's whereabouts, when the wrapped bun was plucked out of her hands.

"Maher!"

"Thanks, Al, I was half-starved." He grinned.

"Go on, take it," Ally sighed. "Were you leaving the house or just coming back?"

"Leaving." His face resigned, Maher held up a bound stack of papers too large to fit in with the others in the satchel hanging at his side. "Father's had me playing carrier pigeon to the trade guild all morning. Where are you going?"

"I'm looking for Cal. Have you seen him?"

"Have I seen him? I've passed both him and Luthais twice already this morning. They've been down at the wharf since dawn working on the seasonal inspections." He mimicked the stance Mr. Parvan Dayal often took when dispensing orders or advice, spine straight and one fist curled behind his back like a general directing troops instead of wharf workers. "These things can't be put off, Maher my lad, even at a time like this. Important work we're doing here. Very important."

They walked towards town together. Ally looked over to find Maher struggling to extract the bun one-handed.

"Give me that," Ally unwrapped it for him. She handed the bun back, Maher took a huge bite as she stuffed the cloth into his jacket pocket. "Why is he sending you there so often and not one of his aides? Or that secretary who's always following him around."

"He doesn't trust them with such precarious information," he said around a mouthful of ham and potato.

"*Precarious*? What could be so..." Ally's full stomach lurched. "It's about Mama, isn't it?"

Maher swallowed the last of the bun and cleared his throat. "I'm sorry, Al. Now that word is spreading about Lady Kingfisher's capture, the guild is worried."

"About her safety, or about their pocketbooks? Do they really think this is going to affect trade that badly?"

"I'm afraid so, with everything else that's already happened to the fishing catches and the ships taken from the Eastern Sea corridor. And especially until we know for certain who contracted those pirates."

"If they were even contracted by anyone at all. How do we know they're actually privateers? Or if the Meredian ambassador was telling the truth? We're just taking them all at their word?" Ally pressed a hand to her stomach. Maybe she shouldn't have eaten so fast. She had to pull it together. Throwing up all over Cal's boots would not help her case.

"I know you have a lot on your mind but try not to add this to it." Maher patted her shoulder around his armful of paper.

"I know, I know," she sighed. "They're doing their jobs."

They walked quietly the rest of the way. As they turned down the high street leading to the guild headquarters, Maher shifted the documents under one arm. "Ally, I wanted to talk to you about something. I would have met you this morning, but your maid said you were sleeping in."

"What is it?" She looked up at him, his brow was creased into a tight line.

"Well, I was talking to Khafra and..." he trailed off. They stopped to set a horse and cart go by.

"And?" Ally prompted. Maher usually had no problem speaking his mind with her, even when it was about his father.

"And I wanted to know..." Maher stumbled over a loose cobblestone and swore. The papers nearly dropped, and he gripped them with both hands.

"Maher, are you alright?" Ally rarely saw him this flustered. Maher and his father had their share of disagreements, but whatever Khafra Villaon had said this time was really bothering him.

"I'm fine." He smoothed his already neatly pomaded hair. They crossed the last intersection before the wharf. "I wanted to know... do you really have to go with the *Wave Skipper* to deliver the ransom?"

"We've talked about this." Ally stopped next to the tall, gray stone building. "Of course I do. Not because the pirates are demanding it, I want to go. I need to be there for Mama." She paused, then added, "That's why I agreed to that bargain in the first place."

"I understand," Maher winced. "I just don't want anything to happen to you, Ally."

"It's going to be alright." Ally circled an arm around his waist and squeezed, hoping she sounded more confident than she felt. She'd decided not to mention the swimming lessons yet, not until she made more progress. The news would only upset Maher all over again. She could surprise him later with what she learned, show him she wasn't so afraid anymore. "Nothing is going to happen to me. Who else is going to look after you?"

While she could.

"Excellent point." He draped an arm over her shoulders and kissed the top of her head. They parted and walked around to the guild entrance facing the wharf. "By the way, why in all the gods' names and their grandmothers too are you dressed like that?"

"I have a plan." Ally scanned the docks for her brothers. She finally spotted Luthais' broad back. His long, sandy hair was tied into a horsetail that stuck out beneath his cap. Cal was kneeling next to him, inspecting a section of the dock that had apparently been damaged.

Before she could talk herself out of it, Ally marched towards them. Salty air brushed over her face and the cries of gulls perched in the rigging of the docked ships filled her ears. She focused on the screeching birds and kept walking.

"Another plan? Wait, what are you doing?" Maher called out from behind her. "Ally!"

One foot in front of the other. Ally sidestepped sailors and dock workers unloading cargo and stretching out fishing nets to be mended. The sudden, hollow sound of the boards under her feet nearly sent her breakfast up, but she kept her focus on Luthais' back and willed her stomach to behave a little while longer.

After an eternity of crossing over open water, just on the other side of the wooden planks beneath her, Ally landed at her brothers. Sweat poured down her back and she rubbed clammy palms against her breeches. Ally opened her mouth, only a high-pitched squeak came out. They still hadn't noticed she was there.

Balling up her fists, Ally took a deep breath and addressed the back of Cal's head.

"Teach me how to sail."

Luthais looked over and her burly brother's jaw dropped. "Ally?"

Cal frowned at Luthais, then turned on his knee to find Ally behind him.

"Ally!" Cal jumped up. "What are you doing here? I told you, I don't think it's a good idea…" He stopped when Luthais tapped his shoulder and pointed to where Ally was standing. "You're on the dock?"

"She's on the dock," Luthais confirmed.

"Yes, I'm on the dock," Ally huffed. "Good afternoon. I'm on the dock. Teach me how to sail."

The skin beneath Cal's freckles, already pinked by the sun, blushed a deeper shade of red. "How did this happen? Yesterday you couldn't make it onto the little dock behind the house."

Ally locked her hands behind her back to hide the trembling. "I practiced."

"What's going on?" Luthais demanded.

"I want to learn how to sail. I want to be able to help when we rescue Mama. Cal said if I could walk onto the dock he would teach me. Here I am."

Cal looked back and forth between them. "But – she couldn't – it was only yesterday!"

"I'll be damned and dusted." Luthais shook his head. "You gave her your word, Cal. I'll handle the rest of the inspections, you've got a lot to catch her up on."

Ally blinked at her middle brother. That was the second time Luthais had taken her side. Ever. It was enough of a surprise to make her temporarily forget the breakfast buns trying to make an escape from her stomach.

"You're right." Cal squinted, as if he thought she was a hallucination he could see through. "We'll start tomorrow."

"Thank you!" Ally gave Cal a quick hug, then turned to Luthais. They'd never so much as clasped hands before.

Luthais saved her from making that decision by nudging her lightly on the shoulder. "You should get off the dock now, Ally. This one's in need of repair."

"Right," Ally nodded stiffly and turned to walk back. The wharf looked much farther away from this end. She made it halfway back before her steps faltered.

Maher came running out of the trade guild and made a beeline for her. Ally latched onto his arm as soon as he was within reach. "Ally! Warn me ahead of time, will you? I couldn't leave those blasted papers sitting on the doorstep. What were you thinking?"

"Cal's going to teach me how to sail," Ally gulped, "because I walked out on the dock without fainting."

"He is?" Maher looked past her to where her brothers stood, still scratching their heads over what she'd done. "Ally, you walked onto the dock!"

"I did." She grinned, feeling almost tipsy now that someone else had confirmed it.

Laughing, Maher picked her up and spun her around.

"Maher, I need to get *off* of the dock," she gasped. "Now."

Maher took one look at Ally's face and guided her back through the crowded wharf to the street. They made it back to the guild and down the nearest alleyway.

Once they were out of sight of her brothers, Ally's breakfast gained its freedom at last.

PASHA

CHAPTER FORTY-FIVE

Waiting on the beach the next evening, Pasha worried about how long it would take Ally to feel more comfortable in the water. Seeing firsthand how terrified she was of standing in the smallest wavelets, Pasha wanted to give her the gift there and then. But she wasn't ready, likely wouldn't be ready for a while. They only had so much time. Would Ally be able to make it onto the ship?

The tapping of light footsteps reached her ears and Pasha saw Ally descending the stone stairs. She'd give it a few more days, then see if Ally could handle what Pasha could offer her.

When Ally reached Pasha, she was a little breathless and there was a new spark in her eyes. "My brother is going to teach me to sail! I made it out onto one of the docks at the wharf, and now he's going to teach me."

"That's good news."

"I couldn't have done it if I hadn't been able to finally stand in the sea."

"I'm sure you would have." Pasha stayed out of the way as she unlaced her boots.

"We start tomorrow." Ally put her outer clothing aside and rolled her breeches over her knees. "I want to keep up the swimming lessons, every day that we can, until it's time to leave."

Pasha followed her to the water's edge, pulled by the girl's momentum. Ally took the first step on her own, then went rigid.

"Are you alright?"

"It still feels so... so new." She slowly backed out, lips pursed. "I don't know why I thought this would be easier after yesterday."

"It will take as much or as little time as it needs." Pasha stood as close as she dared. "The sea doesn't measure time the way you do, or I do, or anyone else. It takes its own time."

"But I *have* to do this."

"You will," Pasha offered her an arm. Ally hesitated, her hand hovering between them. "I'll help you to be as ready as you can, in the days we have. But even I can't make you love the sea."

"Do I have to love the sea in order to swim in it?"

"No, but it can make all the difference."

With that stubborn lift of her chin, Ally hooked her arm over Pasha's and together they stepped into the surf.

CHAPTER FORTY-SIX

12 Days

"What's this?"

"It's a rowboat."

"I know it's a rowboat, Cal! I mean, why are we standing in front of a rowboat instead of the sloop?"

"Because you've never been in a rowboat," he grinned. "We're starting small and working our way up."

"That's not... I haven't, but..." Ally sighed. "Fine, please teach me the secrets of the rowboat."

"Be grateful I'm not starting you out on a raft." Cal tugged the end of the rope holding the boat to the dock and the knot slipped free. "I'll hold the line while you step in."

"*Step* in?" Ally eyed the boards bobbing up and down with the gentle current. "But it's moving."

"Yes, boats tend to do that when they're in the water," Cal said. "Do you want to do this, or not?"

"You know I do."

"Then step in. Place one foot in front of the second seat and brace your leg against it while you bring your other foot down."

Keeping her eyes fixed on the seat in question, Ally followed Cal's instructions. The first step wasn't so bad, the boat dipped a little with her weight but the board against her leg felt solid. She pulled her other leg in, and the boat rocked to one side. Ally's stomach sank and her arms windmilled as the boat thrashed harder beneath her. Cal caught one of her arms and held her still.

"Ally! If you keep swinging about like that you'll tip over."

Legs trembling, Ally took deep breaths and tried to balance without moving the boat too much.

"By the goddess, we haven't even left the dock yet." Cal peered down at her. "It will take time to get your sea legs. Just sit down in the middle of the seat."

Ally promptly sat and gripped the edges of the board. Her brother slipped two pairs of oars into the boat and gathered up the line.

"I'm going to get in now. The boat will rock, but I'll keep her steady."

Squeezing her eyes shut and thinking a larger boat wouldn't have been nearly as wobbly, Ally held on until Cal was seated ahead of her. She opened her eyes as Cal secured the oars in place and was forced to let go of the seat to hold her pair. They bobbed freely in the water.

"I assume you know how the design of an oar works?" He asked over his shoulder.

"Yes Cal, living on an island I was able to grasp that much."

"Just asking. I grew up in the same house as you and I couldn't sew to save my life."

"You should learn. What if your sail rips?"

"I have a crew to do that."

"Well, that's –" Ally shifted too hard, and the boat tilted with her. Cal's added weight pulled the bottom of the boat clear out of the sea. "No, no, no!"

Just before the frame dipped into the water it stopped, held, and bobbed back up.

Cal frowned over the edge and shook his head. "You're alright? Let's move on, then. Hold your oars out of the water while I get us turned in the right direction." He steered them away from the dock, out of line with the other vessels tied there.

It didn't escape Ally that this was her first time out on open water and only her fierce desire to not tip them over kept her rooted to her spot. There was no time to dwell on that, they only had twelve days left, less the five Gai said they'd need to sail to the pirates' meeting point at sea. A week. She only had a week left to prepare. The surface of the sea around them was mercifully calm, barely rippling with the tide and the breeze blowing through.

Cal gave her a while to sit and experience being on the boat before asking if she was ready to row. Ally focused on his oars and tried to copy him. It was harder than she'd expected, keeping time with each rotation, and moving both oars at the same speed. If they got too out of step, Cal would start them all over again and repeat the fundamental ideas behind the structure of the rowboat. Ally appreciated for the first time how quickly Maher had tired of sailing with her brothers.

"You're getting better," Cal said after their fifth circle around the dock. "Remember, if you row out of time with the rest of the oars, you're likely to pull a crab."

"Pull a what?" Ally leaned forward, lifting one of her oars out of the water. She quickly pushed it back down as Cal's were coming back around. The boat rocked hard, and Ally fell backwards off the seat, her legs and oars both stuck in the air. Like a crab on its back.

Chuckling, Cal pushed the airborne oars down and helped her sit up. "A crab. Congratulations, you already got that one out of the way."

"Lucky me."

PASHA

CHAPTER FORTY-SEVEN

Pasha tucked herself beneath the little boat after she stopped it from tipping over. They hadn't seen her, she was sure.

After spending a second evening standing ankle-deep on the shore, something told Pasha it would be best to see exactly how Ally's brother planned to teach her to sail.

He was right, starting her out on a small boat. It forced her to think about what she was doing and not just the water beneath her. On a larger vessel, it would have been too easy for Ally to hide in a corner and worry about what could happen rather than how sailing worked.

When they were away from the dock, Pasha swam farther out and watched from a safe distance. The Kingfishers knew about their new agreement, but that didn't mean Pasha wanted to meet any of them. Ally'd made the choice herself, of her own free will, but Pasha couldn't be sure what any of the other humans would do if they ever saw them together.

The water around the small dock was calm enough, but Pasha still sent a few threads to create a buffer around the boat. Ally would have to be ready for the possibility of a rough voyage, but her first time on a boat didn't have to be terrible. When Ally lost control of one of her oars and fell backwards, Pasha reinforced the thread and steadied them. The brother looked puzzled, for just a moment, then bent to help her up. Pasha let all the threads go after that, a sailor might notice if the sea was too peaceful.

When Ally was safely back on land, Pasha reluctantly swam back down to her own home. She tried not to put too much hope onto Ally's willingness to let Pasha help her learn to swim. Or her insistence that they meet as often as possible to practice. This was all to save her mother, Pasha knew that. She wasn't so much of a fool to believe Ally wanted to be around her more than was necessary. Once Lady Kingfisher was safely returned, would she try to stop her daughter from honoring her side of the bargain?

When it came down to it, could Pasha bring herself to tell Ally what she wanted?

CHAPTER FORTY-EIGHT

Maher should have been sleeping. Should have, but wasn't. The days were catching up with him. Every time he shut his eyes, a new crisis would jump to mind and he'd be wide awake again.

He'd thought a great deal about Pimm's suggestion, that the black lantern establishment might be the key to unmasking Luthais. The black lantern was one of the doors in the district Maher had staunchly avoided. Rumors of what went on inside were enough to keep him away. He knew of at least one person who'd walked in and never came back out again. That Pimm could get him inside raised more questions than it answered.

Then there was Ally, trapped in that deal with the sea witch and determined to be the on the *Wave Skipper* when it delivered the ransom. He'd hit dead end after dead end there. Accepting the bargain herself had locked Ally in, as far as he could tell. It held more weight than being ignorant of a deal made by someone else.

Speaking of unfair deals... after successfully avoiding his father for nearly a fortnight, Maher was caught that afternoon in Khafra's office at the trade guild.

"Have you asked her?"

"She has enough on her mind right now," he hedged. "I have to get this to Mr. Dayal."

His father blocked the door. "Did I not impress upon you how important this was, Maher?" When he straightened his son's lapels, Maher barely resisted the urge to push his hands away.

Instead Maher gritted his teeth and said nothing. There was no reply he could give that Khafra wanted to hear.

Maher shoved his feet into a pair of boots and left his quarters. It was nearly dawn, everyone else would be up soon anyway. He wanted to catch Ally before she left for her sailing lesson with Cal. They'd hardly seen each other since the day she walked onto the dock on her own.

It showed how much she wanted to help her mother and Maher admired the courage it took for her to board whatever vessel Cal selected for the day, but the stress and work were beginning to wear on her. Even though she went to bed immediately after dinner each night, Ally still looked exhausted the next morning. There had to be something he could do to help. Maher passed the front hall and found Cal walking through the door.

"Cal?"

He tensed, then relaxed when he saw Maher. "We're both keeping odd hours, it seems."

"Indeed. Another late delivery?"

"Or an early one, depending on how you look at it." His smile looked forced, but then Maher supposed they were all under the same heavy burden.

"I'd have been happy to take it when I walk to the guild this morning."

"It wasn't for the guild, it was for the harbormaster. We've got to do something about our ships that won't sail."

"Oh?" Maher was curious if they were also tracking the spike in sailors out of work, but Cal went on before he could ask.

"Just because our crews are too superstitious to sail, doesn't mean that others will be. We might have to bring in off-island crews to take over."

"Really? Isn't that a betrayal to the crews that serve under the guild?"

"Well, it's..." Cal shrugged. "It was Luthais' idea, you know how he can be."

"Yes, I do know."

"As Lord of Trade, he's the one above the harbormaster, I only have so much say in these matters. But, right now, I'm starved. What say we hunt down some breakfast?"

"I'll be there shortly, you go ahead." Maher stood alone in the front hall, feeling like he'd missed something important but couldn't say what. Bringing in outside crews didn't sound like something Luthais would suggest at all. He was constantly fighting with the guild to improve the conditions the sailors worked under. Pavan Dayal once said he never knew if Lord Luthais Kingfisher was walking into his office as friend or foe.

Was this connected to his activities in the Lantern district, recruiting off-island crews? Was his concern for the Birde Isles sailors all for show?

Maher had to find out what was going on behind the purple lantern door. The next time it made an appearance, he'd be ready.

Chapter Forty-nine

11 Days

"Four days. We've been at this for four days, and this is as far as I've gotten." Ally kicked the water and was rewarded with a splash that soaked her shirt.

"Considering where you started, standing in the waves up to your knees in four days is an accomplishment."

She was right, but Ally's foul mood didn't allow for logic. She didn't have to hold onto the sea witch's arm anymore either, though she stayed close by in case Ally lost her balance. It was an accomplishment. It was a miracle. And it only made Ally more anxious to get as far as possible before the hour struck. Cal would be taking her out on the sloop any day now. If the worst happened and she fell overboard, Ally needed to believe she could at least keep herself afloat long enough to be fished out.

They'd met a little earlier than usual. Ally wanted the daylight, it made the sea less murky, less likely to leap up and snatch her.

"Take your time," the sea witch said again. "The sea will still be here."

"But I won't. I'm running out of time." Ally braced as a wave broke against her legs. The impact was still a little jarring, but it no longer felt like she was about to be knocked off her feet with each swell. "You said before you had something that would help if I could get past my ankles. I'm past my ankles. What is it?"

She didn't answer right away. Another wave rushed at them, then another. Standing in the sea was, well, not comfortable for her, but it didn't frighten her anymore either. Not in the ways it had before. Ally could feel the push and pull of the water without thinking the waves would trap her. If whatever trick the sea witch had in mind could help her swim sooner, Ally would take it.

Finally she said, "It will be easier to show you, rather than tell you. But you must keep your mind open, Ally."

"Open? Not focused?"

"Focused on what you're doing, yes, but also open to things you might not have thought possible."

"The fact that I'm learning to swim is already something I didn't think was possible." Ally huffed, not adding the existence of an actual sea witch to the list. "I think I can safely say my mind is pretty open."

"So you say," she smiled in a way that felt like a challenge. "We should go then, while there's still some daylight left."

"Go where?"

"Would you like to see?" She held out a hand. Sunlight glistened off the scar on her forearm, for that's exactly what it was. An image of a goddess statue kept in the manor came to mind, one hand extending down to the sea creatures gathered at her feet.

Still not used to the extraordinary softness of her skin, Ally shivered when her fingers wrapped around the sea witch's palm.

"Come with me." They walked down the shoreline, away from the house.

Uncertain of what the sea witch meant to show her, Ally let herself be led along, choosing her steps carefully as they sloshed through the water. The walk was almost relaxing, her muscles warming with each step against the current.

After a while they turned, and Ally's heels dug into the sand when she realized the sea witch was heading into open water. "I can't just go in. I told you, I never learned to swim at all."

"It's alright. As long as you're with me, nothing will harm you."

"But I won't be able to breathe." An all-too-familiar band of dread wrapped around her chest like a vise. The water wrapped around the backs of her knees and Ally swore the waves were pulling her under.

The sea witch stepped in close. Ally could smell the salt on her skin, see exactly where the scales curving around her jaw blended from one brilliant hue to the next.

"Yes, you will."

"H-how?" she whimpered when another wave broke against them.

"I need you to let me kiss you, Ally."

"I – you need *what*?"

"Don't fret, it doesn't have to be on the lips," the sea witch smirked. "Unless you asked me to."

Ally blushed furiously, her panic forgotten. "This better not be a trick!"

"Is that a yes?"

Scowling at her, Ally nodded once.

The sea witch swiftly tilted her head and brushed her lips against the left pulse point on Ally's neck. An odd tingling washed over Ally's skin as she did the same to the right side. Then she dipped lower and pressed a longer kiss into the hollow of Ally's throat. Her lips were as soft as the rest of her and cool as silk. The skin that stretched between those three points hummed and Ally tasted the bitter tang of electricity on her tongue, like when a storm was brewing over the sea.

Her face was level with Ally's again. "This is only temporary, but you could always have this gift if you wanted it."

"What gift?" Ally's voice sounded strange in her own ears. Fuller, yet farther away.

"I'll show you."

She took Ally's hand again and they moved deeper into the water. Waves crashed around Ally's waist, soaked through her clothes, already heavier and sticking to her skin.

Ally balked again when the water was up to her chest. They were past the breaking waves, being lifted off their feet with the swells. The weightless feeling that accompanied each rise was disorienting, but the sea witch's tight grip on her hand kept her somewhat grounded. She swam closer and wrapped her other arm around Ally's waist, buoying her head higher above the water. Ally grasped her shoulder and took a deep gulp of air. The shore seemed so very far away.

"I told you, Ally, as long as you're with me nothing can hurt you. I won't pull you under the water, you need to do that for yourself."

"I can't!" Ally jerked her head up. The water was colder out here than in the shallows, it surged and wrapped around her neck. The sea witch's head disappeared completely until the sea lowered them back down. Water streamed down her skin, like rain on a glass pane. Her long hair was slicked back from her face and clung to the edges of her slightly pointed ears. Ally could practically count the scales on her face.

Another swell passed through. Ally wanted to say she'd had enough, she couldn't do it. A vision of her mother raced unbidden through her mind, frightened and alone. Waiting for Ally to save her.

Ally closed her eyes and ducked under.

The shock of the chilly water enveloping her head nearly sent Ally kicking back to the surface. It was like her ears had been stuffed with cotton, her own heartbeat was the only sound she heard. The sea witch kept a firm hold on Ally while she adjusted to the new sensation of floating underwater, releasing her hand to secure both arms around her middle.

Ally's lungs quickly started to burn. This was her limit, she needed air. A trickle of bubbles squeezed out of the corner of her mouth. Ally tried to pull back, pushed hard against the sea witch's shoulders, but it was as if an anchor was holding her down. Pulling her farther out to sea. Struggling against the sea witch was like pushing against the tide itself.

More bubbles escaped between her lips. She'd been tricked. The sea witch was going to drown her, eat her, feed her to a shark or a sea monster.

"Ally," a calm voice caressed the inside of Ally's mind. "Ally. Breathe."

Well, that was it. She was hallucinating now.

One of the sea witch's hands slid from around Ally's waist and pressed against her breastbone. "Breathe. Trust me."

She had no choice. Ally opened her mouth, anticipating the burn of saltwater flooding her lungs and... breathed in. There was a fresh blast of cold against the spots where the sea witch had kissed her. The water seemed to bypass her throat and nose altogether, rushing instead through those points and back out again. Like gills. Like a fish. It was as if she were breathing the fresh, clean air high on the cliffs.

That same hand moved up to her face. Ally felt the edge of a pointed nail graze across her eyelids.

"Now, open your eyes."

Ally slowly cracked one eye open, then the other. Blinking away the initial sting, her vision cleared. The edges were still a little blurry, but she could see. Ally noted again how very close her face was to the sea witch's.

There was a brief flash of sharp teeth before the sea witch's amused voice was back inside her head. "I told you that you'd be able to breathe."

"How did you do that?" Ally spoke the words out loud, releasing a fresh batch of bubbles with air she didn't think she had anymore.

"It's a gift I can lend out if I choose." She loosened her hold on Ally's waist. "But I need to be sure you understand, you can't tell anyone else about this. Not your family, not your friends. No one. If someone were to find out and try to take the gift for themselves, I won't be responsible for what happens."

"What would happen?" Ally tried to just think the question, to see if the sea witch would hear it, but the words left her mouth anyway.

"They would drown on dry land."

The words Ally'd heard over and over throughout her life suddenly took on a new meaning: **You cannot take what the sea is not willing to give.**

"I understand."

"Good." A grimace passed over her face and the sea witch let Ally go. "Hold on, just a moment."

"Wait!" Ally reached for her through the water, her limbs behaving as if they weren't her own. "Don't leave me alone!"

"I'm not leaving," she gritted her teeth. "But I can't wait any longer. You need to stay back until I'm done."

"Done with what?" Ally flapped her arms in a wild circle, feeling like she'd drift off without the sea witch anchoring her in place.

The sea witch's body convulsed, her back curved at a deep angle. Her dark blue hair floating around her head obscured her face, but Ally could see the twitches and tremors that rolled through her torso. Tiny threads of white light danced over her skin. They twisted and expanded, running down her body until one large band wrapped around her legs and snapped them together.

Ally shrieked, sending a curtain of bubbles in front of her face. She swatted them away, eyes wide as she watched the sea witch's legs change into...

A tail?

The threads flew over each other, stitching her legs together. A single dorsal fin shot down the back, while two fan-shaped pelvic fins sprouted from the front of her hips. Her tail fin was the last to appear. With a final full body twist, her fluke unfurled like a ship's sail. It stretched out into twin points before dipping back up to notch in the middle. The kaleidoscope of blue and green scales that decorated her torso coated the body of her tail in shimmering armor. Her fins were a blend of blues and the same silvery gray as her skin.

"You... you're..." Ally's pounding heartbeat was thick and muffled underwater. Her nerves screamed at her to get away, to swim back to shore.

Even if she could swim, she'd never make it. That powerful tail would catch up to Ally in the time it would take her to figure out where the shore was.

The change appeared to be finished. The sea witch – no, the mermaid (was it possible to be both?) – floated in front of her, chest heaving in and out.

A weary gaze locked onto her, and Ally shrank back. "You're a *mermaid*."

She stretched her spine and flexed all of her fins. "I'm aware of that."

Ally struggled to stay in one spot, her memory turning up every tale and warning she'd ever heard about mermaids. Despite being the guardians of the goddess, they were supposed to be one of the most dangerous creatures in the sea. She blurted out, "Are you going to eat me?"

"Of course I'm not." The mermaid eyed her. "You're not my type."

Ally gulped down a mouthful of seawater and, even with her new breathing ability, choked on the salt burning its way down her throat. She coughed and tried to kick to the surface, but only succeeded in pushing herself deeper underwater.

Strong hands grabbed her shoulders, and she was turned back upright.

"Ally, calm down! It was only a joke." She sighed, though no bubbles appeared through her lips. "I don't eat humans. I never have."

Ally's jaw went slack. She blinked several times, then pushed the mermaid's hands away. "You're not funny!"

"I'm sorry, really." She flipped around and swam in a wide circle. "Ready to swim?"

Ally's eyes were glued to her tail as she moved. The sea witch was a mermaid. Maher would well and truly become hysterical if he found out. He'd heard the stories too and had always believed them more than Ally did. "Does it always hurt like that? When you change?"

"Not always. Only if I stay on land too long."

"How long is too long?"

"It depends. The older I get, the longer I can do it. Right now I can only stay for a day or two, and I've been on land a lot lately."

Ally watched her scales ripple with each movement. Why would she want to ever trade something as incredible as that tail for legs? "What happens if –"

"Ally," one swish of her fluke and the mermaid was right in front of her again, "you said yourself, we don't have much time. When you can swim without my help, or looking like a lopsided squid, you can ask all the questions you want."

Ally huffed and tilted over. The mermaid righted her again.

"You're right. But you're still not funny."

CHAPTER FIFTY

10 Days

Maher was waiting for Ally in the family dining room. They'd arranged to have breakfast together before her sailing lesson with Cal.

Ally walked in with a dazed look on her face, like her thoughts were somewhere far away. She'd been wearing that look a lot lately, enough to worry Maher about how much she was taking on. He pulled her chair out and kissed the top of her head when she sat. Ally's hair was still damp from a recent wash and smelled of lavender.

"Happy birthday, Al."

"What?" She tilted her head back to look at him, as if she'd just noticed he was in the room.

"Don't tell me you've forgotten your birthday?" He sat across from her.

"I haven't, but I don't really feel like celebrating, not now. Not without Mama here."

"I know, Al." Maher poured her a cup of tea from the pot already on the table. "Have you told the others you'd rather wait?"

"I said something to Father last night when he asked. I don't mind if they want to wish me well, but I couldn't handle a party or gifts right now."

"They'll understand." With a flourish, he produced a box from Mrs. Ekmekci's bakery. "That doesn't mean we can't enjoy these."

The smell of freshly baked walnut pastries filled the air as soon as he untied the string holding the box together. Maher slid the largest one onto a plate for her.

"And when Lady Kingfisher is home, we can really celebrate."

Ally's eyes went misty, and she reached for his hand across the table.

"Thank you, Maher." She dabbed the corners of her eyes with a napkin and grabbed a fork. "It's probably better if we wait until your face is completely healed anyway. It's improved already."

"You're too kind, it warms my heart to hear your concern for my battered, beautiful face."

Ally snickered and a small knot loosened in Maher's chest. He wouldn't ask Ally not to worry for her mother, or to not work to get her back. But he didn't want to see Ally's light fade away either. If he could still make her laugh, that was a good sign she wasn't giving into despair.

Half the pastries had been devoured when Ally asked, "What did Mrs. Ekmekci say when she saw you?"

Maher topped off their cups and raised a brow at her. "If you must know, she offered to defend my honor." Ally snorted into her tea, and he leaned in as if to tell her a secret. "And she gave me two extra pastries for free."

Feeling lighter than he had in days, Maher saw Ally off to meet Cal and then walked into town to check in at the trade guild.

Cutting through the market district, he couldn't help but notice how sparse the stalls were. Those that were open had limited wares. The oyster man and his son were in their usual place, but their shellfish were collected by the selkies, not the fishers. Su-Yonn was already closing up the stall in front of the perfumery. When was the last time she'd gotten in any oils or plants that couldn't be found in the Birde Isles? Maher waved to her as he passed, reminding himself to check in properly on the way back.

As he entered the wharf district and neared the guild, Maher saw a familiar face standing at the end of the street.

"Mister Villaon!" The kitchen maid from the Bear's Den waved him over. Her pale cheeks were flushed, and her blond hair was escaping the white, puffed cap on her head. "I'm glad I found you. I was afraid I'd have to run all the way to the Kingfisher house, and I've got a lot of work to do, you know."

"Catch your breath, Olga." Maher steered her into the shade of a building. "Is everything alright? Do I need to come to the Bear's Den?"

"No, no," she dug into her apron pocket. "Pimm asked me to deliver this to you." A sealed note was shoved into his hands.

"Why did they ask *you* to deliver it?"

"That's what I wanted to know!" She huffed and straightened her brown work dress. "They know how much I've got to do, with the kitchen and the laundry and the odd n' ends left lying around by the patrons. On top of everything else, some horse's ass made a right mess in the alley and who has to clean it up? Me! We need *two* maids –"

"Olga," Maher laid a hand on her shoulder, he'd never seen the girl so flustered. "Does Pimm need a reply?"

"Nope, they said I didn't need to wait for one."

"Then why don't you head back?" He pressed a few coins into her hand. "Grab yourself something to eat on the way."

"Oh! I couldn't take it, Mister Villaon, we have food at the Den."

"You interrupted your work and ran all the way here to find me, you deserve it." Maher gave her a gentle push in the right direction. "Ten extra minutes won't hurt, you can say I held you up."

"That I'll do. Thank you, Mister Villaon!" She hurried away, hair flying and holding onto her cap as she went.

Maybe they really do need two maids. Maher ducked into the side street near the guild and examined the letter. There was nothing written on the outside. He broke the red wax seal, stamped with a bear's paw, and unfolded a single sheet of paper. Written in Pimm's precise handwriting was the message he'd been waiting for.

I got you in. Meet me in the square, tomorrow night, seven o'clock. Bring all of the items I've listed for you here, you might need them. -P

PASHA

CHAPTER FIFTY-ONE

Pasha asked Ally to meet her as soon as her sailing lesson was finished. Their time was growing short, and Pasha wanted to share something with her, even if it made her nervous just thinking about it.

"Where are we going?" Ally asked as they waded into the water.

"I want to show you something," Pasha slipped under to let her tail appear.

Ally joined her. "Show me what?"

"I want to show you my home, that is, if you'd like to see it?"

"Your home?" Ally still couldn't speak without sending bubbles everywhere. "I hadn't thought you could build a home in the sea."

"I don't just float around like a hunk of kelp when I'm not in your company."

"I didn't think that! If you'd like to show me your home, then I'd be glad to see it."

Pasha let herself smile a little. That she might have asked too soon did cross her mind, but yesterday had gone well after Ally received the gift. With the threat of drowning removed, Ally had embraced swimming with renewed determination. And she wanted to see where Pasha lived. "See if you can keep up."

Setting a solid pace, Pasha looked back every now and then to make sure Ally was still behind her. When they reached the depth where the light began to fade, she could sense Ally becoming anxious.

"We're almost there." She offered a hand, thrilled when Ally took it without hesitation. The mouth of the nearest passage was just ahead. Ally's hold on her tightened. "It's dark now, but you'll be able to see soon. Trust me."

Ally swam closer to her but didn't try to stop them from going in. They traveled in darkness for a little while, then the first corals sensed their presence. A soft green glow lit up beneath them and spread up the walls of the passage.

Ally gasped in a flurry of bubbles. She tugged on Pasha's arm to stop and bent to examine one of them. "Are these... naturally luminescent corals?"

"If that means they glow by themselves, then yes."

"And they grow beneath the island? How has no one ever found them before?"

"They only grow where humans can't swim."

"But why... oh!" Ally pulled back when the nearest creature put out its light. She'd gotten too close. "I suppose humans haven't been very gentle with them?"

"They haven't. Come, this is only the entrance. There's more to see."

Ally followed Pasha, the corals lighting the rest of the way and fading out as they passed. The passage ended in the largest cavern of all. When the walls lit up, Ally pressed her hands to her lips, taking everything in. Pasha felt a swell of pride. This cavern was the most ornate, smoothed over the years by sand and sea. The carvings done by her people had begun to fade, with no one there to keep the lines fresh, but they flowed from wall to wall. Scenes of dozens of mermaids swimming, building, changing to walk on land and back again. The corals had spread beyond the perches carved for them to dot along tails and faces, and more small creatures had moved in since Pasha woke from her long sleep.

"There's so many of them," Ally murmured.

Pasha knew she wasn't talking about the corals. "Yes, there were."

"What happened to them?" She gave Pasha a searching look, "Are you the last one?"

"Come this way," Pasha headed for one of the smaller passages that connected to the cavern. Ally kicked hard to catch up. Swimming down the passageway, she stopped to look at a series of braided ropes with different patterns carved into one side.

"What are these for?" Ally touched the nearest rope.

"To help those with weaker eyesight find their way."

Pasha moved on, there was only enough time to show Ally one more place. Over the last few days, Pasha had moved several shipwreck finds into the tapestry chamber. She took Ally there.

Ally went straight to the largest tapestry that was still intact. A group of mermaids each held a basket of shells. Woven into the baskets were words in different languages used by the humans. Her fingers twitched as if she wanted to touch it. "Can you speak all of these languages?"

"I've never been anywhere else. Those were added by mermaids who came from other corners of the sea. I can only speak the human language we're using now."

"Trader's Tongue," she didn't take her eyes off the tapestry.

"If that's what you call it, and there's the language my people use. But it's not included here."

"Why isn't it on one of the baskets?"

"It can't be written down."

"Why is that?" Ally lifted a hand towards the uneven surface of the glass, caught herself, then brought it back down.

Pasha shrugged, "It's not possible. I couldn't use it with you if I wanted, you wouldn't hear it."

"Why not?"

"Because you're not a mermaid."

CHAPTER FIFTY-TWO

Ally struggled to take it all in. The hidden caverns beneath King-fisher Island, glowing corals that weren't supposed to grow this close to land. And the mermaids. So many mermaids of different shapes and sizes and figures, some with multiple fins and some with only their tail fluke. Mermaids with long, flowing hair like Pasha's and no hair at all, and everything in between. Ally even spotted an image of one with a bony crest that ran down the centerline of her bare skull. Yet none of them were like the artwork, statues and mosaics scattered across the Birde Isles and beyond.

When the mermaid offered to show Ally her home, it never dawned on her something this vast had always been right beneath her feet.

They had art, histories, the tapestries somehow miraculously pre-served between thick slabs of mottled glass. She was still trying to wrap her mind around the idea of a language that could only be understood by other mermaids. These weren't the seductive manhunters or blood-thirsty guardians of the goddess in the stories Ally grew up with.

This room must have been a library of some sort, everything was set up high on the walls. The carvings were smaller but told more detailed stories, it would take days to decipher them all. Ally went back to the largest tapestry, aching to know how it was made and preserved so well underwater. The mermaid said the words were from other parts of the sea. Where were the rest of the mermaids now?

"You didn't answer my question before."

"Didn't I?" She rejoined Ally at the tapestry.

"Are you the last mermaid? Is that why there aren't any others in this huge place?"

"I'm the last one here, yes." Pointing at the woven words, she asked, "Can you read any of these?"

Ally braced herself against the wall and looked more carefully. "I know some of the Balahn words, not all, a little Saprean, and of course the Trader's Tongue." Squinting at that basket, Ally noticed some of the threads were much more faded than others. The brightest word was sewn into the base of the basket in a reddish thread, but it wasn't one she recognized. "P-A-S-H-A. Pasha? What does Pasha mean?"

"That's my name."

Ally's hold on the wall slipped and she sank towards the floor. "Your... You never told me you had a name!"

"You never asked," she nudged Ally's legs with her tail fins to get them moving again. "When we want to know a name, we ask. But we don't just volunteer our own for no reason."

"Why not?"

"Names are important. When someone knows your name, they have a little piece of you that you won't get back."

Ally's cheeks burned, an impressive feat considering how long she'd been underwater. How could she have never asked? Did she assume the mermaid – *Pasha* – didn't have a name because she wasn't human?

"I'm sorry. Pasha. Really, I am."

"Thank you, but there's no need to look so grim. I would have found a way to prompt you if you didn't ask soon."

"You sort of did that anyway," Ally pointed at her name. "Why is your name newer than the rest?"

"I'm the youngest."

"The *youngest*?"

"The last to be born. Did you think we popped out of the sea foam fully grown?"

Ally glanced down. "There are a lot of stories about the origins of mermaids. How was I supposed to know which was true?"

Pasha studied the basket that held her name. "Mermaids don't have children often, it's difficult and time consuming. But we live in large groups, shoals, build families outside our own bloodlines. There might have been more younger ones after me, but the others left long before that could happen."

"Wait, they *left* you?" She looked back into Pasha's black irises. Something heavy flashed through them, blotting out the slim whites around the edges and turning them into solid voids. Then Pasha blinked, and they returned to normal.

"Someone had to stay behind."

CHAPTER FIFTY-THREE

"**I** don't understand, why would your entire family leave without you?"

Pasha weighed how much she should say. Ally was adjusting fairly well to the reality of what lay beneath her own home, how much else could she handle in one day?

"It had been a long time since any mermaids came to visit from the other communities. More humans were sailing on the seas than before, with larger ships and fiercer weapons. The elders worried something might have trapped the others in their homes. Or worse." Pasha brushed the scar on her arm, feeling a phantom burn. "They were planning to only send a small group to find the others when there was... a terrible accident. It put all of us in danger, so it was decided everyone would leave."

"That still doesn't explain why you had to stay." Ally held onto the wall again. This was the longest they'd been underwater, she had to be getting tired.

"The accident was partly my fault, or so the elders said. I was never sure until... well it doesn't matter. I was chosen to stay behind and watch our home until they came back."

"Did that happen during the accident?" She pointed to Pasha's forearm.

"Not exactly," her hand fell away. Pasha hardly looked at it unless she had to. The thick, lighter gray tissue stretched nearly to her elbow joint. "It's a reminder of why I'm here."

"As if you could forget?" Ally looked at the tapestry again, then back to her. "Pasha, exactly how young were you when they left?"

"I was still a child." When Ally's mouth dropped open, she added, "I age, Ally, but it's much slower than you do."

"How slow? Sea turtle slow?" Ally's hands slipped again. Pasha caught her and they both sank to the sandy floor.

"I'm going to ignore that you just called me a turtle. I don't know exactly, but if I had to guess I'd say ten years or so for you is the same as one year for me. I was 82 of your years old when they left."

Pasha waited for Ally to react, to do something else besides stare off into space. Was she alright?

"Ally?"

"I'm just trying to add this up. You mean to say you spent decades going through adolescence?" She made a face.

Pasha laughed, relieved. "I didn't know any different, but that's true."

"Still, if I had to spend ten years or more pining for Neylan, I don't know what I would have done."

"Who's Neylan?"

"Maher's cousin, it's not important." Ally studied her, Pasha felt the blood rushing to her face. "And how old are you now?"

"I'm not sure, I didn't pay attention for a long time." Pasha scanned the other carvings, wishing she'd made some kind of record, even if it was only a notch in the stone to mark each year. "I'm at least three hundred years old."

"So that means you should be in your… thirties?"

"Close enough."

Ally's bottom lip caught between her teeth. "Where did the others go?"

"I'm not sure." Pasha shifted, sand clouded around them. "I think it's time we head back; this is the longest you've been underwater."

Ally resisted when Pasha tried to guide her to the passage. "How could they not tell you where they were going?"

"It's not that they didn't, I just don't know where they are."

"I don't care if you were being punished for something they thought you did. You don't just leave a child all alone and you certainly don't leave a child alone with no word of where you're going!"

The burst of outrage on her behalf caught Pasha off guard, the need to defend them rising in her chest. "I don't know, because the map was damaged!"

Ally's anger melted away, quickly replaced by curiosity. "What map?"

"The map of the last known mermaid shoals. They were going to check them all." She pointed to a smaller tapestry lying on the floor. "It fell years ago, and the glass cracked. I didn't know the water would deteriorate it so badly. It's too faded to read now."

Paddling over to the map, Ally peered at the crack running through the middle of the top piece of glass. She gave the frame a small push, a puff of seawater and sand seeped out. Skimming her fingers around the edges and lining them up at the corners, Ally seemed to be measuring it.

"It doesn't matter," Pasha sighed.

"Hold on," She got so close her nose almost touched the glass. "I can't be sure without holding it, but the base of it appears to still be in good shape. What if I try to fix it for you?"

Fix it? Pasha knew Ally could sew, she'd mentioned it before, but could she really fix something this old and damaged?

"That map has been exposed to the sea for a long time, wouldn't the air destroy it?"

"We won't know unless we try."

"I don't know," said Pasha. "Let me think about it."

CHAPTER FIFTY-FOUR

9 Days

Cal was waiting for her on the manor dock early that morning. He'd said she was finally ready to go out with him on the sloop, the largest vessel she'd been on yet but one that only needed a few people to sail properly. There'd been some talk of taking her out on one of the packet ships that navigated between the islands, but it all depended on how she did on the sloop.

They had four days left until it was time to set sail. Fifteen days had seemed so far away, now Ally almost wished she had some of that time back. Her lessons with Pasha and Cal had been going well, after the rocky starts with both. Ally had begun to look forward to each one for different reasons.

"Are you ready to make way, First Mate?" Cal grinned wide as she reached the end of the dock, freckled cheeks scrunching beneath his eyes.

"Aye aye, Captain," she smiled back, even if it was a little shaky.

"Come aboard and meet the rest of the crew." Cal led the way up the short gangplank. Ally kept her eyes straight ahead. Falling into the water wasn't as much of a worry now, but she still hadn't told anyone she was learning to swim. It would lead to too many questions about *how* she was learning. None of them had brought up the need for her to learn either, which puzzled her more than she liked.

Already on board and preparing to cast off were two members of the *Wave Skipper* crew. They were both fairly young; Cal had a reputation for only taking on sailors close to his own age.

"Morning, milady." A pale, lanky man tipped his cap, showing off a mop of orange curls.

"None of that, Weams, today she's acting first mate," said Cal. "You'll shadow me this first time out, but then I'm going to turn you loose."

The other sailor, shorter, broader, and darker of complexion than Weams, waved from the stern of the sloop.

Ally stuck to Cal's side. She paid close attention to what he did, and the orders given to their small crew. Once they were well away from land, Cal set a course that would take them around the southern edge of Trader's Bay. The wind was good, and the sky was clear. Once they were skimming along the open sea, Ally thought she felt a taste of the joy her brothers spoke of when they were learning to sail. Her instinct was still to stay back from the railing, but she wasn't overwhelmed either.

"First Mate, come take the helm."

"Me?" Ally made her way to him on uneasy footing, her sea legs had yet to appear.

"You heard me, First Mate," Cal winked. He placed her hands on two of the helm spokes and stepped back.

"Wait!" Her knuckles went white.

"I'm right behind you. We've got a clear way ahead and are in no rush. 'Tis a perfect day at sea." Cal raised his voice over the wind, "If only the crew weren't such lazy swabs!"

"Ho! You hear that, Olebile?" Weams' head popped up from behind the line he was coiling. "Sounds as if we'd be better off going on account with a pirate captain."

"Speak for yourself," a baritone voice answered. "I'll take my chances here."

"Don't mind them, mila– eh, First Mate," Weams shrugged. "Olebile's a good sailor. But they have trouble catchin' onto a joke."

"Ignore both of them." Cal adjusted her stance. "Loosen up if you can, your joints will thank you later."

Ally giggled as the crewmates traded barbs and pretended to cower when Cal gave an order. They were lucky, she supposed, to have a captain they could relax with. There were too many accounts of captains known for their cruelty. At least her father and brothers wouldn't stand for it in Kingsport, even if they couldn't stop them once they were on the sea again. Not two years before, a Fraollish ship left a man on the dock who'd been flayed to death by the bosun. That captain was banned from Kingsport for life, Luthais delivered the proclamation himself. Along with a promise to toss the captain overboard if Luthais ever saw his face again. Their father had to have another discussion with him about issuing threats as Lord of Trade.

Guiding the sloop across the water became easier as the morning went on. Cal gave Ally a break to have some water and a bite to eat, then she was back at the helm. The ships still sitting in Trader's Bay were far enough away that Ally was able to gradually relax. Her mind drifted, not for the first time, to the caverns Pasha had shown her beneath the island. Who would have thought such a place existed? And the story Pasha told about her family. What could have a child done that was horrible enough to justify them leaving her behind? She'd tried to learn more about the accident, but Pasha didn't want to discuss it. Ally wouldn't try to force her, she knew well enough what it was like for people to pry into painful, private memories.

On their way back out, Pasha implored Ally to keep her home a secret. Her face was pinched with worry, and it dawned on Ally she was probably the first outsider to see that place.

"To the grave," Ally used the oath Maher taught her.

"What's that?" Pasha paused at the mouth of the passage. The last of the corals behind them went dark.

"It means I'll never tell anyone. It's a promise."

"To the grave," Pasha tried the words out. "Mermaids say, 'until the sea runs dry'."

"Until the sea runs dry," Ally repeated. Pasha visibly calmed then, face smoothing and fins relaxing. "Your home is safe with me."

"Prepare to come about!" Cal shouted.

Ally jerked back to the present, the wind was taking them farther into the harbor than planned.

"Ally, bring her about!"

She spun the wheel too fast, lost control of the spokes, and forced the sloop into a sharp turn.

"Hold fast!" Cal grabbed the wheel and wrenched it to a stop. Ally pitched forward, landing hard on the deck. She looked up and saw Weams dive for a sail line that pulled loose.

"BOOM ABOUT!"

Weams hit the deck seconds before the swinging beam would have cracked his head open.

Cal brought the sloop all the way around until they were pointed back toward home. Ally's stomach rolled and she threw herself at the railing. When there was nothing left to bring up, she toppled back over and leaned against the rail. Reaching for the shark tooth, she held it tight and caught her breath.

"Olebile, take the helm."

"Aye, Captain."

Cal knelt in front of his sister and pushed a flask into her hands, "Drink some of this."

Ally smelled the alcohol before he'd pulled out the stopper. "I don't think that's a good idea."

"Go on. One glug to rinse your mouth out and one to drink."

Taking a swig from the flask, Ally nearly spat the whiskey in Cal's face. She swished it once around her mouth and spat it between the railing posts instead. The second drink was a little less harsh. Ally gave the flask back; Cal took a sip of his own before putting it aside.

"You're alright, Ally. Where was your head at?"

"I'm sorry, I don't know what happened."

"It's good you're getting comfortable," sighed Cal. "But you should always pay attention, no matter how easy it starts to feel."

"You're right." Ally doubted this would ever feel easy. "Are Olebile and Weams okay?"

"Still in one piece!" Weams jogged over and presented himself for inspection. "That was quick of you, milady, calling out the boom. You saved my noggin."

"Not sure you had much to save," Olebile gave the wheel back to Cal.

When Ally felt well enough to stand, Olebile and Weams asked if she'd like to help them mend a large sail laid out at the stern.

"I want to apologize again," Ally said when they were out of Cal's earshot. "You both could have been badly hurt."

"We all made mistakes when we started out." Weams passed her a large needle. "Besides, I always say it's bad luck to sail a vessel that's not been blessed by the goddess. You balanced out the luck."

Olebile snorted as they each chose a section of the sail to repair. "A few words spoken by a priestess doesn't grant unlimited luck at sea."

"It doesn't hurt!"

"Do you mean the ship dedication ceremony?" asked Ally, thankful for a task she could do without any trouble. Her needle wove swiftly through the tough canvas.

"Aye, that's the one. If the blessings didn't give us some benefit, we wouldn't still be doing them after all this time."

"Or you're just set in your ways. The Birde Isles build good ships, that's why they sail well."

"Olebile doesn't understand," Weams mock-whispered to Ally. "From a dry, landlocked country, they are."

"Really? Which one?"

"Kharabo. On the continent across the Split Sea."

Ally tied off a stitch. "And you wanted to be a sailor?"

"It's a good way to see the world," Olebile grinned wide, jerking a thumb at the man next to them. "Even if it means being stuck at sea with this one for months on end."

"They say that now," Weams hooked an arm around Olebile's neck. "But just wait 'til they come asking to share my bunk again."

Ally giggled when Olebile's jaw dropped. Now some of the bickering made sense, they were lovers.

Olebile sputtered and pushed him away. "You jackass! A fine thing to say in front of the captain's sister!"

"Speaking of jackasses..."

"I agree with you," Ally said before Weams could go on. "I've never understood the need for some of those older rituals. I know they mean a lot to people and can bring some comfort, but do we still need all of them?"

"I'm surprised to hear that, milady," said Weams.

"She's right, though," Olebile tied off their section of the sail. "Have the priestess say a prayer if it makes you feel protected, but who needs a reminder the Birde Isles used to sacrifice people to the sea?"

"What did you say?"

"You haven't heard the story, milady?" Weams' brow wrinkled. "Guess they don't tell it much on land anymore."

"The red handprint the priestesses paint on new ships, it's a symbol of the blood sacrifices made by the first people to settle here."

"I've never heard that before," said Ally.

"I hope we haven't upset you," Weams rushed to add. "A lot of people used to do such things, otherwise how else would it have started here? But they all learned better."

"You hope," said Olebile.

"We'll be docking soon!" Cal called out. "Crew to positions. First Mate, come watch from the helm."

"Aye, sir!" The crewmates hurried to their stations.

Ally followed, a little slower. Standing with Cal, the manor dock soon came into view. There would be time before she was supposed to meet Pasha on the beach. Time enough to walk to the temple. Some of the records Esa pulled for her were hundreds of years old. None of them mentioned anything about living sacrifices. Gooseflesh raced up her arms.

"Feeling better?" asked Cal, not taking his eyes off their destination.

"Hm? Oh, yes, I am." Ally wrapped her arms around herself. "It's just getting colder."

CHAPTER FIFTY-FIVE

They're going to be late. Maher waited in the square for Pimm to arrive. Just as his new watch struck seven, Maher saw them leaving the Bear's Den. Taking their time and smoking, Pimm stopped to exchange words with a few people along the way. It was ten minutes after the hour when they reached Maher.

"You're late."

"But you're not." Pimm flicked ashes onto the ground. "That's all that matters."

"Was there a reason you didn't want to meet at the Bear's Den?"

"Doesn't look good if a patron enters and then leaves a few minutes later." Pimm started walking, Maher fell in step with them.

"You have someone to cover for you?"

"Barkeep's younger brother is in town, said he'd watch the door until I got back."

"Brother? Gods help us." He looked around as they turned down the dead-end street. "You're sure about this?"

They tossed the end of the cigarette. "I'm sure. Are you?"

"It would be a poor time not to be." The further down the street they went, the chillier he felt.

"In that case," from somewhere in their coat, Pimm produced another flat cap. "Put this on."

"Am I not dressed appropriately?" Maher slipped the hat on, the back felt heavier than it should.

"Extra protection, and it won't hurt to disguise yourself a bit more. You're getting pretty recognizable, Maher."

"Thanks, I think." They reached the establishment. The door and knob were both painted pitch black, from a distance it appeared there was no way in.

"Pistol," Pimm reminded him. With great reluctance, Maher handed the weapon over. Pimm tucked the pistol into an inner coat pocket.

"Anything else I need to know?"

"You're there to see the owner and no one else. Don't open any doors you're not invited through, don't accept any gifts, and leave exactly the way you came in."

"That's not complicated at all." Maher checked his pockets, making sure he had everything Pimm said to bring. "How will I know who the owner is?"

"You'll know." Pimm knocked on the door.

Leaning over, Maher whispered, "How do *you* know the owner?"

The door swung open and Maher straightened up. A pale, balding, middle-aged man dressed head-to-toe in black looked down his nose at them. He put Maher more in mind of an undertaker than the door guard to a club. "Yes?"

Pimm reached into a trouser pocket, pulled out a single match, and handed it to him. "This gentleman has an appointment with the owner."

The guard struck the match against the doorframe. It flashed a bright green flame and went out. He addressed Maher, "You may follow me."

"I'll be waiting for you right here." Pimm patted his back.

Maher crossed the threshold. "Lead the way."

The door closed behind him and Maher adjusted to the gloom. They stood in a short, windowless entryway painted solid black like the door and lit by only one candelabra at each end.

"This way, if you please." Now the door guard looked like some kind of spirit haunting the building. Maher followed, wishing Pimm could have come in with him. But they'd only been able to secure a meeting for one.

At the second door, the man knocked, and a new guard answered. She was younger, full-figured with thick black hair shorn close to her skull and dressed in an ordinary suit of clothes. Maher was somewhat relieved, until he saw the hefty pistol on her hip.

"You're here to see the owner?"

Maher couldn't quite place her accent. "Yes, I have an appointment."

"Carrying any weapons?"

"I was told to leave them outside."

"And did you?" Her dark brown eyes roved over his clothing.

He spread his arms out, "You're welcome to check."

"He had the invitation," the front door guard sounded bored and ready to move on.

"Come with me." She led Maher through an ordinary looking, if deserted, parlor. Where were all the patrons? They went up a flight of stairs and down a long hallway lined with doors. Every door was shut and had a carved plank hanging from the handle. Flowers, fruit, birds, anchors, skulls... there were no sounds coming from inside the rooms either. Even in a well-insulated establishment like the Bear's Den, it was impossible not to hear some of the activity going on in the bedrooms.

"It's, uh, a quiet night, isn't it?"

"It's always quiet."

Maher coughed into his fist, "Ah, I assumed you would be busier."

She glanced at him over her shoulder. "We don't deal in pleasures of the flesh here. If that's what you're after, you'll need to adjust your expectations."

"I'm not expecting a damn thing."

"Good choice." His guide stopped at the only door with no sign and produced a key. She unlocked it to reveal another, narrower set of stairs.

"Go to the top and turn left. Not right."

"Left and not right," Maher repeated. "You're not coming?"

"That isn't my floor." She pulled a small tin out of her gun belt and popped it open. The smell of mint hit his nose. "Would you like one?" She placed one of the green buttons on her tongue.

No gifts.

"Ah, thank you, but no." Maher inched towards the stairs.

"Suit yourself," she grinned, showing several gold-capped teeth. "You can go up now. The Madam will meet you."

Madam?

He was a few steps up when the door closed, plunging the stairwell into darkness. Fumbling in his inner coat pocket, Maher pulled out a box of matches and struck one until it lit. With a short candle from the same pocket, Maher gave himself enough light to find his way up the stairs. The candle and matches had been on Pimm's *Things Maher Might Need* list.

This staircase was steep and only wide enough for one person to pass through at a time. Even with the light, he couldn't see how far up it went. Hot wax dripped onto his hand and a trail of sweat snaked down his back by the time Maher reached the top. There was only one door, no left or right option at all. His candle was burning quickly, and he'd need it for the trip back down.

"Fuck this place." Maher grabbed the handle and pushed it open.

He ended up in yet another hallway, this building was beginning to feel like a carnival maze. At least this new floor was well lit, Maher blew out the candle and scraped most of the wax from his knuckles. Out of sheer curiosity, he looked to the right. At that end of the hall was a large door with a decorative brass knocker, nothing alarming there. The left side, the direction he was supposed to go, was less inviting. This door was older, the wood splitting around the edges. The knocker was iron, and it looked like something big had *gnawed* on the doorframe.

Nothing was going to be resolved if he stood there all night. Walking to the door on the left, Maher tapped the knocker three times.

A faint voice drifted out from the other side, "Come in!"

Out of habit, Maher straightened his clothes first and then entered the room. Stopping just inside, Maher thought his eyes must be playing tricks. One of the door guards must have slipped him something when he wasn't looking, because this had to be a hallucination. He'd been prepared for any number of gruesome sights, even expected to have nightmares the rest of his life after entering the black lantern, but he wasn't prepared for this.

A fire blazed in the red brick hearth that took up most of one wall, while tall lamps with frosted globes stood in each corner. Plush Saprean rugs in shades of burgundy and dark green covered the floor, matching the leafy vine wallpaper. In the middle of the room, facing the fire, was a plump sofa and two tall-backed chairs. A silver tray set for tea waited on the low table sitting on its own little rug. The back wall was lined with shelves stuffed with books and trinkets.

Sitting at a spindly, claw-footed writing desk was a woman old enough to be his grandmother. Possibly even his great-grandmother. Long, ivory hair was piled high on her head in an intricate bun and a pair of spectacles connected to a delicate gold chain perched on the end of her nose. She wore the kind of high-necked satin gown that belonged to another age, pointed black boots peeked out from the hem of her skirt. He couldn't help thinking Ally would love to get her hands on an antique dress like that.

The woman hadn't looked up or acknowledged Maher's presence yet. He waited, unsure if he was supposed to speak first or not. The only sounds in the room were the crackling of the fire and the scratch of her pen as she finished the letter in front of her.

Pimm was waiting for him outside. Maher decided to take a chance. "Good evening, Madam."

A pair of sharp blue eyes found him over the rim of her spectacles. "Good evening. I'll be with you in a moment, have a seat if you'd like."

Maher selected the chair closest to the door. The arms were carved with sparrows and flowers, craftsmanship that would have cost more than a few coins. Everything in the room was fine quality, the gears in Maher's mind spun over what this woman's business must entail to afford such things.

After signing the bottom of the letter, she blew on the page to dry the ink and folded it into an envelope. Resting her spectacles around her neck, the woman turned in her seat to look at Maher.

"Mister Maher Villaon, yes? I gather you wish to speak to me about an important matter."

Something about her was strangely familiar, but he couldn't think where he might have seen her before.

"That's right, Madam, I wanted to –" Maher's eye caught something under the desk.

Laying there, half-hidden by the woman's skirt, was a gray block-headed dog. Possibly the biggest dog he'd ever seen. Its folded, triangular ears and square, white-patched muzzle twitched as it chased whatever furry creature was running through its dreams.

She flapped a hand at him. "Don't mind Sweetpea, she won't bother you if you don't bother her."

Sweetpea?

"Uh, yes, as I was saying. I appreciate you seeing me this evening."

"Your friend was most insistent." She joined him by the fire, her back ramrod straight even while sitting on the sofa. The dog, Sweetpea, immediately noticed her mistress's absence and ambled over. She was even bigger up close. With a yawn that showed an imposing set of teeth, the dog flopped down by the woman's feet and kept one eye on Maher. "Would you like some tea? It's a fresh pot."

Maher nearly accepted, then stopped. Did this count as a gift?

"There are no strings attached, Mr. Villaon. It's only tea."

"Thank you, Madam. That would be nice."

She poured three cups of tea, added milk to hers and Maher's, and left the third sitting at the edge of the tray. "What can I do for you, Mr. Villaon?"

"I'll get right to the point. I need to know what's going on inside the purple lantern establishment. The one that appeared this summer and constantly moves its location."

"Are you sure this is something you need to know, or that you merely want to know?"

"Pardon?"

"People come here only when they truly need something. Why do you need this?"

"I think that establishment is connected to the series of recent misfortunes that have fallen on Kingsport." He took out a small pouch, the coins inside clinked together. "I also think they could be the ones funding the street crews that have been spreading through the city."

"May I?" She held out a gnarled hand. Maher tipped the coins into her palm. Holding her spectacles up, she examined the Saprean silver. "This has never seen the inside of a bank. It was stolen not long after it was minted."

"That was my thought, too." His fingers tapped against the arm of the chair. "Do you think you can help me? I only have four days to find out what they're doing and stop them from causing any more damage."

The old woman took her time looking over each coin. "My daughter speaks very highly of you, Mr. Villaon."

"Your daughter, Madam?"

"Mmm..." She stacked the coins on her side of the table. "I'll see what I can do. I won't make promises, but I'll see what I can do."

Maher had a strong feeling it was time to leave. "Thank you, very much. I'll wait to hear from you." He started to rise.

The dog's head popped up, a low growl rumbled in her chest. Maher found his seat again.

"Before you go," the Madam smiled sweetly. "We ask that you make a donation, whatever you think our help is worth."

"A donation?"

"Unless you'd rather owe us a favor for this information?"

Maher did *not* want that. "Is the silver not enough?"

"These coins are tainted. I dare not spend them or let them back out into the world, lest the negative trail they leave leads to my door."

"I don't have anything else..." Maher's head tilted back and hit something hard on the chair. No, not on the chair, in his hat. "A moment, if you please?"

"Be my guest," she took the third teacup and set it on the floor. "Here you are, darling." Sweetpea sniffed it and lapped up the cooled tea.

He took off the cap and smoothed his hair down. Feeling along the back inside seam, Maher found a row of hard, rounded lumps. "May I borrow your paper knife?"

When she nodded, Maher retrieved it from the desk and slid the silver point under the threads holding the hat band together. They snapped with the tiniest pressure. Four gold Birde Isles coins rolled out, the diving Kingfisher birds stamped onto the backs were a welcome sight.

Thank the gods for Pimm.

"Will this do?"

"Perfectly, it's a good trade. Thank you for your generosity." She held Sweetpea's collar in a loose grip. "I will send word through your friend if anything can be uncovered. I assume you can make your way out without my assistance."

"I can, Madam, and thank you for your time." Maher gave a short bow and left the room.

As the door was closing, her voice rang out behind him, "Best of luck to you, little magpie."

CHAPTER FIFTY-SIX

"Tonight, you're going to learn how to keep yourself afloat."

"Can I not already do that?" Ally toed off her boots and tucked them against the usual rock pile.

"You've made progress swimming on the surface, and beneath it, but what if you need to stay in one place? Will you swim in a circle?"

"I see your point." Ally checked the tie on her braid was secure and followed Pasha into the water.

They swam out beyond the waves until they reached a quieter place. Ally couldn't tell how deep the ocean was here, but the island looked pretty far away. She could just make out tiny dots of lamplight from Kingsport, winking at them like stars.

"Bring yourself upright. Move your legs as if you were walking." Pasha's tailfin flicked against Ally's ankle. "Use your arms to keep your balance."

Ally kicked too hard, and face planted into the water. Sputtering, she righted herself and worked until she found a rhythm that kept her mostly in a fixed position. There was nothing she could do about the tide pushing her up and down, but Pasha didn't make any other corrections. "How long are we going to do this?"

"Until you can't tread water anymore. We're going to see how long you can stay here."

"Fun," Ally was grateful now for the chance she'd had to rest earlier that afternoon, after all that had happened on Cal's sloop. She glanced back towards land. "It looks so small. I wonder if you can really tell how large a new place is from a ship?"

"I wouldn't know," Pasha said dryly.

"Oh, right." Ally hummed, the splash of her paddling echoed around them. Pasha was floating quietly in front of her, slender arms hardly moving as her powerful tail kept her in place. She could probably do this all night. "Can I ask you something?"

"Of course."

"After all this time, when the other mermaids didn't come back, why did you stay?"

The tip of Pasha's tongue rested against the points of her upper teeth which, Ally had learned, meant she was considering her answer.

Eventually she said, "This is my home, and I was tasked with watching it."

"I know that, but why stay if it meant you might always be alone?" Ally started to sink and kicked herself back up again.

"We were here long before any humans showed up, Ally." Pasha shook her head. "I wouldn't expect you to understand this, but I can't just leave everything. These islands were our home before humans ever learned to sail, it's where most of us were born. We came on land when we wanted, returned to the water when we wanted. At least that's what I was taught. I was one of the few born after the humans arrived."

I'm the youngest. Ally recalled her saying that. She hadn't thought to mention her own birthday to Pasha. As old as the mermaid was, Ally questioned if she marked the passing years the same as humans.

"When the first humans came they thought these islands were empty, but we were here. Same as the fish or the birds, or any other creatures that made them their home. We couldn't stop them, even with our gifts there were so many of them and so few of us. Our elders soon realized many of those first humans worshiped a sea goddess. So they gave them a goddess. They'd take turns, only appearing at night so it was harder for the humans to get a good look at them. It kept them from getting too close and seeing what we really were."

"Why pretend to be the goddess at all?" Ally panted. Despite knowing she could breathe even if she sank, the urge to keep her chin as high above water as she could was impossible to resist. "That's what I don't understand. Why show yourselves at all?"

"To protect the shoal. Have you not heard stories about the miraculous properties of a mermaid's scales? Or her teeth?" She bared her own. "How about if you can get your hands on a mermaid's blood, or tears, or bones?"

"Those are just…" Ally trailed off, remembering the market vendor with his fake scales. "Myths."

"Maybe now, but not that long ago they were believed to be facts. We didn't want to be hunted, not in our own home. If we accidentally met any of the humans after that, we could pretend to be messengers of their goddess." Her tail whipped hard beneath her, and Ally was pushed back by the force of it.

Ally struggled to keep herself afloat. Pasha could easily send her skimming back towards the shore. "That's still no reason to let them make human sacrifices to a goddess that didn't exist!"

Pasha went still. "Where did you hear that?"

"The sailors still tell the story, apparently it's common knowledge if you know who to ask. By making the goddess more real to them, you've affected how entire generations of people live and work and think."

"We never asked for their sacrifices!"

Ally flinched at the anguish in Pasha's voice, but she didn't look away. She held the mermaid's gaze and reminded herself Pasha was as much a casualty of events and machinations beyond her control as she was. Both of their families had steered their lives without ever asking what they wanted. In different ways, perhaps, but they'd done it all the same.

Ally's family loved and took care of her, but they'd rather let fear consume her than explain why they'd kept her from the sea.

Pasha's had completely abandoned her, a child, to fend for herself. And for what? What had happened to make them leave her behind?

Ally swam a little closer, "Why did they do it, if you didn't ask for them?"

"I wasn't born yet, the first time it happened. I only know the story. A human girl kept lingering at the sea, longer and longer, until her parents had to drag her away. She'd break free and come right back, throw herself into the waves. No matter how exhausted she became, she wouldn't leave until someone pulled her out. The elders didn't know what to do about it, they didn't want the humans thinking we'd pulled her in. Some tried to scare her out of the water, but it didn't work. She wanted to stay, insisted she *had* to stay." Pasha scooped a handful of water and smoothed her drying hair out of her face. "We'd heard of rare cases of humans being called by the sea, from mermaids visiting from other shoals, but we'd never seen it. And their accounts were never like that."

Sea Kissed. Ally thought dazedly. *She's talking about someone who was Sea Kissed.*

"This wasn't a sailor who'd fallen overboard, or a human trying to take their own life. She didn't want to die, but she'd continue to put herself in danger if nothing was done. The girl drowned while the elders were still deciding what to do, and her family caught one of us bringing the body back to land."

A muscle in Ally's hip cramped, she tried to shake it out without distracting Pasha from her story, not when she was finally telling Ally the real history of the Isles. "And they assumed the sea goddess had taken her on purpose?"

"Afterwards, the humans returned to that place each year. Bringing, often dragging, girls who had no call to the sea and no desire to die. We tried sending them back. They were shunned, turned out by their own families to survive on their own." Her eyes shuttered. "They were such superstitious people."

"So you took them instead."

"We had to. We weren't monsters, whatever the humans thought, and we weren't going to let innocents be punished by their own people's ignorance. All of them were given a choice." Pasha hesitated, searching Ally's face. Her next words came out in a rush, "They could become like us, or we would see them safely to another shore."

A chill that had nothing to do with the water traveled up Ally's spine. "You could *change* them into mermaids?"

"The elders who were strong enough, they could. And the next time there was a human who couldn't stay away from the sea, they offered to change her as well."

"How many chose to be like you?"

"Only a few and none in my lifetime. Most asked to be taken elsewhere."

So, they hadn't all drowned, those daughters torn from their families. "What made the people finally stop the offerings, then?"

Pasha laughed, but it was a bitter sound. "Love."

"I don't understand."

"Love is one of the greatest, most terrible motivators." She swam a few strokes away from Ally and floated on her back, gazing up at the halfmoon.

Ally tried to copy Pasha, but her backend kept sinking. She went back to treading water instead.

"Time went by, the humans got smarter, and the sacrifices began to drop off. We were told to stay away from the shore and let them forget. If they tried to bring a girl again, our strongest elder planned to walk on land and tell them the goddess was satisfied with the blood of sailors lost at sea. That she didn't want their daughters anymore. If they wished they could build an altar in every home or bring offerings and prayers to the temple. That would be enough."

Ally's legs were starting to burn. The lower half of her face kept dipping beneath the water. "But why didn't they do that when all of this started?"

"I told you Ally, the humans were too superstitious back then. When one of us would try to give a girl back or say we didn't want them, they took it as some kind test of their devotion to the goddess. We couldn't reason with them. Over time they grew less frightened by the natural world around them."

How many times had Ally said something similar to Maher? Yet here she was, swimming with one of the mermaids she'd never believed was real.

"You said love made them stop. What did you mean by that?"

Pasha sighed, flipping backwards so her tail broke through the surface. Ally saw a flash of blue in the moonlight, the webbing and veins running through her fluke. Then it was gone, and Pasha's head came back up. "One of the younger mermaids, Pallagia, fell in love with a human girl from the biggest island. It was already called Kingfisher Island by then. She refused to tell anyone how they'd even met, let alone formed a relationship."

"What was her name?" Ally felt it was an important thing to know.

"Eal-ah-saych," Pasha sounded the name out, as if it had been a long time since she'd said it aloud. "Ealasaid felt some pull of the sea, she even cared for Pallagia, but she hadn't made up her mind yet to give up her life on land. Pallagia went against every rule put in place to keep us safe and went on shore during the day to convince Ealasaid to come with her. They were seen by the girl's family."

"What happened?"

"She panicked, claimed to be the sea goddess taking a final sacrifice that was owed to her and... she pulled the girl with her over the cliff. In their hurry, Pallagia had forgotten to give her the gift to breathe before they hit the water. Ealasaid died before anyone could help her."

Over the cliff. Without asking, Ally knew it was the cliff behind her own home, the one she'd climbed countless times to watch the morning sun as it rose over the ocean.

Ally dared to kick herself next to Pasha. She was dying to know more about the Sea Kissed who chose to become mermaids. How it was done. If the incessant pull of the sea was finally quieted by making the change.

But something in Pasha's eyes as she spoke of Pallagia and Ealasaid, something distant and full of regret, made her ask instead, "That's when the other mermaids left?"

Pasha exhaled. "That's right."

"What happened to Pallagia?" Ally flapped her arms harder to give her legs some relief, feeling very much like a ridiculous bird. Or – what had Pasha called her? – a lopsided squid.

"She died too, not long after. She was... heartsick. Never forgave herself for what happened to Ealasaid."

Ally inhaled too quickly and spat out a mouthful of seawater. "But, if no one harmed you, I didn't think you could..."

"I age more slowly than you, but eventually I'll still grow old and die."

Chewing on the inside of her cheek, Ally strained to keep her body turned in Pasha's direction. How was she still floating there so easily?

As much as Pasha had revealed to her that night, there was a hole in the story. Ally could feel it. Like when a thread came loose from a pattern, the whole thing might still be together, but you could see where the missing stitch belonged. "I still don't understand why *you* had to stay behind alone, if Pallagia was the reason they left."

Pasha stared at her for a long time without answering. Ally was about to ask the question again when her legs finally gave out and she sank beneath the surface. It took a moment for her to adjust and Ally marveled again at how unafraid she was. The cool tingle of her invisible gills made everything alright. She waited for Pasha to join her, but all she saw was her torso and tail, still swishing easily from side to side. Those green and blue hued scales glistened like jewels. No wonder the early humans thought they must have held some special powers, they *were* magical. Enchanting. Ally's hands flexed, a sudden urge to touch Pasha's scales itching at the tips of her fingers. She was so close, all she had to do was reach out and...

Pasha caught her wrists and Ally was pulled back to the surface. Ally's clothed legs brushed against her tail on the way up, material catching on the fine scale edges. As Ally blinked the water from her eyes, Pasha moved away.

"It's time to go back," Pasha kept her at arm's length. "You should get some sleep before you meet your brother tomorrow."

She towed Ally back towards land until her feet touched sand. Instead of walking Ally onto the beach like she'd always done before, Pasha kept her tail and stayed in the waves.

Ally stood at the edge of the water, feeling the sand shift beneath her feet as the tide came in. "Will we swim tomorrow?"

"I'll be here."

Something kept Ally from walking away, a nagging question that wouldn't leave her alone. "Pasha?"

"Yes?"

"Who was Pallagia to you?"

"My sister." A wave crashed over Pasha's head. When the foam settled and the water pulled back, she was gone.

CHAPTER FIFTY-SEVEN

The second-floor guard was waiting for him when Maher reached the bottom of the narrow staircase. When he tripped down the last few steps after his candle burned out, more like.

"Meeting went well, I see."

Maher righted himself and stuffed the torn cap into a coat pocket. "How can you tell?"

"You're in one piece, aren't you?" She hooked her thumbs into her belt. "Which way do you want to go out?"

"Through the front." He was tired of these games. "Where your charming friend sits in the dark all night."

Chuckling, she led the way. They'd nearly reached the end of the hall when a door with a carved fruit plank cracked open.

"Miss?" A small voice called out.

The guard asked Maher to wait and went to speak to the person hiding behind the door. He couldn't hear what was said, but when she turned around Maher inhaled sharply. The girl in that room couldn't have been more than sixteen, dressed in only a nightgown with a blanket wrapped around her thin shoulders. A healing yellow bruise spread over one side of her face, and a hunk of auburn hair was missing from her scalp. When the girl noticed Maher standing in the hall, she gasped and quickly shut the door.

"What's going on here?" he demanded when the guard returned. "Who was that girl and what happened to her?"

"Don't raise your voice here. Our patron is resting."

"*Resting*? She's –"

"Don't. Raise. Your voice." She lay a hand on her pistol.

Maher followed her down the stairs, casting one last look at the closed door, trying to memorize its location. Starting a fight, unarmed, in the heart of the blank lantern wouldn't help anyone. When they reached the empty parlor, he put some distance between them. Before he could open his mouth, the guard rounded on him.

"The girl is here because she needs our help."

"Help with what?"

"That's her business." Despite being only eye-level with his chin, she squared off with Maher. "Someone did hurt her and now they won't anymore. You have my word."

"We've never met before today and yet you expect me to take your word?"

She grinned and Maher got a close-up view of those gold teeth. "Pimm at the Bear's Den knows me, and you know Pimm. Ask them."

Back outside, Maher tossed a salute to the front door guard and found Pimm leaning against a wall across the street.

"How'd it go?"

"What is that place?" he hissed.

"That good, eh?"

"Pimm!"

"Calm down," Pimm took out their tobacco pouch. "Smoke?"

"No I don't want a fucking smoke!" Maher took a deep breath and pulled the ragged hat from his pocket. "I had to cut your cap open."

"Keep it, might be good luck now."

Maher waited until they lit the cigarette, then he stole it and took a long drag. Coughing around the burn, he thought about tossing it on the ground so Pimm would have to roll another. He gave it back instead.

"Tell me what really goes on in there," Maher coughed again. "All the rumors about the depraved, lost souls that walk through that door are horseshit, aren't they?"

"What did you see?"

He hesitated, "Is it safe to talk here?"

"Right outside their door? Sure."

Maher recounted everything that happened, pausing in the middle while Pimm had a good laugh at his interaction with Sweetpea, and ended with the gun-toting guard offering Pimm as a reference.

"Marielle? I didn't know if she was working tonight, but she's trustworthy. From The Riddles, you know."

"I feel so much better," Maher huffed, his curiosity over meeting someone from The Riddles overshadowed by an increasing suspicion that he'd been duped. "Now will you explain what's going on?"

"To the grave?"

"To the grave."

"Those stories about the black lantern were spread on purpose. Maybe a long time ago some of them were true, but after Madam took over she decided to use that reputation for her own purposes. Marielle didn't lie, they do help people. They help sex workers leave bad establishments, if they aren't treated well or were coerced into something they didn't agree with. Provide a safe place for the dying with no family, or family they don't care to see. The dark rooms and peculiar rules are all for show."

"Why did you put me through all that? I thought I was going to be murdered with a cup of tea!"

"It wasn't my decision. They had to be sure you were there with the right motives. When you were leaving Marielle told you the girl was safe instead of keeping up the illusion, yes? Madam must have already tipped her off that you could be trusted."

"I think I'm going mad." Maher massaged his forehead, feeling a sharp headache coming on.

"I couldn't say anything until they met you for themselves." They tugged on Maher's sleeve and the pair left the dead-end street. "She really will try to help you get inside the purple lantern. If anyone has the resources, it's her."

"And where do *her* funds come from?"

"I couldn't tell you where it all comes from because I don't know. Those who come to die in peace will give whatever they have left to rent the room."

He thought of that richly decorated office. "That can't be the bulk of it."

"There are also plenty of wealthy citizens who wouldn't want their misbehaviors made public, and the workers who're treated badly by their employers can have a lot of stories to tell."

"Ah."

"And the Madam ensures they're barred from every establishment in Kingsport."

"What stops them from going outside of the city?" asked Maher.

Pimm shoved their hands into their pockets. "Nothing. Not even the Madam can be everywhere, but if she finds out they've resumed their behavior she has everything needed to punish or expose them."

They walked together to the Bear's Den while Maher tried to think if there was anything else he wanted to ask Pimm. Only one question came to mind.

"I feel like I've seen her somewhere before, the owner whose name I'm apparently not going to learn tonight."

"Of course you do."

"Care to explain, Pimm, or do you plan to keep talking in riddles?"

Reaching the iron gate in front of the Bear's Den, Pimm leaned close and spoke low so only Maher could hear them.

"The Madam of the black lantern is Mama Bear's mother."

FORAOISE

CHAPTER FIFTY-EIGHT

8 Days

In the bowels of the *Maiden's Revenge*, Captain Dare had the crew pulling back every other cannon from the gunports. They were lashed down along the center of the gundeck and their replacements wheeled into the empty spaces.

Crossbows, each as long as a cannon and with a bow wider than a sailor's arm span. Attached to the back of each one was a spool of cable woven with copper thread, the free ends of the cables connected to the massive bolts notched into place. They were smaller versions of the massive mounted bows once used for war across the continent. Foraoise had seen one once, a museum piece displayed on a stone pedestal in New Pravil. The Meredians did love to boast how those war machines were invented in the days of Old Pravil, before the world went from running on battle and bloodshed to trade and politics. Though they had no proof.

There'd been some grumbling amongst the crew, some concern that cutting their firepower in half would make them an easier target. She'd allowed it, because this was something they'd have to see with their own eyes to believe. And they would see very soon. The smaller ships they'd come across had only required two crossbows, they needed more to truly appreciate what she'd done. They'd witness the real power behind the strange contraption she'd brought aboard five years ago. Their initial fear of it had dulled into annoyance at the space it took up, but they'd soon know they were right to be wary of its power.

The next prize that crossed their path would be the final test before they met the Kingfisher ship. No matter where it made its berth, they'd take it.

Swain arrived and stood beside her. "Captain, the ship's carpenters are confident they can get the cables connected back by the end of the day, so's long as they don't run out of wood for the trenches."

"Then they'd better not run out."

"Aye," he pulled on his mustache, watching as the last crossbows were strapped into place. "What's to stop the crew launching the bolts from getting caught in the line of fire? You'll remember, we lost a few when they were first learning how to run the spinner."

"Watch it, sailor!" Foraoise barked at a man dragging one of the metal spools across the deck. "That cable's worth more than all the wages you've made in your short fucking life."

"Aye, Captain!" he scrambled to rewind the cable and lift it higher.

"Captain?" Swain prompted.

"They'll have the boots and gloves to wear on the gun deck," she said to Swain. "If they aren't smart enough to keep their attention on the lines, they'll learn quick enough."

"Aye, I expect they will."

PASHA

CHAPTER FIFTY-NINE

Pasha hadn't meant to tell Ally about Pallagia so soon, if at all, but once she started it was impossible to stop.

She *needed* Ally to understand. When Gaius I came begging for help, impersonating the goddess was all she knew to do. Pasha didn't *want* to deceive anyone. If she'd been in her right mind, not freshly woken from a sleep that was nearly her death, she wouldn't have answered the call at all. Maybe.

If she hadn't, would Ally even be here? By pretending to be the sea goddess, bringing her back to life, Pasha set off a series of events that affected every human on the islands. If she'd stayed put like she was supposed to, would all of the humans have gone? Would her family have eventually returned to find their home belonged to them again?

Would Ally even be alive?

Pasha traced a nail over the crack in the glass-covered map. Ally offered to mend it, or to at least try, and Pasha had put a great deal of thought into what that could mean if she succeeded. She could try to find her family, to find any other mermaids who might still be out there. When Ally asked if Pasha was the last one, she had no idea that Pasha had been asking herself the same question for some time. Mermaids used to come from the farthest corners of the sea to visit these islands. Pasha's home was the oldest and largest shoal any had ever seen. She was very young the last time a newcomer came to stay, but she remembered the impression their home made.

There were too many *what if's* spinning around inside her head. Let Ally see if the map was salvageable, then Pasha would decide what to do. Brushing off the melancholy that threatened to settle in, Pasha pried the glass apart. The top slab broke completely in half, and she pushed the pieces away. As gently as she could, Pasha rolled up the map and wrapped a scrap of old sail around it.

Leaving would be hard, if it turned out she could, but it might be the kindest thing she could do.

The glow of pleasure that lit up Ally's face when Pasha handed her the map was worth giving it away. She unrolled the tapestry, a little at a time, until it was spread out across her lap. Pasha's heart sank when she saw it now in the daylight. Most of the material down the middle had turned a muddy brown and a rip tore through the top edge.

Ally caught her disappointment. "That's very normal, the discoloration, but look at how well the blues and reds around the edges have been preserved."

"Do you really think you can mend it?"

"It's in better shape than I thought it might be, after being in the water so long." Mindful of the rip, Ally rolled it back up. "I'll have to let it dry first, then we can see what we have to work with."

We? Pasha was sure that tiny word didn't mean what she would have wished. This was Ally's passion, and she was volunteering her skills to help Pasha, nothing more.

She could see Ally trying to decide on a safe place to leave the map while they swam. "You should take it home now, so there's no more damage done out here."

"But, what about…"

"We can swim tomorrow. You've done well, I don't think an evening off would be amiss."

A full, bright smile was Pasha's reward, the first she'd seen on Ally since the day they met properly. "I appreciate that, but I really do want to keep practicing. Is that alright? You're right about the tapestry, though. Let me run this up to the house and I'll come back."

Something warm bloomed in Pasha's chest. "I'll be here."

"Thank you, I'll do my best with it, I promise!" Holding the map close, soaking the front of her shirt, Ally left the beach.

Ally wanted to come back. She actually wanted to come back and be with Pasha… *No.* Pasha shook her head. Ally wanted to *practice*. This didn't mean anything more than her offer to repair the map.

Yes, it *would* be hard for Pasha to leave her home. But it might be the kindest thing she could do for everyone. Including herself.

Chapter Sixty

Maher had barely seen or spoken to Ally since they had breakfast together on her birthday, only catching her for a brief moment at breakfast. Maybe at dinner if both of them were actually there. Even though it had only been a few days, it still didn't feel right, not spending at least a few hours of the day together. After his meeting inside the black lantern, he was eager to catch Ally up on his suspicions about Luthais. But the Madam hadn't gotten back to him yet, and there'd been no sign of the purple lantern opening up again.

They were running low on time. Ally's sailing lessons with Cal had progressed at an impressive rate, almost too impressive. That's what Maher couldn't figure out when Cal sang his sister's praises. How, after only a handful of lessons, her fear of the water seemed to melt away and she threw herself wholly into sailing. When only a few weeks ago she couldn't set foot on the sand without breaking down? Did no one else find that odd? Lord Kingfisher and all the rest were so focused on securing the ransom, Maher guessed Ally's accelerated sailing progress wasn't enough to catch their attention.

And if the talk Maher overheard in his father's office was to be believed, it sounded as if the pirates had demanded a ransom that was impossible to meet. Even if they substituted equal value goods for some of the items on the list, there'd be hardly anything left on any of the Birde Isles to sustain the people. Word had gotten out through Kingsport; it was impossible to keep such proceedings a secret when wagonloads of goods were passing through the city each day. Pimm said the Lantern owners were at a loss, even with the maps and details they'd collected. Their own businesses were starting to suffer, and the street crews were getting bolder. Pimm still wasn't sure how to identify half of them beyond the rough territories. The old crews would sew patches into their clothes, maybe even dress similarly, not unlike the matching uniforms or tattoos worn by sailors or soldiers. But only those on the inside knew who belonged to which new crew. Pimm even offered to try joining up with one, to gain some insight, but Mama Bear forbade it. Maher was glad, he didn't want to think of Pimm putting themselves in danger like that. Not when the information gathered wouldn't be worth the risk, and Pimm was too well-known in the Lantern anyway.

Having finished his last run to the trade guild for the day, Maher decided to wait for Ally and Cal to return from their lesson. He snagged a random book from the library and camped out in a chair in the front hall. Flipping through the pages, though not really seeing the words, Maher jumped each time the front doors opened. Mostly it was advisors or assistants coming and going or servants cutting through. Mrs. Thorley had given permission for them to use the front entrance in order to get their work done faster. She wanted to anticipate anything Lord Kingfisher might need.

By late afternoon, Maher still hadn't seen either Ally or Cal. The servants had cleaned around him, as if he were a part of the furniture. His legs were going to sleep, and he'd only just realized that the book in his hands was on ship maintenance. The doors opened and Gai walked into the manor.

"Gai!" he hopped up, tossing the book into the chair.

"Maher? What are you doing sitting in the hall?"

"I was waiting for Ally to finish her sailing lesson with Cal, shouldn't they be back by now?"

"They parted ways around noon," Gai's mustache twitched. "Cal's been down at the docks with Luthais and the harbormaster since then."

Maher's brows furrowed. "Where's Ally, then?"

"Cal said she went down to the beach below the manor dock, she wanted to go for a walk on her own." He sighed, "I forget she has as much on her mind as the rest of us. I really ought to see how she's doing."

"I'll be glad to let you know after I talk to her."

"Thank you, Maher," Gai clasped his hand. "You've been a good friend to Ally, I hope you know how much we all appreciate it."

Maher started at the small dock and worked his way down the beach. Surely, she wouldn't have walked too far? Once the shoreline curved up into the harbor the terrain became pretty rough. Ally would have to turn around and head back eventually.

The days were getting shorter as autumn set in, Maher was glad he thought to grab a lantern on his way out of the house. He lit the wick as the sun met the waterline on the horizon.

Where was she? There was no way they could have passed each other, even if she took the seawall road back to the house. Maher began to get an uneasy feeling in the pit of his stomach. Where had she gone?

A faint voice drifted through the air and Maher stopped. He couldn't make out the words but he *knew* that was Ally.

Spinning in place, he searched up and down the beach, but couldn't lay eyes on her. The sound reached him again and Maher looked out to sea. Ally was standing up to her ribcage in the surf, jumping up with each wave that broke and letting them carry her along for the ride.

Ally was in the sea.

Ally, who couldn't swim, was in the path of the undertow.

"ALLY!" Maher dropped the lamp and wrenched his jacket off. "Ally, hold on!"

"Maher?" A wave caught her off guard and broke over her head. Maher was a few steps into the water when she surfaced, sputtering, and waved her arms at him. "Don't! It's alright, Maher!"

"What do you mean it's alright? Get out of there!" he shouted, his steps faltering as she used her arms to pull herself towards him. Swimming? She was *swimming*?

Ally looked around and he saw her lips moving. Maher blinked and finally saw who, or what, she was talking to. A woman's head, covered in long hair that blended into the water around them, with gray skin and black eyes.

The sea witch.

"Al, come here right now." He tried to track the creature, but she drifted in and out of focus as the sea rolled.

Ally splashed onto the beach in only a pair of breeches and an undershirt. Grabbing her hands, he pulled until they were well away from the waterline. When he looked again for the sea witch, she was gone.

"Maher?" she was speaking to him. "Maher, you can let me go. I'm fine."

"Fine? How could you possibly be fine? Ally, you..." Maher dropped her hands. "You were swimming."

"That's right." She smiled. *Smiled.* "Surprise?"

"How... how did you learn to swim?"

Ally jerked her chin over her shoulder. "She taught me."

Maher hardly heard her over the roaring in his ears. "And how long has this been going on?"

"Since I made the new bargain with her." Ally started up the beach. Maher grabbed his jacket and the lantern, catching up with her.

"Ally! How could you keep this from me?"

Reaching behind a large rock, Ally pulled out a bundle of clothes. "I haven't told anyone, Maher." She tugged a long-sleeved shirt over her wet clothes and held onto her boots. "Learning to swim, or at least *touch* the water without fainting, was the only way I was going to be able to join the crew sailing to rescue Mama."

"Do you realize how reckless it was not to tell anyone what you were doing? How do you know she won't turn around and drown you when your guard is down?"

"That's not fair! You don't even know her."

"I've heard enough about sea witches to know you shouldn't be trusting her so easily, even if she is helping you to rescue Rochelle. Who knows what disgusting, cruel things she's done to become one?"

"She's not a sea witch! She's –" Ally clapped one hand over her mouth.

"She's *what*, Ally?"

Ally glanced back at the darkened water, looking for something Maher couldn't see. When she faced him again, he could see her working out if she should tell him what she'd meant to say.

"What is she?" The lantern handle creaked in Maher's grip, grinding on its hinges.

Chin lifting, Ally said, "She's a mermaid."

"A *mermaid*?" He glanced behind her, seeing nothing but the faint outline of the water against the sky. "One of the creatures you insisted don't exist? I can't believe this."

"You said you believed in everything! Take no chances, remember?"

"Not when one of those things is taking you out – alone, I might add – into the ocean!"

"Those things? She is not a thing, she's a mermaid. And she's helping me to overcome the fear that's kept me paralyzed on this island for most of my life. Something no one else has ever offered!"

"Oh well, begging your pardon, princess!" Maher spat. "I'm sure that makes up for tricking your family into trading you for a few extra fish each year."

Ally backed out of the circle of lamplight. Shadows fell over her face, but not before Maher saw the hurt that settled deep into her eyes.

"Al... I'm sorry, I'm just worried about –"

With her boots still hugged to her chest, Ally sprinted down the beach.

"Ally, wait!" Maher started after her. There was a sharp splash to his right. A wave surged up past the tideline, soaking his trousers and dousing out the light. "Fuck!" He jumped back from the water, ready to swing the lamp at the ten-foot long, killer mermaid he'd conjured in his mind.

Finding nothing but the empty beach and his own shame, Maher chucked the lantern into the sea. He turned back up the beach, his clothes clinging wetly to his legs. How was he going to make this up to Ally? They'd never had a real fight before and the way she'd looked at him... it brought back a memory of a little girl trying to stand her ground against three bullies twice her size. Strong, stubborn, and so, so vulnerable.

Maher was halfway up the seawall when something crashed against the stones beneath him. Back pressed against the wall, Maher edged down a few steps until he could squint through the darkness, to the place where the base met the sand.

Lying just beyond the stairs was the mangled frame of his lamp. A dozen shards of glass scattered around it, where the globe had shattered against stone.

It took twice as long to navigate the manor grounds in the dark, only the lamps closest to the house were lit. Maher shivered as his wet trousers caught against his skin. He'd left the broken lantern where it was, maybe Ally would see it the next time she went down there. To him, it was proof he'd been right to warn her off the sea witch – the *mermaid* – and now he needed to redouble his efforts to get her out of that bargain.

As Maher stalked up the gravel drive to the house, leaving a wet trail of bitterness behind him, he met Gai, Luthais, and Cal walking back from the Kingsport road.

"Maher?" Luthais spotted him first. He eyed the other man's soaked clothes but made no remark on them.

"Did you find Ally?" asked Gai.

"Oh, I found her." He marched past them, "And she wasn't alone."

Cal grabbed his shoulder, "What's that supposed to mean?"

Maher jerked free and rounded on the three Kingfisher brothers. "I hope you all know what your sister has gotten herself into!"

CHAPTER SIXTY-ONE

Pasha watched the boy leave the beach. Maybe it was petty of her to splash him, but it was better than shocking him like she'd wanted. The way he'd spoken to Ally had sent sparks of electricity to gather at her fingertips. While it was clear Ally didn't need her to interfere and would have called for help if she did, Pasha wasn't going to let him completely get away with it.

She'd gathered, as she and Ally spent more time together, that he was her closest friend. That didn't give him the right to berate her like a child. Pasha didn't like that jab about the bargain either. It was none of his business.

The threads, woven through with her displeasure, spiked again when he threw that lantern at her. Or near her. He'd had no idea how close she really was at that moment. Still, Pasha waited until he was on the steps to throw it back. Ally might have been upset with him but knocking her friend senseless wouldn't have done Pasha any good.

And Ally, she'd defended Pasha to him. Even when he lashed out at her, she hadn't wavered.

You don't even know her.

How Pasha yearned to go to Ally now, to make sure she was alright. It wasn't the distance that kept her where she was, it was the thought of being caught by a guard, or a member of Ally's family, or the boy. Maher. They were too close to the day of departure for Pasha to risk it. She wanted to be there for Ally.

The words had surprised her the first time she thought them, but it was true. She did want to help Ally as much as she could. Bargain or no bargain.

She knew Ally was concerned they wouldn't be able to meet the ransom demands. The pirates had asked for more than the people on the islands had to give. Here was something Pasha could help with, calling on the talent she'd largely kept to herself. It had always unsettled the other mermaids in her shoal, made them wary of her even as a child. Now Pasha had a chance to put it to good use. She just needed to find the right shipwreck.

CHAPTER SIXTY-TWO

7 Days

With only two days before they planned to set sail, Cal said Ally had learned all she could before their departure and asked her to rest. Ally wasn't proud of it, but she'd been avoiding Maher since their fight on the beach. She wasn't angry anymore, exactly, but she honestly didn't know what to say to him. For all of the friendly barbs they'd traded over the years, none of them had ever been as sharp as that. Pasha likely wouldn't press her, but Ally knew the mermaid heard everything. With a morning where she had nowhere to be, Ally closed herself in the parlor to work on the map.

There was no telling how old it was. The style didn't match any eras she was aware of. Then again, it was made by the mermaids, wasn't it? Why would it match anything done by humans? Comparing it to the map book in the library only helped so much. Most of the detail was on the sea itself, not the land that bordered the edges.

Ally guessed there were five bigger mermaid communities marked, with several smaller ones scattered between. The shoal beneath the Birde

Isles had to be the largest one stitched next to three nameless hunks of land in an upper quadrant.

There was still a lot of work to do, and Ally was losing confidence that the stripe of brown down the middle could be saved. Then an idea came to her on her second day out on the sloop with Cal. Olebile was scraping salt and grime buildup from another sail in need of repair, the process made far easier by the coating meant to protect the material from saltwater. She'd asked Cal for the name of the shop that made the cloak the brothers gave Rochelle for her birthday. He was shocked she'd even brought it up but promised to write it down for her that evening. For now, she was repairing the rip at the top and stitching new threads along the colored shapes still visible on the blue of the sea. There wouldn't be time to visit the shop before they left, she'd have to do it when they returned home.

Ally's hands stilled for the space of a sigh, then started moving again. None of the others spoke of life after her mother's rescue, only the plans and preparations and gathering the ransom. Some might have thought it bad luck to say such things, but to Ally it felt wrong. As if they doubted Mama had a future to discuss.

Her chest ached and energy pulsed out from the shark tooth. Ally pressed it to her skin. Lately, she hadn't felt the need to hold it as much. Though she didn't dare take it off again, even to bathe, remembering what happened the night she met Pasha.

Pasha still didn't know Ally's theory that she was one of the Sea Kissed. No one did except for Esa, and the head priestess wouldn't say anything. But the more time she spent in the water, the more Ally was sure she was right.

She'd tell Pasha soon. After Mama was returned safely, then she'd explain everything. And Pasha would know exactly why Ally chose to remake the bargain.

A soft knock startled Ally out of her thoughts.

"Ally? Are you in there?"

Maher.

Taking her needle back up, Ally focused on the tapestry. "Yes, I'm here."

One of the parlor doors slid open, only half of his face came through. "May I come in?"

That was the first time he'd ever asked.

"Yes."

Maher stepped into the room, closing the door behind him. He seemed as unsure as she'd ever seen him, hanging by the doorway as if he expected Ally to order him back out. He looked like he'd slept in his clothes and his hair was noticeably out of place.

"I almost didn't look in here, it's been so long since you've worked on your sewing."

"I've had other things to do."

"Right," Maher edged closer. "Can I speak with you?"

She let the needle rest against the material. "What can I do for you?"

"Nothing, I mean, Ally... I want to apologize."

Ally waited, but he didn't move to speak again. "Whenever you're ready."

"I don't expect you to forgive me right away, if at all, for what I said. I'm sorry, I really am. I was worried about you, and I know, that's no excuse for jumping all over you like that."

"No, it wasn't."

"And I hope, someday, you'll forgive me." He huffed a sort of laugh. "We've been there for each other for so long, it didn't occur to me you might not need my help."

Ally's lips pressed together. That wouldn't have been an easy thing for Maher to admit. "Will you believe me now, when I say I can handle something?"

"Of course," Maher nodded quickly.

"And accept that I'm entitled to my privacy as much as you are?"

"Absolutely."

"Then, I forgive you," she gave him a small smile. "I don't like it when we aren't speaking, the last few days have felt so off. More than they already are."

"Thank you, Al!" He sat next to Ally and wrapped her into a hug. "I felt the same way."

Ally lay her head on his shoulder, breathing in the pine and spice scent she'd become used to on him. "I do need you Maher, I need your support."

"And you have it." Maher kissed the top of her head and released her. His nose scrunched up.

"What is it?"

"You taste like salt."

Ally chuckled. "I didn't have the energy to wash my hair yesterday. It's been hard to get it all out and I've been around the sea quite a bit lately, you know."

"I know," he scratched the whiskers on his jaw. "Al, about this mermaid,"

"Did you not just agree that you'll support me when I say I've got it under control?"

"I did, I did. I do! But Al, in the space of a summer you went from not believing in mermaids to swimming with them. It's a lot to take in!"

"It was hard enough for me to take in, and I'm the one doing it." Ally found she didn't want to get any deeper into this topic. She poked Maher's ribs and he twisted out of reach. "Besides, how boring would I be if I didn't have a few scandalous secrets?"

"Using something I would say against me, eh?" He gave her an easy smile. "Very good."

"I learned from the best there is."

"Will you tell me about your sailing lessons? Cal must think he's the greatest sailor alive to get you successfully onto a boat."

They talked together for the rest of the morning, only stopping once to ring for tea. Ally continued to work on the map, she was nearly done refreshing the colors around the border. After a servant cleared away the tea tray, Ally finished regaling Maher with the tales of her sailing progress.

"What about you?" She snipped off a thread. "Have you been on any daring adventures in between messenger runs? Your legs must be quite sturdy by now."

"Ah, yes, in the few brief moments I've had to myself I've accomplished many heroic deeds. In fact –" Maher stopped mid-sentence. His smile dropped.

"Maher? What's wrong?"

He stood and paced over the rug in front of her. "There are some things I've been wanting to tell you, for a while now. Things I think you have the right to know, Al."

"What things?" Ally spread the tapestry across her lap and stuck the needle into a pin cushion, giving him her full attention.

"I debated on whether I should say anything, I didn't want to add to the stress you were already under."

"What are you talking about? Does this have something to do with Mama?"

"In a way, more indirectly, at least part of it does." He rubbed the back of his neck. "I'll start with the easier one, if you could call it that."

"Just tell me, please."

Maher stopped in front of her. "I think one of your brothers may be involved with the plot to kidnap Rochelle."

"*What*?" He might as well have lapsed into Saprean, for all that she'd understood just now.

"It's hard to hear, I know, but I've seen Luthais..." Maher's eyes landed on the tapestry in her lap.

"Luthais? You've seen Luthais doing what?"

"What is that you're working on?"

"What does it look like?"

"Like you're trying to repair an old pillow cover?"

"Nice try," she huffed. "It's a map. What about Luthais?"

"A map for what?" He looked closer at the dilapidated material. "It doesn't look like a map of anything I've ever seen before."

Why would he stop in the middle of telling her something so important to talk about a sewing project? "It's a map for Pasha."

"Who's Pasha?"

Shit. Ally hadn't told Maher her name. "The mermaid."

"Let me get this right, you're repairing a *map* for the mermaid?"

"That sums it up pretty well. Now, what were you going to say?"

"Where does this map lead?"

Ally blew out a breath. She didn't want to tell Maher an outright lie, but she'd promised Pasha to keep her home a secret. It stood to reason that included the other mermaid communities and, to her surprise, Ally didn't really *want* to tell Maher more right now. "It could possibly tell her... where her family might have gone."

"You mean, there's more of her?"

"There were, yes."

Maher glared at the map, as if its very existence offended him. "Why would you want to do anything for the mermaid who's forcing you to leave your home?"

"It's not that simple, Maher."

"Not simple? In what way is it not simple?"

"It just isn't!"

"Ally, what aren't you telling me?"

"Something I promised I wouldn't."

"Promised? You're making promises to her now?"

"So what if I am?" Ally stood and placed the tapestry behind her on the sofa. "What is this really about, Maher?"

"It's about you getting yourself in even deeper with that mermaid than you already are! How can we get you out of it later if you keep this up?"

"Haven't we already had this argument?"

"What is it, Ally? Has she hypnotized you? Convinced you we won't get your mother home without her?"

"I'm the one who convinced *her* to help, and you know that!" Ally hissed. "Do you really think I'm so weak that I'd let anyone control me again? After my own family lied and kept me away from the sea all this time?"

"I never said that!" His brown eyes darted around the room, looking for an answer where there was none. "Don't let her come with you."

"Are you serious?"

"Yes, tell her not to come. I said before you didn't need her, I know I'm right."

"I'm not going to do that." She crossed her arms.

Maher threw his hands up. "If she's going, then I'm going to be with you on the *Wave Skipper*."

"You are absolutely not coming!"

"And why not?"

"Because *you* might get hurt! I'm pretty sure I'm a better sailor now than you are, Maher."

"Perhaps I could have learned if I didn't always stay here to keep you company."

"What horseshit! Maher, we met when you were trying to escape from another day out on a boat with my brothers."

"I'm not the same person I was twelve years ago."

"Well neither am I!"

They stared at each other, both breathing hard, neither willing to be the first to back down. A log snapped in the hearth and the clock on the wall ticked, but Ally and Maher said nothing.

"My lady, is everything alright?" Mrs. Thorley knocked on the door. "Only, I heard yelling."

Ally took a deep breath. "Everything is fine, Mrs. Thorley, thank you."

"If you're sure?" She still sounded doubtful.

"Yes, I am. Thank you for asking."

"Very well, if you need anything, my lady, please let me know." The sound of her heels clicking away on the hardwood floor let them know she'd gone.

"Al?"

"Yes?" She looked at Maher, he blinked hard against the tears swimming in his vision.

"Why won't you let me help you?"

"You *have* been helping me, Maher, you've always helped me. But I can't rely on someone else forever, this is something I need to do on my own."

"You won't be on your own, though, will you?"

"Cal and his crew are taking me there. Pasha will be nearby, to use her power over the sea if needed. She'll even be a sort of safety net if I end up in the water. But I'm the one rescuing Mama." She bit the inside of her cheek. If she was going to tell Maher about Pasha's gift, now was the time. Still, she couldn't. That had been a promise too. "I don't want you on the ship because I'd never forgive myself if anything happened to you."

Maher shook his head. "That's what I'm supposed to say to you."

"It can be true for both of us." She held out a hand. After a moment's hesitation, Maher took it. His warm, slender fingers wrapped over hers. "Is there something you're not saying, Maher? I really feel like this is coming from somewhere else, at least in part?"

"It might be," he looked down. "But it's nothing to worry you about, not right now."

MAHER

CHAPTER SIXTY-THREE

Maher splashed water onto his face, his head hanging over the basin in his room. Drops of water ran down his nose and dripped back into the shallow bowl.

Scooping up another handful, he pushed it through his hair until it was slicked back. He'd left the parlor before his mouth could get him into any more trouble and in the process he never finished telling Ally why he suspected Luthais. There'd be time to tell her on the journey.

He still believed he should be on the ship with her. It was the one point they couldn't come to an agreement on, and Maher didn't know how to go about it. If she really wanted to keep him on land, all Ally had to do was tell Cal's crew not to let him on board. They wouldn't refuse an order from Lady Alphonsine Kingfisher.

Maher stripped off his rumpled clothes and changed into one of the black suits he usually wore to the Lantern at night. Ally could read him so well. Even after he started the first two fights they'd ever had, she still burrowed down and saw there was something else fueling the fire.

And that something just burst through his door.

"Maher!" His father slammed the door shut. "What's this I hear about you yelling at Lady Alphonsine?"

"Good afternoon, Father," Maher buttoned his jacket. "I'm doing well, and you?"

"Answer me, boy. Did you get into a shouting match with Lady Alphonsine?"

"It works so well for you, I thought I'd give it a try."

"How dare you jeopardize everything we've worked for!"

"Everything *you've* worked for." He picked up the bottle of scent from his dressing table. "Make yourself Lord of Trade if you think it's so important. I'm done. I'm done with your games and your schemes. I'm done with all of it."

Khafra smacked the bottle from his hands. Perfumed liquid splashed down the front of his trousers and soaked into the rug, engulfing them in a pine-scented cloud.

Maher left the empty bottle where it landed. "Normally that would upset me, but at least it won't show on this suit."

"What is wrong with you, Maher? You'd rather be sent back home in disgrace than secure our place here?"

"This is my home. The Birde Isles are my home." He grabbed his coat and brushed past his father. "I'm not going anywhere."

He made it to the door before Khafra recovered from the shock of his son's icy tone. Maher twisted the knob, but his father held the door shut.

"I assume you're trying to make some sort of point, but hear me now. Disobey me in this, and I'll crush the little web of spies you've built for yourself."

Those words, so casually spoken, hit the back of Maher's head like a club. "What?"

"Do you truly think I don't know what you've been doing? That I was convinced all your cavorting in the Lantern was for pleasure? You've not been as careful as you think, Maher. Now, either you do as I say, or I'll make sure every so-called establishment you've ever set foot inside in the Lantern is shut down and the inhabitants thrown into prison."

Maher stared at a faint crack winding through the paint on his door, his mind racing. Khafra had to be bluffing. He couldn't possibly know about Mama Bear, Pimm, all the others. "You can't..."

"Can't I?" Khafra moved closer, boxing his son in. "I think you'll find I can do anything I like. Who would take the word of a criminal over that of an ambassador? Do you still not understand why Lady Alphonsine's endorsement is crucial? It's her *mother* that's been taken hostage and that ransom was designed to weaken the Isles beyond defense. Lord Kingfisher will do anything she asks of him now, anything that would both comfort his daughter and bolster their chances of retrieving Lady Kingfisher alive. As Lord of Trade I can secure enough silver from Saprea to pay the ransom twice over. Luthais has no such connections."

Maher braced a shaking hand on the doorframe, the other still gripped the knob hard enough to make his fingers go numb. It was the only thing stopping him from throwing his father bodily out of the room.

"If you ruin this now, Maher, I will make certain that everyone who once trusted you pays for it the rest of their lives." His hand slipped away, and Maher wrenched the door open. Ambassador Villaon's parting words followed Maher down the hall, "Enjoy your last night out. If you don't secure this position for me before Lady Alphonsine leaves, you'll be on the next ship to Saprea before she returns."

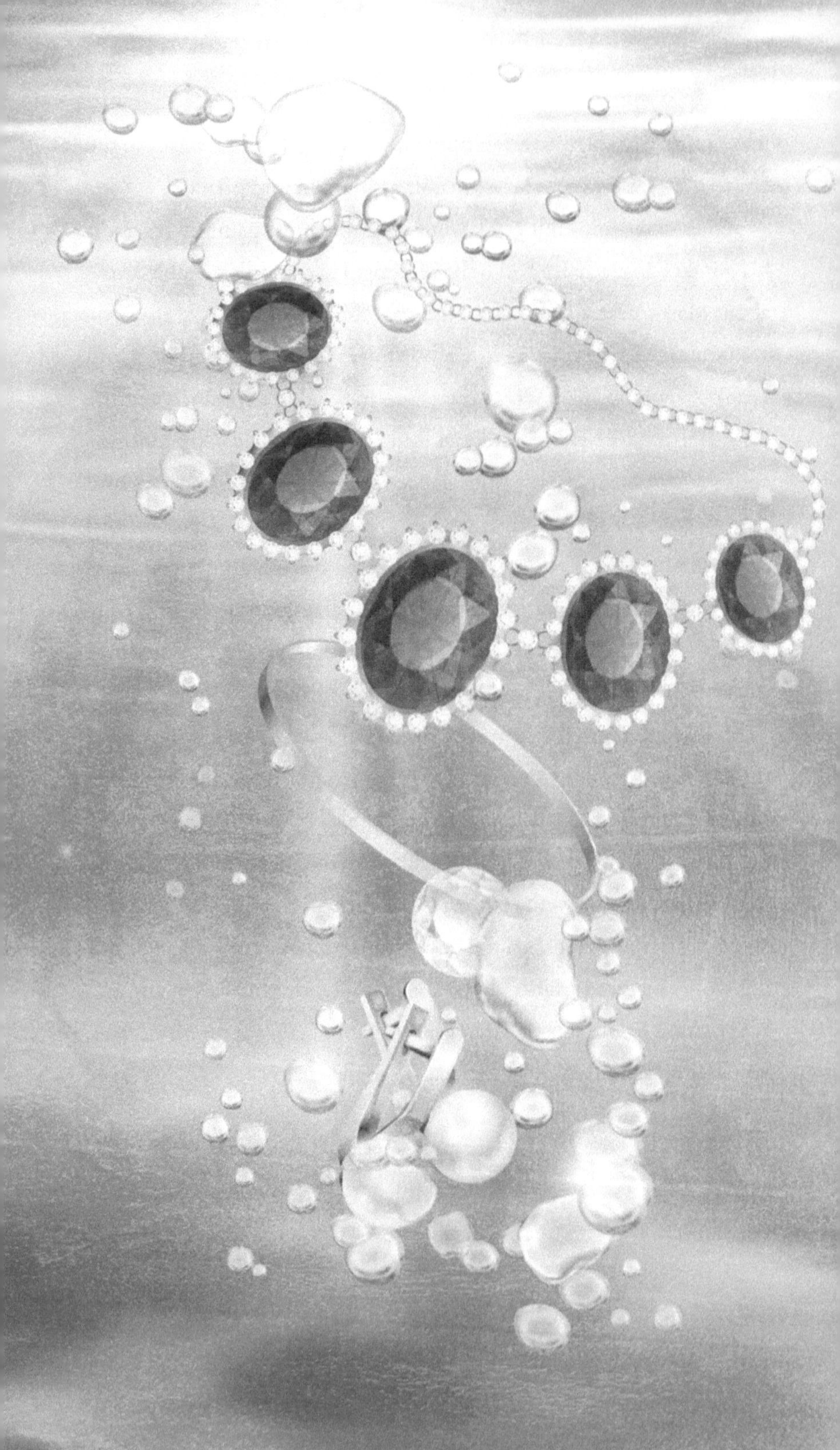

ROCHELLE

CHAPTER SIXTY-FOUR

Rochelle Kingfisher sat on the floor of the captain's cabin, working at the lock shackling her to a table.

She'd lost count of how many days she'd been on this wretched ship. After several failed attempts to remove the chain, she finally got hold of a fork and hid it from the sailor who brought her food and water once a day. Bending the other tines back against the table edge, Rochelle waited until she was alone and used it to dig around inside the mechanism.

Knowing nothing about locks, she wasn't sure she was actually doing anything. There was a small hope that it would break and come apart on its own. If that didn't work then she'd try the next thing, and the next, and the next. Whatever it took to get out of this cabin and off this ship. Rochelle had a vague idea of how to lower a longboat and enough knowledge of the stars to point herself toward home. If she could only get this damned chain off... the fork slipped and one of the bent tines scratched the top of her hand hard enough to draw blood.

Tears stung her eyes and Rochelle stopped short of throwing her only tool across the cabin. She blotted her hand with the hem of her ruined cloak and took deep breaths. It would pass, it didn't matter. Only her family mattered. Gaius and Ally, and the boys. And her people. She didn't know who Gaius would send to rescue her, but any sizable ransom would bankrupt the Birde Isles and put whoever brought it in untold danger. If only there was some way to warn them, to signal them not to come. Either Rochelle would get herself out or die in the attempt. That Captain Dare meant her family nothing but harm and Rochelle wouldn't stand for it.

A loud clang echoed from the decks below. The noise had gotten worse over the last few days. There was something abnormal about this ship. Something that even made the crew uneasy. She could see it in the faces of the ones who kept watch over her, especially after the noises increased. Rochelle might not have been a born sailor, but she knew enough to recognize something that didn't belong on a ship.

The lock on the cabin door clicked and she hurried to hide the fork in the pocket of her gown. It was too late to get back into the chair. Captain Dare walked in, and Rochelle tried to act like she'd meant to sit on the floor all along.

"Lady Kingfisher," she swept off her hat and gave a mocking bow.

Rochelle stood with as much dignity as possible with a chain around her leg. "What is it now?"

The captain clucked her tongue. "That's no way to greet the person who's been kind enough to share her cabin with you for a fortnight at least."

Had it truly been that long? Rochelle wrapped her hands in her skirt and glanced disdainfully around them. "Kind? Kind would have been to have never attacked my ship in the first place."

Captain Dare sneered, "I think I've been quite kind, considering where I could have left you. Would your ladyship have preferred to stay in the brig? With the bilge pump and rats for company?"

Rochelle knew Dare was trying to goad her, to frighten her into saying something she shouldn't. Instead, she lifted her chin and met the captain's eye, "You prefer to blame others for your own troubles, do you not? We both know your quarrel isn't with me."

"Do we?" Foraoise stalked closer, one hand going to the dagger in her belt.

"Yes, we do," she scoffed. "Don't punish me because you hold a grudge against a dead man."

Dare stopped a few paces from Rochelle. Her eyes went wide, the lines around her mouth tightened. An emotion that resembled something like pain twisted her features and Rochelle knew she'd plucked a nerve.

The victory was short-lived, and Rochelle had no room to move out of the way when Captain Dare struck. Closing the distance between them, one hand snaked around the back of Rochelle's neck and gripped a handful of her hair. The point of the dagger pressed beneath her chin.

Rochelle didn't move, willing her hands to hang limp by her sides. She could feel the blade kissing her skin, pressing just a little harder with each ragged breath the captain took.

Her forehead dropped to Rochelle's shoulder. The scratchy stubble on one side of her head grazed Rochelle's face. A scent that was earthy and slightly bitter filled her nose, the blood-like liquid the captain poured over her head before each attack on another ship. Rochelle had witnessed it a few times since she was brought here.

Foraoise's lips found Rochelle's ear, her raspy voice laced with rage, "Jon has nothing to do with this."

"Jon?" Rochelle breathed. "Were we talking about Jon?"

Dragging their cheeks together, Foraoise lifted her head until they were nose-to-nose, "Don't pretend now that you don't know." The hand in her hair let go and traveled down her arm. "The only reason your blood isn't painting my floor right now, is because you're currently worth more alive than dead."

Rochelle grit her teeth as the captain's hand ghosted over her side. Any move to free herself could send that dagger through her neck.

"But, if you ever mention him again," she grabbed Rochelle's hip. "I'll just have to take the loss of coin. Understand?"

Straining to keep her head up, Rochelle said, "I understand."

When Foraoise released her, Rochelle swayed with relief. Then the captain held up the fork from her pocket.

"You're resourceful, I admit. In another life we might have been friends." She twirled the fork between her fingers, all traces of anger gone. "But no more of this. You agreed to behave yourself and my patience has limits."

Sinking into a chair as soon as Foraoise was gone, Rochelle rubbed her aching scalp and considered what she'd learned. The fork was a loss, but she wasn't getting far with it anyway. Probably too soft to do anything but scratch the surface of the lock.

Something more important had come to light from that conversation. Captain Dare's outburst wasn't the reaction she'd planned for, but it was very, very educational.

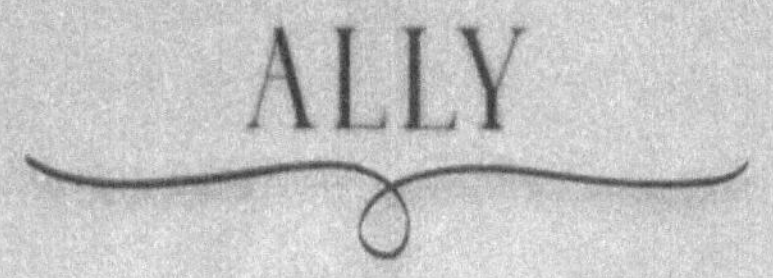

ALLY

CHAPTER SIXTY-FIVE

When Ally dragged herself down to the beach late that afternoon, she half-hoped Pasha would see how tired she was and repeat her offer to take a night off from their swimming lessons.

She would have no such luck.

"I want you to meet someone," Pasha said as soon as Ally reached the rocks. She'd never seen Pasha so excited, the scales peeking out across her shoulders and around the curve of her face were practically pulsing with energy.

"Who?" Ally shrugged off her coat.

"They're old friends of mine."

"Friends... like you?"

"No, not like me." She smiled wide, clearly enjoying whatever secret she was keeping. "They don't pass by here often, please come? I promise you'll like them."

"Fine," Ally yawned. "But if I get eaten, I'm blaming you."

"I can accept that. Come on!" Pasha grabbed Ally's hand and took off for the water. They waded in and dove under.

Ally barely had time to get her bearings before Pasha took her hand again and pulled her out to sea. Not even bothering to kick her legs, Ally held on and let Pasha do the work. The mermaid was a faster swimmer anyway. Cool water rushed over her face and through her borrowed gills, soothing and sweet. Ally shut her eyes for just a moment.

When Pasha came to a stop, Ally collided into her back and jerked awake. Had she really dozed off?

"I didn't realize how tired you were," Pasha's brow creased. "After we meet them, I'll take you back to shore."

"I'm not so tired..." Ally yawned again, and a huge bubble left her mouth.

Popping it with the point of a nail, Pasha's amused timbre was hard to miss, even inside Ally's head. "I'm sure you're not, but this will be a good lesson."

"How so?" Ally used her arms to balance when Pasha let go.

"You already know it's dangerous for humans to swim out of deep water too quickly."

She nodded. "The selkies train for years to dive as far as they do."

"We've come out pretty far to see my friends, so we'll take plenty of time going back. You may have an advantage now, but you still want to be careful with yourself."

Ally turned in place, the open ocean stretched out all around them. This was different from being out in the deeper water around the island. Her breath came a little faster. If she'd paid attention, and stayed awake, she could have gradually gotten used to it.

"Ally? I wouldn't bring you anywhere you couldn't handle." Pasha touched her arm.

"I know. There's just so much of it."

"Do you want to go back?"

Ally shook her head, then pushed her hair away when it wrapped around her face. How did Pasha never seem to have that problem? "I'm alright. We've come this far, and I want to meet these friends of yours. They don't have too many teeth, do they?"

Showing off her own sharp set, Pasha nudged Ally back a bit. "Try to stay here, I'm going to call them."

Ally was about to ask how that would work, when the white threads started running over Pasha's arms. They were much brighter out here, away from the glowing corals and with the sunlight dimmed by the depth. When she pressed her palms together, the threads concentrated around Pasha's wrists and arced across her knuckles. Forming a circle with her fingers, she pulled her hands apart until she had a ring of sizzling light. Ally tasted the electricity. It tingled across her neck, into her gills and through her body, and she felt very much awake.

Pasha released the ring into the water. It floated in front of them for a few breaths, then expanded before shooting out and away. Pasha stretched her arms, "Now we wait for them to respond."

"Pasha, how do you do that?"

Lifting a hand, Pasha concentrated until a collection of new threads danced over her palm. "Do you know the electric currents that occur within storms?"

Ally blinked. "Yes! Scientists on the continent have been working to harness them."

"Oh?" Pasha's lips twisted into a wry smile, as if she doubted they'd be very successful. "There are also tiny electric charges throughout the sea, thousands and thousands of them. I pull them to me."

"You just *pull* them to you?" It was Ally's turn to be skeptical.

"I'm not sure I could explain it any better than that." Pasha scanned the open water around them. "The old humans called it magic, but that's not quite right either. It's something I was born with, not a trick I learned."

Ally swam closer, "It's just electricity?"

"Electricity and energy. My energy I suppose. I have a limited amount, it takes time to build back up." Carefully, as if giving Ally the chance to pull away, Pasha reached out and caressed the polished surface of the shark tooth hanging around her neck. "It's the same energy I put into this. I don't know why it's changed. Why you can't take the tooth off without it causing you pain. I never meant for that to happen. But I swear I'm going to fix it."

A jolt of heat pulsed from the tooth, Ally felt it even though it wasn't touching her skin. She didn't realize how badly Pasha felt about her dependence on the shark tooth. The mermaid still didn't know Ally was Sea Kissed. Ally's reasons for not telling her seemed childish now. "I know you didn't. And, honestly, right now I need it for –"

"They're here!" Pasha pointed ahead of them. Ally squinted through the murkiness, seeing nothing at first. Slowly, several oblong shapes started to form in the distance. A long, low, croon wove through the water and encased them in a bubble of sound. Ally felt it vibrating over her skin.

Whales! Pasha had called a pod of whales.

Pasha waved and did a small backflip, her tail fins flicking hard in their direction. Ally laughed, bubbles escaping through her lips. At that moment Pasha looked so much younger, happier.

"I've never seen a real whale. Only pictures and carvings."

"This family has been around a long time. I try to see them when I can."

Ally gasped as the lead whale got closer. It was bigger and more grace-ful than anything she could have imagined. Pasha swam out to meet them. She stroked the whale's face, beneath its eye, more white threads passed between them. When she motioned for Ally to come closer, the whale crooned again and let out a high-pitched whistle. The call bounced off her chest and burrowed into Ally's heart. As she swam to Pasha's side, the rest of the pod closed around them. Pasha took Ally's hand and brought her close to the first whale. Ally wracked her brain for what kind of whales they might be, dark gray with white patches along their underbellies and fins. She forgot to ask when Pasha guided her palm to the whale's head. A serene blue eye the size of a dinner plate gazed at her, and Ally ran both hands over the bumpy skin around it.

"They're so wonderful." Ally might have been crying, but who could tell underwater.

"I told you that you'd like them. Would you like to meet the little one?"

Ally looked over, the little one was the size of a carriage and enthusiastically bumping its snout against Pasha's tail.

"Easy!" Pasha scratched the space between the calf's eyes. "That's the only tail I've got."

"Do they understand you?"

"Sort of, not in words so much as emotions. Sometimes pictures."

The calf squealed at them, and Ally helped to pet it. "Do you sing with them?"

"I wouldn't attempt it."

"Can't you sing?" Ally teased.

"No. Can you?"

"Not very well. I thought all mermaids could sing?"

The hard ridge above one of her eyes lifted incredulously, and it took that movement for Ally to notice that Pasha had no eyebrows to match her blue hair.

"If you're thinking of a hypnotic, irresistible song that lures sailors to a watery grave, those are sung by the sirens. Our cousins."

Ally's head swiveled, seeing nothing but the whales and endless water. "Are there any sirens here?"

"Don't worry, they prefer warmer climates."

After the whales moved on, they made their way back to Kingfisher Island at a leisurely pace. Pasha encouraged Ally to really pay attention to how her body felt, the closer they got to the surface. Any discomfort, and she made them stay at that depth a little longer. By the time they broke the surface the moon was high, and land was in sight.

"I'm glad you went with me to see them." Pasha gave Ally a break and towed her to shore.

"I'm glad you invited me."

"I think I might have pestered you into going."

"Either way, I'm very glad I went. I only wish..."

"You wish, what?"

They hit the point where Ally could stand. Pasha grunted as her tail split.

"I was just thinking, how much Mama would have loved that," Ally stopped before she made herself cry.

Pasha waited until they were on the sand to speak again. "When we bring her home, you can introduce her to the whales if you like. She'll have to stay in a boat of some kind, for her safety, but – Ally, what is it?"

The tears had come anyway, sliding down her cheeks, mingling with the saltwater beading on her skin. Ally started to wipe her face with her sleeve, then remembered it was soaked already.

"Should I not have said that?"

"It's not that, it's... it feels like I'm one of the only people thinking of life after Mama is saved. Everyone else is too scared to talk about her that way, except Maher. It's nice to hear someone else talk about the things Mama will do *when* she's home again, and not *if*." Ally picked up her jacket and pressed it against her face. When she pulled it down, Pasha was bracing herself on a rock. Her face twisted as if she were in physical pain. "What's wrong? Did you change too fast?"

"No, I'm fine, but I have something I want to say." Pasha looked her in the eye. "I'm letting you out of the bargain."

BEAR'S DEN

PIMM

CHAPTER SIXTY-SIX

Pimm wasn't the kind of person who went in for vices.

Not gambling or drinking, lust or greed. It was part of what made them an ideal door guard for a place like the Bear's Den. No one was going to bribe their way past Pimm, though plenty had tried. On a daily basis Pimm saw what vices did to those who let them take over their lives and wanted no part in it.

Except for one.

An empty tobacco pouch was what had them slipping out the bear-knocker door on their break, instead of spending it eating or napping in a spare room.

There should have been enough to last for the whole night, Pimm didn't smoke every hour on the hour like some people. A fight broke out early on in the evening between two patrons, not even the Bear's Den had been spared from the tension gripping the city. Before they broke it up, Pimm took a good shove from behind and the pouch went flying, scattering tobacco leaves like streamers at a parade. Mama Bear was livid that two of her patrons would disrespect the Den and disrupt the experience of everyone else. She revoked their tokens then and there, tossing them into the great stone fireplace.

There was a shop that stayed open late on the edge of the district. They charged extra for their goods, but they were the only option if you didn't want to wait until morning. It would take Pimm the entire break to walk there and back.

It might save me some shoe leather if I cut back, thought Pimm. The shop was only a few blocks away by then. *I'll cut back after this one.*

Pimm didn't linger in the shop, Maher was expected sometime that night and Pimm had finally heard back from the Madam of the black lantern. Maher had handled the revelation that she was Mama Bear's family better than Pimm expected. He didn't overreact, anyway. It was a night of revelations. There were a lot of questions, only a few that Pimm could answer. They didn't even know the Madam's real name, just as they didn't know Mama Bear's real name. Probably never would, and that didn't bother Pimm. Those two could have been long-lost royalty for all Pimm knew.

With a full tobacco pouch that they'd definitely overpaid for, Pimm started the walk back to the Bear's Den and enjoyed their first smoke since the night began.

If Pimm had been paying more attention, they might have noticed the darkened streetlamps that had been lit during the walk to the shop. They also might have noticed how much quieter this part of the city was than usual. When someone coming the opposite way veered into Pimm's path, they tried to step out into the street to avoid a collision. Another person materialized out of the shadows and shoved Pimm towards the nearest alley. When they twisted around to run the other way, both the strangers blocked Pimm inside.

"There's no passing through without paying the toll," a new voice echoed from inside the alley. Pimm backed up to a wall as a lantern was lit, and they saw the lapels of a familiar green jacket trimmed with gold thread.

Not good.

"I didn't see a sign." Pimm tried to count the weapons they held, but couldn't get a clear view with only the small lamp for light.

"Think you're so smart, don't ya?" The larger of the two bodies blocking the way out came closer, and Pimm was looking at the face of a sailor they'd thrown out of the Den. One of his shipmates stood next to him.

Definitely not good.

"My apologies," Pimm smoked the last of the cigarette, the end glowed red in the darkness. "You should have said you couldn't write or read, I wouldn't have asked otherwise."

"I know who you are, *mite*." The big one loomed over them. "Hand over everything you've got and maybe I'll leave you with enough teeth to still ask fancy folk for tokens."

With a turn of the wrist and the soft click of a lever, the knife up Pimm's left sleeve dropped into their hand.

"Hurry up!" the man wearing Maher's jacket barked. "Before anyone else comes by."

I really should have quit smoking tonight. Pimm threw the smoldering end of that last cigarette into the sailor's face and pushed off the wall as the other came charging in with a knife of his own.

CHAPTER SIXTY-SEVEN

"What did you say?"

"I'm ending the bargain, Ally. I'll still help to get your mother home safely, and I'll bring the fish back to the islands." Pasha's throat burned. "But I won't hold you to anything else."

Ally gaped at her, not unlike the first night they met. "Why now?"

"Because it was wrong of me to make that deal in the first place. You said it yourself, you're not a sack of coins, you're a person." She looked down, "And I was only thinking of myself then."

"It wasn't only you. Gaius took the bargain without a second thought, and I made the new one. It was my idea."

"He did, and you did, and I'm releasing you both."

"I..." Ally pressed the heel of her hand between her eyes. "I can't think about this right now."

"Ally, there's nothing to think about. Nothing for you to do but focus on getting your mother back. You're free of this."

"There's plenty to think about! I had everything worked out and I can't, it's not, no." Ally started to sit on the rocks, changed her mind, and grabbed the rest of her clothes instead. "We'll talk about this after Mama is home."

"I don't understand. I thought you'd be glad –"

"*After* Mama is home." She left without another word.

Pasha let her go. She thought it would be a relief to Ally, not to be bound to her anymore. They'd still go together to save her mother, and Pasha would still keep her word. Maybe it was too much, after everything else that had happened since the summer. Pasha refused to entertain the idea that Ally might *want* to keep the bargain, when she didn't even know what Pasha would ask in return. Ally was smarter than that.

With nothing else to keep her on land, Pasha made her way back home. The corals lit up to welcome her, but the passages and caverns beneath the island felt emptier than ever. Pasha curled up in one of the smaller chambers and drifted into a fitful sleep.

# MAHER

CHAPTER SIXTY-EIGHT

Maher was running through the streets of Kingsport, dodging people, carts, and carriages.

When the barkeep said Pimm was late returning from their nightly break, a cold sweat broke out on the back of Maher's neck. Pimm was never late when it came to their job. He asked if anyone knew where their door guard had gone. Barkeep mentioned the fight from earlier that night and how Pimm's tobacco pouch had been a casualty.

There was only one shop near the Lantern district that stayed open after dark. Maher told them to let Mama Bear know where he'd gone and bolted out the door. But which route would Pimm have taken? The most direct option was through the southern end of the square, so that's the one Maher chose. Every few blocks, Maher would slow to a jog and listen. He heard nothing out of the ordinary, if anything the streets outside the Lantern were unusually quiet, even at night. Quiet wasn't comforting.

Maher was about halfway to the shop, he crossed an intersection of two larger streets and hit a block with all the streetlamps put out except one. Behind him and at the far end of the neighborhood they were still lit. Only this section was dark.

Staying close to the buildings, Maher slowed to a walk, trying to breathe as soundlessly as possible. His blood was pumping through his veins, he could feel it in his fingertips. Maher stopped when the sounds of a scuffle reached him. Across the street, a light bobbed around the mouth of an alley, and he heard someone who sounded very big and very angry.

Maher took out his pistol, glad he'd already secured it before his father came into his room, and darted across the street. Every window nearby was dark. Either no one was there, or no one wanted to get involved. Were there no Kingsport guards stationed nearby? They were outside the Lantern now and there was a guard post in each neighborhood.

He reached the alley. Mr. Very Big and Very Angry had Pimm pinned to the wall, one big hand wrapped around their neck. There was a second figure slumped on the ground nearby. A third with blood running down one side of his face was holding the lantern. And wearing Maher's godsbedamned jacket.

"I've had enough of you, mite." The big one pulled a folded blade from his pocket and flipped it open.

"We know you're helping those Kingfishers starve us out," said the other. "What did you think's gonna happen? We'd just let them get away with it?"

Pimm wheezed and kicked the big one in the shin. He cursed and bounced Pimm's head off the wall. The knife flashed in the lamplight.

Maher didn't wait to see what would happen next. He stepped into the mouth of the alley, pistol raised, and fired.

BEAR'S DEN

PIMM

CHAPTER SIXTY-NINE

A loud crack echoed down the street and the sharp smell of gunpowder coaxed Pimm's eyes open. Stars still danced in front of them, left over from their head meeting a brick wall.

The sailor Pimm hadn't managed to drop grunted, let go of their neck and grabbed his own side. Pimm collapsed onto the ground like a rag doll. Pain shot through their ribs every time they took a breath.

"Fuck, fuck, fuck," the big sailor leaned against the opposite wall where his shipmate's body was already growing cold.

"Who's there?" The man holding the lantern lifted it higher. His other hand reached inside the jacket.

Maher stepped into the light and, even though it hurt like fire, Pimm's heart lifted.

"If it isn't Lord Kingfisher's magpie."

"Of course it's him, innit?" the sailor growled. "Come to save your little mite again?" He choked, streaks of blood and spittle running down his chin.

"I'm alright with that," Pimm croaked.

Maher didn't take his eyes off the two men. "And it's you attacking them again, isn't it?"

"If you were smart, you'd leave," the leader sneered. "You're still outnumbered two-on-one."

"I'd say it's one-on-one, if my aim was any good."

"Eat shit!" The sailor tilted to the side, one knee hitting the ground.

Maher ignored him and kept his pistol on the last one standing. "You know, I thought I'd never have the pleasure of seeing you again. I like that jacket. I think I'll have it back."

"You think so, do you?"

Wincing against the burn in their side, Pimm slipped another knife from inside a boot.

"There's nowhere else for you to go." Maher sidestepped closer to Pimm. "I'll say this for the old wharf crews, they never would have been stupid enough to target a Lantern employee."

"Things are changing 'round here. We've got backing the old crews never had and I suggest you get used to it." He drew his own weapon. "Get 'em!"

The injured sailor threw himself at Maher. He shielded Pimm and shot the man a second time, just as the other pistol went off. Maher ducked, but the shot went wide. When he looked up again, the last man was laying on his back with Pimm's knife buried to the hilt in his breast.

Pimm gasped for breath. Something in their chest had cracked when they threw the knife. If the man hadn't been holding the light, Pimm didn't think the knife would have found its target.

Maher made sure all three of the would-be robbers were dead, then grabbed the lamp and ran to Pimm.

"Are you hurt?" He checked the back of Pimm's head.

"Something's broken, but it's not my skull." Pimm gritted their teeth, "I'm afraid I got blood all over your jacket."

"It doesn't matter." Maher found Pimm's cap on the ground and handed it to them. "You hold onto that, I'm going to see if we can get you up."

"You know, I've never been so glad to see you, Maher," Pimm tried to lighten the mood. But the moment Maher wrapped an arm around their waist, fresh stars flashed before their eyes and Pimm's world went dark.

# MAHER

CHAPTER SEVENTY

Pimm was still unconscious when Maher got them both through the back door of the Bear's Den. Maher didn't consider himself particularly strong, but Pimm's smaller size made carrying them easier than it might have been.

Now he was sitting on the sofa in Mama Bear's room, elbows braced on his knees and his face in his hands. He'd been banished there while the physician, whom she paid a hefty fee to be available at night, examined Pimm.

"Well?" Maher asked for the fifth time.

"Patience, Mr. Villaon." The physician had a screen drawn around the bed for privacy. Her calm tone did nothing to make Maher feel better. He'd rather she was shouting orders at him, at least then he'd feel useful.

The extent of the damage that he'd seen was bad enough. Though the physician said it wasn't a deep enough wound to cause damage to the brain, the back of Pimm's head was covered in blood, split open from hitting the wall. One eye was swollen shut and a bruise was already spreading across their face beneath it.

When Maher first tried to lift Pimm, they'd cried out and fainted. Pimm had said something was broken, but Maher couldn't leave them in the alley to get help. Eventually he settled on wrapping his coat under Pimm and tying the arms around his own neck to make a sling. It was after midnight by the time he reached the alley behind the Den. He'd taken as many side streets as possible on the way back.

Maher kicked on the door until Olga peeked through the tiny lens set at eye level. When she saw Pimm in Maher's arms she shrieked and threw the door open. All of the employees liked Pimm, Mama Bear was keeping them at bay and ensuring none of the patrons knew what was happening upstairs. Barkeep was probably slinging a lot of free liquor.

"*Well*?"

"Mr. Villaon," the physician's frowning face appeared around the screen. A braided streak of gray ran through the left side of her dark hairline, Maher focused on that instead of her stern expression. "If you say the word 'well' again, I will have you removed from the room. Do you understand?"

Maher laced his fingers together and leaned back against the sofa. "Yes."

"Thank you." She disappeared again.

A muscle in the side of Maher's jaw ticked. If those bastards weren't already dead, he'd go back and crack their heads open.

Bile rose in his throat and Maher dove for a potted plant on the balcony. When he'd retched up everything in his stomach, he sank back onto his heels and took a shaky breath.

"Here, drink this." A glass of water was placed in his hand.

Maher looked up at the physician. "Don't worry about me, I'd rather you see to Pimm."

"I'm finished, for now." She helped him back to the sofa. He held the glass with both hands while she pushed his hair out of his face. "Follow my hand with your eyes." She lifted two fingers and moved them in a random pattern. When she seemed satisfied, she felt his forehead and the pulse in his neck. "Drink the water, see if it stays down."

"What about Pimm?" Maher took a sip.

She checked behind the screen, then came back to sit in a chair across from him. "There are cracked ribs, three that I can tell. They will take time to mend and Pimm must sleep upright until they're healed. There isn't much else I can do beyond recommending a pain reliever."

"Pimm won't take it."

"No? Not even willow bark?"

"That might work, but nothing stronger."

"We'll see. I had to give them something during the examination."

He finished the water, his stomach gurgled once, then settled. "What else?"

"I've stitched the cut on the back of their head. I had to remove some of the hair to clean it, but not too much. The rest of Pimm's injuries are mostly bruises and scrapes, but I want to test their vision when they wake up. This could have been much worse, had you not arrived when you did."

"Thank you, doctor, very much. Whatever this costs, whatever else Pimm needs, I'll pay for it."

"There's no need, the Bear's Den will cover everything."

"But–"

"Mama Bear insists."

As if saying her name summoned her like a spirit, Mama Bear bustled into the room with a tea tray. She spotted them sitting together. "What news, Tambara? How is Pimm?"

"Come, set that down. I'm going to check on them and then I'll tell you everything." She nodded at Maher. "Give him some tea, he could use it."

Mama Bear set the tray on the low table in front of Maher, pausing long enough to plant a kiss on his cheek before pouring the tea.

Maher couldn't be sure, but it looked as if she'd been crying. The tip of her nose and the corners of her wide, blue eyes were red. A hot cup of tea was soon in his hands. It smelled like lavender.

"Can't I have something stronger?"

"You're looking a little gray, darling. Tambara is right, tea first."

"Yes, dear. By the way, you might need to re-pot that fern on the balcony," Maher winced.

Mama Bear sighed and sat next to him. "I'll tend to it later. First, I have to thank you, Maher. I know Pimm was your friend before they started here, but we've all grown so fond of them... When you came in, Pimm was so still, I thought –" tears spilled down her plump cheeks.

Maher put his cup aside and held her while she composed herself. She reached into his waistcoat and helped herself to a handkerchief.

"I'm sorry, my little magpie," she dabbed at her eyes.

"Don't be," he rubbed her back and checked that Doctor Tambara was still behind the screen. He lowered his voice, "What should we do, about the bodies? The alley is just south of the Lantern."

"I've sent a note to Mother, she'll take care of it."

"Mother?"

"Yes. She liked you, by the way. Although she tried to insinuate that you were too young for me, but I told her," she searched his face. "What's wrong? Your color is off again."

Maher groaned, letting his head fall between his knees. Talking of removing the bodies and her mother, the Madam, reminded him why he'd come to see Pimm in the first place. The look on the sailor's face the second time Maher shot him flashed through his mind.

"Maher? Do you need the doctor?"

"No," he grabbed her hand to stop her from rising. "I'll be fine."

"Then, what is it? Surely my bringing up Mother didn't make you ill?"

"It didn't, but I appreciate the concern." Maher straightened and his stomach flipped, but he wasn't going to be sick again. "I've been carrying that pistol for almost two years. I've been forced to draw it before, and even fire a few warning shots, but I've never had to kill anyone until tonight. I didn't see any other way to get Pimm out of there."

"That was an impossible decision, I know. I've been there myself." She smoothed his brow. "You mustn't let it consume you, darling."

"Are you ready to talk?" the doctor said as she came back out.

"Of course." Mama Bear handed Maher's tea back to him, "Drink this and I'll have food and wine sent up."

Tambara pushed part of the screen together. "Will you keep an eye on Pimm until we return?"

"Go ahead," Maher moved to the chair nearest to the bed. Pimm was propped up against a stack of pillows, with more on each side in case they tipped over. "I don't have to be anywhere else for a while."

6 Days

After eating the meal Mama Bear sent him, Maher dozed in his chair for the rest of the night. Only waking if Mama Bear or the doctor came to check on Pimm.

By morning, he had a kink in his neck, but some color had returned to Pimm's face. Maher worried Pimm had been given too much medicine, they didn't stir all night. But if Mama Bear trusted Doctor Tambara to see to her employees, then Maher would try to trust that they both knew what they were doing.

He thought about sending a note to Ally explaining his absence, but what if his father saw it? Maher couldn't give himself away, not yet.

Breakfast was served and Mama Bear came in to change her clothes. She'd slept in the room next door. There was a kind offer for Maher to bathe or get some sleep in another bed, but he wanted to be there when Pimm woke up.

It was midmorning, Maher walked several laps around the room and out to the balcony. The unfortunate fern had been removed while he slept. Someday he would ask Mama Bear how she, and apparently her mother, got things done so quickly. The blankets on the bed rustled and Maher raced back across the room. Pimm gazed dazedly at him, one gray eye still swollen shut.

"Pimm, thank the gods." He moved next to them. "I thought you were going to sleep into next year."

"It feels like I did," Pimm rasped, grimacing at the sound of their voice. Maher retrieved a glass of water from the bedside table and helped Pimm drink.

"Better?"

"More or less." Pimm tugged at the collar of the nightshirt Mama Bear provided. "This is a little tight, could you?"

Maher undid the top buttons holding the collar shut. When it fell open, he hissed through his teeth. An angry, red handprint wrapped around Pimm's throat. The physician hadn't mentioned that.

"Do I look as bad as I feel?" Pimm tried to chuckle and coughed instead. A hand flew to their side.

"Careful, you've cracked a few ribs." Maher straightened the pillows so Pimm could sit more comfortably. "Otherwise, you look fantastic. Really, I must know your secret."

"Jackass." Pimm laid a hand on his arm, "Thank you, Maher."

"You've rescued me from a similar situation. We should stop spending so much time in alleys."

"This city is full of alleys. I should stop smoking, that might be easier."

"True, at least until your ribs heal. Would you like something to eat? Some tea? The doctor recommended willow bark for the pain."

"Doctor Tambara?" Pimm shifted and blanched when the stitched wound on their head grazed the pillow. "I don't even want to know why the back of my head is chillier than the rest. Willow bark tea it is."

When Maher returned with the tea and a bowl of porridge from the kitchen, Pimm asked for an account of the night before. Maher was able to tell it all without feeling ill. It was starting to feel like the whole thing had been relayed to him by someone else, that he hadn't really been there.

When the physician arrived to examine Pimm, she was pleased they were eating already. Her instructions were for Pimm to stay in Mama Bear's room for two more days, then they could move next door if Pimm wanted. Mama Bear came in with lunch and fussed over Pimm until Maher gently chased her out. Pimm looked exhausted from all the attention, and the willow bark tea would only help so much.

"Sleep, I'll be over on the sofa if you need anything."

"Wait," Pimm stopped him. "Before that, and before anyone else comes in, isn't there something you want to know?"

"What's that?" Maher perched on the edge of the bed.

"You haven't asked about our mission."

"What mission?"

"The purple lantern! It's only appeared twice since you last saw it," said Pimm. "They must be wrapping up their business in the Lantern."

"Let me guess, we missed it."

"You guessed wrong. Madam did get someone inside."

He leaned forward. "She did? Who?"

The corner of Pimm's mouth lifted, "Marielle."

"Marielle? How in all the gods' names did she manage that?"

"Don't ask because I don't know. She didn't hear much, but it was enough to make the mission worth our while."

"How so?"

"We know something no one else in Kingsport is privy to and it's going to help you go on the journey with Lady Alphonsine if that's still your plan. We just have to get you onto the ship without being seen."

"How? The *Wave Skipper* is going to be surrounded by guards and crew."

"That's not the ship you want to be on."

CHAPTER SEVENTY-ONE

With only one more night until Ally expected to set sail, Pasha wasn't sure if she would come to the shore. The way they'd left things still had her feeling restless. She'd decided Ally must be too concerned for her mother to focus on what Pasha was trying to say. She hoped Ally would come for a short visit, at least. There was more to the plan she needed to relay.

Ally arrived late that afternoon, walking slowly down the beach to where Pasha stood in the surf. She looked like she'd hardly slept at all.

"I'm glad you're here," Pasha said. Some of the tension in Ally's shoulders slipped away after she stepped into the sea. Quite a difference from the first time they were here. "I'm sure you want to rest for tomorrow. We don't have to swim, but I do need to make you aware of a few things."

"I still want to swim." She bent to swish her hands through the tiny waves that hit their legs. "Can we talk out there?"

"Of course we can." They dove under and Pasha took Ally to her home again. This time, Ally was prepared for the darkness of the passage until they reached the corals. Inside the main chamber, Pasha showed Ally a polished stretch of rock where they could rest. Despite her insistence that she wanted to swim, Ally looked too tired to go much further.

Ally gazed up at the glittering rock of the chamber ceiling. Before Pasha could speak, she asked, "What's the most ridiculous myth about mermaids? Besides that you eat people."

Pasha thought for a moment. "That we can all raise ships full of sunken treasure from the ocean floor."

"You can't do that?" Ally smirked, still admiring the ceiling. "How disappointing."

"Not whole ships, anyway."

She finally looked at the mermaid. "Really?"

"We all have our own talents, just like humans," Pasha shrugged. "Some of us can find certain treasures more easily than the others. My sister, she could sense different metals."

"What about you?"

"I know when gemstones are nearby. And..." she trailed off. Would Ally want to know about Pasha's other gift? Would she be as uncomfortable as the others in Pasha's shoal had been when they saw it?

"And?" Ally prompted. "You can tell me. Is it something difficult to describe, like how the elders could turn humans into mermaids?"

"Nothing like that." Pasha pressed the tip of her tongue hard enough against her teeth to cause a small spike of pain. She didn't want to scare her, but Ally hadn't shied away from anything about Pasha since the day they made their new bargain. "It would be easier to show you."

Holding one palm out towards the sandy cavern floor, Pasha closed her eyes, opening up her senses and waiting for the tell-tale prickle in her skull. Gradually, a dozen random bones of different ages and from different creatures wriggled out of the sand. None were bigger than one of her own fingers. Next to her, Ally gave a surprised squeak when the bones circled together and began to dance between them. Relief flooded through Pasha when she looked up and found Ally watching the bones in wonder rather than fear or disgust.

"Have you always been able to do that?"

"As far back as I can remember." Her fingers twitched, the bony cyclone slowed and switched direction. "They listen to me."

"You can sense the presence of jewels and bones *listen* to you?" Ally held her palm out towards the swirling bones, as if she were warming it by a fire. Bits of sand bounced off her skin. "Not even our stories about mermaids mention anything like this. Could any of the others move pieces of bone around at will?"

"Only me, that I know of." Pasha tried to swallow past the lump in her throat. Why bother telling Ally that Pasha was already considered strange even before they abandoned her here?

"But, what can you do with an ability like that?" Ally pressed.

Nothing good.

"I was always the first one called when it was time to clean out the old tunnels."

She gave a small chuckle, turning her attention back to the still-spinning collection of bones. They watched them dance a little while, until Ally spoke softly, "Pasha?"

"Hmm?"

"Could you turn someone like me into a mermaid?"

"I don't know," Pasha frowned slightly. "I don't exactly know how it was done before. What little I heard came in bits and pieces."

"I see." An emotion Pasha couldn't catch flashed through Ally's eyes and was quickly blinked away. "What did you want to tell me?"

At the abrupt change in subject, Pasha lost control of the bones and they landed in a small heap. "Well, I want to send some of the whales ahead of your brother's ship, to get an idea of what's waiting for us there."

"They'd do that? Really?"

"If I ask nicely, they will."

Her brow wrinkled. "How will they know where to go? I wouldn't think whales could interpret map coordinates."

"You know roughly where we're going, yes?"

"Of course. I've stared at Gai's maps for so long, I've got them memorized. It's at least two day's sailing southwest from the end of the continent."

"I'll have them go out ahead in the direction the ship is traveling and split into smaller groups once they reach that area. They can cover a much larger distance that way. The ones who find anything will send messages back."

"I must find a way to thank them."

Pasha cast her eye towards the mouth of the largest passage. "I have another friend or two that might follow. I wanted you to meet sooner, but I asked them to stay away until you were more comfortable."

"What kind of friends are they?"

"There's one waiting outside, can she come in?"

Ally scooted closer to her. "I guess so, if you want me to meet her."

"I didn't want you to be surprised to see her near the ship, and I hoped you wouldn't draw the crew's attention."

"Why?" Ally brows rose. "It's not one of your cousins, is it?"

"No, no! I don't mean to keep you in suspense." She sent a small thread into the largest passage and felt it echo back. Soon the corals lit up, as the great shark glided past them into the chamber. She was twice as long as Pasha, a matriarch in her own right. Scars crisscrossed over her thick gray skin. Ally moved faster than Pasha'd ever seen. She was jerked backwards by Ally's sudden grip on her shoulders, her knees digging into Pasha's back.

"You didn't say it was a shark!"

"Ally!" Pasha didn't try to remove her, but she pushed them off the rock before Ally squashed her dorsal fin. "I told you, she's a friend."

"*She's* a shark."

"I'm not saying sharks haven't bitten humans before, but they don't hunt humans. They only bite to figure out what something is. She won't hurt you."

Ally's fingers relaxed slightly. "She won't?"

"I promise." Pasha took Ally's hand and gently pulled her to the side. The shark stayed on the other end of the chamber during all of this. "Can she come over now?"

Ally gave the tiniest of nods. Pasha beckoned the shark closer.

"The sharks I've met are as much my friends as the whales, more so really."

"Why?"

"Don't tell me you haven't noticed the resemblance," Pasha flashed her teeth.

"I thought it would have been rude to point it out," Ally blushed.

The shark passed in front of them, Pasha ran a hand down her side.

"But not all mermaids look the same." Ally's yes flickered to the murals carved into the walls.

It wasn't quite a question, but Pasha answered it anyway. "We're all different. Pallagia and I looked a little alike, but it's rare even for mermaid siblings to resemble each other that much."

The shark came by again. Ally brushed her fingers over the very edge of a pectoral fin and jerked them back.

Pasha bit back a laugh. "Not so bad, is it?"

"She almost feels like you do."

"Almost?" She'd never thought about the difference.

While Ally's focus stayed on the shark making lazy circles around the chamber, she rubbed her thumb over the pads of her fingers that touched the fin. "You're softer."

Pasha looked down at their still-joined hands. Ally's thumb swept over her skin, unconsciously mimicking the movement of her other hand. "Softer? I'm…" Pasha's head jerked up and she caught the shark eyeing them. "That is, thank you?"

Ally shook her head, letting go of Pasha's hand. "What was that?"

"Nothing." Their arms brushed as Pasha told herself not to reach out for Ally again. "So, you'll be alright if she follows the ship?"

"I will. I won't be so afraid of her, knowing she's your friend and you'll be nearby."

"Good, that's good." Pasha waved the shark away, still tingling where Ally's thumb had stroked her skin. "Let's head back to land."

Back on the beach, Ally gave her a brief report on her progress with the map. Pasha couldn't believe she'd already done that much. It might be ready sooner than Ally thought, news that should have made her happy. Instead, a knot of dread pressed hard against Pasha's chest.

"Do you feel ready to sail?" she changed the subject as Ally retrieved her belongings.

"As ready as I can be," Ally fiddled with the buttons on her coat. "I've been thinking about everything that's happened since Mama was taken, and I wanted to ask you something."

"Go ahead."

"Why did you do it?" Ally asked, her voice barely above a whisper.

Pasha found she couldn't look directly at her. "You'll have to be more specific."

"You know what I'm talking about. Why did you make that bargain with my great-grandfather?"

Pasha'd been waiting for that question. Had expected it the first time they spoke. Then days and nights went by with every other possible question asked, except that one. Now it was here and there was only one way to answer.

"I wanted a friend. A companion. I didn't want to be alone anymore."

"A friend?" Ally blinked, obviously not expecting that answer. Then again, she'd refused to hear what Pasha wanted when they struck a new deal. "You did all of this because you wanted a friend?"

"You remember when I said, mermaids live in large groups? We're not meant to be alone for long, it doesn't turn out well. The others knew exactly what it would be like for me when they left."

"But, *forcing* someone to be with you? How could that help?"

"Do you realize how long I'd already been on my own when Gaius came begging for help?" She glanced at Ally, then away again. "I know, it's not an excuse and I'm not trying to make it one, but it was all I could think about back then. The chance to have someone."

Ally huffed, "I still don't see how you could have expected it to work when you'd be taking away someone's choice."

"It wasn't a thought-out decision, Ally, it just happened. When I had time to think about it afterwards, I knew I wouldn't have forced anyone to go anywhere against their will. I couldn't, I *wouldn't*, be like Pallagia. But I thought, if the daughter he brought got to know me, came to like me, I'd at least have someone to talk to. Sometimes. After so many years went by and no one came, I didn't think it would happen at all." Pasha finally lifted her head, "I was angry, I admit it. More with myself than with Gaius, but I was still thinking like a child."

"And you stopped the fish you'd been drawing to the islands."

"That's right. It takes a lot of energy. It's a constant drain with no relief. I'd put it back now, but I need to save as much energy as possible until we get your mother back. I won't break my word on that."

"I know you won't." Ally looked back towards the manor. There was just enough of the day left to light her way home.

"You should try to sleep. There will be time to talk later."

"Right, of course." Something kept her lingering by the rocks.

"What is it?"

"I'm worried about Maher."

"Your friend? Why?"

"I thought we'd made up from the fight we had, but he left the house last night and no one has seen him since."

Pasha gave her what she hoped was an encouraging smile. "I'm sure he'll be waiting on the dock to see you off tomorrow."

Ally hummed in answer, her face still pinched with concern. "Where will you be?"

"I'll follow the ship until it's out to sea. Your brother is giving you the captain's cabin, right? Look for me at night on that end of the ship. We'll decide together if it's safe for me to come aboard."

ALLY

CHAPTER SEVENTY-TWO

5 Days

Ally sat wedged between her father and Gai. The carriage taking them to the northern end of the wharf rocked over the cobblestones.

The *Wave Skipper* would be ready and waiting for them. Cal's crew were already preparing to make way, the most valuable cargo would only be loaded once the Kingfishers were there to supervise. They'd left the manor in the gray hour just before dawn, with Mrs. Thorley and many of the servants to see them off. The housekeeper hugged Ally and said she'd be praying to the goddess every day for their safe return. Luthais and Cal rode ahead of them on horseback, while another wagon with Ally and Cal's belongings brought up the rear.

Ally held onto the shark tooth the whole way, not particularly caring if they noticed. She'd looked for Maher at the house to say goodbye, but no one knew where he was. Ambassador Villaon was also conspicuously absent, though he might have already been waiting for them at the dock. She hoped Maher would be there too.

Even with the interwoven plans laid out by her father, brothers, and Pasha, Ally still felt they'd forgotten something. Worse than that, she'd overheard Gai and Cal talking when she came home from the beach the night before. They couldn't meet all the ransom demands. As they'd tried to gather everything on that ridiculous list, it became increasingly obvious the loss of many of the goods would hurt the Birde Isles' resources. The individual numbers were small enough not to cause much concern, but when combined all together could do some real damage. Lord Kingfisher refused to retrieve some of the items, others they simply didn't have. They'd taken as much coin as they could without impoverishing the Isles, but Kingfisher Island still took the largest hit.

What if the pirates wouldn't accept what they brought? Gai had whispered. What if they took it and demanded the rest without releasing Lady Kingfisher?

Ally wished Maher was here.

She wished Pasha was here.

The carriage rolled to a stop. Had they arrived already? Tucking the necklace back inside her shirt, Ally climbed out after her father and Gai. Most of the area around the northern wharf was blocked off days ago, with guards positioned around the perimeter day and night. An armored wagon was bringing the most valuable portion of the ransom, also heavily guarded.

Ally focused on her boots as they approached the ship. She was grateful she'd gotten to know some of Cal's crew. They'd know she was fairly competent on a ship now, even with– Ally ran face-first into Gai's back. All three of her brothers and their father stood motionless at the top of the dock.

"What's going on?" She stepped around them. "What the..."

"By the goddess," Gai stared at the scene in front of them.

Sailors were sprawled across the dock and the deck of the ship. Some hung over the side rails, too sick to stand. The supplies and other cargo that were meant to have been loaded the night before still sat up on the wharf platform.

"What is the meaning of this?" Cal bellowed. "First Mate! Where's the first mate?"

A sailor dragged himself to his feet, it was Weams. "Captain, First Mate's indisposed at the moment." He blanched. "We all are."

"How did this happen?" Lord Kingfisher demanded. "Have you no control over your own crew?"

Cal hooked Weams by the collar of his jacket and dragged him over. "Explain this. Now."

"It were the gift you sent over milord, er, Captain. Sir."

"What gift!"

Weams waved a shaky hand at three hogshead barrels sitting nearby. "They were delivered last night. The fella who brought 'em said they were a gift from our captain to thank us for taking on the voyage. Figured we'd have a toast and get back to loadin' the ship."

"Why would I send you barrels of drink the night *before* a voyage?" Cal shook him and Weams groaned.

"Let him go, Cal." Ally felt sick herself. "He looks green around the gills."

"Thank you kindly, milady," Weams swayed in place after Cal released him.

"Did you get a look at the man who delivered it?" asked Luthais. "A name? Anything?"

"We didn't. He weren't in uniform or nothin'."

"Where were the guards or the harbormaster during all of this?" asked Ally.

"Keeping everyone else out, weren't they? 'Scuse me, Captain, milords, milady." Weams turned and threw up over the edge of the dock.

"What are we going to do?" She looked to Cal and found herself backing away from him. His face flushed a dark shade of red, hands balled into fists as he stalked to the barrels. One was turned over on its side, a puddle of golden liquid dripped from the open spigot.

"Son of a bitch!" Cal kicked the barrel, the wood snapped and buckled inward.

"Son, come here," Lord Kingfisher put a hand on Cal's shoulder, guiding him away from the others and speaking in a low voice.

Luthais dipped a finger into the ale leaking from the busted hogshead and swiped it on his tongue. His face screwed up and he spat the taste out. "Dead man's bells."

"Oh no," Ally looked back at the scattered crew. "That's..."

"Foxglove. They wouldn't have noticed it right away, not when it was mixed with alcohol."

"And by the time anyone thought the beer tasted a little bitter, they would have been too drunk to care," said Gai.

"Who could have done this?" Ally stood between her two oldest brothers. "And what do we do now?"

"We'll find who did this," Gai promised. "But for now, we need a new ship. This lot will be out of commission for some time."

"Why do we need a new ship? Can't we use another crew on the *Wave Skipper*?"

Gai paused as Lord Kingfisher and Cal rejoined them. Cal was more composed, but Ally could feel his rage bubbling beneath the surface. Seeing him like that made her uneasy in a way she couldn't describe. Cal never lost his temper. If anything, he was the most annoyingly patient member of the family.

Gai said, "It wouldn't be a good idea. A new crew won't be familiar with the ship, and nothing's been done to get this one ready to sail."

Cal muttered something under his breath that Ally didn't catch.

"Enough." Their father's tone was steady, and Ally wondered at his composure. She herself was one more setback from breaking down. "The armored wagon will be here soon. What ships do we have that are ready to sail this morning?"

"The fishers would be too slow, full of equipment," Gai scanned the vessels farther down the wharf. "We can't take a foreign ship, but we could look at one of the traders that have refused to sail this summer."

"We'll use mine," said Luthais.

"Yours?" Cal sputtered.

"I thought your ship was docked at Swan Island?" said Gai, ignoring Cal's outburst.

"It was, but I brought it back a week ago. It's docked in a slip just outside the harbor. My crew can be gathered and prepared to sail in three hours."

Ally stood in the middle of the harbormaster's office at the northern wharf, feeling completely useless.

She knew her family was right, this time. There was nothing constructive she could do to help load the cargo onto Luthais' ship. As much as she'd learned over the summer, she wasn't really a sailor, unused to the manual labor that must be done as fast as possible.

That didn't stop Ally from feeling like a squid suctioned to their sides, doing nothing but getting in the way. Sensing her frustration, Lord Kingfisher suggested she wait inside and review the maps hanging on the office walls. Ally could do that. Bless Esa a hundred times for overcoming Ally's reluctance and including map reading in her lessons.

She'd gone over each map thrice, now she searched fruitlessly for something else to do. Her fingers itched for an embroidery hoop, but the only sewing supplies she'd packed were a small kit for mending clothes and a set of the massive needles used for sail repair. If nothing else, Ally could probably sew a rip in a sail faster than any sailor on that ship.

Ally worried her lower lip. She didn't know anyone on Luthais' crew. One of the reasons she'd felt comfortable with the idea of sailing on the *Wave Skipper* was because she'd made friends there. Olebile and Weams, and the others who helped Cal with her lessons. They were all still recovering from the tainted beer. A handful of manor guards helped get most of them to the bunks on their ship, the worst cases were carried to a nearby warehouse. Luthais sent for a physician, to ensure there was nothing more harmful than foxglove at work. Cal started to object, but Gai and their father overruled him.

Of course Cal was upset, but Ally couldn't believe he'd want his crew to suffer any more than they already had. He was their friend as well as their captain.

Ally let go of her lip before she wore a hole through it and went to the tiny window behind the harbormaster's desk. Through the warped glazing, she could just make out the masts of Luthais' clipper. It wouldn't be quite as fast as the *Wave Skipper*, but still a better choice than one of the fishing or trade ships.

Come to think of it, she'd never seen Luthais' ship before. He kept his crew busy with supply runs between the three largest Isles and short trips out to the handful of smaller islands scattered between. The first mate was left to manage things on Luthais' behalf, when his other duties as Lord of Trade kept him in Kingsport.

Ally couldn't tell which of the sailors hurrying around the dock were the officers. Still, this crew worked quickly, they were making up for the time they'd already lost that morning. Gai and Cal used to tease Luthais about how strict he was with his crew, but it was paying off now.

Ten days, or more, alone at sea with Luthais and a crew she didn't know. Ally suddenly wished she'd let Maher join her on this rescue mission. Where was he, anyway? Surely he wasn't still upset with her for asking him to stay behind? Maher spent years encouraging her to be more independent, to stand up for herself and make her desires known. Now she was doing just that, and he was surprised? Offended she was doing something this important on her own? And what was Maher trying to tell her about her middle brother? She'd resolved to ask him before they left, and then he disappeared.

With Luthais' crew working at this speed, they'd be off very soon. Ally didn't want to leave without saying goodbye to Maher.

At least Pasha was waiting for her out there somewhere. She wouldn't be totally alone.

There was a knock on the door and the harbormaster's secretary poked their head inside.

"Milady?"

"Is it time?"

"Not quite yet, there's a Mister Villaon here to see you."

Maher! She smiled. *At last.*

"Please, show him in," Ally started across the office, but her steps slowed and her smile dropped when she heard an indignant voice in the hallway.

"That's *Ambassador* Villaon, not 'mister'."

Ally tried to assume what could pass for a pleasant expression when Maher's father swept into the room.

"Ambassador, what can I do for you?"

"Good morning, Lady Alphonsine." The ambassador wasn't his usual, put-together self. His once-immaculate beard was in dire need of a trim and he'd missed one of the buttons on his high-collared jacket. The smooth mask he usually wore had slipped and a deep furrow ran between his brows. "I've heard of the terrible prank played on the *Wave Skipper* crew, but it appears Lord Luthais has everything in hand."

"Prank? That was no prank, Ambassador. Someone was trying to stop us from getting to Lady Kingfisher, or at the very least to slow us down."

"Indeed," he scanned the office around them, frown deepening.

His face is going to stick that way, Ally thought. What was he looking for?

"Father will be most appreciative that you've come to see us off, have you already seen him?"

"Not yet. I wanted to speak to you first, Lady Alphonsine."

Ally hated the way Khafra said her name. He made it sound like she was a vase or some other collectable object. But maybe he knew where Maher was hiding. "About what?"

His gaze landed back on her. She'd never gotten used to seeing Maher's chestnut eyes set into such an unforgiving face. "I was hoping you could tell me where I might find my son?"

"Me?" Ally laughed before she could stop herself. "I was about to ask you the same thing, Ambassador."

CHAPTER SEVENTY-THREE

Maher was contemplating the irony of his situation.

His father had threatened, repeatedly, to nail him into a box bound for Saprea. Now here he was, nailed into a box, but not bound for Saprea or anywhere near it. Not exactly nailed in, either. Cork stoppers painted a dull gray held the lid shut. If any became too full of moisture to push out from the inside, Maher could use the folding knife Mama Bear gave him to whittle them out. A series of tiny air holes were drilled around the top, scattered to mimic an insect eating through the wood.

***

"What insect makes perfectly round holes?" He'd asked the night before.

"Powderpost beetles," said Pimm, giving Maher instructions from Mama Bear's bed. "They get unintentionally imported from the tropics all the time."

"Won't that make them think there's an infestation?"

"Not if we stamp the container as inspected by the harbormaster's office. They won't want to waste a usable crate."

"Do I want to know how you got one of the harbormaster's stamps?"

Pimm snickered, then flinched at the resulting pain in their ribs. "Nope, I don't think you do."

Pimm really had thought of everything. There was a bundle of bread and dried meat, and a flask of water in the crate with him. Maher would have to ration carefully, but by the time he revealed himself to Ally it would be too late to turn back. Pimm even included an empty jar in case Maher needed to relieve himself before he could leave the crate. There was a joke hidden in there somewhere.

They'd arranged it all after Marielle returned from the purple lantern. If Maher made it through this alive, he promised himself he'd ask the Riddle Islander how she'd made it inside the floating establishment.

Hopefully Ally wouldn't be too upset when she learned what he'd done, but Maher wasn't holding his breath. Between Ally and his father's wrath, he'd take Ally any day. Still, he might have to move into the Bear's Den until things settled down.

How they got him onto the ship without being seen, Maher couldn't begin to guess. He'd bid Pimm and Mama Bear goodbye, let the men sent by the Madam of the black lantern shut him into the crate, and a short wagon ride later Maher could smell the sea. His companions weren't very talkative.

Something occurred to Maher as they were lifting him from the wagon. "Wait!" He hissed through the air holes. "What if they put another crate on top of me?"

"Your friend's already thought of that." One of them grumbled under the weight of the box.

"Care to share?"

"No. Now shut up and quit squirming."

Maher took deep breaths and listened for any signs of trouble, but soon they'd placed him in the ship's hold.

The same man knocked softly on the lid. "You're on board."

"Thank you," he whispered. "And thank the Madam for me."

"You can do that yourself," he chuckled as they walked away. "You owe her for getting you on the ship."

Maher jerked and hit his head on the lid. He *owed* her? Hadn't Pimm done most of this?

Unless you'd rather owe us a favor for this information?

The coin he'd given her was just for Marielle sneaking into the purple lantern.

Well, shit. He rubbed the sore spot on his head.

Now he owed the Madam a favor anyway. Maher made the sign against ill fortune and settled down in a corner to wait. He'd worry about what the Madam of the black lantern would ask of him when he made it back. If he made it back.

ALLY

CHAPTER SEVENTY-FOUR

By the time Ambassador Villaon stalked out of the harbormaster's office, Ally's head was spinning. She had a feeling he'd given away more than he meant to and was now worried more than before that something had happened to Maher. Should she ask her father or Gai to step in? The manor guards could search the city much faster than Khafra or his staff. Would they bother going into any buildings or would they only search the streets?

Or was Maher even missing at all? He could be hiding for all Ally knew, and there was even less chance of finding him if that were the case. Not that she seriously thought his father would harm him, but she wouldn't put it past the ambassador to somehow keep Maher from being there.

"Are you ready, milady?" The secretary returned.

Pushing her shoulders back, Ally followed them through the building until they came out a door that opened right onto the docks. In the bright morning sunlight, the wharf was in a flurry of activity. The last of the cargo and ransom were loaded and the armored wagon was pulling away from the ship.

Ally scanned the group of people standing with her father and brothers. No Maher. Maybe he really was avoiding her, or his father, or both. Even so, could he not at least send word that he wouldn't be there to see her off? She schooled her features as Lord Kingfisher approached.

"It's almost time to board. Are you absolutely sure you want to do this, Ally?"

"I am." Ally let her father wrap her in an embrace and buried her face into his chest.

"My brave daughter," he murmured, so soft she thought she might have imagined it.

Gaius pulled back, and they walked towards Luthais's waiting ship. It wasn't as sleek as the *Wave Skipper*, but it was sturdy and well-cared for. Not a tack line or canvas was out of place. Her brothers were waiting at the bottom of the gangplank. Gai's anxious expression mirrored their father's, his mustache bristling every time turned his head. Luthais was as unreadable as ever, as he watched the sailors climbing the rigging. And Cal, he was still seething, his hands clenching and releasing at his sides. No doubt he was ready to track down the person responsible for dosing his crew with foxglove.

"Ready?" Gai asked.

"As long as no one else asks me that, I am."

"Everything on board?" Lord Kingfisher turned to Luthais.

"It is, the first mate is reviewing the manifest as we speak."

"What's the..." Ally was about to ask Luthais the name of his first mate, when she looked at the prow and caught the name of the ship. The *Pike*.

"This is the first time you've seen my ship, isn't it?"

Ally nearly missed the slight uptick of one corner of Luthais' mouth before it dropped. Everyone else already knew, she supposed, that he'd immortalized his unofficial title. Carved it into the side of a ship for the world to see.

"Lord Luthais, Captain!" someone called from the deck of the ship.

"Aye, First Mate? What's the condition of the cargo?"

Ally shielded the sun from her eyes as a tall woman descended the gangplank. Luthais' first mate had nearly half a foot on him in height. Her skin was the warm, dark brown of soil just after a storm. Coiled onyx hair was arranged in a series of braids that began in narrow points at her hairline and gradually widened until they reached the crown of her head. They hugged her scalp and then cascaded down her back; each end secured by a sturdy, green enamel cuff.

"All cargo is secured and accounted for, Captain," she handed over the ship's manifest.

"Good. You've met my father and brothers," Luthais nudged Ally forward. "Allow me to introduce my sister, Lady Alphonsine Kingfisher, who will sail with us. Ally, may I present Kamharida Anyanwu, first mate of the *Pike*.

"My lords, good morning," Kamharida nodded to the rest of the family. Then she turned to Ally and bowed. "We welcome you aboard, Lady Alphonsine. If you require anything during the voyage, my lady, please let me know."

"I... thank you." Ally felt the confidence radiating off this woman like warmth from a fire and it calmed her racing heart just a little. As if the sea wouldn't be foolish enough to cross such a skilled sailor.

Giving her father, Gai, and Cal each one last hug, Ally followed the first mate up the gangplank. Luthais trailed behind her. The ropes strung up either side grazed her palms as Ally told herself, yet again, nothing bad would happen if she fell into the sea. She could swim now. And, thanks to Pasha, she could breathe underwater. Even the sharks following the ship would be there at Pasha's request. Nothing in the sea was going to harm her, it was the creatures above it she had to be wary of.

Ally took her first steps onto the ship's deck. The sheer size of the vessel compared to Cal's sloop gave her pause, but the boards were sturdy beneath her feet. Any passing crewmembers nodded Ally's way but kept about their business. She'd have to tell Luthais they didn't have to do that the whole voyage.

Stepping out of the way as her brother reached them, Ally looked down at the people who were counting on her. The last hope that she'd see Maher loping across the wharf to wish her well slipped away. Luthais shut the gate in the railing and locked it into place.

"Prepare to weigh anchor!" Luthais' voice boomed across the deck.

Choruses of "Aye Captain!" echoed around them. Ally grabbed the railing to steady herself. Her father raised a hand in farewell and Ally did the same. Gai waved too and Cal... Cal was gone. Ally spotted his blond head weaving through the crowd. Was he so angry that he wouldn't say a last goodbye?

The gangplank pulled back from the hull, stopping only a few feet away. Someone below shouted something about a jammed wheel.

Sails were snapped open by the crewmates climbing through the rigging like squirrels up a tree. Wind filled the canvas and the *Pike* groaned under the weight of its valuable cargo as it began to move forward.

"Ally, listen to me," Luthais suddenly gripped her shoulder.

"What is it? Something else couldn't have gone wrong already!"

He snorted, it was almost a laugh. "No, nothing's gone wrong, but I'm getting off the ship."

"You're not coming?" Panic snaked up Ally's spine. She and Luthais weren't the closest siblings in the family, but to sail on his ship without him?

The dock slipped farther away.

"You're in good hands with Kamharida, she'll explain everything once you're under way. Trust me," Luthais held her gaze and she nodded. "First Mate, the ship is yours!"

"Aye Captain!" Kamharida appeared on Ally's other side.

Running back down the deck, Luthais vaulted over the rail and leapt across to the stalled gangplank.

The sea breeze carried Gai's panicked words to where Ally was frozen against the ship's rail. "Luthais! What in the goddess's name are you doing?"

There was no stopping the *Pike* after Luthais jumped ship. Ally soon lost sight of her family altogether. Kamharida stood with her until Kingfisher Island was a narrow strip of land in the distance.

"Lady Alphonsine?"

Ally looked up into her russet eyes, "What's going on?"

"Come to the captain's quarters, I'll tell you what I know."

PASHA

CHAPTER SEVENTY-FIVE

P asha swam carefully through the rotting skeleton of a sunken ship, using the slightest flick of her fins to propel herself forward.

She would have to move quickly, Ally should have set sail that morning. Locating the ship Pasha wanted took longer than planned. Now it would be at least a day before she caught up, depending on how much wind was behind them.

This ship had been on the ocean floor for a long time, rolling onto its side as it sank. Downed by enemy cannon fire if the jagged holes in the lower hull were any clue. Pasha had already tried the window to the captain's quarters, but it was sealed shut by years of rust and the corals that had made their homes along the outside of the vessel.

Twisting herself around a cannon that had broken loose from its ties, she found the entry to the cabin. The lopsided door opened easily, crumbling from the hinges, its middle rotted away. Swimming through, Pasha's eyes adjusted to the darker space, her pupils widening. The thing she wanted was in here, she could feel it, hidden somewhere out of sight. A splintered pile of furniture had rolled into the bottom corner of the cabin. She pulled a broken chair aside, startling a pair of eels out of hiding.

"Pardon me," she grinned as they circled her once, their silvery blue skin glistening in the gloom, before darting under a fallen cabinet.

Pasha lugged a few more pieces of wood out of the way, pausing to listen if the ship creaked too loudly around her. Finally, she found the man she'd come to see. Pinned beneath his wide desk, the captain's hollow eye sockets stared up at her. He'd been there, guarding what was left of his ship, since it went down. A rusted iron ring holding two keys was clutched in one bony hand. Nodding at him, Pasha pried his fingers apart and took the keys.

"Much obliged, Captain," she murmured. "Now, where is the lock I need?"

Stretching her arm across the desk, Pasha laid a hand on the captain's chest and *pushed*. An electric jolt shot through her arm and out the pads of her fingers, the skeleton vibrated as the energy passed through each bone. Long lost tendon and muscle was replaced with shining threads of energy. The eels poked their snouts out of their new hiding place, scenting the charge that lingered in the water.

Everything was still for a moment. Wrenching into place, the slack jaw of the skull lined up and shut with a muffled click. Head rolling back to look above them, the captain raised an arm off the desk and pointed.

"Thank you, Captain. You may rest now."

The skeleton went limp once again, bones relaxing with a sound like empty seashells clacking together.

On the wall above her head was the only piece of furniture that had stayed in place when the sunken ship came to rest. Another cabinet, now empty except for a small statue of a mermaid bolted to a shelf.

"Dead men tell no tales, indeed." Pasha swished her tail, pushing up to the statue. She shook her head, it really looked nothing like them. More like some human's fantasy of a mermaid: a pretty, comically well-en-dowed, human woman with a fish tail in place of her legs.

Sliding the key ring over her wrist, Pasha gripped the statue with both hands and twisted this way and that, as hard as she could until it moved. There was a dull clanking of long unused bolts and the cabinet swung out from the wall. A small chest was hidden in an open compartment in the back of the cabinet. Pasha caught the chest before it could put another hole through the rotting hull. Propping it against the captain's desk, she tried the first key on the ring, but it didn't fit. The second key slid snugly into the lock. It took some fiddling to work the rusted key around, but eventually the mechanism popped free.

Flipping the lid up, Pasha picked through the shiny contents. Loose gems and coins, rings, and brooches. All valuable, but not what she was looking for. Buried beneath the small pile of coins was a cinched pouch, the fabric mostly protected from the water while sealed in the chest. She plucked it out and withdrew the treasure inside. Three strands of thick, white pearls met at a gold clasp in the back, then flowed down to a golden pendant encrusted with a rainbow of small jewels. They winked at her like a fish's scales. Set in the middle was an emerald as big as a shark's eye.

This was what she'd felt waiting somewhere inside the ship. Pasha was always the best at sensing gemstones that had plummeted to the bottom of the sea. Her sister could come up with precious metals, but never jewels.

Thinking of Pallagia made her heart skip. Brushing her memories aside, Pasha returned the necklace to the pouch and slipped the draw-string around her neck. Before closing the chest, she picked out a fat garnet ring.

After the rest of the treasure was locked tight and stuffed back behind the cabinet, she swam down to the captain. Sliding the ring over one finger, she fit the keys back into his hand. The bones twitched, then closed around the keys.

Satisfied, Pasha waved goodbye to the eels.

Leaving the ship, Pasha let the tide carry her along while she focused and found the warm pinpoint of the shark tooth. Wasting no more time, Pasha fixed on the beacon and swam towards it. Towards Ally.

CHAPTER SEVENTY-SIX

4 Days

A sharp gust blew Foraoise's hair back, nearly taking her hat with it, as the *Maiden's Revenge* picked up speed. She was glad of the extra wind on their side, they had an appointment to keep.

"Keep her steady, helmsman."

"Aye, Captain!"

Leaving him to mind the quarterdeck, Captain Dare went to her quarters where Lady Kingfisher was still housed. Their guest hadn't tried to attack anymore of the crew, but she still had to be locked up. Lest someone else, besides the unfortunate ship's cook, meet with the wrong end of a chamber pot upon opening the door.

"Good afternoon, Lady Kingfisher," she locked the door behind her.

"What do you want?"

Rochelle sat at the captain's dining table, arms crossed and looking a little more worse for wear. She'd refused the fresh clothes offered by the captain, so the offers stopped. A chain connecting one of her ankles to the bolted-down table kept her from roaming too far.

"Your time with us is coming to an end, my lady. In a matter of days we shall meet your husband's representative to trade you for fair payment."

"Fair payment? There is nothing fair about this."

"I disagree, but why argue when we shan't see eye-to-eye?"

Rochelle scowled and turned away.

"Do you not want to know which brave soul is coming to your rescue?" Foraoise laughed when her spine stiffened. "Never fear, your lordly husband won't be leaving the safety of Kingsport, not even for you."

"You know nothing of governance. He couldn't leave, even if he wished to."

"But your daughter can."

Slowly, Rochelle's head twisted like a puppet on a string. For the first time since they brought her aboard, she looked truly frightened. "You're lying. My daughter has never set foot on a ship."

"I may lie about a great many things, but not this." Foraoise waved the note in her face. Lady Kingfisher's eyes locked on the paper, but Foraoise whisked it away before she could read the words. "Lady Alphonsine knows, if she doesn't bring the ransom herself, I send you home in pieces."

With a long, guttural wail, Rochelle covered her face with her hands. The captain folded the letter and tucked it into her shirt.

"Don't fret, my lady, we'll –" She looked up as Rochelle launched herself out of the chair, eyes wild and fingers curled into claws. Catching one of her wrists, Foraoise used Rochelle's momentum against her and spun the younger woman around. Rochelle flung her free arm back and raked her nails across the captain's face.

"That's quite enough!" Foraoise snatched her other arm and pinned them both behind her back. "You're about to see your daughter, do you really want to greet her with a missing limb when we're so close?"

Sagging forward, Rochelle sobbed, "No... Not Ally, no!"

The captain deposited her back in the chair and stepped out of range of the chain.

"As I was saying, before I was so rudely interrupted," she mopped her cheek with her sleeve, it came back stained red with blood. "We'll make Lady Alphonsine feel very welcome."

CHAPTER SEVENTY-SEVEN

3 Days

Where was Pasha?

Ally prowled through the captain's quarters aboard the *Pike*. They'd already been at sea for two days and she'd waited up all night, looking for any sign of Pasha. The great shark's dorsal fin had broken the surface a few times, but the mermaid never joined her.

What if she wasn't coming? What if she was trapped somewhere?

What if she'd decided to completely break the bargain?

First Maher, then Luthais, and now Pasha. First Mate Anyanwu was still with her, but Ally could see she was having trouble with some of the crew after Luthais quite literally jumped ship. Word had spread, as it always did, that Ally was somehow connected to the troubles plaguing the Birde Isles. Many of the sailors were starting to give her a wide berth or make their wards against bad luck when she passed. No matter how loyal they were to Luthais, his unannounced departure had shaken them.

What if they reached the meeting point and Pasha was still missing? Ally clutched the shark tooth, the point digging into her skin, willing it to send her some kind of message.

Where are you?

CHAPTER SEVENTY-EIGHT

Bits of cork and wooden splinters rained down as Maher twisted the point of his knife into one of the makeshift nails holding the crate together. It had been long enough, surely, he'd heard the morning task calls for the crew twice now. Besides, he was nearly out of food and couldn't stay in that box any longer.

After the last cork was whittled away, Maher listened to make sure he was alone before cracking the lid. The Madam's men had chosen this spot well. He was back against one side of the ship's hold, more crates stacked higher than his blocking him from view. Sliding the lid back just enough to stick his head out, Maher waited for several more minutes, then crawled over the side of the box. He dropped down to the floor of the hold, grimaced at the tightness in his legs.

Brushing off his clothes, Maher twisted the lid back onto the crate and slung the small pack he'd brought across his back. It wouldn't do to have anyone notice it was open in case he needed to return. Now, how to get to the captain's quarters without any of the crew, or worse Luthais, spotting him? Pulling the knit sailor's cap he wore further down over his ears and forehead, Maher crept along the line of crates until he reached an open space. This part of the hold appeared to be mercifully empty of people. He could hear the crew running about above deck, orders and answers being shouted above the roar of the wind and waves.

There was only one way to get to the quarterdeck, the most likely place Ally would be. He'd have to climb out the hold hatch, walk through the gun deck to the main deck, and down the length of the ship.

All the gods and their grandmothers, Maher exhaled. *Why couldn't there have been a back way?*

Waiting until night fell was an option, but Maher decided his odds of being noticed while stepping over sleeping sailors was greater than while crossing the bustling deck. Turned out, making it to the main deck was the easy part. No one spared him a glance as he navigated up from the belly of the ship. The sun was low in the sky as he breathed fresh air for the first time in days.

Scanning the way ahead, he didn't see Ally anywhere, or her brother. Maybe it was faint-hearted of him to not want to face Luthais Kingfisher before he'd seen Ally, but experience had taught him it was better to have her at his side. That is, if Ally didn't have Maher tied to the yardarm for stowing away. He'd been unable to predict her reactions the whole summer, and it had made him more than a little off kilter.

There was also the question of Luthais' involvement in all of this. All Marielle had learned, during her brief infiltration of the purple lantern, was they'd be taking this ship instead of Cal's. Why or how that came about, Maher didn't know yet. After all, he'd already been locked in the cargo hold when the switch happened. As soon as he got to Ally, he'd ask her.

Staying close to the railing, Maher wove through the crew going about their business. His legs wobbled, but he didn't let himself hold onto the rail for support. From the portside of the ship, he caught the faint opening notes of a shanty.

Maher was so fixed on the doors to the captain's quarters, he nearly tripped over a bucket of water a sailor was using to mop that part of the deck. Backing away and muttering an apology, Maher caught a flash of movement out of the corner of his eye. A woman who had to be at least his height was striding across the deck and heading right for him. Walking faster, Maher tried to quickly think of a way to lose her. Before he'd so much as planned a first move, she appeared in his path.

"What are you about, sailor?" her clipped tone made his next step falter. She had to be an officer.

Maher ducked his head and mumbled something noncommittal before trying to slip by. If he had to make a run for the quarterdeck, he would.

Her eyes narrowed, and she blocked him again. "I know every face in this crew, and I don't recognize yours."

"I, uh, I just joined up at the start of the voyage, um, ma'am."

"*Ma'am*?" Stepping closer, her nose wrinkled as if she smelled something foul. She tore the hat from Maher's head and swore. "Goddess and sea spirits save me."

Well, Maher thought as the woman towed him across the ship, his upper arm in an iron grip, *at least I'm being taken where I wanted to go and not below decks again.*

She didn't say another word until they reached the double doors. Rapping her knuckles on the polished wood, she called out, "My lady, I must speak with you. May I come in?"

Maher's head swiveled around. If Ally was alone in there, where was Luthais lurking?

"Come in!" Ally's voice reached them, and Maher was never so glad to hear it.

"Let's go," she opened the door and steered him inside. They passed through the main room of the cabin, into what looked like a small study. Ally was leaning over a wide map table scattered with weights and markers. The sun was just setting through the windows behind her head, but she'd already lit the lamp on the wall and a candelabra bolted to the corner of the table. With her shirt sleeves rolled up and a stony set to her face, she looked more like her brothers in that moment than he'd ever noticed.

"My lady, I'm afraid we have a problem."

She pressed her fingers over her eyelids. "What is it now?"

Maher cleared his throat and Ally finally looked up.

"Maher!" she gawked, as if a trousered flounder had just walked into the room and not her dearest friend. "What in the goddess's name are you doing here?"

"Al, there's a perfectly reasonable explanation for this."

"Reasonable? Yes, I'm sure an ambassador's son playing stow away is completely reasonable." The tall woman snorted and Maher shot her a glare.

"Since you know who I am already, I think you can let go of me now."

Ally sighed heavily, "May I introduce Kamharida Anyanwu, first mate of the *Pike*."

"We've met," Maher pulled out of her grasp.

"You still haven't answered my question. What are you doing here?"

"I'm here to help you, Al."

"By sneaking on board? How did you even manage it?"

Kamharida said, "I might not have noticed him tripping across the deck at first, but that smell is what really gave him away."

"What smell?" He moved closer to Ally.

"Any sailors that might wear scents save it for shore leave. Did you think no one would notice when you absolutely reek of pine and cardamom?"

Ally's nostrils flared. "You do smell like you poured on the whole bottle, Maher."

"That's because the whole bottle *was* poured on, but not by me." He scrubbed a hand over his face. Why hadn't Pimm or anyone else mentioned it? Did they think he'd done that on purpose?

"How did you get on board?" The first mate repeated Ally's question.

Maher turned to Ally, "I'll explain everything, in private. Please."

After a moment she said, "Leave us, please, Kamharida."

"I'll be just outside if you need me, my lady." Kamharida gave Maher another long look before exiting the captain's quarters.

"That's exactly the kind of first mate I expected Luthais to have, they share the same personality."

"You can't blame her for being upset," Ally came around the map table. When she let him give her a quick hug, he could feel how tense she was. "She'll be held responsible if anything happens to you."

"Not Luthais?"

Ally shook her head, "Luthais isn't here. Kamharida is acting captain for the voyage."

"Luthais let you sail away on his own ship, without him?" That made no sense. Why would Luthais go through the trouble of having his ship ready to sail, only to not join them? When Ally only chewed on her lip and gave him an appraising look, he glanced around the room. "I didn't exactly plan for an entrance like this, I was hoping for something a bit stealthier."

"Maher, you're dancing around the subject. You asked for privacy, and you've got it."

"One of my contacts in the city got me into the hold, sealed in a crate. I had enough food and water to last for a few days."

"When we'd be far enough from shore and unable to do anything about it," Ally put the table between them again. "The whole time we were preparing to leave, I thought you were angry at me over our last conversation. Or something terrible had happened to you. And you were already on the damned ship."

"I'm sorry you had to feel that, but I'm not sorry for ensuring I could be here to help you."

"You'll be lucky if our first mate doesn't throw you into the brig." Ally rubbed her necklace, the shark tooth outlined beneath her shirt, then her head snapped up. "Maher, how did you know we'd be on this ship and not Cal's?"

"That's... a little more complicated of an answer."

"Well?"

Maher opened his mouth to reply, then stopped himself. He didn't want Ally tangled up in the Madam's web, the one he'd walked right into. "I can't tell you."

"I have a right to know. If you've been in the hold of this ship for *three days*, Maher, then you knew what was going to happen long before the rest of us!" Something new flitted across her face. "Please tell me you weren't involved with Cal's crew being drugged."

"Drugged! I don't know anything about that, Al, I swear. All my contact found out was that you'd be switching ships, not why or how. Is the crew alright?"

"I think so. The night before our departure they were given beer tainted with foxglove. Not enough to kill them, but more than enough to make them all very sick."

Foxglove? Now *that* was interesting. Maher tried to think past the fatigue and hunger that were starting to crowd his thoughts, who would have thought to use something as commonplace as foxglove to put Cal's crew out of commission? The spindly plants with their strings of purple, bell-shaped flowers grew everywhere in the Birde Isles. They were so pervasive that, to warn children away from the temptation, parents told stories of furious sprites who would whisk them away if they even touched the flowers. He'd heard similar stories as a child, since a variety in white and pink grew on the continent. Whoever planned this could have picked them from the fields behind Ally's home, for all the gods' sakes.

"Luthais!" Maher cried and Ally jumped. "This must have been what he was planning all along! But I still don't understand why he'd go through the trouble, only to leave the ship."

"He left the ship because felt he was needed more in Kingsport, but Father would have tried to stop him if he said anything." She paled, "Is this what you were trying to tell me in the parlor? You really think Luthais betrayed us?"

"I'm afraid so, Al."

"Why would he drug Cal's crew to stop us from going, then offer his own ship, then leave it? He's done nothing but try to help throughout this whole ordeal."

"And that doesn't make you suspicious?"

Ally checked the window behind her, where night was falling and the stars were beginning to appear. It was the third time she'd done it since the first mate left the room.

"What are you looking at?"

"Nothing," her mouth pressed into a thin line.

"Is she out there?" Maher asked carefully. He should have realized, just because he hadn't seen the mermaid on board didn't mean she wasn't skulking somewhere beneath the ship.

"I don't know."

His brows shot up. "Don't tell me, the mermaid hasn't kept her word? I can't say I'm surprised."

"Leave it alone," Ally's voice grew hoarse. "You have no idea what I've been dealing with while you were hiding in a box belowdecks."

"I wouldn't have had to hide in a box if you'd understood that I couldn't let you go alone!"

Why were they doing this again? Was he really miscalculating so badly, or was Ally still hiding something from him?

Ally fiddled with one of the weights holding the map down. "Maher, why did your father come to the wharf this morning to inquire if I'd made my decision whether to give him my support in naming him Lord of Trade?"

Fuck.

"He said... what?"

"While I was waiting for them to prepare Luthais' ship, which of course you already knew about since you're *here*, your father caught me alone. He said he was looking for you and thought you might be there to see me off. Apparently, you were supposed to use our friendship to have my brother ousted from his title and replaced by your father."

"Bastard," he growled. "I should have known he'd try something else when I didn't return home."

"So it's true, then?" Her tone was light, but her fingers curled tight around the rounded hunk of metal in her hand. "Khafra thinks you're only friends with me to bide your time until our friendship was useful?"

"It's true he's been pushing me, but I wanted no part in it. I told him, I wouldn't take advantage of our relationship just to improve his position." Who else had his father approached with this? Who else thought he'd used Ally? "I don't even know anymore if this is about our family legacy or about bringing me to heel. I've been trying to distance myself from him for years, and he knows it." And Khafra knew much more than Maher had realized. "I didn't come home three nights ago because, if I hadn't secured your support by then, he threatened to send me back to Saprea whether I agreed to go or not."

"He can't force you to go anywhere, Maher. My father wouldn't allow it."

All the work he'd put in these last few years really had been for nothing, hadn't it? He'd never get out from under his father's thumb, Khafra would always be one step ahead. "Clearly, he can get to anyone he wants. He's also threatened to have everyone I've ever known in the Lantern thrown in prison for the crime of speaking to me. Shut all of their establishments down. Ruin dozens of lives. All because of me."

"He can't have! Of all the underhanded, scheming –" Ally smacked the weight down. "We won't let him get away with this. What's the worst he could do?"

"He can do more than you think. Khafra's used to getting his own way."

She snorted, "Well, Khafra Villaon is about to be sorely disappointed."

He looked away while Ally fumed. Everything he'd tried to do, every plan to help Ally had turned to shit. Preparing her for this dangerous ransom voyage? Shit. Tracking down Luthais' involvement in Rochelle's capture? Shit. Breaking the old and new bargains made with the sea witch, or mermaid, whatever she was? Utter shit.

Maher's head lifted. "Would... would it be so bad if Luthais were removed?"

"You can't be serious."

"Why not? Al, I thought everything I've been working towards, the nights spent in the city, the connections I've made, would free me of Khafra once and for all. Now, I'm not so sure. What's to stop him from snatching me off the street the moment I let my guard down? What could your family do? Remove him from his ambassadorship? He'll only try to take me back with him anyway."

"You can't," she said again, very slowly, "be serious."

"If Luthais' involvement with Rochelle's capture goes as deep as I think it does, he'll be stripped of his title anyway! Don't you see?"

"Are you so sure you weren't willing to go along with it from the start? You obviously don't trust my brother."

"Do *you* honestly trust him?" Maher shook his head. "If it gets Khafra off our backs and stops Luthais from doing anymore damage, what's wrong with letting him have the title?"

"Maher, if your father gets his way in this, what's to stop him from demanding the next thing he wants? What if he's not content with being Lord of Trade and decides marrying you off to Gai or to me will propel him to an even higher station?"

"He wouldn't, wait..." Maher gasped. "What if we did it?"

"Did what? Got married? Maher, I wasn't suggesting it!"

He barely heard her, his mind already revolving through everything he'd learned about binding contracts. "If we're tied together, if we're legally bound, maybe the bargain between you and the mermaid would be severed! It's the only way out I hadn't thought of. She can't have a claim on you then!"

"Leave Pasha out of this!" Ally snapped.

"You mean the Pasha who's gone back on every promise she's ever made to you or your family?" He waved a hand at the empty window. "Think of it Ally, we can be free of both her and my father at the same time! At least we could protect each other and still see whomever we wanted."

"For the goddess's sake! I don't want to be free of her!" Ally caught herself, pressed a hand over her necklace. "Besides he's your father, Maher, he wouldn't really do something to harm you."

"Not everyone's parents are like yours, Ally! Have you been so wrapped up in yourself that you've never noticed what he's really like?" Maher gripped the edge of the table.

Ally sucked a sharp breath through her teeth, eyes flashing. "You're a grown man! You don't have to jump anymore when your father snaps his fingers."

"That doesn't matter. Not for people of our station." Maher knew his tone was bitter, and still he couldn't stop himself. "Khafra has made it perfectly clear. I don't know why I thought it would be any different."

"That doesn't mean it has to involve me!"

Maher flinched as if she'd slapped him in the face. Her words stretched out between them.

When he spoke again, his voice was rough. Even so, he wasn't going to let Ally know she'd almost brought him to tears. "I know that, Al. I just thought... you understand me and I understand you. We could fix everything, get you out of that bargain, stop Luthais from harming anyone else, and still be able to be ourselves. What's so wrong about marrying your best friend?"

Ally crossed her arms. "I understand what you're saying, and I know you think that's your only option, Maher, but it isn't. I love you, but I'm not convinced Luthais has done anything wrong. And I'm through letting other people make decisions for me about my life. I'm not going to settle for anything less than what makes me happy. I'm going to save my mother, and then I'm going to do what's right for *me*." She refocused on the map. "I hope you'll do the same for yourself."

CHAPTER SEVENTY-NINE

Pasha held her breath until she heard Maher leave the cabin. He wasn't supposed to join this crew, was he? Ally said he wasn't a sailor.

One of the windows to the cabin was barely cracked open, she'd climbed the side of the ship and held onto the ledge until Ally was alone. Then Pasha pulled herself inside and eased the window shut behind her. Seawater dripped across the sill and puddled around her feet.

Ally was bent over a map, eyes unfocused and staring at nothing. She'd only caught the end of their argument, but she heard clearly enough when Ally said she wasn't going to let anyone make decisions for her. What else had Maher told her before Pasha arrived?

"Ally..."

Her eyes swept across the cabin and focused on where Pasha waited in the shadows. Ally's shoulders slumped and a look of relief passed across her face, but it didn't stay for long. Her brows knit together as she straightened up.

"Where have you been?"

"I had to make a stop on my way to meet you," Pasha said softly, wary of any other humans hearing them. "It took longer than expected."

Ally ran her fingers through her hair, only to get them caught in the thick braid hanging over her shoulder. She yanked them out, sending stray curls flying around her head. "I've barely slept since we left Kingsport. I thought you must have been hurt or trapped somewhere. Or you just changed your mind and weren't coming."

Pasha wanted to brush the loose curls away, to comfort her. But the look on Ally's face kept her where she was. "There's something you need to know. My friends came back to me on my way here."

"The whales?"

"Yes, the accounts they brought conflicted and changed with each group. Something's not right about this meeting place the pirates chose."

"Something's not *right* about it?" Ally's voice cracked. "They're pirates. They're holding my mother for ransom. Of course there's something not right about it!"

"That's not what I meant," Pasha frowned. "If none of their impressions of this place line up and they can't agree on a description, there's got to be a reason. They could be setting a trap, or–"

Ally scoffed, "Are you sure your fish weren't just confused?"

Pasha took a few steps closer. "Ally, I'm worried about you."

"Right, you're worried about me. We both know you're only doing this because of your godsbedamned bargain."

"The bargain I've been trying to let you out of?" she hissed.

"Why? Because you feel guilty? You should!"

"What's happened?" Pasha paced across her end of the small room. "When we parted you were nervous, understandably so, but not angry. What happened between then and now?"

Tears slid down Ally's cheeks and she scrubbed her sleeve over her face. "Everything has happened! It's all going wrong! Cal's crew were given tainted beer to make them too sick to sail and I hardly know Luthais's crew. In case you haven't noticed yet, we're on his ship, not Cal's. Either way, both crews think I'm cursed." She waved a hand between herself and Pasha. "We don't have enough to pay the ransom for my mother. Maher somehow stowed away on board the ship, so the first mate is beside herself. Oh, and let's not forget, I've just found out Maher's father is planning to use our friendship to strip my brother from his title as Lord of Trade and instate himself."

Pasha bared her teeth. "He has no power to do that."

"I'm not so sure. Apparently Khafra Villaon has been very busy, trying to make this happen without a word to me." Ally pinched the bridge of her nose. "Will you stop that pacing? You're making me dizzy."

She planted her feet. "And what does Maher think?"

"He thinks we don't have a choice, or at least he doesn't. I've never seen him like that. Willing to just let his father win. That's not the Maher I know. I tried to reason with him, convince him Khafra won't be satisfied with that title alone for long. Next thing you know, he'll be petitioning for Maher to marry one of us. Probably me. I doubt Khafra believes he can get away with pressuring Gai into anything."

A choked sound escaped Pasha's throat. "How do you come to that?"

"It's obvious. A familial link would all but guarantee their family a permanent position on the Birde Isles, a higher one than they'd ever had in Saprea."

The cabin was stifling. Pasha wished she'd left the window open. "Do you want to marry him?"

"Of course not! I don't love Maher that way, we're like brother and sister. But... I can't be the one to abandon him when he needs me, either. After how much he's been there for me? When all's said and done, he's my best friend. I won't let his father hurt him or my family."

She looked away, "Maybe you should marry him, then."

Ally threw her hands up. "That's not what I meant!"

"What did you mean, Ally? It sounds like a comfortable life with your *best friend* would be better than the alternative."

Ally's fists clenched. Pasha needed to get out, she needed to breathe. Every harsh word only sucked more air out of the room.

"Are you saying," Ally's next words were laced with venom, "I'm not free to make my own choices? That I can *only* pick between a forced marriage to someone I'm not in love with, or being tossed into the sea because of a bargain my great-grandfather made?"

Pasha whipped around. "I *told* you the bargain doesn't matter anymore. I tried to break it!"

"Because you weren't expecting to end up with someone who was afraid of water? Poor you. Why bother asking Gaius for one of his daughters at all?"

"I was desperate!" Pasha growled. "I'd been left on my own for most of my life! What would you have done, if you were me, and suddenly given the chance to not be alone anymore?"

"Well, it's nice to know you only demanded someone else's child because you were lonely. It wouldn't have mattered which one of us it was, right?"

"Can't you see, Ally? I decided to end the bargain because I knew it was wrong of me to make it in the first place. Because I couldn't do that to you, or anyone else. Because I can't –" She bit off her own words and turned away. "It doesn't really matter, does it?"

"What doesn't matter?"

Pasha unlatched the window. Gloriously cool sea air swept over her face. "You have one less choice to worry about, Ally. I hope that makes it easier for you."

"What do you mean?"

Pasha removed the bag from around her neck and tossed it to Ally. The jewels inside clinked together when she caught it. "Put this with the ransom for your mother, it should be more than enough."

Ally tugged the drawstring open and gasped. "But, where did this come from?"

Not trusting herself to speak, not waiting or wanting to hear anything else, Pasha dove through the window.

CHAPTER EIGHTY

Ally stared into the brocade purse clenched in her hands. A small pile of gold and jewels glittered and winked in the candlelight. There was a soft splash and Ally's head jerked up.

Pasha was gone.

"Pasha?" Ally ran for the window. "Pasha!"

She stuck her head out as far as she could. There was no sign of the mermaid, only the bottomless black swells surrounding the *Pike*.

"*Pasha*!" Ally nearly threw the purse into the water after her. The ocean breeze brushed across her brow, cooling her frustration enough to see what a stupid decision that would be. Pasha was right, the jeweled necklace would more than cover the difference in the ransom value the Isles hadn't been able to meet.

Pasha was late catching up to them because she'd gone goddess-knew-where to retrieve the necklace for Ally. For Mama.

Ally's chest throbbed. She rubbed it, trying in vain to soften the ache. It only seemed to make it worse. Then, her chest *burned*. With a yelp, Ally dropped the pouch and yanked the shark tooth from beneath her shirt. The tooth smoldered like a live coal, burning so hot she had to hold it by the chain.

Fabric brushed against her skin and Ally hissed. Holding the tooth out with one hand, the chain taut against the back of her neck, she lifted the neckline of her shirt with the other. A triangular shape, red and angry, was burned into the skin over her breastbone.

What had Pasha done? Had she taken back the mermaid gift she'd lent to Ally?

The cabin spun around her. Ally's knees hit the hard wooden planks, the shark tooth slipped from her fingers and dangled in front of her face. If Ally couldn't breathe underwater anymore, if Pasha didn't come back, her one advantage over the pirates was gone.

She could drown.

Candlelight blurred and streaked around her. Everything narrowed until all she could see was the jeweled necklace lying on the floor. Ally clawed at her chest, scraping over the fresh burn, sending sharp spirals of pain through skin and muscle, down into her bones.

This was all her fault. She'd driven them all away. She'd thrown away her chance to safely rescue Mama. She'd thrown Pasha away.

Someone was knocking on the door, but how could that be? There was no one left.

Ally was alone.

FORAOISE

CHAPTER EIGHTY-ONE

Foraoise read the new letter twice and then a third time. Then a fourth, for good measure. The words themselves made sense, and yet the news they delivered was beyond anything she might have imagined.

If this account was true, and her letter-writing friend had yet to be proven wrong, it would change everything. Any plan she'd made, or could make, meant nothing in the wake of this knowledge. *This* would secure Foraoise Dare as the greatest captain on the Eastern Sea. No, the greatest captain on *any* sea.

"You'll see, Jon," she whispered. "I'm going to accomplish more on my own than we ever dreamed of together."

CHAPTER EIGHTY-TWO

2 Days

It took Maher the rest of the night to calm Ally down. By dawn the following morning she was finally asleep on the bunk in her cabin, but he was afraid to leave her alone for long.

This was unlike any of her other panic attacks he'd witnessed. When he and the first mate pushed their way back into the cabin, they found her barely conscious on the floor. Sweat streaked through her hair and her skin had taken on a gray tinge. Ally didn't pass out, but she panted so hard Maher was sure she'd make herself sick. Between himself and Kamharida, whom he'd quickly grown to trust for how well she handled the ordeal, they got Ally through the night. What made him equally uneasy was Ally's surprise upon seeing them, once she'd gotten some of her wits about her. She acted as if she thought they'd all left the ship.

He didn't ask about the shark tooth-shaped burn that was seared into the skin of her chest, just below her collar bones. Neither did the first mate, though she gave him a searching look when he told her to leave

Ally's necklace on. He knew Ally would only wake alarmed if it was missing.

After they got her into bed, Ally kept murmuring the mermaid's name over and over. Pasha, Pasha, Pasha. Maher could only gather that she'd turned up after all, it explained the shouting he'd heard after Ally dismissed him. She'd gone from one fight straight to another, and it sounded like Pasha had left in the middle of theirs. No wonder it brought on this reaction from Ally.

It also must have been the mermaid who left the heavy, jewel-encrusted necklace that Ally shoved into his hands as if it were on fire. Added to what the Kingfishers had loaded onto the *Pike*, it would easily cover anything missing from the pirates' insulting demands.

So what caused an argument between them, if Pasha had indeed brought the necklace to help?

Maher wasn't sure he wanted to bring it up, at least not until they'd made the trade for Rochelle and were safely back in Kingsport. Maybe then, he'd ask Ally what happened between her and Pasha. And maybe by then, she'd be ready to tell him.

1 Day

Ally was finally coming back to herself again. There were still long periods of silence, where she stared at the sea from her cabin window or stood at the railing by the helm. Kamharida ordered the crew to work around her, telling them Lady Alphonsine was growing more concerned for Lady Kingfisher's safety. That was true, but Maher knew it wasn't the reason she constantly checked the waves around the ship. She was hoping Pasha would come back.

The shark tooth hardly left her grip now. Maher had also decided it would be wise to not mention the angry mark on her chest yet, either. He simply placed a small jar of burn salve, obtained from the ship's infirmary, by her bunk and left it at that.

With the weather on their side thus far in the voyage, the *Pike* was making excellent time. They might even reach the meeting point half a day early if the wind kept up. It was as if something stronger was pushing them towards their destination, Maher didn't miss some of the looks the crew gave Ally as she stood on deck. It wouldn't surprise him if many of the sailors thought she'd summoned some help from the goddess, or whatever sea-faring deities they believed in.

By the evening of their fourth day at sea, Maher felt comfortable leaving Ally alone in the cabin long enough to stretch his legs with a walk around the main deck. She'd taken a renewed interest in checking their map coordinates, poring over wide swaths of sea on either side of their destination.

Nodding back to any of the crew who greeted him, Maher circled the deck twice before climbing the steps to the quarterdeck. The night was fine, even with the crisp breeze that had him buttoning his coat. Being on this ship had taken him back to the voyage he and his father made from Meredia to the Birde Isles.

It was much larger than the *Pike*, a passenger ship that ran a regular route down the Eastern Sea corridor, through the southern straits, and up into the mouth of the Split Sea. There were people on that vessel from places he'd only seen on a school room map, and some places he hadn't heard of at all. It was exciting, the idea that there were so many parts of the world to explore. And the more Maher learned about the Isles, the more he looked forward to seeing their new home. Meredia had been stifling, after spending most of his young life in Saprea.

Not that Saprea didn't have its own rules or codes of conduct, but for the Meredians it seemed like rules were a way of life. Such rigid expectations put on everyone. No spontaneity, everything planned just so. There would be no taking off with his friends for a swim in the river, like he'd done back home, scattering clothes along the way. Even their art was regulated. If the old masters didn't approve, then it simply wasn't art.

"What happens when there are *new* old masters?" Maher had asked his tutor.

The Meredian woman who taught all of the ambassadors' children, in her tightly buttoned gown and pin-straight hair, had looked down her nose and informed him, "The new masters are taught by the old masters, of course."

At least his father didn't make Maher wear the clothes. All stiff collars, solid colors with no embellishment, and puffy cravats. In the evenings, the most fashionable and wealthy Meredians wore austere, wide ruffs around their necks. The wider the ruff, the wealthier the family. It was like they were morally opposed to turning their heads.

Maher stretched his neck over his own low, loose-collared shirt at the thought. The Meredian post hadn't lasted long, only two years. What would his life have been like if they'd stayed? Or went somewhere else afterwards? Would he have still tried to become his own person, outside of his father's expectations, or would he have given in? Given up?

Coming to the Birde Isles was one of the best things that had ever happened to him. Meeting Ally, with her quiet stubborn streak and artist's spirit that had reached out to his own, was perhaps *the* best thing that had ever happened to him. Even if he had to endure a few months with her brothers to get to her.

Maher breathed in deeply, feeling the cold air fill his chest. His bout of self-doubt, the abrupt crash of hopelessness, was gone. Neither of them would be happy if they went along with Khafra's scheme. Even considering it had been a lapse in judgement, one he wouldn't make again.

He still didn't trust Luthais, but Ally was right about one thing. They both deserved to choose what to do with their lives.

And she was also right about his father. Khafra might do just about anything to get his own way, but to truly harm his only son? Maher didn't think he'd go that far. He very much hoped not.

I'll get us both what we want, Al. Maher warmed his hands inside his pockets, fingers brushing against the silver coin he still carried with him. *I promise.*

"I need to speak with you."

Maher started, turning to find the first mate standing next to him. After Ally seemed to be on the mend, he'd given Kamharida a brief explanation of what he believed had happened. He was intrigued to learn she'd already heard rumors of Ally's involvement with some kind of powerful sea creature, whether it was the goddess or a sea witch or whatever else people were saying. The story had reached them on Swan Island, spreading beyond Kingsport and no doubt growing in size and spectacle along the way. Personally she'd taken it all with a grain of salt and, after talking with Maher, agreed to keep the knowledge of what Pasha actually was to herself.

"What is it?"

"We have some trouble belowdecks. The crew knows Lady Alphonsine had an argument with someone who wasn't on the ship when we set sail and isn't on it now. There's been talk of turning back."

"Turning back? But we're nearly there!"

She spoke softly, eyes trained on the stars stretching out above them. "I'm doing everything I can to keep that from happening, but if they mutiny we're outnumbered."

Maher lowered his voice to match hers, "Why is this coming up now?"

"Some of the crew have convinced themselves Lady Alphonsine was arguing with the goddess of the sea herself. They think the goddess must be angry and we've lost her protection. They're spooked by how smooth the seas have been so far, any rough weather now might be taken as a sign they're right."

"That's ridiculous! Luth– that is, Lord Luthais wouldn't have taken on sailors whose loyalty could be turned just like that."

"It doesn't matter how disciplined they are, most sailors are more superstitious than is good for them." Kamharida glanced around, making sure they were still alone. "Everything that's happened the last two seasons has been building up. Our route might keep us moving between the different Isles, but we still see what's happening."

"You don't have to tell me it's all building up." Maher hunched farther into his coat, not from the cold so much as to block the road his thoughts were trying to take. "Kingsport is sitting on a knife edge. Its salvation or its ruin depends on us and if we can carry off this rescue. And I can't let Ally down."

"I'll do what I can. Our bosun, Ga-Seung, and the other commissioned officers will stand by us, but we still might have to bring you in. If orders or threats don't work, old-fashioned bribery is useful."

"What do you suggest I bribe them with? I stowed away, sorry again about that, with little more than the clothes I have on."

"You are the son of the Saprean ambassador,"

He nodded, not looking forward to putting that hat back on.

One corner of her mouth lifted as she examined him, "And you're the Magpie of Kingsport. I'm sure you'll –"

Maher stopped mid-nod. "Wait! How did you... that fucking nick-name."

"As I was saying, you'll think of something."

CHAPTER EIGHTY-THREE

The sun was at its highest point when they arrived at the edge of the location sent by the pirates. Ally stood by the helm, listening as Kamharida relayed orders to the bosun and helmsman. She'd learned at the start of the voyage that Ga-Seung had been part of Luthais' crew since his first commissioning, Ally could see the first mate put a great deal of trust in him as an officer. Grant, the helmsman, was a boy from Swan Island only around Ally's age but he'd proven himself quite adept at steering a ship. The bosun said something she didn't catch, but the way his wide-set brows pinched together gave her an idea that he wasn't happy with their position. His sleek, black hair was trimmed short on the sides and left longer on top. A cut more popular with sailors who didn't grow their hair enough to tie back.

Maher was by her side, eyes fixed on the expanse of glittering water ahead of them. Though Ally still worried about Maher's safety, she was glad to have him with her. Not once had he mentioned the biting words she'd thrown at him, nor did he ask what had passed between her and Pasha afterwards. He'd only picked her up and given her time to come out of the fog. Ally's stomach twisted when she remembered what she'd said to Pasha. She hadn't meant a word of it and yet she couldn't stop herself. The fierce spark in the mermaid's eyes had guttered out, leaving vacant, bottomless pits behind. Then she'd left, without even saying goodbye. Not that Ally had deserved any sort of parting words from Pasha, but it pained her, nonetheless.

Maybe you should marry him, then.

Only now could Ally hear the emotion hidden beneath that flat tone. And it wrapped around her heart in an iron grip. After watching the waves for two days, Ally reluctantly accepted that Pasha wasn't coming back. Mama was waiting for her, relying on her. After Ally saw her mother safely home, she'd find Pasha. If she had to use the nearly finished tapestry waiting in her room and travel to every mermaid community on the map, she'd find Pasha and beg her forgiveness. Even if Pasha turned her away in the end, she'd know how much Ally regretted their parting.

The fragile state of mind the mermaid had been in, when Ally's great-grandfather woke her, had been one of despair and fear. Ally knew what that was like. Through her behavior, if not her words, she'd created a barrier around herself and brought Maher into it. He'd stayed by his own choice, but Ally never encouraged him to branch out. She'd been terrified to lose him. How was that any different than what Pasha had done in her unfathomable loneliness?

But Pasha had learned and grown from the child who made that bargain. Now, it was Ally's turn to do the same.

Patting the front of her blue wool jacket, Ally felt the necklace in its brocade pouch tucked safely into an inner pocket. Handing it over would be a good-faith gesture, proof that they'd brought the value of the demanded ransom, if not the exact contents.

"Ease up the sails," Kamharida's voice carried over the deck. The *Pike* gradually slowed as the tension in the rigging was loosened.

"Where are they?" Maher stepped closer to Ally, his face edged with suspicion. "We're not very early."

"They could be closer than you think," said the first mate.

"And if this was all an elaborate trick?"

"Don't say that." Ally's eyes strained as she searched for anything ahead on the water, "She has to be out there."

Another two hours passed, by the position of the sun. Maher tried to convince her to rest for a while in the cabin, but Ally stayed where she was.

"We're early, that's all," she said to him for the third time. "And I'm not going anywhere."

They floated aimlessly, drifting slowly through the swells. Ally's throat was parched, she eyed the earthen jug of water one of the kitchen crew had placed nearby.

"Ship ahoy!" the barrelman called down to them. "Ship ahoy!"

"Where?" Ally scanned the horizon and saw nothing. "Where is it?"

Thinking there must have been some mistake, Ally looked up at the crow's nest. But the sailor there, a girl who'd climbed the mast as nimbly as any acrobat, wasn't pointing ahead of the *Pike*.

She was pointing behind it.

"Off the stern!" the barrelman called from her perch. "Ship ahoy, off the stern!"

Ally and Maher turned as Kamharida strode past them, opening a spyglass and lifting it to her eye. After a moment, her shoulders went rigid, and she slowly lowered the glass.

"What is it?" asked Maher.

"It's the *Swan Song*, flying Dare's flag."

Ally's heart raced. "Did they keep Mama on the *Swan Song*?"

Maher shook his head, "How could they have followed without us noticing before now?"

The First Mate looked through the glass again. "She's not as weighed down with cannon or cargo. It wouldn't have been too difficult to cut around, knowing which direction we came from."

"Ship ahoy! Portside!"

Ally whirled, the faint outline of a smaller ship was visible to their left.

"Looks like a clipper. They're coming in fast," Grant, the helmsman, said. "Orders, First Mate?"

Kamharida turned to Ally. "If they flank us, there's no guarantee we'll have a clear passage out. They may not be heavily armed, but neither are we. Half the guns were removed to make room for the ransom. They could still disable the sails or rudder the moment everything of value is off the ship."

Ga-Seung approached, flanked by two more officers. "What's our strategy here?"

"We're not leaving. My mother is close by, I can feel it." Ally's spine straightened when they all looked her way. "We're not abandoning Lady Kingfisher."

Kamharida nodded, "Very well. We'll need to come about at an angle, it will give our broadside to both of them, but we'll be able to fire if needed. A longboat can be sent out to meet their representative and we'll demand they do the same."

"We can prepare the cannons on the starboard side," the gunner spoke up. He was the oldest of the ship's officers, the craggy lines on either side of his mouth deepened when he looked back at the waiting crew. "We'll need all five team members per gun, but we won't be able to fire until we know which ship is housing Lady Kingfisher."

"Exactly," said Kamharida. "Take whomever you need."

"Starboard teams, make ready on the guns!" bellowed the gunner. "Move!"

"Full canvas!" Kamharida took the helm. "Prepare to come about!"

The crew lurched into motion. Sailors ran for their posts and more orders carried down the line.

"What can we do?" Ally asked Maher.

"Stay out of the way and stay calm. The first mate will say if she needs us." He took her hand, "When you see your mother, do your best to keep your composure. Don't show them how desperate you are to have her back."

Ally nodded, squeezing Maher's fingers to stop her own from trembling. The *Pike* picked up speed as the sails filled. Kamharida was waiting for the right moment to turn them around. Ally found the shark tooth beneath her shirt, the fossil had gone back to its usual level of unnatural warmth. Even with her ability to breath underwater lost, its solid presence against her skin made Ally feel that Pasha was with her in some small way.

"SHIP AHOY!" the barrelman cried. "Dead ahead!"

"Fuck." Maher took off for the prow, Ally on his heels.

They reached the front of the ship as a massive vessel, twice the size of the *Pike*, crested the swells before them. Ally couldn't make out the cracked heart and dagger from this distance, but she could see the bloodred banner snapping in the wind. A ship this large, it had to be Dare's flagship, the *Maiden's Revenge*. But which of the three vessels was carrying her mother?

"Come on," Maher grabbed her hand again. "We must speak to the first mate."

The crew scrambled to prepare the rest of the cannons, load shot into pistols, and distribute blades. But when Ally and Maher reached the quarterdeck, they found a small group of sailors confronting the first mate.

"We're about to be swallowed up," the leader of the group was saying, her sunburnt arm sweeping out as if Kamharida hadn't seen the other ships. "We still have time to get away, if we dump the cargo and cut our losses."

The sailors behind her gave their agreement.

Kamharida's countenance never slipped. "You are all employed by the Birde Isles, paid to carry out your duties. This is not a pirate vessel, where a vote can be called on every little matter. Lord Luthais informed us of the possible danger of this voyage, and you all turned down the chance to stay behind. You are here because you chose to serve the Birde Isles and rescue Lady Kingfisher. Was that all a lie?"

Many of those gathered looked doubtful, a few shuffled back from the group. The leader noticed Ally paused on the steps, and her lip curled into a sneer. "And what of her? We didn't agree to sail with some sea witch's whore, who's lost us the goddess' blessing."

Maher surged forward, but Ally put a hand on his arm.

"What was that, sailor?" Kamharida rested a hand on the sword strapped to her hip.

Leaving Maher's side, Ally stepped in front of the first mate, the top of her head barely clearing the other woman's shoulder.

"I understand," she said evenly. "I understand this mission isn't what you thought it would be, and you're afraid. I'm afraid too. I've been afraid my entire life. Now I'm here surrounded by the thing that terrifies me most and I have to deal with it because someone I love with all my heart needs me." Ally looked at each of them in turn. "Lady Kingfisher needs all of us. I'm not asking anyone not to be afraid, because I'm still terrified, but I am asking you to help me. To help her. Please."

Kamharida shifted behind her, "Argue with that if you dare, but we both know you don't have the numbers for an attempted mutiny anymore."

The leader looked around and saw that only two crewmates still stood with her. The rest had all backed away. She swore, "Cowards."

"The only coward I see here is you," said Maher.

"We'll have all the guns loaded and teams at the ready by the time they close in on us," said Kamharida. "With any luck, this will be just a show of strength, Foraoise Dare flexing her muscles."

Maher joined them on the quarterdeck, "And if it's not for show?"

"Then hopefully we can make a hole in the line to escape. She wouldn't risk sinking a ransom this size, not after going through all this trouble to get it." She turned a sharp eye to the crew. "Back to your posts."

"Thank you," Ally said as the would-be mutineers dispersed.

Their leader stopped in front of Ally and looked her over. "If I die for this, I'm going to haunt your steps the rest of your days."

"That's fair."

FORAOISE

CHAPTER EIGHTY-FOUR

A ripple of pleasure slid down Foraoise's spine as her ships closed in on the *Pike*.

She only wished she could have seen their faces as each ship came into view. And these were only a few of the ships she'd commandeered, imagine the terror that would sweep through Kingsport when every ship under her banner closed in on the city.

Now the *Maiden's Revenge* was nearly upon them, towering above the smaller vessel. The girl standing by the helm had to be Lady Kingfisher's daughter. She had the same hair if nothing else. With her wide-brimmed hat covering her own hair, Foraoise leaned against the ship's rail. When they pulled up alongside the *Pike*, she called down to them.

"So glad you could join us. Name your captain."

A tall woman with long braids stepped forward. "I am Kamharida Anyanwu, First Mate of this ship. The captain turned command over to me as we set sail."

Foraoise's brows rose, "Impressive." Behind her, the crew jeered and taunted the smaller ship. "And where is the young Lady Kingfisher?"

As expected, the brunette girl she'd spotted earlier stood next to the first mate. A lanky young man with a black beard stayed close behind her, arms crossed and glared up at Foraoise. A bodyguard, perhaps. Or a lover. No matter.

The captain spread her hands. "Well, we'd best get to business before we lose the daylight. I'll send a ladder down for you, Lady Alphonsine."

The girl whispered something to the man behind her.

"A ladder?" the first mate frowned. "No, you send down Lady Rochelle Kingfisher and we'll load the ransom cargo onto whichever of your ships you want, but Lady Alphonsine stays here."

"You're in no position to dictate terms," Foraoise indicated the ships surrounding them, most within firing range. "Either Lady Alphonsine comes aboard my ship to seal the trade, or I slaughter her mother here and now, then take your ship to add to my own." She straightened, saying as she turned away, "It's your choice, Lady Alphonsine. I'll give you a few minutes to decide."

Foraoise moved to where Rochelle was held at the mast. Her teeth bit into the cloth they'd tied over her mouth, a string of muffled obscenities were sent in the captain's direction.

"I told you that your daughter would come, dear heart." She grinned, knowing the other woman would seethe at Foraoise using such an endearment. Lady Kingfisher jerked her head away when Foraoise tried to push some of her lank hair out of her face. The captain shrugged, "Just trying to make you presentable."

She strolled at a leisurely pace back to the rail. Below, Lady Alphonsine was in a heated argument with the bodyguard and First Mate Anyanwu. The girl shook her head and pointed at the *Maiden's Revenge*, while the *Pike* crew visible on the decks watched them warily. Foraoise smiled to herself. Setback and surprises notwithstanding, the plan was working out well.

"Have you come to a decision, my lady?"

They all stared up at her again. Squaring her shoulders, Alphonsine shook off the others. "I'll come aboard, as long as you prove my mother is on that ship with you."

"Excellent." Captain Dare waved a hand and Lady Kingfisher was dragged close enough for them to catch a glimpse. Another flick of her wrist and their hostage disappeared. Alphonsine was stock still, a hand pressed to her chest. Foraoise had her now.

A rope ladder was tied to the railing and dropped over the side. The wooden slats that made up the steps clacked all the way down. Two of her most trusted sailors went down to escort Lady Alphonsine aboard. Kamharida Anyanwu had her pistol drawn by the time they reached the deck below, but wisely kept it pointed down. Alphonsine's bodyguard tried to stop her one last time. She brushed past him.

Bookended by the two sailors, the girl made the climb up the ladder. Foraoise half-expected it to take longer, but these Kingfisher women were all apparently tougher than they looked.

When her crew pulled the slightly out-of-breath girl over the railing, Foraoise swept into a bow, "Welcome aboard the *Maiden's Revenge*, Lady Alphonsine."

"You're the captain, I take it?" she panted. "Captain Dare?"

"At your service." Foraoise jerked her head towards the mast, "Your mother, in one piece, as promised."

The girl reached inside her coat. Foraoise stiffened, wondering if the little chit was actually going to pull a weapon on her own ship. Then Alphonsine saw her mother sprawled on the deck and ran to her side instead.

The crew let her pass, leaving a little space around Lady Kingfisher as her daughter dropped to her knees and pulled the gag out of her mother's mouth.

"Mama! Mama, don't worry, we're here to take you home."

"You have to leave, Ally!" Rochelle sobbed. "Get off the ship!"

"Not without you," she tugged at the ropes around her wrists. "Stand up, Mama, please."

"You don't understand, she's not going to let you go!"

"You should listen to your mother, Alphonsine," Foraoise said. The girl's head whipped around, hazel eyes blazing.

"That's the deal," Alphonsine spat. "We give you the ransom and you let us leave."

"Not anymore." Foraoise saw more of a resemblance now between mother and daughter, and something nasty twisted in her stomach. She barked at the nearest sailor, "Pull the ladder up!"

ALLY

CHAPTER EIGHTY-FIVE

"What are you doing?" Ally demanded.

"What would you guess I'm doing?" The captain's grin flashed beneath the brim of her hat.

"Don't you want the ransom?"

"Why bother with that when two hostages are far more lucrative than one?"

"No, no…" her mother cried. Ally tried again to help her stand. Mama was in the same clothes she'd been wearing when she left Kingsport all those weeks ago. She was dirty, her gown was torn, but she was alive. She was alive and Ally was getting them off this ship one way or another.

"Mama, please stand up," she whispered.

She tried to rise, but her knees buckled, and Ally was forced to lower her back onto the deck. Something heavy clinked together when her skirt touched the boards. Ally felt along the hem, her fingers scraped over haphazard stitching and hard shapes shifted inside the fabric. They'd sewn weights into her mother's clothing.

Ally should have let Maher come on board with her, he'd wanted to come, demanded to come with her, but she'd refused and climbed onto the *Maiden's Revenge* alone. So determined to do this without anyone's help, and now she needed someone, anyone, to help get Mama to her feet.

An older man with a gray-streaked mustache appeared, joining the pirate captain. "Crew of the *Pike*! Captain Dare is feeling generous today. She'll let you all free with your lives, and the cargo on your ship, but only if you leave now. Split the ransom if you wish."

"What? No, Ally! Ally!" Maher shouted from the deck of the *Pike*. There was more yelling as the crew pressed for them to take the opportunity and leave. Kamharida's calls for order were drowned out, lines and rigging visible from Ally's place on the deck jerked into motion. The poor barrelman still up in the crow's nest looked right at Ally, guilt and anguish and hope of survival all written on her face. Ally tried to wave at her, to give some sign that everything would be alright, but she couldn't. Her hands stayed locked around her mother's arm.

The captain prowled across the deck, hands resting on her belt. Her hat was pulled so low, Ally could really only make out her face from the nose down. A braid of rusted red hair hung over one of her shoulders, stiff, like cheap dye had been poured onto it and never washed out.

"Now, where were we?" Her voice was rough, weather worn.

"Listen Ally, listen to me!" Mama rasped into her ear. "She's not who you think she is."

"What do you mean?" Ally tried to soothe her. There were deep, purple circles beneath her mother's dark brown eyes.

"I think I can answer that," Foraoise answered. Kneeling a few feet away, she slowly pulled off her hat.

The first thing Ally saw was the terrible scar running over one side of her head, the hair around it shaved down to the scalp. It looked as if someone had tried to cut the woman's head off and missed. Maybe that's exactly what happened.

So that's where Beitris got that idea from. Mister Tapper had forced his daughter to wear a wig until it all grew back, nearly two years. She tamped down on the absurd urge to giggle.

That urge disappeared entirely as she took in the scars of all kinds that riddled the pirate captain's face and neck. Years of sun and sea had toughened the skin around them and freckles stood out across her slightly upturned nose.

"Do you see it?" Her mother whispered, sounding almost feverish.

What am I supposed to see? Ally scanned her face again. Scars, freckles, wide set brows and...

Kingfisher eyes.

Ally's heart pounded so hard she was sure it was going to break through her ribs. She was looking into another version of her father's face. A little narrower, a little malnourished, riddled with crooked scars and harsher lines, but still full of Kingfisher features. Ally blinked hard, trying to wipe away the image, but shave off her father's mustache and put him next to this woman? Goddess help her, they could almost be twins.

It was the eyes that disturbed Ally the most. Her father's moss green eyes, looking back at her with such contempt. "I'd hoped to have you both on the *Swan Song*, only to find out my own niece is afraid of the sea. Rather pathetic for a girl born to an island kingdom, don't you think?"

"You're..." Ally's mouth went dry as sand. "You're one of the daughters who was sent away."

"Sent away?" Foraoise sneered and stood back up. "Is that what you call it?"

"I don't understand, why go through all this if you knew who you were? Why not contact the family and explain?"

"What family? *I'm* not the one who has anything to explain."

Ally flinched.

"Don't worry, they're going to have ample opportunity to make things right."

Ally rose, shielding her mother with her legs. The *Pike* was turning away, they were really leaving. A small part of her sighed in relief. Maher, Kamharida, and the rest of the crew would be safe. They'd make it to Kingsport and warn everyone about Captain Dare's deceit. At least Ally could look after Mama now.

"What are you going to do?"

"I'm going to claim everything that should have been mine." Foraoise clasped her hands behind her back, watching the other ship make its escape. "But first, I'm going to show you my prized possession. Gunner!"

"Aye, Captain?" A brawny, middle-aged woman pushed her way forward.

"Run out the bows. We're going to give the ladies a demonstration."

"Aye! All bow teams, to me!" She left with at least thirty pirates, all disappearing below decks.

"What is this?" Ally fought the bile that burned up her throat. "What are you demonstrating?"

"Watch and see."

Beneath them, a loud clanging of metal against metal made the boards of the deck shudder. Her mother groaned, as if she knew what those sounds meant. Chains screeched as the covers to the gunports opened. The rest of the pirates had gone still. Every other ship was watching the *Pike*.

The blood drained from Ally's face. "You said you would let them live! You said they could go!"

"They didn't leave fast enough."

"Bows ready!" the Gunner called from the gun deck below.

Rochelle clung to Ally's leg, as if she were trying to hold her daughter in place.

"Don't do this!" Ally begged.

"It's already done."

A brief moment of stillness hung over them. Ally pulled in one breath, then two.

Then the Gunner shouted, "FIRE AT WILL!"

Giant bolts shot from beneath their feet and punched into the back and starboard side of the *Pike*, the thick cords attached to their ends grew taught with each hit. Wood splintered and the ship was yanked to a stop.

"MAHER!" Ally shrieked. Breaking free of her mother's weak grip, she ran for the ship's rail, ready to throw the ladder back over... only to be jerked to a stop by a pirate's arm around her waist. She watched, horrified, as one of the bolts sliced through the mainmast, felling it like a tree and sending the young barrelman flying through the air. She tucked herself into a ball and crashed into the sea on the other side of the ship. A couple of the bolts missed and came splashing back to the *Maiden's Revenge* as they were reeled in like fishing lines.

A whirring noise, unlike anything Ally'd heard before, started towards the front of the ship. It grew stronger and louder, even the pirate holding her tensed at the power of it. The closest thing she could compare it to was the sound a spinning bobbin made as linen thread was woven at a fast pace. There was a woman in Kingsport who could run her wheel so quickly, it sounded like a buzzing bee. That's what this noise became as it continued to grow louder, a monstrous bee. The whole of the *Maiden's Revenge* was quivering now, the sensation running up her legs and making her teeth ache. Only the captain seemed immune to the discomfort experienced by everyone else on board. Her attention stayed on the battered, bolt-ridden ship. It was still floating, nothing had caught fire, yet.

Ally could just make out some of the crew on the *Pike*. She hoped, begged any gods that were listening, they were securing the longboats and getting as many off as possible.

Please let Maher be alright. Please, please.

The whirring built to a pitch that made the pirate let go of her to cover his ears. Ally pressed her palms over her own as pressure built deep inside her ear canals. What *thing* was making this noise? It was starting to jumble her thoughts. She staggered forward, feeling like her skull was going to crack like an egg. A sharp, tangy scent hit her nose and Ally was searching her memory for what it meant when the noise abruptly stopped. All around her, she could feel the collective sigh as the pressure eased.

Someone far, far away yelled, "FIRE ALL!"

There was another ear-splitting clank of metal. The cords attached to the bolts bowed and stretched. Ally's stomach curdled as wave after wave of *electricity* bounced along the cords, almost too fast for her to see. The currents were wild, many losing purchase and ricocheting away, sizzling into the sea or dying before they reached the end. But three waves held on until they smashed into the *Pike*. The ship buckled inward, gunpowder ignited and flames shot into the air.

Lightning from the sea. The survivors from the *Gull's Flight* had raved about lightning shooting out of the sea.

When the same pirate grabbed her again, Ally realized she'd almost made it to the rail that time.

With a final shudder, the *Pike* collapsed into a twisted hunk of iron and wood that didn't even resemble a ship anymore, and sank beneath the churning waves.

Chapter Eighty-six

Maher fought the crew as they readied the ship to pull away, leaving both Ally and Lady Kingfisher behind.

"What's wrong with all of you!" He tried to stop a sailor from pulling in a line.

"We want to live!" She'd pushed him away and gone back to her task.

He barely noticed when Kamharida herded him away from the crew and into the captain's cabin. Only when the door shut behind her did he take in his surroundings.

"We can't just let them take her!" Maher tried to get past the first mate and was soundly rebuffed.

"We have to, if anyone is going to warn the Kingfishers."

"But she might..."

"Get ahold of yourself!" Kamharida grabbed his shoulders. "All it would take to sink us is one cannon shot from each of those ships currently surrounding ours. They obviously don't care about the ransom. Who will tell Lord Kingfisher where to find his wife and daughter if we're all dead at the bottom of the sea?"

Maher sagged, some of the fight draining out of him. She was right, it wouldn't do Ally or her mother any good if they attacked Dare now. "How quickly can we get back to Kingsport?"

"Once we clear the pirates, we'll raise full canvas and put up an alert flag. If any of the gods are on our side, we'll pass a friendly ship carrying messenger birds, or better yet a postal ship. That way we can send word ahead. With a good tailwind, and if the weather holds, we could be back in Trader's Bay in less than five days."

It was a good plan, better than any other option they had. Maher relented and she released him.

"What can I do to help?"

She scanned the cabin and her eyes landed on the desk. "You can start drafting letters to our allies and a report for Lord Kingfisher. Include every detail you can think of, the make of each vessel we saw. If the rumors are true, and she's stolen ships from every nation that sails the Eastern Sea corridor, what we saw today may only be a fraction of the fleet she's built. After we've cleared cannon range from Dare's ships, I'll write a report of my own to Lord Luthais and we can compare what we both remember."

"I'll start right away," said Maher, feeling more clear-headed now that they had a plan in place. He held out a hand, "I know your first responsibility is to ensure the crew's safety, but thank you for everything else."

Clasping his hand, Kamharida said, "We should be nearly turned about by now, I'll check back in after I speak to the helmsman."

The wall behind Maher shattered. Wood and glass and metal flew through the air. The ship rocked violently to one side and they were thrown to the floor as debris rained down on them.

Through the settling dust, Maher found an arrowhead the size of an anchor's crown stuck into the hull. Long, curved spikes like those on a grappling hook dug into the wood and locked it in place.

"They're firing on us," Kamharida coughed. "That double-crossing bitch is firing on us!"

Maher tried to stand and was hurled off his feet again when a second, third, and fourth blow hit the *Pike*. Sailors were crying out and the whole ship tilted as something monstrous came crashing down outside.

The first mate made it to her feet and wrenched the cabin doors open. "Sea spirits help us."

He ran out after Kamharida. Their mainmast had broken clean off, leaving a jagged stump where it once stood. There were sailors crushed beneath it. Maher saw the woman whose rope line he'd tried to take just moments before, her lifeless eyes staring up at him.

Maher pushed into the chaos. Sailors rushed to pull crewmates out of the hold, he heard someone shout that one of the huge bolts had destroyed the stairs leading below decks. Dust and grit stung his eyes and clogged his nose. Someone's blood sprayed across his face as they staggered and collapsed nearby, a hunk of wood stuck through their side. Maher stopped to help lift a section of railing off another man. When Maher was sure the sailor could stand, he went on to the next. Not knowing how long he moved from one person to another, only that he couldn't stop, couldn't stand still and watch everything crumble around him.

Above it all, he could still hear Kamharida, and it spurred him on. "Ready the longboats! Load in the wounded! I need two uninjured crew to row – Don't just stand there, sailor! Prepare to abandon ship!"

Maher reached where the first mate was coordinating a longboat full of wounded sailors, their blood running and mixing together at the bottom of the boat. He looked down at himself and saw he was covered in red as well, though he was fairly sure none of it was his.

Some time had gone by since the last bolt hit them, but the pause in attack didn't give him much hope. He wanted to ask Kamharida how many longboats were still usable, taking one step towards her before his knees hit the bloodstained deck. It was like someone had looped a vise around his head and fastened it tight. Covering his ears barely helped, the pressure was coming from *inside* his skull. Running along beneath it, Maher swore he heard some kind of humming noise. A low, steady, unending purr that made the bones in his face throb.

Looking up, he found Kamharida still fighting to lower the longboat by herself. The sailor who'd been operating the pulley with her was writhing on the deck. Maher forced his hands from his ears and dragged himself over. Taking up the discarded rope, he followed Kamharida's count.

"One, two, heave! One, two, heave!"

Their ropes slipped and the boat fell the last few feet, splashing into the churning water. The two uninjured sailors who'd gone with the wounded took up their oars and rowed for all they were worth.

"We have to get another one down!" Kamharida's words barely registered over the pounding in his head. He followed her to the next longboat, tripping over splintered hunks of ship and dead bodies in his haste to keep up. There were already a few wounded crewmates inside, too weak to try to block out the skull-splitting sound.

Another rope was thrust into his hands. Maher stared at it until she yelled at him to get the boat into position, while she helped more passengers onboard. The muscles in his arms and shoulders screamed as he pulled and pulled until the longboat inched into motion.

Just when Maher thought his brain was going to turn to mush and run out his ears, everything went quiet. Kamharida blinked hard, gesturing to ask if the noise had stopped for him as well.

Nodding slowly, Maher craned his neck to look back at the *Maiden's Revenge*. Thick cords attached to the bolts hooked into the *Pike* reached all the way back into the larger ship's gunports. Captain Dare was standing on the deck, watching them. Waiting. What was she waiting for?

A toneless, drawn-out clang pealed through the air. It sounded like it came from *inside* Dare's ship and he imagined a clock's inner workings winding up to chime the hour. The hair on Maher's arms stood up and he could taste the static on his tongue. Letting go of the rope, Maher grabbed a hatchet from the belt of a dead woman lying nearby.

"Hold on!" he shouted at the wild-eyed sailors in the boat and cut the line. The longboat dropped.

Kamharida darted to him and leaned over the side, "Villaon! What are you doing!"

The air crackled around them, and Maher did the only thing he could think of. He ran at Kamharida, shoulder down, and tackled her over the rail. They hit the water together, spiraling downward until she pushed away from him. Above them, something massive struck the *Pike*, the force scattering them through the sea like leaves caught by the wind.

Pain seared through Maher's shoulder and his entire body convulsed, no longer under his control. The last of his air escaped through his lips and for a moment, before the water closed in around him, he could have sworn he saw the sea goddess' face.

ALLY

CHAPTER EIGHTY-SEVEN

Planting her feet, Ally drove both elbows back into the pirate's gut as hard as she could. Swearing, he shoved her away, back towards her mother. Ally collapsed next to her, and Rochelle wrapped her bound arms over Ally's head to hug her close.

"I'm so sorry, darling," her tears dampened Ally's hair. "So, so sorry."

Cheers erupted from some of the crew around them. It was worse than hearing whatever mechanical contraption had dredged up that electric charge.

Ally was wrenched from her mother's arms, her neck twisting painfully. The new pirate holding Ally's arm only let go when she took a wild swing at her face.

Captain Dare soaked up the praise from her crew. "What did you think, Lady Alphonsine? Will my discovery be quite a *shock* to the people of Kingsport?"

Ally's teeth ground together when the woman at her back cackled, as if the slaughter of innocents was something to be laughed at. Like the deaths of everyone on that ship meant nothing.

As Foraoise turned to survey the bubbling place where the *Pike* had once been, a furious roaring filled Ally's head. Like the never-ending waves crashing against the cliffs by her home. This woman might look like her family, but she was a monster. Worse than any creature from Esa's stories. Next to her, the knife sticking out of the pirate's belt glinted in the fading sunlight.

Pushing her arm out of the way, Ally grabbed the knife and dove for the captain's back. She was only three steps away, two, one... the mustached man appeared out of nowhere and tackled Ally from the side. He beat her fist against the deck until the knife clattered away.

"You have my thanks, Swain." A pair of brown boots arrived in front of Ally's face. Scarred hands yanked on Ally's forearms and she was hauled to her feet.

"Aye, Captain," the man, Swain, puffed as he stood up. He glowered at the rest of the crew. "One of you younger swabs better be prepared to do that in future! I'm getting too old to be throwing myself across the deck. Back to your posts!"

"Aye aye, Quartermaster!" several of them answered.

"Come with me, my little *niece*." Foraoise dragged Ally to the other side of the ship. "I don't appreciate when people try to kill me, it doesn't bring out my best side."

"I didn't think you had another side from this one," Ally spat.

"Oh? That's too bad." Foraoise lifted a finger towards Ally's nose. "Tell me what happened here,"

"None of your business," she wrenched her head away.

The captain leaned close and whispered into Ally's ear. "I'm going to take everything that should have been mine. Kingsport will be mine. The Birde Isles will be mine. Every person you hold dear is going to fear me, bow to *me*. And when I catch your mermaid, Ally, I will have the greatest weapon of all."

Ally couldn't have said where the impulse came from, some primal place that wanted to hurt the captain for having the impudence to even know Pasha existed. She lunged and her teeth clicked together less than an inch away from Foraoise's own nose.

When those gratingly familiar eyes widened and her face twitched away, Ally felt a surge of grim satisfaction. "If you really believe that, *Captain*, then you will have nothing."

"Just as spirited as your mother, it's a pity." Captain Dare's hold on her wrists tightened, grinding the bones together, "But I think I'll do just as well with one hostage after all."

What came next felt like it was all happening to someone else. It wasn't Ally standing there in the captain's grip. It wasn't Ally seeking out her mother's grief-stricken face in the crowd around them. It wasn't the backs of Ally's legs hitting the low rail. And it wasn't Ally's body that was tipped off the edge of the ship.

"Why don't you go for a swim?" Foraoise shoved her overboard.

Falling through the air, the captain's wicked grin and bloodstained hair growing smaller and smaller, Ally settled into a strange place of peace. It seemed inevitable somehow, that she'd meet her death in the sea.

She didn't want to leave Mama behind.

She regretted that she'd never get to apologize to Pasha.

But everything else faded away.

At least Maher will be waiting for me. Ally found herself smiling at the thought. *At least we can walk into the next life together.* Her eyes slid closed, and her arms spread out at her sides.

The last thing Ally heard before she hit the water was her mother screaming her name.

PASHA

CHAPTER EIGHTY-EIGHT

Pasha couldn't bear to go back home, not yet. Home was too full of memories again. New memories replacing the old voices that once followed her through the empty maze of caverns and tunnels.

Every passage now echoed with Ally's excited gasp at seeing the glowing corals. In the great chamber, all Pasha would see was Ally's face as she took in the dozens of mermaids carved into glittering rock. All she'd feel was Ally's thumb sweeping over the back of her hand, comparing the softness to the shark's. And the tapestry chamber, how could Pasha go in there again without thinking of her? When one of the most important tapestries was hidden somewhere inside Ally's house? The map. Ally'd been so pleased there was something she could do for Pasha. There was no retrieving the map now, not that she'd been able to read it before anyway. The loss wasn't so great, not nearly as great as everything else she'd never get back.

With the islands still at least three days' journey away, and no desire to face them yet, Pasha sank low into the water. As aimlessly as she'd been swimming since leaving the ship, Pasha wasn't entirely sure where in the sea she was, only that she'd been traveling in the direction of home. She sent bright tendrils of energy out in each direction, slowly wending from her fingertips through the water like sea snakes, searching. They were looking for a trove.

Mermaid troves were once scattered throughout the seas. Safe stopping points for those who traveled between communities. They were filled with tools and treasures the mermaids left for one another. Jewelry, trinkets, fishing nets, even weapons. Whatever was needed, they could take and replace it with something else.

Pasha had only seen a trove once when she was very young. Pallagia had taken her to the closest one, half a day's swim from their home. It was small, being so near a community like theirs, with barely enough room for both of them to fit beneath the slab of stone that hung over the entrance. Pallagia left behind a round, metal human shield taken from a shipwreck and told Pasha to pick anything she wanted to take. Just one thing.

Sifting through the treasures left behind, Pasha lifted out a dagger with a jewel-studded hilt, a silver hand mirror tarnished by the seawater, a ceramic teapot missing its lid, and put each one back down. None of them felt right. Her sister was patient, draping herself against one side of the cave. The gray and green scales of her tail, her silvery skin and fern green hair, all blended together until Pallagia looked like a moss-dappled carving in the rock wall.

Just as Pasha thought she'd never been able to choose, she felt it. The itch that started at the back of her head when she came close to a particularly old bone. It was different from the vibrations that swept over her skin and tickled at her palms when jewels were nearby. Pasha pressed a hand against the cave wall and when the itch grew stronger, she drifted in that direction. Tucked into a small hollow in the back of the cave, the shark tooth's jet-black surface glistened even in the trove's dim light. It was so large, when Pasha lifted it out she needed both hands to hold the tooth.

"Do you know what that is, Pasha?" Pallagia swam up behind her.

"A shark's tooth," she'd whispered.

"Not just a shark's tooth. I bet if we show the elders, they'd say this belonged to one of the great-jawed sharks that once ruled some parts of the sea." Her voice dropped into a whisper, "A great-jawed shark could hunt and feed on a fully grown whale."

Pasha gawked at her sister, unable to fully comprehend a shark of that size. "Are there any of those sharks left?"

"The last of them died a long time ago," she cupped Pasha's hands around her pick from the trove. "So you'd better take good care of that, it's far older than anything we have at home. Maybe even older than our home itself."

One of Pasha's tendrils finally came back with what she was looking for. A trove, close enough to reach before dark. It would take her farther from home, but Pasha didn't mind that.

The trove was hidden inside of a rock formation surrounded by a thriving kelp forest. A school of curious brown and white bass circled her as she followed the wisp of energy through the stalks. This trove hadn't been used for many, many years. Pasha shifted the rocks that were stacked over the entrance until she could comfortably swim through.

Most of the things left here had been worn down by time or made into homes by tiny creatures. Fish bones of varying sizes littered the floor of the cave. Something'd had more than a few meals there. Then Pasha's eye caught on a strangely familiar object leaning in a far corner of the cave, the only treasure still in one piece. A spear. This wasn't a human spear, Pasha realized as she took a closer look. This spear was forged by mermaids. She hadn't seen one since she was a child. Her family had taken the few they still had left with them.

Pasha's palms tingled as she picked up the long weapon, testing its weight. The energy of the last mermaid to use it danced beneath the surface, sparking to life at her touch. It wasn't anyone Pasha knew; she could tell that much. The shaft of the spear was nearly as long as she was, carved out of a pearlescent green stone. It was one unbroken piece, made with methods that had been lost long before Pasha was born. An end cap of gilded, inky black metal was on the bottom, and the same material made up the wicked tapered blade set into the other end. At least, it resembled metal.

Long shadows shifted and grew around her, the last of the light would be gone soon. Pasha would stay for a day or two, see what else might have been left in or near the cave. Whatever else she found, wherever she went from here, the spear would be coming with her. Getting as comfortable as she could, Pasha laid the spear beside her, still not quite believing that something so precious had been waiting in an abandoned trove. There had to be something she could find to trade for it. Her fingers trailed over the green stone, somehow perfectly smooth even after an untold amount of time underwater.

Ally would love to see this. She sighed.

Pasha jerked her hand away, as if the spear had bitten her. Turning over, she wrapped her arms around her middle and shut her eyes.

There was no escape, even in sleep. Ally flitted through Pasha's dreams throughout the night, running or swimming ahead of her, beckoning for her to catch up. Always just out of reach. In the last dream Pasha had, Ally was standing on the edge of the cliff behind her house, where she'd sat morning after morning, often with Pasha clinging to the rocks below. The same cliff that Pallagia and Ealasaid went over so many years ago. Only this time Pasha was on the cliff too, without her tail, the grass digging into the soles of her feet like a thousand knives. Every step was agony, but something deep inside told her she had to reach Ally before it was too late. Ally was staring out at the sea, the wind blowing in off the swells and tangling her brown curls. She was wearing nothing but a nightgown and the pulsing shark tooth around her neck.

Pasha reached out a hand, tried to call out to her, but Ally didn't seem to hear over the wind and the waves. Then she turned, giving Pasha a serene smile that didn't quite reach her eyes. A resigned smile. The nightgown beneath the shark tooth was turning red, as if blood was seeping from it and leaching into the material. Pasha tried to run, tried to help her, but more knives sliced her feet and calves. If only she had her tail, if only they were in the water, she'd already be by Ally's side.

Backing up to the edge of the cliff, Ally's bare heels hung over the drop. She took off the shark tooth and held it out to Pasha. As soon as the necklace left her neck, the blood-soaked nightgown began to freeze. Ice crystals spread up Ally's legs and down her arms, frost touched the ends of her hair and her lips quickly turned blue. Except for the light still in her eyes, she looked almost dead.

"Put it back on!" Pasha screamed. She took another step and fell to her knees, new cuts appeared on her legs and hands where they touched the ground. "Please Ally, put it back on!"

Without answering, Ally dropped the necklace onto the ground. She pressed frostbitten fingers to her blue lips and blew Pasha a kiss. An icy blast hit her face and Pasha grabbed handfuls of sharp grass to stop herself from being tossed down the slope. Ally's eyelids closed and her hands spread out by her sides.

"Don't!" Pasha crawled the rest of the way to her, leaving a bloody trail that wove all the way down to the bottom of the hill. "Ally, please don't leave."

She picked up the shark tooth, the energy she'd infused into it all those years ago was gone. Pebbles scattered and now only Ally's toes were gripping the edge of the cliff. Finally reaching the stone ledge, Pasha lunged for Ally as she tipped backwards. Pasha's fingers grazed Ally's frozen ankle, and then she was falling.

Pasha could only watch as Ally plummeted towards the sea, the jagged rocks jutting up through the surface.

"ALLY!" She jolted awake. Shards of bone were spinning around the trove, shattering against the cave walls, pelting her skin hard enough to draw blood.

"ENOUGH!" Pasha's breath came in heaving gasps. Wild electric arcs bounced off each other as the last of the fish bones dropped back into the sand. The green stone of the spear lying next to her glowed and pulsed, trying to respond to the energy Pasha sent out in her sleep.

It was only a dream. Pasha told herself, reining in the arcs before they broke anything else inside the cave. *It was only a dream. Ally is fine. She should have her mother back by now, they're probably on their way home.*

Home. Pasha's heart felt like it was going to break apart. Is this what Pallagia felt when she lost Ealasaid? Did Pasha even have a home anymore? Would anywhere in the world truly be home if Ally wasn't there?

CHAPTER EIGHTY-NINE

It took three sailors to drag Rochelle Kingfisher back into the captain's quarters. Some of her old fight returned when her daughter went overboard. She even managed to break one man's nose before they got her subdued.

Foraoise watched the spectacle with mild disinterest. That's what becoming attached to another person did to you. Inevitably, something would go wrong. People lie, people cheat, people break their promises, people leave... people die.

"Enough," she muttered to herself, crossing the deck to the rail facing the place where the *Pike* went under. Chunks of debris and scattered cargo had begun floating to the surface. The bodies would soon follow. They'd send out a party to search for anything of value. She'd already sent the *Swan Song* after the longboats that managed to escape while the weapon aboard the *Maiden's Revenge* charged.

The extra minutes needed for the machine to warm up was costing more time than she liked. But, until they could get someone on board who knew more about its construction, they'd have to make do.

Smoothing her hands over the sun-warmed wood of the railing, Foraoise could almost feel Jon standing next to her. That first voyage was a lifetime ago now; the details of Jon's young face were already fading from her memory.

"Captain," Swain joined her and all thoughts of Jon drifted away with the breeze. "Was that wise, throwing the girl over?" When she made no reply, he cleared his throat. "Only I'm sure the crew are curious as to why we went through all the trouble of demanding a ransom to lure the Kingfishers' daughter here, only to be right back where we started."

"Every decision we make has the potential for more than one outcome, Swain."

"Meaning?"

"Meaning, that we aren't necessarily back where we started. We're going to use my dear niece's dip into the depths as a test." Foraoise looked back out at the horizon. There was only blue water as far as the eye could see. It would take days to reach land by ship. "We're going to see if the rumor about Lady Alphonsine is true."

"How will we know that, Captain?"

"We'll know, Swain, if the mermaid comes to save her."

ALLY

CHAPTER NINETY

Every scrap of air was knocked from Ally's lungs when she hit the cold water. She tumbled deeper and deeper, whipped around like a rag doll by the wake of the ship.

Ally couldn't find which direction led back to the surface. Soon, as expected, her lungs began to burn. The stillness that had wrapped around her on the way down shattered when the shark tooth on its chain slipped off her neck and she grabbed frantically for it. Ally's hand closed around the tooth and the sharp point sliced across her palm. Ally screamed, the seawater flooded in. She could taste her own blood clouding the water. The sound echoed around her, rippling out through the depths. Her eyes closed again.

Ally was flying. No, she was floating.

Her body was no longer cold, the water enveloping her instead in a snug embrace. Everything was calm, comfortable. She didn't want to move, but after some coaxing her eyes blinked open. Around her was nothing but an endless stretch of darkness.

Was this death?

She felt the tooth clutched in her hand, her palm throbbed from the fresh cut. No, it couldn't be death if her hand hurt that much.

A trickle of blood still wrapped around her, dissolving into the water as it floated farther away. Shadows rippled as she drifted along with the tide. Looking up, or what she supposed was up, Ally thought she saw twinkling stars shifting across the water's surface. Her legs were suspended above nothing. It really was like she was flying.

Ally felt the cool tingle of saltwater sliding along her throat, weaving through invisible gills. She was breathing. Pasha hadn't taken the gift back after all. Everything that had happened between them on the ship came rushing back. Pasha was gone, but Ally still had her gift.

I can breathe, I'm alive! The relief swelling in her chest with each breath slowed. *I'm sorry Maher. I can't be with you just yet*. He'd have to wait for her a while longer. Ally saw what that weapon on Dare's ship was capable of, Maher couldn't possibly have survived the *Pike* going down. None of them could... A sharp ache shot through her heart. Ally had to move, had to find her way back to the pirate's ship. She couldn't let Dare win.

Giving an experimental kick of one leg, her body bobbed to the left. A kick with the other leg and she drifted back to the right. Could she swim until she found land? Possibly. But whose land would it be? Ally wanted to move, to find a way back to her mother, but something kept her in place. Something told her to wait. A faint tickle at the back of her mind. *Wait*.

The night waned on, Ally floated and waited. Slowly, so very slowly, out of the darkness below it came, moving its great bulk through the water. Ally saw a pinpoint of light first, a tiny underwater star that grew larger and brighter as the creature it was attached to swam closer.

Warmth spread through her bones and the world grew brighter as the creature's head came into view. The source of the light, an orb easily the size of her head, was fastened to its skull by one long, flexible appendage. Rows of sharp teeth jutted from a crescent-shaped mouth, set below opaque predator's eyes. One of those teeth was easily as long as Ally's arm, yet she wasn't afraid. That same tickling sensation in her head told her the creature didn't mean her any harm. It floated serenely in front of Ally. An eel-like body dipped down into the water below them, two wide side fins and a narrowed tail swished back and forth.

"Did I call you?" Ally whispered, unsure if the creature could even hear her words, let alone understand them.

The massive head turned, the light bobbled on its lever as the creature fixed one round eye on her. Ally could see her face reflected back, her wide eyes and hair billowing around her head. She laid her palm on the hard ridge just above its eye, just like she'd done with the whales. The slick skin, there were no scales, could have been gray or it could have been blue. Or, in the right light, it could have been the color of wet sand. She started to ask the creature to take her to Mama, but how could it possibly find the *Maiden's Revenge*? It waited patiently, the glowing orb attached to its head encasing them in a cozy bubble of light.

Ally slid her necklace back on, securing it beneath her shirt. Her arm pressed against a lump in her coat and Ally pulled out the brocade pouch. The last thing Pasha had given her... before Ally drove the mermaid away. Fingertips running over the raised pattern of the material, Ally thought of Pasha retrieving the priceless necklace from wherever it had been locked away, hidden for years at the bottom of the sea. Then she'd carried it all the way to meet Ally, swimming for days....

Carried it. Pasha had *carried* it.

Whirling in place, Ally found the creature where she'd left it. One giant eye rested on her as if it had all the time in the world. Was this calm creature really one of the dreaded sea monsters pulled from a sailor's yarn? A mindless predator, a shark twisted into a nightmare. But, sharks weren't mindless hunters. She knew that now. They were *skilled* hunters. Sharks had an incredible sense of smell, even under water. Maybe sea monsters did too.

"Can... Can you take me to Pasha?" She held the pouch under the creature's snout. Its oblong nostrils quivered, inhaling the scent from the fabric. Ally held her own breath, as if any sound she made might distract it.

With an undulation that wove down its entire body, the creature circled Ally and dipped below her. Running along its back was a long section of fins separated by sharp spines, with a break around where its skull began, and another spined fin sticking out from the back of its head. Tucking the pouch back into her pocket, Ally slipped down in between the head and back fins. Her hands were only somewhat shaky when she wrapped them around the front spine.

Another wave whipped down its backbone and the creature shot into motion. It moved with such speed, slicing through the water as if nothing could stand in its way, Ally nearly fell off. Gripping her knees against its sides, Ally hunkered down and hoped the creature knew where it was going.

Take me to Pasha, please, take me to Pasha. The silent plea took root in her heart like a prayer.

Crooning as if it understood, the sea monster banked down until the surface was lost from sight, carrying Ally into the unknown.

Acknowledgements

This book was more than a labor of love, it was built by a community.

To my parents, thank you for always encouraging me to follow my dream of being a published author. Mom, I love that you saved every scrap of paper I ever scribbled a story on as a kid and kept them safe as I found my way back to writing as an adult. Dad, you are without a doubt the best cheerleader, insisting everyone in the family had to have a copy of *Carolina Crimes* when my first short story was published.

To my fabulous beta and sensitivity readers, you are incredible! Can you believe you stuck with me through two years and a complete rewrite of this book? Your feedback and enthusiasm for this story was invaluable!

I also want to thank Foraoise, Captain Dare's namesake, for all of the time spent brainstorming and for just how much you believed in this story. And, let's face it, for helping to create one badass pirate captain!

To my critique partner and fellow writer, Toni, how many years have we been doing this now? You were the first to read Ally and Pasha and Maher's story, and even though you're not a regular fantasy reader you still jumped in with both feet! You're not afraid to tell me when something just doesn't work and you have no idea how much I appreciate that.

To my editor Rowe, who held my hand through two wildly different versions of this novel, you are the absolute best and I love how you challenge me as a writer.

To the talented Celipher, you brought my characters to life before I was even sure this book was going to be published. I'll never forget when you first reached out about drawing Captain Dare, I was so surprised! We've worked on multiple projects since then, but more importantly I feel I've gained a friend.

To my cover artist Sandra at Maldo Designs, thank you so much for walking me through my first cover design experience. For taking all of my random notes and "what about this instead?" questions, and turning them into something beautiful! I can't wait to brainstorm on the next Kingsport Chronicles cover with you.

To my map artist Rachael at Cartographybird, you took probably one of the worst sketches in history and made it into the gorgeous maps that represent this world that only existed in my head for so long. I hope we can work together again!

This section wouldn't be complete if I didn't include my wonderful online community of writers and readers. I'm so lucky to know each of you and I love how we're all on this journey together.

Like I said, this book – this series – wouldn't have been possible without this community and I'm grateful for all of you. Everyone who has encouraged me, everyone who has said they can't wait for TKTS to release, everyone who has already said the story resonates with them in some way: Thank you, from the bottom of my heart.

Index: Places

Index of all places in *To Kiss the Sea*

<u>The Known World</u>

The Birde Isles (bird): Capital: Kingsport (kings-port); Symbol: Kingfisher bird holding one fish in its beak; Worship: The Goddess of the Sea and her messengers (Henotheism); Collection of islands off the east coast of the continent; Only stopping point on the Unending Sea crossing, built into a bustling trade hub by Gaius Kingfisher I; Ally's birthplace.

Balah (bah-la): Capital: Ehlafi (Eh-lah-fee); Symbol: Stag; Worship: Polytheistic Trio of Deities (Sun, Moon, & In-Between); Prosperous country on the southeastern end of the Split Sea; Rochelle's birthplace.

Saprea (say-pree-ah): Capital: Laleseir (lah-lei-seer); Symbol: Double flower tulip; Worship: Polytheistic pantheon of deities, varied by region; Large, mid-continent nation that relies heavily on trade; Their major export is textiles; Maher's birthplace.

Fraolland (fray-oh-lund): Capital: Laivastho (Lah-ee-vahs-thoh; Symbol: Crossed cannons; Worship: Nature based; Located at the northeastern end of the Split Sea; Still holds territory on the Zavatleo and Saprean borders, holdover from the old Continental Wars; Powerful naval presence.

Meredia (mare-eh-dee-ah): Capital: New Pravil (prah-vill); Symbol: Crossed gavel and quill; Worship: Henotheism; Western neighbor to Balah; High level of control at the mouth of the Split Sea; Strong but regimented arts culture; Generally more concerned with their own affairs over mutual needs; Those raised in the capital tend to call it New Pravil.

Tjordun (sch-ohr-doon): Capital: Midthe (mid-teh); Symbol: A horse with an empty saddle; Worship: Polytheistic pantheon of deities; Shares the inner Split Sea border with Fraolland and Meredia; Strong ally with Balah, allows heavy land travel from the Eastern Sea coast to the Split Sea coast.

Utollmir (oo-toll-meer): Capital: Darajha (dah-rah-ha); Symbol: Circle of waves around the sun; Worship: Ancestral; Largest southern nation on the west side of the Split Sea; Major stopping point on the Southern Strait; Strong Birde Isles ally; Kamharida's birthplace.

Kharabo (kh-air-ah-boe): Capital: Botsa (boat-sah); Symbol: Crossed scrolls in front of a flowering tree branch; Worship: Ancestral; Land-locked northern neighbor of Utollmir, also their strongest ally; Known for the Great University at Botsa and multiple advancements in modern science; First nation on the continent to implement education for all citizens; Olebile's birthplace.

Char-range (ch-ah-r-raynj): Capital: Illsik-yun (ill-si-ck-yoon); Symbol: Mortar & pestle filled with various herbs; Worship – Deism; The largest country on the continent, Char-range takes up the entire west coast; Known historically for alchemy, later channeled those skills into mass herb farming and production of concentrated oils; Ga-Seung's birthplace.

Teratsu (teh-rah-tsoo): Capital: Ine (ee-neh); Symbol: Three trees of staggered age framed by a mountain; Worship: Mix of Deism and Non-theism (ethics based); Landlocked country between Char-range and Zavatleo; Mountainous and heavily forested, Teratsu controls the largest mining interest on the continent; Known for a specialized type of woodworking that integrates metal throughout each piece.

Nuvwaan (noov-wa-ahn): Capital(s): NuvLunsoh (noov-loo-n-soe) (Left Star) & NuvDamseh (noov-dahm-say) (Right Star); Symbol: A constellation with stars representing each island; Worship: Celestial; A collection of islands, the two largest are connected by a string of smaller land masses called the Bridge of Islands; Closest neighbors are Utollmir and Char-range; Known for beautiful coastlines and export of rare fruits.

Agriya (ahg-ree-yah): Capital: Muevat (Moo-eh-vah); Symbol: An ornate metal brazier with high flames; Worship: Nature based; A smaller nation that sits in the middle of Saprea's southern border, have had tensions in the past over access to the Southern Strait; Primary export: carmine powder and other paint pigments; Known for elaborate funeral processions that include the use of massive decorative pyres to burn the dead, people will travel to Agriya just to brag they've seen one.

Myrre (meer-ay): Capital: San Aveth (sahn-ah-vett); Symbol: Multiple hands joined together; Worship: Mixed, largely taken from their surrounding neighbors; Smallest and newest nation on the continent, broke off from Agriya more than a century ago. Borders Saprea, Agriya, and controls the western shore of the mouth of the Split Sea; Strong culinary culture.

Zavatleo: Capital: Straihorn; Symbol: Two bulls locking horns; Worship: Henotheism; Closest ally to Teratsu, boasts the northernmost settlement ranging into the expanse of largely uninhabited northern tundra; Lost their entire territory along the Split Sea to the Fraollish during the Continental Wars. Known for hardy livestock breeding, also their biggest export.

The Riddles: Capital: Unknown; Symbol: Unknown; Worship: Unknown; Volcanic archipelago known for pink sands and clear seas; The Riddles are surrounded by an abnormal water formation, known to most sailors as The Currents, that makes sailing to the islands nearly impossible unless the crew includes someone who has made the passage before; Mostly isolated for centuries, only in the past decade have their uniquely designed ships been making the passage across the Unending Sea to trade at major ports like those in the Birde Isles. But, those who make the crossing remain secretive about their homeland; Marielle's birthplace.

Major Bodies of Water

Eastern Sea, Western Sea, Split Sea, Southern Strait, Unending Sea, the Fraollkin Inlet.

Index: Cast of Characters

Index of all named characters in *To Kiss the Sea*

The Sea

Birde Isles Shoal:

Pasha (pah-shah): Mermaid; Last left in the Birde Isles shoal; Location of Pasha's remaining kin: Unknown. (she/her)

Pallagia (pah-la-gee-ah): Mermaid; Deceased. (she/her)

The Manor

The Kingfishers:

Gaius Kingfisher I (guy-uhs): Former Lord of the Birde Isles; Ally's great-grandfather; Deceased. (he/him)

Gaius Kingfisher III: Current Lord of the Birde Isles; Father to Gaius IV, Luthais, Calder, and Alphonsine. (he/him)

Glenna Kingfisher (glen-nah) Former Lady of the Birde Isles; Mother to Gaius IV, Luthais, and Calder; Deceased. (she/her)

Rochelle Kingfisher (roh-shel): Current Lady of the Birde Isles; Mother to Alphonsine; Step-mother to Gaius IV, Luthais, and Calder. (she/her)

Gaius "Gai" Kingfisher IV: Eldest Kingfisher child; Heir by birth order; Ship: None. (he/him)

Luthais Kingfisher (loo-tye-iss): Lord of Trade; Second-eldest Kingfisher child; Ship: the *Pike*. (he/him)

Calder Kingfisher (kal-dur): Sea captain; Third-eldest Kingfisher child; Ship: the *Wave Skipper*. (he/him)

Alphonsine "Ally" Kingfisher: (ahl-fahn-seen/ahl-lee): Youngest Kingfisher child; Only child to Rochelle and Gaius III; Ship: None; Maher's best friend. (she/her)

The Villaons:

Khafra Villaon (kah-frah : vill-ay-on) : Saprean ambassador to the Birde Isles; Maher's father. (he/him)

Maher Villaon (Ma-hehr): Khafra's son; Ally's best friend. (he/him)

Staff:

Mrs. Thorley (thorr-lee): The Kingfishers' housekeeper. (she/her)

<u>Kingsport</u>

The Lantern:

Mama Bear: Owner of the Bear's Den, a private, green lantern after-hours club; Given name unknown; Friend of Maher. (she/her)

Pimm: Door guard at the Bear's Den; Friend of Maher; Origins unknown. (they/them)

"Barkeep": Bartender and general strong arm at the Bear's Den; Originally from Swan Island. (he/him)

Olga (ol-guh): Kitchen maid at the Bear's Den. (she/her)

Dr. Tambara (tahm-ba-rah): Physician kept on payroll by the Bear's Den. (she/her)

The Madam: Identity unknown. (she/her)

Marielle (mar-ee-ell): Identity unknown. (she/her)

Temple of the Sea:

Eschina (eh-schh-ee-nah): Former Head Priestess in the time of Gaius Kingfisher II; Deceased. (she/her)

Aithne (eye-ehth-ne): Former Head Priestess; Studied under Eschina; Deceased. (she/her)

Esa (ee-sah): Current Head Priestess; Ally's former tutor; Studied under Aithne. (she/her)

Citizens:

Parvan Dayal (pah-r-van : duh-yahl): Head of the Birde Isles trade guild. (he/him)

Edgar Dayal: Parvan's husband; They love matching outfits. (he/him)

Su-Yonn (soo-yo-nn): Owner of Su's Perfumery. (she/her)

Su-Minn (soo-min): Su-Yonn's daughter; Helps her mother at the perfumery. (she/her)

Kamharida Anyanwu (kahm-ha-ree-dah : ahn-yahn-woo): First Mate of the *Pike*. (she/her)

Ga-Seung (gah-seh-yung): Bosun of the *Pike*. (he/him)

Anya (ah-n-ya): Barrelman of the *Pike*. (she/her)

Grant (gr-ant): Helmsman of the *Pike*. (he/him)

Olebile (oh-leh-bee-leh): Crewmember of the *Wave Skipper*. (they/them)

Weams (weems): Crewmember of the *Wave Skipper*. (he/him)

August Tapper (aw-guhst): Birde Isles Trade Guild member; Has trade connections to Agriya through family. (he/him)

Beitris Tapper (bee-triss): Daughter of August Tapper. (she/her)

Safiye (sah-fee-yeh) & **Latife** (lah-tee-feh): Twin sisters from Saprea who often follow Beitris' lead. (she/her)

Ealasaid (eal-ah-saych): Identity unknown; Deceased. (she/her)

The *Maiden's Revenge*

Foraoise Dare (fora-shuh): Captain of the *Maiden's Revenge*; Privateer; Origins unknown. (she/her)

Jon Dare: Former captain and privateer; Foraoise's husband; Deceased. (he/him)

Swain: Quartermaster (first mate) of the *Maiden's Revenge*. (he/him)

Frossard (froh-sah): Crewmember of the *Maiden's Revenge*. (he/him)

About the Author

C.H. Carter is a fantasy author with a life-long love of the genre in all its forms.

In middle school, she wrote a fan letter to Tamora Pierce and received the most encouraging reply! That experience cemented her desire to become an author. (She also still holds out the hope they can meet in person one day!)

When not writing, you can find her working on a number of rotating projects (Crochet, anyone?) and obsessing over her two rescue dogs.

To Kiss the Sea is C.H. Carter's debut novel.

You can connect, check out the blog, and find the latest updates at: www.chcarterwrites.com

The Kingsport Chronicles will continue with:
TO BRAVE THE DEEP (Coming SPRING 2024)

9 789898 882008